MW01138980

3also by EDWARD MASSEY

ERNESTINE
GOES TO WORK

TELLURIDE PROMISE

EDWARD MASSEY

STAMFORD, CONNECTICUT

Copyright © 2009 by Edward Massey

All rights reserved. No part of this book may be reproduced in any
form or by any electronic or mechanical means, including
information storage and retrieval systems without permission in
writing from the publisher, except by a reviewer, who may quote
brief passages in a review. Any members of educational institutions
wishing to photocopy part or all of the work for classroom use, or
publishers who would like to obtain permission to include the work
in an anthology should send their inquires to Opi's Books, 21 Briar
Woods Trail, Stamford, CT 026903.

Printed in the United States of America

ISBN 1442122145
EAN-13 9781442122147

Opi's Books
21 Briar Woods Trail
Stamford, CT 06903

For Anne

You do not have to walk on your knees
For a hundred miles through the desert, …
…Wild Geese, Mary Oliver

1

During the good times, I stood by the picture window of my bank watching customers come to me. On that last Tuesday of August in 1929, I stood there, watching ... and ... waiting for one last customer. It was a kind of useless nervousness, looking out from an empty bank onto empty streets, but I expected him. After he made his deposit, I planned to close the bank for the day. A little early, perhaps, but I figured I could tell my small staff the extra hour was in compensation for the extra work they would have while I was gone. The extra hour would let me make my final preparations and then I would walk home to my usual dinner with Annie. This night had to look like any other night. I would kiss her good-bye before going to the poker game and leave for Denver right after it. The good times were gone.

Mostly people have just forgot my story, and that makes a lot of sense. Hard times were coming and they came so fast and so hard nobody wanted to spend much time remembering a little banker who was saying we need to get the money back to everybody before the big banks lose it all.

It had been six weeks since that last bank in Denver turned me down, telling me a bank in Telluride had no source of repayment in a town that had nothing but mountains for collateral. I had to borrow the money and I suffered two or three weeks of real panic until I realized the only way to borrow what I needed was to do it before they knew they had loaned it to me. It didn't take much to figure out; any banker could have done it.

At that moment, time was dragging out for me. I remember catching myself just staring up into the box canyon, sort of hypnotized, one last look at Angel Falls holding me. I would never be back in the presence of such lacy beauty again. Well, I had to stop that bit of reverie, take hold of myself. I just stepped outside the bank and looked the other way, searching down the street, past the buildings, as if that'd bring Josh any sooner.

The air had a little bite to it. I recognized that feeling, it felt close. Even with a waistcoat under my jacket, the chill made me shiver. I can't say for sure it was the bite; those were days when I was feeling cold all the time. I've always wondered if that cold was about something going on inside of me. Most days I'm real comfortable in my skin. Anyway, what I remember is that air made everything clear, crisp, and hard-edged. Looking through it was like looking through a crystal. Not that I needed a crystal; I just needed patience. The familiar figure emerging from the New Sheridan Hotel was my old friend, Josh Gibson, making his way toward the bank, just like clockwork, coming in to take care of his regular cash deposit.

As he drew nearer, I toyed with the idea it would be fun to surprise Josh, steal his greeting at the door. Reflection doesn't always lead me to overcome my impulses, but it did that day. Much as I delighted at the very idea of a surprise, that was not the day to show even the slightest change in my normal routine.

What I was starting was a course of deceit. Conviction that it was the right thing to do didn't squeeze out my concerns for how it might affect my friends. What I wasn't prepared for in all that came later was the famous editor who said nobody cares if a banker does the right thing.

"Hey, Buck," and the sound of both doors flinging open, crack against the walls, chased me into my office. Josh had made his usual entrance.

Josh Gibson had been coming to the bank the past twenty-six years to add a little cash to his savings, starting when he was a miner, always bringing his deposit on a Tuesday, always carried in the double burlap bag he'd kept hidden under the floorboards in the miners' boarding house. He had decided to escape the mines when they handed him a rifle and announced they were going to unionize. He took up an axe and built a cabin on land he had bought with his savings. He figured there was nothing better than a union of one. He also figured he needed to keep making that weekly deposit, even if some weeks it was just his winnings from the poker game. He wanted to make money every week and this was his way of knowing he had done so.

Josh's first words the day I met him, long before he became the biggest rancher in Telluride and the biggest depositor in my bank, right after I moved here to take a job as a young teller, were delivered through the teller's window along with that burlap bag.

"I figure I'm caught out between not trusting the men I live with and not being real sure I know how a bank works."

"Works simple," I said. "You put your money in, we promise it'll be here when you want it."

For him, it was business as usual.

I turned to wave to him and the practical me started to think it just didn't make sense for him to be putting more money in his account. I might just as well tell him to keep his money in his pocket.

I made a bee line out to stop him. He was right in the middle of his deposit when I got there. He wasn't paying any attention to me. He was busy studying the pale green silk flapper dress my teller had sewn up from a pattern in the mail order … and the dark green stripe across her chest. He might have been caught up in some guilty thoughts. When I took hold of his right arm, I guess I startled him some.

Old Josh doesn't stay startled for long. He's a big man and he jumped and swiveled all at once and looked down about eight inches right into my eyes. With a slow, almost gentle nod down at my hand on the sleeve of his heavy leather coat, he asked in the same big voice.

"Somethin' on your mind, Buck?"

I straightened up to my full height.

"Well, I … uh, think," and in the phrase of his greeting, I recognized something deeper than he intended. I had already told myself I couldn't afford even the slightest change in my normal routine. "I'll just take that money in tonight's game. Might as well keep it in your pocket." Maybe I stammered a couple more times, but in the end, that was the way I put an end to my impulse to do something highly unusual.

My young teller dropped two quarters from Josh's deposit onto the marble counter. They made a lonely echo in the great hall, the last two quarters anyone ever offered to put in my bank.

"Now, there's something," Josh said, fully in charge again, and laughing, and lifting my arm from his sleeve as he jostled my shoulder. "Hell, Buck, I'll do both. Ain't you been preaching this entire century to put something away against a rainy day?"

"Not quite," I said. Something in me just can't resist the need to get the facts straight and since I had already given myself the lecture on acting normal, I just went ahead and corrected him. "Not the whole century, just since '03. Besides, I want your pockets full tonight."

"They'd be a lot fuller if you'd make me that loan."

"Not that again." I knew he'd jump to that conclusion; say it was about that damn loan. We'd locked horns on that loan for weeks. I had turned him down every time he brought it up; told him straight out it wasn't the time for anyone to be taking out more loans. We were heading into hard times.

Now that's some twist, isn't it. Here I was fixing to get a loan from some banks before they even knew they'd lent me the money and I wouldn't make a loan to my biggest depositor. It's different though. The loan Josh wanted was to buy land he didn't need for a ranch that was already the biggest in the county. Like everybody else, he was convinced he could just go on growing by buying things with borrowed money. That damn fool loan was going to ruin him. He didn't believe me anymore'n anybody else did.

I swept the money from the counter and shoved it back under the teller's window. I wanted to stuff it in his jacket pocket; but I had to let him go on misunderstanding. Now his deposit was made, I could close the bank and get started. I took hold of his elbow. Josh recognized the maneuver. He let me guide him across the floor. The lines of easy laughter on his face deepened a little when we arrived at the front door.

"You know, Buck, for a little shit, you sure are a little shit."

"I believe you have made that observation before, George," I said. Up in these high mountains where life is often as fragile as it is precious only true friends enjoy the privilege of using a man's formal first name. True friend or not, I held onto his elbow until I had opened the door and we both stepped outside.

"Easy, there, Buck," said Josh. "If I didn't know better, I'd think you were trying to send me packing."

"Nonsense," I said. I let go of his elbow and turned to close the tall doors behind us. "I'd never treat my biggest depositor that way."

Josh Gibson took a deep, noisy breath and looked across Colorado Avenue, across three or four streets, to a steep green wall of trees so massive and so close you could touch it. So massive it invades a man's thoughts.

"This view," he said, taunting me like so many times before, "is the main reason I keep coming to this bank. Hell, everybody else treats me better."

"To be sure," I said. It was our little ritual and I may have enjoyed it that day a bit more than usual. "Hell, we only live in a spectacle, in a box canyon of soaring rock and ribbons of waterfall, but I don't doubt I got the best view. And, my friend, because I got the best Directors, I also got the best bank."

"You little shit," he said and those laughter lines in his face got a little deeper. He stretched out his arms till they nearly touched the fluting in the two wooden columns that flanked the entranceway.

"Nah, it ain't the Directors. Maybe it's the mountains. Maybe it's these pillars," he said. His tone gave way to one as careful and deliberate as testimony, "This here feels like the solidest place on earth."

As compliments go, that's about as much as you'll get in this town. I straightened my bow tie and just smiled at him, letting his words hang in the air.

"Regular time tonight?" I asked.

"I'll have the beers," he said.

"Just have your money." I said.

"And what about you?" teased Josh. "You going to have enough cash money to stay up with us a while?"

Bet small, lose small, and win big. That was my policy and he knew it. He was just trying to get my goat. I wasn't about to let that happen. I made a grand sweep of my arm across the bank's entrance and bowed.

"A whole bank full."

2

I watched Josh pick his way down West Colorado Avenue, careful to preserve the shine on his only pair of boots. When the richest man in town is modest enough to own one pair of cowboy boots and shines them himself, he is careful not to get mud on them. You want to be true to a good person.

That chill shivered me. I wondered if there was a good reason for it or if it was just sick emptiness. I looked up into the sky. Snow, probably. It figured to be a little early, even up this high, but sure enough it felt like snow. That gave me a moment's relief. Maybe it's not just me. Either way, it was going to be a long winter.

When I turned to go back in, I stopped to look at those pillars, as Josh called them. He was right, even if he couldn't quite put his finger on it, those columns were supposed to stand for dependability. That's what I had in mind when I designed the place. I had just been made president. I was full of plans. Sometimes now when I look back at that young man I can see all that he was doing, all that he did, but I can't really tell what he was thinking.

My Annie tells me that I am good at seeing the thinking, but I'm not so good at the feeling. Well, I didn't think of it then and even now I don't know what he was thinking. I know what he was feeling. He was feeling the first flush of success and that's what it is: full of plans and good ideas. He had things to do. Age and the hammer blows that make up life's experience have created a veil. I can't see through to his thinking as clearly as I can see his plunging. I can see the result, though: careful, thoughtful, and deliberate. It tells me he was thinking.

The twin columns were in the Doric style for a reason. They supported a lintel to create a gateway to a temple of commerce and industry. Some folks said it was a bit much. Some folks always find something a bit much. I say what was wrong with that young man trying to build a temple to the hopes and dreams of the people of Telluride? He knew they were good people, I know they are good people, down to the last girl in the cribs and the miner who bought her with his wages.

My Annie told me it wasn't up to me to make their hopes and dreams come true. She was right, of course. I knew that even without her telling me, but, truth is, I tried to do just that. I surely did. I was good at admonishing myself for having gone too far, always was, still am, but I just couldn't help it.

I stepped through the open doorway and lingered a bit to look at the sweep of the great hall with the stand-up desk perfectly centered. I always loved that view. I could almost see fifty thousand in gold bars still stacked on its marble top.

The late afternoon light from the now overcast sky darkened the grand interior of my empty bank. These past two years the bank had grown emptier each month as I watched the people line up to take out their life savings so they could leave town. Nothing but memories were the times now gone past when so many people milled about and lined up at the teller windows that I wondered how I could get them all out by closing time.

Enough of that! I could think all I wanted to about the good times gone by, but having no one to deal with served my purpose, just fine. Dawdling might have been a bit of understandable procrastination, but it wasn't going to get a damn thing done.

3

One step inside the bank, before I could close the door behind me, a softly accented voice floated across my shoulders.

"Mr. Wain."

I didn't need to see who had called my name. I turned to face the petite but fine figure of a woman coming up the steps.

"Rosa," I said, reaching to take her hand. She placed her fingers gently in my palm, like a lady. "Where is your little boy?"

"I left him with one of the girls," she said. "They still help me out. It'll only take long enough to make my withdrawal."

Rosa was a darkly beautiful woman with a hard past and the hardest part of her past was my doing. I walked her to the teller's area and stopped at David Twicken's window. She smiled to acknowledge him. My head teller would take good care of her.

"Is everything all right?" I asked.

"Everything's fine — thanks to the miner's insurance," she said. "That was God's own miracle, Mr. Wain, Akus taking that insurance.

"Now God's blessed me again. I got a powerful man on my side. You know, there's no work in this town. And I couldn't find any anyway," — she faltered slightly — "except what I was doing before Akus and the baby. Now, Mr. Drake says he'll help me."

"I'm sure," I said. Drake saying he'd help her spelled trouble.

Rosa waited for me to say more, but the less said about Drake the better. I could see comprehension dawn in her dark eyes as she stared at me through those long black lashes. The wide ovals that created so much of her beauty narrowed into a tight almond shape. "He told me you were his friend — his partner in the miners' hospital."

I glanced up at the clock high on the wall behind the tellers. Each minute ticked off with a lurch around the simple face. Two more lurches and it would be three.

"Yes, we're partners," was about all I could say. I knew Drake. I knew why he no longer held the position that had made him my partner. I knew what Drake saw in the beautiful young Mexican woman. Even if there had been time, I was not about to discuss Corlen Drake with the widow of Akus Knutzon. "Well, Mr. Twicken, here, can take care of you."

"If he don't help me," Rosa said, disregarding Twicken's attention, speaking only to me, "I'll have to take what little I have and leave town."

Beautiful and friendly, as always, her face betrayed no further comment. Her voice had not carried the tone of a threat, nor had she dropped it lower to keep a secret from Twicken. She was simply dealing with her lot.

It was my fault this woman was a widow. I had done what I could to get money to her, but that would not last forever and it was her decision if she was starting to believe she had to leave Telluride to support her son. I could not see how to do more for her. What she was threatening was what I was fixing to do, anyway. Life was lived hard up in these mountains. That didn't make it any the less painful for me to know I could do nothing for her.

"Yes, Rosa, it'd be too bad to see you leave town. If it'd make you feel more independent about it, maybe you should take all your money out today. At least, you'll have it."

"May I help you, Mrs. Knutson?" Twicken's words covered my retreat.

I made myself busy, looking busy. I continued to watch through my glass wall. Finally, Twicken stepped around from his stool and, in the usual courtesy of the bank, took the lovely woman by the elbow and escorted her out the door.

The moment he stepped through the double doors with her, I hurried across the empty lobby, pushing through the tellers' door concealed in the wall of paneling.

Down the row I went, as fast as I could, pulling down the green rolling shade at each of the teller windows. The movements may have been a little rapid. Amy stared at me with an obvious display of surprise. I almost said something to her about her open mouth, the way I might say something to my own niece about ladylike behavior.

"Mr. Wa-in?" she stammered in a twang that neatly divided my name into two syllables.

"Day's done," I said, patting her hand. She was almost one of mine, a good friend to my two nieces, especially Susan, but it was not a day for an uncle's admonition. For good measure, I reached below the counter and took her cash tray.

4

Twicken returned to his station, saw the drawn shades and Amy's cash tray in my hands. Without a word, he pulled his cash tray and stacked it on top of Amy's. I carried them both into the vault and placed them on the table in the center of that wonderful room. You might think me a little daft to call a vault a wonderful room, but it was a room built to store dreams. That is what treasure is, stored dreams. This was the storehouse of the dreams of the citizens of Telluride. There was a time when safe deposit boxes from floor to ceiling on all three walls were not enough to store all the dreams. No longer.

Lingering there was not going to take care of the problem. I stepped to the door of the vault and announced:

"I'm giving you an extra hour today. My little gift to make up for the extra work you'll have with me gone. I'm leaving tomorrow for a trip East."

It didn't surprise me none when J. P. Dixon hopped off his stool. My vice president protested that he knew nothing about a trip back East. After all, bank examiners were scheduled to be here next Friday.

With the great staff I had, I assured him there was no need for me to be here, but I'd leave the next day just in case he needed me back in time.

Protest was never quite enough for Dixon. For good measure, he whined, too, adding that even if he had been told about it, it wasn't a good idea for the bank president to be away at the end of the month. He couldn't possibly close out the month alone; he wasn't prepared.

"Oh, tosh," I said. "Mr. Drew hired you, and I made you a vice-president. You're my vice president. You can handle these responsibilities."

His stiff, by the book way of dealing with the world was exactly what I needed when the bank examiners showed up next week. I left it at that and continued on to my office. I don't normally close my door, but I did that time.

Some minutes later, after what he determined would be a suitable delay, David Twicken knocked on my door. My final notes were almost finished and I put the piece of paper in my center drawer and waved him in.

"Sir," said Twicken, closing the door. He never made a big show of being discrete, but he never lapsed. "Maybe one of us got our schedules crossed. If you recall, you gave me permission to go to Denver on Friday for the Knights of Pythias meeting."

There was no mistake. I put down my pen.

"No, no mix-up, at all. Your meeting has been scheduled quite a while and I started planning this trip three weeks ago. I believe Mr. Dixon can handle it."

"Thank you, sir," he said. "I assure you, everything will be left in order. My accounts are in order. I've already signed the ten blank checks for use in my absence. Do you want to count them?"

He needn't have recounted his attention to every detail. I knew he had followed the protocol. In the moment I waved away the unnecessary question, Dixon knocked on the glass door. He pushed open the door and leaned his head into the office.

"Will you be closing the vault alone, Mr. Wain?"

It was well past three and leaving the vault open this long after collecting the cash trays was unusual. Dixon's question reminded me that unexpected behavior raises suspicion.

"No," I said, getting up from behind the desk, the last thing I wanted was Dixon to start thinking, at all, but especially about what I was doing. I swung full open the door he held. "Let's do it together, right now."

Twicken followed us into the vault. We counted the day's cash and Dixon made a tally and I reviewed it.

"Five hundred seventy-three dollars and ninety-two cents," he droned after the final tally, using his official vice-president voice, signing his initials to the tally.

"Same total I have," I said. I signed my initials and added the date.

"Not much cash for a bank with nearly eight hundred thousand in assets," he said.

I frowned because I don't like negative comments, even though I agreed with the facts, as far as they went.

"Not much."

"Too bad that Denver bank wouldn't make us the loan," he said.

"Too bad," I said. Once he was started with his observations, the only way to stop him was to agree with him. Pointing out that those Denver banks owed us nothing would let them off the hook as much as him for his worthless observation. So, I just agreed with him.

Fifteen years before, when times were good and the bank's gold bars were on display, I made the decision to loan money to a Denver bank in trouble. No one, from Dixon to my Board of Directors, thought it was a good banker's decision. I was sandwiched. Everyone told me it was bad business for damn near twenty-five percent of the bank's assets to go out in one loan to a shaky Denver bank. About all I could say in my defense is that good people make good loans.

It turned out I was right. That loan had been paid off since 1921.

In early August, I had approached that same bank for a loan to the Bank of Telluride. It wasn't just that Telluride was having hard times; that had been going on for two years or more. No, I had been watching what was going on in the whole country and any damn fool could see, the loans were too much, the credit was too shaky, and every month more banks were failing. It was like a big wave coming in to shore and I was pretty damn convinced we were all going to get drowned by it. Right here and now and not just in our little town. Those big banks were going to be unable … or maybe even just unwilling … to give us back the money we put on deposit with them. I needed the money to give my depositors back their money. It was better off in their mattress than in my bank … any bank … for the next couple of years.

When I made that loan to the Denver bank, it took them seven years to pay it back. I knew we could do the same for them.

They turned me down flat.

5

I don't like complaining. Whining of any sort just doesn't sit right with me. I'll allow as how there might be some shades, still I don't see much gray. You got to sit up and look right at reality. Even if I was prepared to face the reality of that decision, I did think poorly of that Denver bank.

That banker no doubt believed Success favored avoiding the risk. Little nymph. Men think they understand her siren song. Men think she promises immortality if they sleep with her. Men even believe she promises that they alone may sleep with her. They get caught up and they think Success promises her favors to those who have when others don't.

True, I knew there was a crash coming, and after the crash, you could buy a lot if you had the capital. That banker never believed there was a crash coming; he was not trying to protect against squandering his resources; he was just refusing to help others.

There was no point dwelling on it. He didn't know what he was doing. Like almost all bankers, he did not deserve his pay. All he did was count the money he sat on not the good he did. Let me say again, gathering up more money to sit on, not using it to good purpose, is what gets bankers paid.

Maybe that sounds like complaining and like I said, I don't like complaining. Success had given me some tools, too. When I got back home at the beginning of August, I knew I had to take care of things myself. It had taken me three weeks to figure it all out. And when I did, I knew today was the day to set it in motion.

No complaint, but I didn't need Dixon to remind me of the Denver bank.

Before I left the vault, I turned to Twicken and asked him the exact number of bank depositors. The prosecutor later pressed Twicken to agree with him in thinking it strange that the president of the bank wanted to know such detailed information.

"On the contrary," my Mr. Twicken said, "Mr. Wain had trained me that's what a bank president is supposed to do: keep track of his depositors."

That pleased me no end.

Edward Massey

"One hundred eighty-five, not counting the county and the children." Twicken's answer was as crisp and precise as his white shirt and red suspenders.

"A good distinction," I said, noting it on my pad. "The county has its own surety bonds. And the children? How many?"

"Oh, I don't know. Maybe fifty, maybe a few more." To my query about how much money they had on deposit, he rolled his eyes up. He did a few calculations in his head. "You are testing me, Mr. Wain, but certainly not more than six hundred dollars."

I reached the cash from my pocket and counted out twenty-seven dollars. "Here, add this to the total."

"For what?" asked Twicken.

"For the children," I said. "Gives us more than six hundred. It's good policy to have enough cash on hand to repay the children's deposits. It isn't likely all the children of Telluride will come in at the same time to recover their savings, but we do it anyway. As a matter of principle."

I pointed in the direction of the marble-topped desk.

"For goodwill," I said, chuckling at my little joke. "We can't afford gold bars anymore!"

Twicken joined me to swing the vault door closed. Dixon stepped between us to spin the handle and set the lock.

I looked up at the clock and said, "Almost four, you'll get that hour I promised."

I stepped over to Twicken at his station and asked, "Before you leave, I want to make sure your depositor list is up to date."

"Rest assured, sir. I know what each of our depositors has in the bank. Today and everyday."

6

Raw as it was that Tuesday afternoon, my three employees welcomed the gift of an extra hour in the high mountain air. Absently returning my good wishes for their long weekend, thinking about how they would use the time, no one noticed I held the door open and shook each hand. I knew it was to be the last time I saw them out before I closed up the bank, a normal day's courtesy.

"Sleep well. You'll be busy while I'm gone," I said. No one heard me, so that is information the prosecutor never got.

I had the bank to myself. I don't doubt nostalgia for my life's work invades me more now than it did then, but, as I stood there, I knew it was my last moment with my bank. Slowly, I surveyed its interior, taking stock of every detail, however familiar, however mundane. My gaze carried through the glass wall of the meeting room, next to my office and slightly larger, as it should be. That room was for the townsfolk, whatever the purpose. Businessmen, ranchers, Western Federation of Miners, mine management, even the Telluride Ladies Auxiliary used it at one time or another. The bank existed to be of assistance to the community and I wanted it at the center. Annie teased me some about that. She'd get that devilish look of hers and wonder aloud if the president of the bank didn't want to be at the center of the community, too. Well, I guess I did.

Those aren't modern thoughts and most of the people I have asked to help me get this story out don't even believe them. But, damn it, it's true. All you ever need and all I ever wanted was to be of assistance to the community. That's where the passion comes in and, over the past twenty-six years, almost daily, at first, and less frequently, later, I had felt the embrace of Success. If counting is the measure of a man, I could count a long list of achievements. If I wrote them down on a piece of paper, I knew they would impress any reader. In fact, before this story is over, they probably will get pretty much written down. Yet, standing there, peering into that empty meeting room, feeling all those shards of pride sticking into my present, all that seemed almost like another person. These last few years I lived with a voice I could not ignore – one that insisted nothing lasting had been accomplished.

There was nothing to do with those thoughts but to deal with the day I was in. I had to keep to my normal Tuesday ritual. I had more than forty-five minutes until I would leave the bank at five. My plan took some research and some thought, but once I knew what I had to do, figuring out how to instruct those bankers to lend me the money turned out to be quite simple. I knew I was nothing special; at least a thousand bankers in the country had access to the codes and could have done the same thing. I knew I could make it work, and I still felt rushed. It was time to calm my mind.

It never hurt to write things down. One last check to see if I had thought of everything. Sitting behind my glass wall, as if all of Telluride watched, I breathed and picked up my pen. My hand betrayed me. I steadied it, and then, as if independent of the thoughts that resisted my efforts to tame them, it quickly covered a single sheet of paper in neatly written out single lines of full sentences. When I paused to review the finished work, it looked like a page of blank verse:

Make sure all open bank business is routine.

I reached for my pocket calendar and fingered the pages of each date one by one. It confirmed what I already knew: nothing unusual in the next few days. The holiday would come on Monday, and that was important, but nothing was scheduled until the bank examiners, Friday a week.

Verify names and addresses of each bank.

Unlocking the top drawer I removed a small black leather-bound binder and another sheet of paper. I checked each of the names and addresses I had written on the sheet of paper, checking them against the directory. All set and verified.

Verify amount to borrow.

I reached into the unlocked drawer at the center of my desk for a piece of paper and took out a Western Union telegram blank. I turned the form over and quickly drew a T on the blank side. On the left side of the T, I wrote the heading *CASH.* I began the list of cash items, *Pay out the depositors,* and put an amount next to it. Then I added, *Clear the bank loans,* and noted an amount, and finally, *Clear the collateral,* and by that I meant the bank stock I had pledged. I wrote down the amount it would take. I drew a line under all the numbers and added the column. It was a total so I drew two lines under the sum. I looked at the number for a few seconds. It was all I needed and on the right side of the T, across from the word *CASH,* I pressed hard on my pen to make the darkest lines I could and wrote down the same amount, drew two lines under it, and wrote *LOAN.*

A loan. Precisely what I asked of the Denver banks. Nothing more. I folded the paper carefully and put it in the pocket of my suit coat. It was still there when the agents searched me.

Prepare the telegrams in advance

Item four. By now my mind was quiet. Something about numbering that could be trusted. Something about facing the most important step that focused the mind. The coded instructions had to be perfect and look perfect. This time when I reached into the drawer I needed the telegram blanks not for scrap paper but for the six telegrams that would send the money to my bank. I stacked them in a careful pile under my left hand and swiveled in the chair to face the typewriter on the desk's sidearm. Inserting a sheet of telegram stationery, I punched the shift lock and typed:

EQUITABLE TRUST CO.
NEW YORK CITY, NEW YORK

I typed a little slowly and inspected the lines as I went along for I could afford no mistakes. Fine, so I typed:

ALLUNGANDO EXEMPLAR CHASE NATIONAL BANK BUNCADOR THE BANK OF TELLURIDE EXAGITATE.

Again, I went slowly, inspecting as I typed, taking extra care with the strange words. It was fine so I had only to sign it and that meant simply to add the name of the sender. The Denver bank saved with our five hundred thousand dollar loan – and deaf to our need -- deserved the honor of being first. I typed:

INTERNATIONAL TRUST CO.
DENVER, COLORADO

I took the next blank and typed *CHEMICAL BANK AND TRUST CO.,* followed by *"ALLUNGANDO EXEMPLAR CHASE . . . ,"* just as before. This time I typed the signature on behalf of:

DENVER NATIONAL BANK, DENVER, COLORADO.

I went on to type the rest:

FIRST NATIONAL BANK, signed by *FIRST NATIONAL BANK OF DENVER, COLORADO.*

GUARANTY TRUST CO., signed by *COLORADO NATIONAL BANK, DENVER, COLORADO.*

NATIONAL CITY BANK, signed by *U.S. NATIONAL BANK, DENVER, COLORADO.*

HARRIMAN NATIONAL, signed by *AMERICAN NATIONAL BANK, DENVER, COLORADO.*

Six telegrams from Denver banks carrying the exact instructions to a New York bank to deposit funds in our account. I made one last inspection, tapped them up even on the desktop and inserted them one by one in Western Union envelopes. I returned to my list and crossed off number four.

7

The round face of my pocket watch told me a few minutes remained — time enough to review again each step, the travel arrangements, and the instructions. Centering the sheet of paper precisely on the desk top, I stacked the six envelopes with their telegrams at the bottom of the sheet. After putting my leather address book back in the drawer and locking it, everything was ready.

Folding the page in thirds, I placed it on top of the envelopes, and laid them all against the spine of a well-worn leather wallet that I tucked in the chest pocket of my vest. I patted the wallet through my suit jacket and tugged at the bottom. My body is a bit round and soft, not heavy mind you, and I am not particularly concerned about how I look, but hard edges would be noticed.

In the chill of that August morning I had brought my black cashmere overcoat out of summer storage. Lush and suspended from a wooden hanger on one of the metal hooks of the coat tree, it never failed to remind me of the good times that reigned after the war. Good times down in the valley, anyway; they never quite made it up to Telluride. That reminded me of all the things I had tried that never quite worked. I made that loan to Everett, in hopes it would help the good times return. Walt's business survived, even flourished, until now, but it wasn't enough. How could I ever have thought he, or more correctly, his speakeasy, could bring the good times back, just because there was such a boom going on down in Denver? Annie's first comment was right; the one she made when I bought the coat. It was a gesture of false hope. I liked hope, I could even say I believed in it, but looking at that coat that night, I heard her words and felt a little embarrassed. I'd let myself go almost a decade caught up in hope.

Enough of that. The coat might have been a painful reminder, but it still had lots of wear left in it. There was no need to compound my foolishness by letting it go unused. Same with the hat. In truth, it might have been just a bit too western for my trip, but it was a fine felt of a gray so light it appeared almost white. And it had cost good money.

To leave my office and shut my door for the last time brought no special sense of dread. No excitement followed me through the pearly dimness of the lobby. I was not without feeling; there was a feeling and it was large and familiar but beyond that I cannot give a name to it. I might have paused a moment at the marble counter and I probably ran my fingers across the hard, cold top. My habits are predictable.

Inevitability. That was what I felt. It was time to go.

By the time I made it to the double doors, movement had created electric energy and it came out in a playful mood. If anyone had been watching, they would have seen a big, silly grin cross my face as I threw open the doors. With one bold step I made it onto the marble landing. Mountain air did what it always does to me; it rushed to my head and cleared it. I realized I might have put on a little too much of a show. I gave a quick glance up and down the street. No one. No surprise, perhaps, in those sad days as Telluride dwindled, but lucky nonetheless.

When I held out the large brass key, I noticed again my hand shook slightly. Funny. Here was a task I had taken care of thousands of times. The clunk of the lock cylinder ended the shakiness. I stepped back, all the way down the steps, off the boardwalk and into the dusty street. I was not aware of it until I stopped. I was looking up at my bank.

The brick building boom started in Telluride on Thanksgiving, 1890. That was the day Otto Mears brought in his Rio Grande Southern on track he had laid on his old toll road. It was also the year L.L. Nunn harnessed the water to generate electric power for the hoists in his mines.

Now there was an entrepreneur. I don't recall if he owned the mines before he owned the bank, but the year before he negotiated with Mr. Westinghouse to build generators for his mines, he dealt with a ne'er do well who tried to rob his bank. Nunn owned race horses and when Butch Cassidy robbed his bank, he chased after him on his own horse. Of course, he caught up with Cassidy, but all the good it did him was to lose a very fast horse to the same man who had just plundered his bank. That story always meant something to me. A banker had to do everything he could to protect his depositors; even if it meant losing his fast horse.

Anyway, I didn't really know those men, but I made it my business to learn about them because they were the reason Telluride prospered. By the time I arrived here, two-thirds of the town's wooden false fronts had given way to brick or masonry. I don't mean to make too much of this, but I reckon it was my first day on the job when I decided the bank needed a permanent and a prominent building. Of course, I had to become president before I could do anything about it, but when I did, in 1909, I made it my very first major project.

Even taking pride into account, you have to recognize the building I built was pretty small when you look at it compared to those New York banks, but still, I made it symmetrical and that adds to the overall impression. The yellow brick made it feel like a kind of mass. A heavy lintel ran the entire length of the façade and supported a peaked front. Everyday I walked into it, and that night, too, the place made my spirit soar. If I could see it today, it would still. Classical design and grand proportion was what was needed to make a living temple, and it was that, worthy of the bank's role in the community.

As I write this now, like I said once before, I imagine that night I didn't think much about him, but today I feel a little awed and surprised at the young man, barely thirty-three, who was driven to build his temple to frugality and wealth.

Then again, those were heady times, with prosperity, power, and fun, a lot of fun, at least for a while. I looked up at the name etched into the lintel. I loved that name in a way that I can never say I loved myself. I simply could not allow anyone, much less some out-of-town bank examiners, to come between my bank, my depositors, and me.

True, their visit was supposed to be routine; they were always scheduled to come in the fall, before the snow made travel to Telluride a chance expedition as well as a burden. Maybe it was a coincidence that the notice of their trip came immediately after I returned from Denver. Maybe the confidential discussions with the Denver bankers had not been all that confidential. The business failures up here were no secret. Maybe those bankers smelled something. Maybe they figured there were bad loans on the books. And 'liquidity problems.' Now, there's a fancy word. Hell, 'liquidity' was nothing more than cash on hand.

If the Denver bank had made that loan, the Bank of Telluride would have plenty of cash on hand. Then, with time, the loans to the folks of Telluride that they called bad today would prove to be good.

All of this went through my mind as I stood there, uncertain and convinced at the same time. Maybe my problem had always been too much fantasy, too much wishing, but when it came time to bite the bullet, I could face the reality I saw. The chances were something would stop me, yet I had no choice. Was I off on a voyage of fantasy or was I facing reality? Truth is, that is what I ask myself today. I don't really think I was asking myself that as I looked up into the blue-gray sky. It was a voyage and I had to use the boat I could build. I brought my eyes into focus, a squint up at the name carved on the lintel. My eyes began to water.

"Knew it," I said aloud, pulling the soft collar up around my neck and tugging at my hat brim. "Going to be a long winter."

8

The air in these high mountains carries a special caress in the evening. I felt it every night of every day I made my way along that street. Even the wintry days, like the storms in life, never pierced that loving embrace.

Sadness walked with me on my normal course down Colorado Avenue that Tuesday night. Knowledge I would never walk that way again bore less than the lonely emptiness of the street. Maybe I have to admit to pride as I looked at building after building that stood there because my bank had helped the people of Telluride. Helped people to build. Helped people to buy. From time to time, someone told me I had special skills. I just dismissed that kind of talk, as a man always should. About the only skill I had that wasn't pretty much what everybody else could do was that I could carry in my head an inventory of the town's buildings, businesses, and people. In the end, there wasn't anything special in that; in the end keeping track just came down to remembering the people.

At *Zack's Tack*, I paused. As usual, I pushed on from the wooden false front right next to my building to the corner, passed two brick buildings: an attorney — vacant and not too much a loss that he was gone — and the assay office. Treasures brought down to those original assayers touched off the building boom once the railroad made it possible to haul bricks up the mountain. Old-timers' practical logic made the assay office the first wooden building they tore down and rebuilt in brick. My kind of thinking.

Now cross Fir Street and down the next block. Nothing caught my eye in the large display window, but I had something in mind, so I pushed through the recessed doorway set in the middle of five small linked buildings.

"Mr. Wain!" Pierre Robichaud met me with a loud and warm greeting. "What a pleasure to have you in my store."

I liked the wiry French Canadian from the Maine coast, liked especially the wit and determination he showed over the ten years it took to persuade three different men to sell him the five contiguous buildings.

"Of course, I am in your store. You know I do all my shopping in your store," I said, permitting myself an exaggeration, a token of the warmth I felt for my neighbor.

"Not quite all," replied Robichaud, grinning as he ostentatiously ran his hand over my black cashmere coat. "But, to be sure, I do all my banking at your bank. You own more of this store than I do."

"No," I corrected him. "We just hold the mortgage."

"Well, I have you to thank."

What was to thank? This was a man you could trust. I did the best I could to wave away his gratitude.

"Not that you'll ever find yourself needing my help," he said, unwilling to drop the subject, "but if God's will ever puts you in need of anything, I hope you'll come to me."

A chill went through me. It felt too close. Premonition is as close to superstition as I'll ever get. I liked the sentiment behind the idea. That's the way folks were supposed to behave. He was a good man. His good gesture brought all the more to mind what he would face in the days ahead. He had a history of pluck and tenacity. He started his business by leasing the corner building and when he got the chance, he purchased it -- at the peak of Telluride's prosperity. That was just the beginning and he kept right on until he completed his vision by buying all five of the buildings before, during, and after the War, the last in 1921. With every new building, I rewrote the loan. The bank had held the mortgage for the past eight years. It was one of the good loans. That history would not save him in the face of what was coming. Eight years of hard work could be lost in six months. As I stood there I knew Robichaud would have to struggle to keep the store. The thirty-two years remaining on the mortgage were standard. They didn't bother me none. It was the next five or six years that would cause him trouble.

"Well, for today, what God has put me in need of is something bigger than the bag I take every day to the bank, but not exactly a valise."

"I have exactly what you need." Robichaud was a good storekeeper; he always had what you needed, either by putting it in your hand or by redirecting you so that you were convinced that you had asked for what he put in your hand. I marveled at his genius;

alone among Telluride's storekeepers, he had kept his deposits growing every year.

Until this past year. When Robichaud's deposits stopped growing, I knew to stop listening to the big people who said the good times would just keep rolling.

"How's business?" I asked as I followed Robichaud to the leather counter.

"Great," he laughed. "Everybody's off. On holiday."

His eyes swept the corners of the store. It was a look I recognized. It was the look of a man searching for something that once was but is no longer.

"People know when they need to stop spending. They know it in advance. The girls down in the cribs might be doing okay. And maybe Gus," he said, meaning the grocer. "You can't do without sex and food. But go over to the hotel, that restaurant is wall to wall empty."

His analysis was painfully accurate, but I did not want him to know I thought any of that myself.

"Think it's any better in Maine?" I asked.

"Dunno. Don't matter. My life's out here. Mines keep cuttin' back. People keep leavin'. We're down to maybe five hundred people, right? It's a might smaller'n Bath. But it'll grow. Things'll get better."

There it was. Telluride optimism. The first five hundred and the last five hundred, all ready to march into the unknown.

Robichaud had less money on deposit than Josh Gibson, but he had enough to see him through — if I could get it back to him.

9

Back out on the street again, I hesitated for a moment before continuing on home. I wondered if I should retrace my steps and make one last effort to convince old Zack Weimer to sell me his place. It was a thought I had every night, but this would truly be the last night I could do it. After that building boom I mentioned, about eight or nine false fronts remained around town. Zack's was one of them and it was right next to the bank. I had tried to buy the building twenty years before with the idea of tearing it down to enhance the effect of my new bank. He wouldn't sell and so there it remained smack dab next to the yellow brick temple, almost touching. Now I wanted to buy it to help Zack.

Zack Weimer wasn't an easy man to help. Tall and as leathery as the tack he sold, I knew he would emerge through the opening in his back wall, using a chamois to wipe hands tinted red up to wrist bones that protruded like a ball. Like as not, when I told him I was concerned for the future of his business, the stubborn old piece of horsehide would tell me "You just take care o' my money and I'll take care o' my business."

I tried to convince him he'd fare better taking the money, but old Zack would just say, "Farin' okay now."

Maybe. But for how long? It didn't take much figuring. Zack probably needed thirty dollars a year to live on and there was barely twelve dollars in his account. I knew he was somewhere over seventy; he'd outlive that money sure.

No, Zack wouldn't sell. It wouldn't do no damn good to bother him again. But, one thing's for sure, he would expect me to get his twelve dollars back.

Up the hill, past St. Patrick's and the rectory and the handsome parish house, up the hill to my neighborhood, home to Telluride's leading citizens. Pierre Robichaud lived here, so did two attorneys, two mining engineers, a doctor, the Rio Grande Southern regional manager, and, until recently, J. Walter Everett, an "entrepreneur." Annie and Connie and I lived there, happily. Both attorneys and one of the engineers had left town. Their large houses now stood dark and empty. The bank held mortgages on two of them and over the summer I had watched the lawns grow untended. Each inch of growth eroded their value so I finally asked that little girl who does our dandelions, E.L. Davis's granddaughter, to mow it. They were good loans, on good houses. They were the sort of loans that had the bank examiners coming, but they would be good — in time. Somebody needed to give them time.

The front door opened before I touched the handle. Like every night, I looked into expressionless eyes set deep in a wide oval face. It occurred to me that maybe the Ute woman was not counted in the dwindling population of Telluride. There was no way to guess how many Indians lived in town. They didn't have accounts with the bank.

If nothing, no expression, no word, no offer of assistance could be countenanced a greeting, My-Yut's greeting differed not a whit from any other evening. That night her totem-like service annoyed me as I struggled out of my coat. My spectacles fogged in the heat of the hallway, blurring my vision.

"Mimi," I asked, using the name I had given her twenty years before in a vain effort to make her more of the family, "is Mrs. Wain all right?"

The Ute woman dropped her chin, letting it disappear into a turquoise fold around her neck and then appear again. One nod. Yes.

I handed her my coat and she stretched up on her toes to hang it on a hook. She did this every evening. It was a stubbornness I never understood. I took the wooden hanger from the hook under the coat and, holding it before her eyes, explained, as I did every evening, that the coat was to be placed on the hanger – an act I completed myself. Her expressionless eyes watched me place the hanger on the hook.

"Sweetheart, you're home," called Annie from the kitchen. Her firm voice answered my concerns.

Annie met me in the living room. She carried a full vase of virgin's bower. I enjoyed watching her move, even with the heavy burden she held straight out in front of her. Her stride contained the same energy as her voice. She left me in a state of wonder. Her ability to create a striking arrangement out of simple mountain clematis; her tireless pragmatism mixed with dauntless energy. Something, whatever it was, was always a joy to come home to. She was home. She was my Penelope.

I wrapped my arms around her shoulders from behind and leaned over to breathe in the peppery smell of the flowers.

Edward Massey

"You cold, Penny?" I asked.

Annie's sole attention remained on the placement of her vase on the table. Two slight adjustments and she was satisfied. She twisted inside my grasp and gave me a soft kiss.

"Not anymore," she said.

Tonight was like any other night and the kiss was part of our routine but that did nothing to diminish its effect. More than twenty-nine years had passed since the first kiss at the Turn of the Century Ball in Omaha and her kisses still made the world right. I returned her embrace. I wanted to kiss her again, to hold her a little longer, a little closer. Tonight, that would not do.

We shared a life of habits and patterns. We were not people to fight routine. Routine provided comfort. Tonight was poker night, just like any other Tuesday night.

I also wanted a drink. We had some really good rye from our last visit to her brother who had a connection in Canada. I will admit to some afternoons when I sat in my office and looked forward to the evening's small glass of rye, but aside from the relief I expected it to bring from this tightness in my chest, I simply did not want to leave it there, pretty much untouched.

"Did you talk to Connie today?" The same question I asked every evening since our son had married two years ago.

I couldn't go fix a drink. She knew I was playing poker and driving to Denver.

"Yes. He brought the baby over at lunchtime."

"Did he mention business school?" Maybe I could just offer her one.

"No. He probably hasn't decided."

"It may be too late," I said.

"Hardly," she said. Maybe she noticed something in my face. As if to change the subject, she announced, "Dinner's almost ready."

"Would you like a highball?"

She smiled and pushed out of my embrace.

"No, dinner's almost ready."

"Fine, fine," I said. "We don't want to be rushed."

"Well, you go wash up."

I kept close track of her smile. Annie had a stern frown; it felt not unlike the ones I had grown up with, and when I spotted one I felt anxious. She had told me countless times that whether she smiled or frowned, she loved me. Still, I could read meanings into her smile, and I took tonight's to mean she didn't notice anything different.

I climbed the stairs marveling. She treated everything in her life as a fact. Love, for instance. Annie Martin Wain, born and raised and married in Nebraska. To her, loving a person enough to spend her life with him was not subject to something as transitory as circumstances. To me, thinking all the way back to that first New Year's Eve, and all the way forward to what was coming, I believed something powerful had brought that love to us. Could something powerful destroy it?

Through a dinner of pot roast, boiled potatoes, and spinach, Annie teased that I hated holidays and somehow found a way to plan a business trip around every single one.

"Well, it does save time to use the off days for travel."

"Some people," she said, "think the off days are supposed to be off days."

"Properly admonished," I laughed. "Just to prove I can take days off, when I get back to Denver, let's go over to the farm. Come to think of it, you could go over for the long weekend. I'll meet you there Tuesday night."

"You're bribing me," she said.

"Not at all," I protested. "Being practical, like you."

"You don't fool me," she said. "You just like to work, or you wouldn't be leaving right after the poker game. That seems awfully late to be starting on your trip."

"That's what you said before," I reminded her. "I have done it before and I do it because I need to make tomorrow's train out of Denver. Besides, driving overnight gives me a good excuse to go through Delta without stopping to see Warren Hellman."

"Why don't you want to see your old friend, Warren," Annie asked, sounding a little startled.

"Old friend Warren is going to give old friend Josh that loan. Maybe already has. They're both damn fools."

It was the usual time to leave for the game: ten minutes after seven. When she made to get up, I touched her arm to tell her it wasn't necessary. She turned her face up to me, high cheekbones supporting a few creases folding in at the corners of her eyes. When I first arrived in town, I had told a miner that I was too stone cold realistic to call my wife beautiful — that I simply liked the way she looked to me. I remembered that conversation almost thirty years ago and now as I looked at her, I wondered what ever possessed me to say such a damn fool thing.

I kissed her forehead. She was beautiful.

"My," she said, softly noticing how I was looking at her.

Maybe leaders of men needed to be wise and strong, or at least seem so. Yet great leaders showed their emotions and I didn't consider myself in that class. I couldn't afford it. It wouldn't do to let her know what I was thinking.

I broke off and headed for the stairs. I was following an imperative — one I had to follow to be the man I had promised I would be. It was assuming a lot to assume she would understand.

Assume it I did.

10

Sheriff Pickett and Larry Stein, the editor of the *Telluride Journal*, sat in their chosen seats at the round, green felt covered table Josh had ordered from the Sears & Roebuck catalog. The table was the center piece to this side room of Josh's rambling house. Josh leaned up against the wall that held a massive painting of a lone Indian standing with his horse on a plain extending endlessly to a mountain. All in all, that pretty much completed the setting for the Tuesday night poker game.

I took a straight-backed chair from the wall opposite the painting and pushed in between Larry Stein and the Sheriff. Stein immediately started in with his tired jokes about my suit. My riposte about Stein's garters went unheard in the commotion caused by an urgent knock.

"That'd be Kearns," said Josh, heading to the door.

"About time," said Pickett. He pulled his revolver out of its holster and placed it on the table. "I ain't got all night."

"Sorry, men," said Kearns in a quick, breathless voice. "I'm pulling up stakes, fellas. I had a few things to finish up, you know, by the end of the month. Don't have the house sold, though."

"You didn't say a word about this last week," said Stein, giving him the guilt tone we all knew so well with an exaggerated frown. "It's not right to keep your friends in the dark. Is it, Buck?"

"You're an old lady," I said, deflecting the question. It didn't seem logical following Kearns's announcement; there was always the chance Stein knew – or figured – more than he was telling.

I thought of my walk home, of the empty houses. One mining engineer gone, now another. Still some miners left, but no mining engineer. Kearns was the last. It wouldn't be easy to sell that house, but one thing I knew for sure, Kearns would make the mortgage good.

Studiously, I arranged the fifteen dimes I brought to the game each week.

"So where you goin', Jeremy?" I asked.

"There's a big copper mine over in Utah needs me. It wasn't sure 'til yesterday."

"What do you know about copper?" asked Pickett.

"Nothing," laughed Kearns, shucking his coat and pulling up the last chair. "It's not the metal that gives me the job, it's the mining. Hasn't been a new mine open up in this town since Mr. Wain here opened up the Black Bear in '27."

"I didn't open it up."

"Maybe not," said Kearns, reaching for the pitcher of beer, "but you sure did give them the money. Nobody else would do it and they got it opened up. Nobody's even tried since." Kearns's voice was loud. It was always loud, like he was giving orders to a crew down below the earth.

"Maybe I shouldn't have."

"Wasn't your fault," said Pickett. He held tight to the deck of cards in his right hand. "Are we going to play?"

"Damn straight," said Kearns, pouring out a second glass from the pitcher he still held in his hand.

"Go easy on that stuff," said Pickett. "I am the Sheriff, you know."

"Arrest me or lose your money," laughed Kearns. "This'll be the last chance I get to add to my stash. I aim to win a potful from you guys to add to that little bit I got over there at Mr. Wain's bank."

"Well, the night's young," I said. "I aim to take home what you brought with you, Jeremy. Of course, you can come over to the bank for the rest whenever you're ready."

"I'll deal," said Stein, holding out his hand for Pickett to give him the cards. He dealt out, snapping cards around the table, and he talked all the while looking straight at young Kearns.

"I sure hate to see this town die out. I figure I'm the only one around who was actually born in Columbia. Kearns, after you leave town, you can tell everybody you know that was the name before the Post Office forced the town to change it. Countin' my Pa, we have been around damn near since ol' John Fallon staked his first claim in the Marshall Basin. I loved that old mining camp. Then the railroad came and turned it into a boomtown. I loved the boomtown, too. But it's all gone now. I sure hate to see this town die out."

"Hell, I sure hate to see Kearns go," said Josh. He hoisted the pitcher. "He's the only other one around here who drinks beer. But don't worry about the town. It ain't gonna die out."

"I feel truly guilty about taking your money, what with me leaving for better prospects and all," said Kearns, making a long face as he raked in the first pot.

"I agree with Josh," I said "This town won't die. But I do worry about the folks who are here."

Stein scooped up the cards and handed them and the deal to Kearns, our custom for the man who won the pot. A silence fell over the table. It didn't bother me. I was just as happy to make no further comment.

"Copper. My god, copper," exploded Josh's voice. "Gold saved this town when the bottom fell out of the silver market in '93, and now Kearns is gonna mine copper."

The energy and joking came back and circled the table. I played out the hand in silence and the deal came back to me.

"My God, Buck, you won again." Josh's eyes sparkled as he said it and he shot his big right hand behind my neck, practically tugging my head off. I knew I was in for it. "Who wants to hear how ol' Buck got his nickname?"

"Everybody's already heard that story," I said. "Too many times."

Josh paid no attention. He knew me well enough to know I actually carried some pride in the punchy nickname he had given me.

"Yeah, everybody knows that," Stein agreed with me. "What I want to know is how you come up with these things. Is that how you spend your nights up here? Thinking them up?"

"David's mother's a mite too pretty for that," said Josh, drawing a shock of laughter all around. It wasn't regular for a man to point out his wife's attractiveness, especially when the wife, like Emily Gibson, was still lean and in fine figure. Stein's face flushed red.

"I don't believe it," said Stein, and everyone laughed at that, too. Stein chewed on his effort to rejoin. "No, I mean you. I know you've got some sort of secret life that you don't let us know about. I mean, how does a dirt digger like you come to have a son in Princeton?"

"There ain't no call to talk about that," said Josh. His normally booming voice got quieter and quieter as if he really didn't want to talk about it, but he continued. "David's a good boy and he likes to read and write. I always thought the most I could do was give him an education and maybe a little bit of a start. It just seemed like a good thing to do. I ain't been a dirt digger for a long time now; so, maybe he'll come back here and take over the ranch. That's nothing I ever said to him, but it's a bit of a start and that's what I'm hopin'.""

"If you still have the ranch," I said. I shouldn't have said it, even if I did try to make my voice quieter than Josh's, so only he would hear it.

"Oh, you glumgus," he sputtered in his booming voice, making it impossible to let my comment stay hidden. "I gave you the wrong damn nickname. I figured, you stack fifty thousand in gold bars on your marble counter, you got to be some buck and fearsome to boot. But now I guess what Buck really means is you're a stubborn damn mule deer."

To that I did not reply. My comrades around the table were no help; all three of them just held their cards and waited.

"He's just telling me once more that he don't approve of me buying the old Weller spread," Josh said, unnecessarily in my view. He could have just let it all drop and it would have been between him and me.

"The Weller spread?" Pickett's tone was a comment inside a question. "You going to try to ranch land all the way to Ophir? Seems like a long ways away to me."

"That's why I bought it," said Josh. "That land runs clear up to mine."

"Well, it's the first not smart thing I ever saw you do," I said. Now he had everybody in on it, he might as well hear it straight.

"Why?" asked Larry Stein.

I busied myself dealing. I had won another hand and that seemed like the best way to put a stop to this discussion.

"He won't tell you," said Josh. "You know, the banker's creed and all that. He don't like that I borrowed the money from Warren Hellman down in Delta. But what could I do? The stubborn son-of-a-bitch here wouldn't lend me the money. Hellman thought it was a little strange, me being a director of his damn bank and all, but I told him ol' Buck had a rule against it."

"Does he?" asked Pickett, turning to face me.

Like I said, the cards continued to keep me busy.

"Hell, I don't even know. He'd already told me how dumb I was, so I just made that up," answered Josh. "That Delta bank ain't all that big, but old Warren's a hard worker. I'll say that for him. He went to some Denver bank and between the two of them I'm getting what I need. 'Course I had to pledge the farm and my shares in the Norwood Cattle Company. But I got the loan all right."

I peered out over my fanned cards around the table. The room waited. I folded my cards, fanned them again, placed them face down in front of me. I don't know why they expected me to say anything, and I let the silence draw out. Stein and Pickett watched me so intently I could feel it. Josh made a big show of filling his and Kearns's glass. He turned over my cards and looked around the table. He held out four nines.

"You might be getting *more* than what you need," I said as I picked up the pot.

Cards and conversation ebbed and flowed until well past midnight.

"Well, I'm out, Buck," Josh exclaimed with ringing laughter. "You got my money. Was that your plan? Lucky I saved my money today, less to lose to you tonight."

"I was sorely tempted to suggest you just keep it in your pocket."

"All the more to lose to you tonight," Josh said. Once again he clapped his huge hand on my shoulder.

"Better than to lose to some other banker," I said. Why do I do that? Immediately the words were out of my mouth, I knew I should have just let it all pass by me. Fortunately, Kearns was in no mood to let the table dwell on the leaking of worry.

"The hell you say!" he shouted. His glass was empty. The folding money he'd put on the table had grown a little larger at the start of the evening, but all that remained were a bill and a few coins.

"You been waiting all night to get that in," said Larry Stein.

"Damn straight," said Kearns, "You can't find tellurium anywhere around these mountains. So it had to be them old boys who come prospecting up here what gave this town its name."

"Maybe," said Stein, counting his few remaining coins. "But it was 'to hell you ride'."

"What's that about losing to another banker?" asked Pickett, ever the sheriff, his question bringing back a loose comment I hoped had safely disappeared.

Edward Massey

"Like I said, Old Buck here's a glumgus. Thinks everybody's gonna lose their money," said Josh. "Hell, it's only true when he plays poker with us."

"Mr. Wain, how much did you win tonight?" Kearns's voice boomed again. "Go ahead, count it."

I tried hard not to show anything, least of all a smile. It was tough because I was thinking how much I liked it when someone, usually Kearns, tried to dominate the game by throwing down a big stack of bills at the start of the evening, figuring the size of his stack set him up to outlast the rest of us. All that attitude did was improve my chances. Lose little, win big.

"That wouldn't be seemly," I said. For good measure, I tucked the bills straightaway into my wallet.

"It ain't too hard to figure this out," said Pickett. He unbuttoned the breast pocket of his shirt and pulled out a little notebook. "The banker, here, had brought his fifteen dimes. All the rest of us brought folding money and now Kearns's is the only paper dollar left on the table." Pickett stopped talking and concentrated on his figuring. He drew a line under the column of numbers and totaled them.

"My God," he cried, "you won more than twenty dollars!"

"Oh, I don't know," I said. The money and wallet had long since disappeared into the pocket of my suit coat. "You forget, though. I lose most of the time."

"Lose little, win big?" said Pickett.

My God, the man was tenacious. For the briefest moment, I wondered if I would ever have him on my trail.

I got up from the table, the only way to end this. Blessedly, it was my normal time to leave.

Passing through those men, my lifelong friends, shaking hands and saying goodnight, I gave thanks for my predictable habits. No one asked and no one was lied to; it may seem strange today, but that gave me confidence. What I needed to do, I needed to do with no one realizing it, and I had passed my first test.

I reached Main Street and noticed something I must have known for twenty years or more. The electric street lamps were evenly spaced. I don't know how long I sat staring into their symmetry, into the regular pools of light shed onto the deep loneliness of the street.

No other vehicles greeted me.   Only Kearns lived in my neighborhood, and he always stayed back and drank beer with Josh. Home lay ahead, across the intersection, across Main, up the small rise, north of Colorado Avenue. The thought flickered that maybe I should just go home. It guttered with one more look at the street. Empty now, but it might soon be deserted.

Turning left, I drove the Studebaker down Colorado and out of town.

11

An isolated mining camp almost nine thousand feet above sea level for men who would climb another one or two thousand feet to burrow into the earth. There, using primitive tools, powered only by their bodies, gasping for air, they would dig and haul a ton of dirt a day. From inside the mountain the dirt had to be moved to a place where it could be separated into its hidden treasure of gold and silver. The job started with mules led up the mountain by men on horseback. Entrepreneurs carved toll roads from the steep slopes to allow a steady progression of mule trains. More freight meant more tolls. Toll roads led to rails, and mule trains gave way to steam trains — small trains, running on a narrow gauge, but trains nonetheless. Once rails replaced the toll roads, men and supplies moved to where the dirt was valuable. Women, families, rapid growth followed. Telluride emerged.

Building our boomtown did not require a carefully planned schedule. The trains that built Telluride could not offer the precise timing I needed for this trip. Hell, they couldn't even be relied on to get me to Denver — at least, not on a certain day. For that I trusted only my car. That was fine. I loved to drive. Annie might be inconvenienced a bit, but she hated driving, anyway. Besides, Connie would help her.

A few hundred feet beyond the turn onto the main road I passed into the broad valley defined by two rows of hills leading into town. The car gained speed down the gathering slope. The invisible force taking me to Denver played out my drive down this valley through Saw Pit to Placerville where I would turn right at the end of the canyon and head for Ridgway. After the left turn onto the big highway just outside Ridgway, next stop: Montrose. No, I would not stop, just a figure of speech. I would keep on going until I got where I needed to go.

I consider myself a planful man. I had a plan for driving to Denver. I had a plan for taking care of my depositors. Plans took shape in my head the same way every time. They started high and broad. Sometimes they took several years, then swooping down to touch me, as in recent weeks, my concerns narrowed ever further and my alarm grew ever brighter, until my plan took hold. Take hold it did and I saw where I was going.

The Studebaker had a good heater, and I had on a good coat, and I knew what I was doing, and I loved driving on this road, and I was still cold.

That chill was the withdrawal of the seductive nymph's caress. Ten years in my journey home, years of Telluride's decline since the end of the war, years I had been in the service of Success. Her touch is like none other. The sensual and docile life I led became a struggle with her as soon as I started to see the problems coming. Now I saw that struggle for a false promise. If I devoted myself to Success, she could make everything right. If I did not, she would move on, ignore me. That loss created my chill.

I glanced at my watch. It would take about ten hours to make the three hundred sixty-odd miles to Denver and it was not the end of my journey but the beginning.

Maybe I could be in Denver by ten-thirty.

12

What needed to be done was simple, really. With the right loan my depositors could get their money. Sure I knew it might not have been enough to see them through the hard times I saw coming, but the first rule is do no harm. They had put their money in my bank and no other bank's failure deserved to rob them of it. When everybody made good on what they owed the bank, and make no mistake I was most worried about the biggest banks that were furthest away, I could pay off the loan. The interest on the loan was like the premium on an insurance policy for depositors.

It was too damn bad there wasn't some way I could have just bought them insurance. I would have gladly paid for it out of bank profits to see them safe today.

Take that miners' insurance for Rosa Knutzon. I'd loaned Akus and the others a stake to reopen the Black Bear for gold. Akus had a belief in the future and I wanted to share it, in the meaning of encourage him. Hang the common wisdom that held the mine had petered out. I loaned them money for supplies and equipment and they became known as the Black Bear Five. Akus wanted money for living expenses, too. I couldn't do that. Of course the bank stood to profit from the loan, but I had to draw the line. So, I suggested they make a deal with the widow Fall to stay in her boardinghouse on the hill. She was a tough nut, and Akus probably choked trying to negotiate with her, but she put them up, and I figure all she asked in repayment was a cut in the deal.

The avalanche in '27 came midway toward dawn in the second night after the blizzard. Steep mountains cradle Telluride in a box canyon of gray granite. They have a way of putting up with only so much snow. They hived off tons of the stuff with a shuddering crack loud as a cannon blast, woke up the whole town in the middle of the night. What with the steep and the distance, waves of snow built up to seven stories high, traveling at forty miles an hour and increasing in speed. They hit the boarding house, split it in two, dragging it down the slopes, and shredding it along the way.

Summer came late that year. The final burial took place after they found the bodies during the wildflower festival in the last week of June.

I felt responsible. Standing in the bright sunshine of the funeral with Rosa, I wished there had been some kind of miner's insurance for Akus's widow and the new baby on the way. I simply made it up on the spot.

"Well, Akus had a policy for three thousand dollars," I told her. For good measure, I also told her, "Now that the body has been found, you may collect the benefit whenever you like. In cash. You can take it with you or put it in the bank. Now, mind you, you have no obligation to put it in the bank, but if you do I will try to help you with it and whatever you don't spend will be there when you need it."

So, you might say, this trip was the first step in what I had to do to invent some insurance for my depositors. Nobody believed me and nobody had offered any banking insurance for depositors before, so you might say, it wasn't without risk.

There were the shareholders to think about, too. They had invested in the bank in the hope of making a profit. In the good times they made a fine profit, indeed. If I could just get this loan and protect the depositors, all those loans would be made good and the shareholders would make out fine, in time. Of course, that was too much to ask for. Without the loan, the bankers who could help would simply stay away and punish the depositors for something they had not done. Righteous self-interest does things like that. With the loan, the bankers who "helped" me would swarm down to get the money back from the depositors and when they couldn't – believe me, I planned to fix it so they couldn't -- would be doubly angry. They would do the only thing they could do, punish the shareholders for something they hadn't done, something they had not even known about. Known about, hell! I didn't even ask them. Worse still, the tragedy of it all is that my shareholders and I would have been better off if I had just stiffed our depositors, voted myself a big salary for making the tough decisions and walked off with it.

We have been through a lot as a country since then and the misfortune of a war has made our country rich again. So, we are back to the place where people simply have too much to believe what I am saying. When we lose it all again, people will believe what I am saying was true then.

What our bank stood for was taking care of the people it served, not me or anybody who worked for me. If we took care of them, we deserved our fair profit; if we didn't, we deserved the loss. So, if taking care of them ended up creating the loss, well that was part of the promise, too, wasn't it?

After all the years of buying shares in my own bank I now owned five hundred of the nearly twelve hundred shares outstanding, and I figured — well, hoped — that the other shareholders would see things my way. After all, they had profited from the bank's good times, they were obligated to take some risk when it came to protecting the depositors. That was only fair. Leastwise, it seemed that way to me.

There had been snow the night before. The warm air, maybe 50 degrees, kept the road clear if wet. I followed the original road engineered in the 1880s from Telluride to Montrose via Horsefly Mesa. I knew it well. I loved driving my Studebaker. I simply loved the game of skill: to keep the car's speed steady moving down the course itself parallel to the twin strip of rails laid down running parallel to the little river that snaked gently across the high mountain meadows. When I drove those roads, the pleasure I felt always, and I do mean every single time, mingled with the awe I felt for the people who had carved them from the steep slopes. Simply clutching the wheel I felt strength in my chest and arms; I felt I was one of those courageous settlers of long ago.

Ahead I could see the occasional tree or feel a massive presence rising with the slope off to the left of my headlights. Too dark to see well, with little to look at, I treasured the interruptions flashed by the moon on the San Miguel River.

I saw the occasional light in a house halfway up the hill and wondered why. Who built that house up there? Why is there a light shining in their window at this hour?

My headlights spread out on both sides of the shoulderless road, shining part way up the hill. Easing into the rhythm of the curves, I let the yellow Studebaker carry me down and around through winding switches. I began to feel as though the lights of the car snaked around the corner. Somehow I knew what was on the other side of each curve and with confidence there was nothing I feared. I coasted and straightened out the road as much as possible to avoid tapping the brakes.

I had dropped about twelve hundred feet when I passed through Sawpit. I knew the landmarks. The road ran right down next to the river and there were two lights on a pole, a curious apparition in the empty darkness.

Once out of Sawpit, slightly to the left I could see the ring of mountains painted in the faint glow of the new moon. I wished I could see this country one more time in daylight. This was where the evergreens competed, their light and dark greens jostling for attention. I dipped down and then up a little and there, straight ahead, showed the stand of lodge pole pine so clearly on this dark night that I gasped — out on the ledge, seemingly away, each one alone and full and yet each contributing to a majestic array.

From the first time I'd seen it years earlier, that stand had spoken to me, silently reminding me of what an individual should do. Stand tall and straight and alone and contribute to the whole.

I had planned it all in detail, and now it was becoming a reality. I have been asked a thousand times what did it feel like? I have been told I never talk about my feelings. Well, it was my reality and I accepted it and at that moment it was like simply floating along, without effort or feeling or deliberation, coasting. And I was coasting into Placerville.

Water seeped out of red rock that came right down to the road. The narrow valley I was leaving dead-ended into the canyon formed by the river. God had built an entrance to Telluride.

A rock fell off the hill, forcing me to swerve. I had expected to reach Placerville before two in the morning. My depositors lived here, too, the Butlers, twelve miles down the valley. That Jocine. Sharp and tough, but maybe a little less than truthful when it came to matters of money. A lot of people aren't truthful when it comes to matters of money; some don't even know it. Something about Jocine Butler just made me want to watch a little extra.

I checked my watch. On time. A right turn at the junction and the road started to climb again toward Ridgway. The slight distinction between heavens and mountains showed the ridge. My headlights flashed on fence posts and hit the dark bottoms of trees. Traveling north-northeast, up and down, under the sheltering red ridge I knew was above me, the moon would stay behind me all the way through San Miguel County.

The headlight flash caught bright yellow flowers that clung to bushes along the roadside. I had always meant to stop to see if there was a gully there, or maybe a ditch.

I sensed the Uncompahgre Forest rising above me to the east. You could not call me an outdoorsman, maybe even far from it, but I believed in being self-reliant and I loved the forest. I had taught Connie to gauge altitude by the type of trees he saw.

"Must be above 10,000 feet," the boy would say. "That evergreen with reddish bark is Engelman Spruce."

In the dark, the narrow path between the massive slopes becomes part of the larger valley rising to the peaks. All that mass above you and it does not feel closed in. I tried to look into the hills as I snaked along the west side of the Uncompaghre River. The high mountain meadows were perfect for milk cows and well used for beef cattle. The darkness yielded too little distinction to see them or the evergreens that marched up the hill in serrated rows. I could not even see the white bark of the aspens high up on both sides.

I coasted fast through the big broad curves and passed a trailer hauling a large piece of equipment. My eyes started to burn and I held up my watch, the glow of the hands at a quarter to three.

I could see lights to the left as I came over the ridge. One more curve, a big one, and I was among the few stores, such as they were, lining the road. After two cross streets I was out of town and at the big road. A left turn, a slight slope up, and I quickly passed through Ouray County into Montrose County. Now it truly was 'next stop Montrose.' The road crossed pastures high in the hills, the Uncompaghre on my right. I imagined elk down there feeding in the bends of the river. I had eaten elk brought to me by Josh and my other hunting friends, but I had never shot one. I had never shot anything.

I wondered if I would have been a more successful banker if I had hunted — and played golf. I admired the camaraderie of both activities, but the first was too violent and the second too wasteful, not to mention I'd have to drive all the way to Denver. Drive or not, maybe it would have helped with that loan from Denver International.

A sudden downpour and rattling thunder broke into my thoughts. I knew it would stop as quickly as it appeared and the thunder would vanish back into the black night. Knowing changed little, except for the confidence it gave me. Driving into the heavy rain, holding the wheel with both hands, trying to maintain what speed I could, commanded all my attention. At Montrose it was still dark. I could barely make out the green alfalfa, cut and baled in neat rows in the field. I wondered if the farmers had anyone to sell it to, any use for it other than to feed the horses I knew they would be pasturing in their front yards. What was not planted in alfalfa was acre after acre of corn. Corn for silage. No wonder Josh thought the profit from his ranch was earned in the feed lots of Montrose, where he took his lean-muscled mountain cattle to fatten up.

I cleared Montrose before I could figure out the relationship between the thousands of beef and the thousands of acres of corn to feed them. Bores you, doesn't it? But those are the kinds of questions people have to think about to support their families, so they fascinate me.

I headed into the flat rolling hills that opened out to Olathe. Seeing the small road sign, I remembered an old colleague at a bank in the Kansas town of the same name that only last spring I had tried to help with a letter of introduction to the Chase in New York City. Those New York bankers must have thought: Who are these people who could live in such wilderness? Of course, the truth is they probably didn't think at all about people from Olathe. I wondered if the ones in Colorado had pushed out here from Kansas. It was hard to imagine the life they lived. It made me question what I had done bringing Annie to such a place? Like Penelope, she stayed true no matter what my travels. My Annie. My Penny. They meant the same. Just beyond Olathe the goldenrod stood along the ditches, tall yellow flowers against the headlights, and then suddenly the powerful smell of sweet grass.

I could see the lights of Delta off to the right. I could sense the broad, wide valley created by the two dark blues of the night sky. Past a crossroads, a lone tree supported a light, and I was in Delta.

The car moved down the main street until coming to a stop at the railroad tracks, crossing gate down, train inching through. Delta started small and stayed small — but prosperous. Warren Hellman, my friend who lived here, had a nice little bank, but if he was making loans like the one to Josh, he might be stretching himself thin. Josh knew what I thought; Warren hadn't asked. I should let it rest at that.

Lucky for Delta, it was green. In some places you could see water from the road. Beyond the town, for twenty miles, you could see nothing. Miles of barren dirt, sometimes a few tumbleweeds, yielding only to the occasional canyon carved down from the flat plateau. Those arroyos were testament to the force and uselessness of the water when it comes. Lucky for Delta, it had usable water.

Leaving the mountains behind, I could feel them, like a citadel rising out of the plain. Funny, as I was leaving, what I recalled was the first time I'd approached them. Here was a city, a home, a hometown.

Funny, like I said, how much that mattered. The land where I grew up, in southeast Pennsylvania, molded my soul. I call it a land because it was a place with a separate culture, like a separate nation. But I had to migrate. I made a pilgrimage from a place I needed to leave to a place where I did not know I needed to go. I did not know it was the mountains I needed until I was among them.

Annie would laugh at that romantic story. Annie saw everything as a fact and she knew the truth. I discovered the mountains when I moved to the mountains and I had moved to the mountains for the simple reason that I was a bank clerk in Grafton, Nebraska, when Leon Drew offered me the chance to become president of the bank, his bank, and now my bank. All I had to do was move to a little town in the mountains of Colorado and work there for six years. Annie understood, and she never questioned. She had a father who was a banker, John Martin, president of the Bank of Grafton. Over the years John Martin groomed Annie's brother, Bradley, to take over. Bradley had been head teller when I got my first job; now he was president. It made perfect sense that her husband, a banker, would uproot his family and move wherever he needed to in order to become a bank president as well.

The bank in Grafton had given me a start and a wife. The bank in Telluride had given me a career, perhaps, but more important, it had given us a home.

Skipping the bigger road and the added mile to Grand Junction, I took the cutoff and let the Studebaker coast gently on its way to Clifton.

A bottomless feeling invaded my quiet calm. I had passed the last day of the life I had lived for more than a quarter of a century. I was not a man given to tears, but I recognized the feeling. No longer would I live among these people, nor in these mountains.

13

The road crossed the Colorado River just before Clifton. It turned east and ran with the Colorado all the way past Gypsum, an easy drive in the dark on all that flat.

Light from the stars and the moon outlined the contour of the huge bowl of earth around me. To the northeast, I could see skyline, dark rising into faint light. Glancing over my right shoulder I fixed Mars in the southwest sky. In the lingering darkness before dawn I no longer felt a sense of night.

Denver lay a little over two hundred miles away. It was time to review my plan. An easy enough schedule with only two tasks to complete before the train left at three. There would be no problem. Hell, I thought I might even have time for a nap.

The distance between the car and the rising hills started to spread out. I could feel it. Only someone from Telluride could call them hills. No matter how high, it was flatland.

I ran my fingers over the soft lapel of my coat. It reminded me of prohibition. I had hoped prohibition would bring the good times back. Something about prohibition brought out the openly illicit and sparked enterprise and built capital down in the flatlands. It never quite made it up to Telluride. The illicit had always gone on pretty much out in the open up there. In the end, prohibition was nothing more than a venture of busybodies who felt God gave them the duty to legislate what other folks could and could not do. Such a venture was always doomed to fail.

My hometown in Pennsylvania counted no more than fifteen hundred souls but proudly claimed no less than thirty-seven religious denominations. With such diversity, every view is in the minority. The Mennonites' belief that the simple terms were the best terms set the standard for the town. Mennonites held their beliefs firmly and practiced them. For themselves. Modern folk, like the Wain family, would never adopt their attitudes and customs. That bothered the Mennonites not at all. Nothing in their belief allowed them to think they could tell others how to live. That was God's work. Mere mortals had enough work to be true to themselves.

A howling wind forced me to grip the wheel a little tighter, guiding the Studebaker through the wide farming plain past

DeBeque. Off to the right, beyond the plain, a range of white cliffs came into view. The darkness started to thin.

Wind carvings on the hills; how things change.

I was proud that I made the loan to Everett to open the Biltmore. I counted myself a good judge of character and I had been right — that barrel-shaped rough cob had been a good operator and a good credit.

In the cool blue gray of the early morning, I felt warm wrapped in my soft coat and the hard steel of the Studebaker. The road traveled east to Rifle, at bottom, along the river. Nature is the best engineer. The train track ran along the road with plenty of room before the hills started rising on the other side. Directly ahead I spotted the blue green face of a hill maybe thirty miles away. What gave it that color? A small black pony stood on the plain among the brown hills that rose gently from the high plateau that was the valley floor. A sheer red face rose to an abrupt right angle as pure as geometry, the bald face of the red rock giving way to another plateau.

I cracked the window, rolled it all the way down, eager to see more of that red rock face rising to the high plateau. I wished I could draw; I would draw the great sandstone massifs.

Still no sun, yet dawn's early light let me see. In the middle of the broad river valley, ore cars perched on the siding.

Idle ore cars.

There was a little cemetery, all the lonelier for being in the middle of the plain, just before Rifle. I could hear a train. By the time I could see it in the clear dawn, the Studebaker was overtaking the long train, inching toward its head before it disappeared into the tunnel to Glenwood Springs.

I admired the great castle carved out of the rocks all around me, though they were nothing like the slopes above Telluride. Looking out the car window at the high water in Grizzly Creek, I continued around the spiny ridges coming down the hills. The only other time I had seen land like this was on the train going down that narrow little valley into Salt Lake.

No shade anywhere. It would be hell later, even with the convertible. You could never have the top down.

The run in from Rifle was almost straight, all the way to Gypsum. It was day-bright, even as the mountains did their best to block the sun. Through the windshield I watched a flock of birds circle just above a brown-gray field, gathering into formation as they prepared for their annual journey south. The smell of mowed hay filled the air.

I tried to be a good steward to my little bank, keeping careful track of the comings and goings of its deposits. I noticed quickly enough when my depositors started to leave town in small numbers. But sometimes facts start coming at you and you can know those facts and still not connect them up.

The sun's sudden burst over the mountains created a first flash too harsh to look into no matter how long the landscape had been brightening.

With the Tomboy closing, I began to connect things up, like it or not. Mines failed, ranches failed, farms failed. Miners moved, ranchers moved, farmers moved. Everyone who left closed an account in hopes of starting a new life elsewhere. I was sorry to see them fail; I was sorry to see them go.

I was proud to return their own money to them and I told them, each one, I hoped it would be enough to make a new start.

It had been going on since the war. A decade of decline that shrank Telluride from five thousand to five hundred. Each day, I stood in my office watching through the glass walls as a half dozen of my depositors, all long since friends, came to take their money out. I sold all the gold bars, gone from the lobby but locked securely in the bank's vault for years. They needed the cash.

Above the stand of trees on the river, the plume of steam rose from the crushing plant in Gypsum. I knew it would trace down to the plant in full view up ahead. Broad high plain ten to twenty miles across, stark and harsh, too rugged for living, home to hay fields waiting to be brought in, their bales scruffy dry and brown. Two horses out to pasture graced the foreground, a painting of hills in pastels and dark colors — except for the single sign on the cement wall of a block house: For Rent.

It was hard to keep eyes open in the sun. Hard to stay awake. The sparkling light of early morning in the mountains made my eyes water. I took out my handkerchief, wiping first my eyes, then my spectacles.

Maybe I was destined to be unhappy since the world would never be perfect. Maybe I had actually sat on my stone and wept. Enough of that.

I passed Gypsum, and now the hills started to look like tailings, God's tailings, just leaving sand and rock behind. A couple of miles out and the flat gave way to what I knew would be about a hundred more miles of mountain. The sun continued to force my eyes closed. I pulled the Studebaker over to a rock ledge above the river.

It was a mystery how the quiet, green, shallow water could have cut so much, so deep out of this rock. Maybe on other days a rush of mountain runoff would make it easy to understand, but not today. It was almost dry.

I had had enough of nearly falling asleep. Besides, I wanted to be out in the mountains one last time. I flipped down the visors and unsnapped the roof locks. A moment later I had folded the top into its boot and snapped the canvas cover in place.

The rocks went straight up, around the hip of the mountain, interrupted with a shelf here and there bearing a tree or two. A trestle crossed maybe five hundred feet up on the canyon and then the tracks swooped down to about eight feet above the river. Must be the White River and this was where it fed into the Colorado. I got back in my car and looked into a perspective of mountain after mountain, distant peaks stared down like sentinels on the tiny one-lane road.

The gentle hills I drove formed a boulevard and cattle grazed right up to the soaring cliffs. Who cared for them? A log cabin nestled under the red sedimentary rock, its roof caved in.

I stared out at the range of massive mountains and narrow openings. I knew they would take any normal man's breath away, but my thoughts mingled with a certain local pride, this is easy going.

Strange how you feel when you start to notice something that's hard to believe. You don't know what's real and what's deception, but needing to know keeps at you. Just after the beginning of the year, in the midst of the nation's euphoria over its economic boom, I noticed bank failures. More each month for five months running. I searched my journals and professional publications for some short article, at least some small sign that someone had observed this alarming trend. Nothing. I called other bankers I knew, but no one seemed concerned. By the end of June I had no more doubt.

Something had to be done. I headed out of my bank, across West Colorado, under "The Town Without a Bellyache" banner, not even taking notice of the mud, and burst into the office of the *Telluride Journal.*

"There's going to be a crash," I blurted, still standing in the doorway.

"'s'at by way of 'hello'?" asked Stein.

"Larry, banks have started to fail again. More of them. Or at least faster. More frequently."

I realized I had not yet laid a precise word on what I observed. I put both hands down on Stein's oak rolltop desk and leaned into my announcement.

"I've been keeping track."

"No doubt," Stein averred without lifting his head as he continued to mark a sheet of newsprint.

"By March, already 228 banks have suspended operations. You know what that means?"

"Nobody much cares?" answered Larry, head down, scratching continued.

"Well, that's why I'm here. It means failures will go over 660 for the year. That's back to the rate of 1927."

"So?" said Larry. "Good year, '27. Except for Telluride, nobody had a better one."

"Oh, hell, you're as bad as my brother-in law, Bradley. Most people in Nebraska aren't too puffed up, leastwise Bradley Martin. Still, I couldn't believe last spring. Annie and I were in Grafton to check on the spring planting. I stopped by the bank to talk to Bradley. Deposits holding steady. Loans not going bad any more'n usual."

"Maybe it was true?" The editor put down his pencil and for the first time looked directly at me.

"Maybe," I said. "But, damn. Telluride's not the only town in trouble."

"And that's what you want me to write an article about?"

"Sure. Don't you see? People are going to lose all their money. We need to do something to get somebody's attention. I can't do it. Who am I? Just a little banker in a little mountain town."

"Well, Buck, I hate to break this to you." Stein paused and took a big sip of his ever-present black coffee. "Let me put it this way. I know this woman. Used to live in the big city. New York. Now, maybe she lives in Denver. Anyways, she has her finger on the pulse of what everybody wants to read. She'll say this ain't interesting. It may captivate *you*, but it won't grab readers."

I refused to accept the admonition. I knew people did not want to come to grips with vital subjects, especially when they were difficult to understand. I resigned myself to just one question.

"Has your friend ever lost everything?"

14

White fluffy clouds sported high above in the deep blue sky. The earth stretching upwards to meet those clouds gave us mountains, forming steep canyons. Everything reminded me of the people of Telluride -- a tree clinging defiantly on its ledge, pointed straight into the sky from its precarious perch. Where the road from Leadville came out on my right, I could see two passes. I couldn't remember the names of both but one was pretty sure Independence Pass. I had always meant to research how it came by its name. I liked the name, a fine name, the right name.

I wondered how folks were doing over in Leadville. After the turnoff, I passed from traveling on top of the world down into the deep valley shadows. The aspens by the roadside quaked with the slightest breeze. Everything reminded me of the people of Telluride.

The mere notion of national bank failures was unthinkable. The more concrete my concerns grew, the more I could see that we would be at the end of a long whip. The more I was certain the less I was able to get anyone to pay attention. By now, I was convinced the increase in bank failures this year meant twice as many next year. Ha, there was a notion they could hide from behind the old excuse, too much math and abstraction: increase, failure, doubling again. Truth is, and I knew it, they were hiding from too much gloom.

Jesus, the trouble with ignoring something because it is too difficult to think about is that if it happens it means it could happen again. Bank failures could probably double again. And if that happened maybe they would double even again.

Most people call that too abstract and what they really mean is the *maybe* in there is just too hard to manage. Most people think maybe means it won't happen. Ask 'em. So, they plunge ahead expecting the best and they don't prepare for the worst.

Let me tell you what maybe means. It means conduct yourself as if what you can foresee will become your reality. For good or for bad. That's real preparedness.

And joy, too, when you think about it.

But I admit, you don't much think of joy when some nobody from nowhere tells you there'll come a day when three or four thousand banks will fail. It is simply too unthinkable.

Believe me; I wanted the big people to be right. In July, the very month I knew I had to go to Denver for that loan, B.C. Forbes wrote,

> On the whole, the United States rarely has entered the second half of any year better circumstanced.

Now, I figured he believed that. After all, he wrote it in the journal that gave his family a fortune. He wouldn't carelessly take a risk with his reputation or his fortune. Leastwise, that's what he'd have you believe.

Spending was up. Politicians congratulated themselves on a cut in the tax rate. Happy as I was with seeing taxes reduced, the spending wasn't real healthy. It just came from the creation of a new system of installment credit. Now everyone could snap up cars, radios, appliances, even fur coats. And pay for them later. Funny that about the coats. Mine was cashmere and men in fur coats look just silly. Buying their women fur coats on credit was worse than silly.

As I came through Eagle Pass, the sun showed bright on a stand of trees in front of a narrow canyon, the gray-brown sandstone facing opened onto the only lake I had ever seen in these mountains. I started to pass into the steep downgrade and looked for it; there it was, the white fence, the pasture, the beautiful horses — a horse farm way up here.

I loved steep passes like this, they kept people out. Of course, the one that guarded Telluride was the reason no one paid attention to my alarms. Mine was a little town, almost impossible to get to. It didn't matter how I saw things.

In that summer of 1929, like always, the big people were the ones people listened to, like the president of the Union Pacific Railroad, Carl Grey, "I have just returned from a trip over all our lines, and the general feeling among bankers, lumbermen, and other businessmen is optimistic as to the business outlook."

Not that I begrudge him none. I know that little people are little for a reason. They don't command much, and a whole lot of them don't have much to say. When they do have something to say, they don't have much to base it on, for that matter. Me included. How could I possibly disagree with Mr. Gray? The Union Pacific had sixty times more employees than my town had citizens.

Remember what I said about maybe? Maybe he was right, but maybe I was, and that meant I had to do the things I had to do if I was right. Besides, truth to tell, I just didn't believe Mr. Gray's outlook. What it came down to, was I had no choice. I would just have to act on my own.

I was caught, caught out between forces that were bigger than me and principles that were stronger than any force. Now, don't get me wrong, I never told myself I was acting out of principle. That was a thought that was just too big for me. My thoughts were never as big as principles. They were just simple notions. The simple thought I had was when I took money from depositors, I made them a promise.

People ask me all the time how I felt about all this. How did I feel about losing my bank, all I had worked for? It wasn't my creation, not in the very beginning, but I took it over and built it up, bigger than people had any reason to expect, and along the way did people a lot of good, and then I lost it. My only answer to the question is that sometimes my chest felt right tight and I couldn't eat at all if I didn't sneak a whisky before dinner. I smoked a lot fewer cigars and that might have been a good thing.

Maybe I don't know what feel means, but for months I woke up in the night sweating and yet cold and not knowing why. How could I wake up in the middle of the night or twice or even three times my hair wet, my chest soaked, even little wrinkles on my fingers and I was freezing cold. By mid-August I knew. It would be soon — a month or two, three at the outside. I needed to act fast. The night I knew that, I slept soundly and woke up early to drive to Denver, this drive — only to be refused by the Denver International. That bank owed its very survival to me and they refused to help. I didn't tell them that, of course, I just turned around and drove straight back home to work out my plan. This plan.

Labor Day weekend would give me just a little extra help.

15

Peering deep into the canyon I could see the road snake through the short green flat around a red faced hill that climbed to a green and violet top. Up there, the aspens set out among the pines in stands — once again, a few segregating themselves among the many.

I never struggled with my decision. When asked later if I hadn't felt just a little lonely, I allowed as how I wasn't able to talk about it, but that didn't bother me much. Sure, it never hurt to talk things over, but there was no one to talk this thing over with. Leastwise, no one who wouldn't get into trouble if they knew what I was fixin' to do.

I watched deposits go down. I watched hard-working men, family men, miss their loan payments. I had no need to keep track of payment dates; these people never missed their obligations without saying something. They showed up, on time, to face me. The way Seth Tiedemann appeared at my door, a big, lean-muscled man, face tanned and pink from working out in the weather, clothed in coveralls and work shirt.

"Mr. Wain?" asked Seth from the open doorway. "Might I talk to you?"

Rising to greet my visitor, I knew instinctively that it was Seth's due date. This man had come from Pennsylvania, Lancaster, not too far from my own hometown. Seth Tiedemann and his three sons farmed a thousand acres that were frozen five or six months of the year. He raised a few bulls for the ranchers.

"Here, you take a seat," I said. I knew I would have to guide the farmer into my office and into the wooden chair. "What can I do for you, Seth?" I hoped my voice sounded friendly to him, I meant it to.

"Well, Mr. Wain, it's like this," said Seth. Words came to Seth with difficulty, even when the news was good. "I been makin' my loan payments regularly."

"Yes, you have. You have a fine record."

"Well, I come up a little short today."

"Is your payment due today?"

"Yes, sir, it is."

"Maybe a week would help you. I think we could do that for a man with such a fine record."

"That ain't it, Mr. Wain. I'd like to say I could pay you in a week, but I got two bulls ain't sold and one whole stand of alfalfa out there might rot. I just don't got no money coming in to pay you with."

"Perhaps you could just pay the interest, Seth."

"I don't know. That sounds pretty generous of you, but I just don't know."

"Well, you go back and talk it over with Baerbel. I don't want to take the food off your table, but if you could pay the interest, we could just roll over the principal a while till things get better."

I had no expectation of an answer. I knew the man would just sit there, saying nothing. Taking Seth's arm we walked together chatting about Baerbel and the boys all the way to the door of the bank. I patted him on the back and, knowing it was unnecessary, reminded him to come back next week.

It was getting warm, even with the top down, and the sun was no longer in my eyes. I swerved to avoid a boulder. Just as I was passing Georgetown and Silver Plume and thinking they were sad little places, the mountains did their best to open me up. Beyond a mountain meadow of rolling green grass as short and even as my lawn there erupts an elegant single pyramid of a peak — red, bald, soaring into the blue. It sits quiet and says nothing.

I approached Idaho Springs at nine-thirty on my watch. A few flowers in the window box of a darkly brown and weathered house interrupted the dismal laborer housing of this mining camp, surrounded by the yellow slagheaps of the gold mine and mill. The Stanley Metal Mines building was shut down.

The road sliced through a sheer face carved out down to roadbed, great slabs laid slantwise on end, on the final approach into Denver. Reminding myself a grade was always less steep than my senses told me, I started down. A small rockslide broke loose and rolled across the road behind me. *Maybe less steep, but still steep.* Two tight lanes snaked through the canyon next to the little creek rushing by. Barely able to hear the noise of the water with the top down, up and down and around and through into a golden space of valley after valley, slowly losing altitude, simple pinion pines spotted green in the burnt brown foothills. The air felt good. The road followed the crest through a gentle curve onto the high plateau and carried the Studebaker across the flat land until I could see the city start to rise out of the high plain. I would come in from the north and turn right toward downtown.

The Denver banks don't have the same integrity as Seth Tiedemann. I'll admit some anger flashed quickly by, but it was smothered by embarrassment. To be fair, I probably brought the embarrassment on myself. Maybe when I made that loan in 1914, it was for reasons that involved more pride than good sense, but, fact is, in July I had pretty much convinced myself Denver would come through. So much so that I'd gone ahead and written to the Chase to let them know I'd be bringing them a large check and that I'd need a fair amount of cash. Maybe a check for two hundred thousand sounds big only in Telluride, but giving the folks at Chase some advance notice just seemed the right thing to do. I couldn't tell Denver that I wanted the money to pay off my depositors. There wasn't much I could tell Denver at all. In the end, all I could do was ask for the loan…and hope. Of course, I knew that wouldn't stop the crisis that was coming. It would have just given me the insurance I wanted, the means to pay back my depositors.

Well, no one believed me. When I said something had to be done to save the whole damn banking system, I couldn't get anybody to listen. Now all I could do was take care of my own.

Union Station stood at the intersection of Seventeenth and Wynkoop Street, imposing and majestic. The locals cut it down to human scale by referring to it by its location, Seventeenth Street Station. I pulled the Studebaker under an expanse of trees and turned off the engine. I looked up the street toward Brown's Hotel, upon my return I needed only to drive the three blocks up to stay the night there.

Two doors were spaced evenly apart in the perfect symmetry of the broad white façade. I glanced at my watch as I entered the nearest one. I had plenty of time to buy my ticket and cross Wynkoop to the Western Union. Six telegrams rested in my vest pocket. It didn't much matter if they all originated from one office. To the six New York banks, even if they bothered to check with each other, telegrams coming from Denver's main Western Union office would seem logical enough.

I had done my research. Annie sometimes calls me predictable. And maybe she's right. I always do my research. Well, what I discovered was that Lindbergh's ambition had blessed me. In July, Universal Aviation had listened to their famous advisor and added a service connecting a train from Denver to Garden City, Kansas, with a plane to Cleveland. There it hooked up with a train again, so that the whole trip to New York took only one business day. I felt a furtive thrill at my discovery. Maybe a hundred people in all the country had used this service so far. No one would know how I got in and out of New York so fast. All I had to do was buy my ticket and take the eight o'clock train down to Garden City. I even had time for a little nap before I dropped off the telegrams.

I chose the quietest corner of the waiting room to set myself down, but what with the hardness of the bench and my concern over the telegrams, an internal clock triggered a small alarm every hour or so until, at three in the afternoon, I decided it just wasn't worth taking any risk with falling back asleep.

I stood up and stretched out the stiffness, straightened my bow tie, put on my hat and coat, now to instruct the banks to loan me the money I needed.

16

The nameplate — Masterson — above the brass buttons contrasting with the dull blue uniform of the messenger service gave me some comfort. She has a good name, easy to remember.

"Help you?"

I blinked at the cold, quick voice from the other side of the telegraph window. Not very friendly, I thought. I tried for a smile.

"G'd'afternoon, I have telegrams to send."

She looked me up and down.

"This is Western Union. You came to the right place."

"Right," I affirmed.

Maybe my greeting was as stupid as she made it sound. On any other day, I would have stopped right there and tried to figure out why she had to behave that way. It was a struggle, but I had to let it pass, if that's how it had to be. I produced the six envelopes. At the moment I started to count them out to her, I realized there was one more telegram that needed to be sent.

"Ah, may I trouble you for a blank?" I asked.

Her eyes narrowed into a pointed stare over my shoulder at the empty desk that ran against the back wall behind me. With a slight shake of her head, she reached in a drawer and slid a form forward.

"Thanks," I said. I pulled out my pen, quickly inspected the nib, and wrote: *Mrs. Charles C. Wain, Telluride, Colorado. Missing you. Meet you at the farm Tuesday. Love, C.C.*

I held out the form. The agent reached under the brim of her cap and twisted her glasses, the better to see.

"That you?" she asked.

"Yes, indeed," I said. Maybe there could be some pleasant conversation, but now I wasn't so sure I wanted it. It wouldn't do to have her remember too much about me. I managed a smile.

"Where's the farm?"

"Grafton."

"That's Nebraska, ain't it?"

"Why, yes it is." I was surprised. "Have you been there?"

"Naw. We get people here from all over. I remember 'em mostly."

"A-ma-zing," I said. Now I was sure she would remember me.

"That where you from?" she asked.

"In a manner of speaking," I said.

"Is that a fact?" She reached back under the cap and removed the glasses altogether. "You been here before?"

Well, no use trying to avoid it. I just nodded.

"I got my job right here, from a telegram sent to this Western Union."

Even as the words came out of my mouth, I knew I was being too open, my normal self. I should have lied, well, at least some way not to give her so much information, but her question surprised me. It was too late now, so I continued without taking notice of how much more she wanted to hear.

"I was in Denver looking for a job when I heard about one up in Telluride. I sent a telegram to Mr. Drew and I waited right here in this office for four hours. I was willing to wait until the train left to Grafton. Well, he sent a telegram back and offered me the job sight unseen."

"Is that a fact?" She put the glasses back on. "That'll be fifty cents."

"Oh, I've got more," I said.

"Don't have time for more," she said.

"No, I mean more telegrams," I said, though the truth was, remembering the story about getting my job in Telluride reminded me of my parents, and I was about to tell her that story, too.

"Give them to me," she said.

She took the envelopes and rotated each one separately, a question growing on her brow.

"Official business," I said.

"Uh-huh," she said. She shuffled through them again. "You know I'll have to open these to send the telegrams."

"Yes, of course." My wide smile made my spectacles ride up on my nose. I reached to smooth out my mustache. "The fact is, Mrs. Masterson, I was hoping you would send them on Friday. That's why they're sealed."

She looked at me again, the question still on her brow.

"Official business?"

"Yes," I said. Then, bending my head nearer the window, "Also, they need to be sent at a particular time, between three-thirty and four o'clock Friday afternoon. Can you do that for me?"

"No."

She pushed the six sealed envelopes back through the glass.

"You'll have to come back and do it yourself. We don't take responsibility for when telegrams are sent. We send 'em when you give 'em to us."

I felt my heart begin to beat faster. I hadn't allowed for this; it wasn't part of my plan. "Well, if I give them to you today," I asked, struggling to keep my voice even and unhurried, "can you mark them for delivery on Friday? Maybe they can be held in New York."

"Never heard of that before," she said. "Wouldn't know how to do that."

"Well, can you tell me how they will be delivered in New York?"

"Same as always," she said, holding up her arm and displaying her uniform sleeve. "Messengers."

"But I thought you had these new Teletype machines in all the businesses," unable to conceal my disappointment. "Wouldn't they be delivered directly, no need for messengers?"

"Don't know about that," she said.

"You mean to say the Western Union cannot tell me how a telegram is delivered in 1929?"

"There is no information available regarding the specific telegram or the general delivery methods," she said, as though reading from a manual, "and I got no details regarding such deliveries. Now, do you want to send them telegrams or not?"

"Can't you just send them for me on Friday?" I asked again. The question might have felt like pressure to her and it triggered a big caution light. I realized I had not considered the risk. Even if she agreed to send them, how would I know she had actually done so before it was too late?

"Nope. Got to do it yourself," she repeated.

The first flush of panic had passed. Now a measured calm took over; I had made an error in judgment. Only her obstinacy had saved me.

That little flirtation with a serious mistake reminded me of one of my primary rules as a banker.

The outside world will say no to you. It will protect you by its unwillingness to do what you want to do.

You might not believe it by what I was fixing to do, and I know my life would have turned out a whole lot different if I had followed my own rules.

Trust all the nos you get.

"I can't come back," I said, letting out an audible sigh. "I need to get back to the station to catch the train. To meet my grandchildren for the weekend."

"Don't matter to me," she said. "If you just have the one telegram, that'll be fifty cents."

17

The continuing warmth in the late summer sun seeped through my suit coat to my shoulders on my walk back to the car. Sun like that was too good to waste; I would leave the top down on the Studebaker. By the time I'd found my way out of town, heading east toward Limon, I had thought out my route and recalculated this leg of my plan. The train through Colorado Springs and Pueblo would take seven hours; I could beat that by two. Maybe get to Lamar before nine — none too late to take Susan to dinner. We could go to that little place she liked at the other end of town. She'd like driving through Main Street with the top down.

Why hadn't I thought of it in the first place? A better idea, really, what with Lamar right on the way to the plane in Garden City. Susan could send the telegrams. I could trust her to get it done, and she wouldn't need to talk to anyone about it. And I would get to spend the night at Susan's instead of on the train. Then, on the way back, I could drive straight from Lamar to Brown's. Yes, a much better idea.

Susan had been given her mother's maiden name and Susan Martin Harp seemed to double the Martin in her character. Like Annie, she would treat my asking a favor as no more than a matter of fact. Nothing to discuss, just something to do for Uncle Charles. On the other hand, if I was going to get in trouble, I didn't want anyone else involved. But, heck, she'd be all right, I told myself, as if to address the discomfort that rode with me right into the driveway of the neat white frame house. The headlights flashed across the front door as I turned. Susan was at the car before I killed the motor.

"Uncle Charles!" she cried, stepping up onto the running board.

Like Annie, she brought sheer delight to my life. It was one of my great pleasures to be her uncle. To my announcement that I had come to take her to dinner, she responded, "Will you spend the night?" showing no surprise that I had simply turned up. Even the question reminded me of Annie. She needed only the facts.

"That would be nice," I said, reaching to take her extended hand. "I have to go over to Garden City in the morning. I'm going to take an airplane flight, can you believe that? Think you could drive me? Maybe you could bring my car back here and take care of it for a few days. That is, if you wouldn't mind picking me up when I return."

"Oh, Uncle Charles, that would be swell," she squealed, leaning in to kiss my cheek.

"Get in," I said and waved my arm to motion her next to me. She probably didn't even hear my words above the piercing whistle of the Atchison Topeka, passing a quarter mile down the road. I yelled, "I'm starving."

Susan tucked her head and raised her hands in the classic charging motion. I wondered how anyone that pretty and that alive could still be unmarried at twenty-six. She ran around the back of the car, swung the door open and stepped straight up, her long skirt swirling, to stand on the floor board before the front seat.

"Full ahead!" She belted and my charging cavalry captain had been transformed into a landlocked sea captain commanding the ship.

"I'll drive slow," I said prompted to caution by a look at her hands clutching the top of the windshield.

"Not on my account!"

Susan remained standing, face into the wind, hair blowing, all the way to Blackwell Station, down North Main and pretty much all the way down South Main, too. She was excited and talkative and hardly touched the beef patty she ordered. I hadn't eaten all day. The menu offered a steak — no description, just steak. A skinny T-bone arrived, long and thin with a bone down the center, but juicy and good. The potatoes were the best, simply cut and fried in a skillet.

"How's school?" I asked her.

"Starts Tuesday," she said. "They've given me sixth graders. Had two years with the third grade, so if I keep sixth grade, I'll get those kids back next year. Wish I had them now."

"Why's that?"

"You see," she started out, a certain earnestness in her voice, "it's an elementary school. The sixth grade kids are top of the walk. Might be easier, my first year, keeping them in line if I had the kids I had once before."

"You'll do fine, Susie." I put down my coffee and patted her hand. "You've risen to every challenge."

"Because of you," she said, placing her hand on top of mine. "If it weren't for you, I wouldn't even have these challenges."

"My," I said with a twinkle, "that sounds utterly burdensome."

"Oh, Uncle Charles," she squeezed my hand, "you know what I mean. I wouldn't even have gone to college."

"Nonsense," I said. "Besides, your Aunt Annie and I just want to help."

"You did more than help," she said. "Mom was content for me just to marry a banker."

I laughed. "She might not have felt that way if she had married one."

"That's just the point," said Susan. "Grandpa was a banker. Uncle Bradley's a banker. Aunt Annie married you. And Mom ended up in Cheyenne working. You know Mom and Dad couldn't send me to college. And she always used to say, 'You look just like your Aunt Anne. You don't need to go to college; you just need to marry a banker.' "

I stretched back against the chair and, best I could, tried to make as if to look at her for the first time.

"By Jove, you do look like your aunt."

She laughed. "Uncle Charles, you're the cat's meow. Anyway, you'd say the same for Margaret. You can't kid me."

"Prob'bly," I said, unsuccessful in suppressing a grin, "she's pretty cute, too."

"Oh, Uncle Charles," Susan laughed, "when you do that, the edges of your mustache turn up." Abruptly she stopped. "You sent us both to college, Uncle Charles. You didn't need to do that."

"Oh, but I did. In a manner of speaking, I think I clearly did," I said. Finished with my steak, I glanced around. I caught the attention of the waitress and signaled for the check. "You see," I continued, "my father thought if you worked on the foundation you could trust to the rest."

I stopped and took a slow sip of coffee. There was more that I might have said — about years of high promise that led to promises unfulfilled. About struggle and disappointment — the sort that slowly eats away at a man, or a whole town. I might have admitted that my family never would have what I once hoped for them. I might have felt depressed about how it was all turning out, but I couldn't. I like to think it wasn't my way, but the truth is, all I really know is that it wasn't the way I wanted Susan to think about difficulties.

Morning's first light streamed through the single window of the lean-to bedroom tacked onto the kitchen. Susan's call, "Five o'clock, coffee's ready," followed her knock. A glimpse of her already dressed, yellow scarf knotted around her neck, seeped into the dark space that lay anchored by a huge weight behind my eyes, pinning me to the bed. In the first daunting moments of consciousness it all seemed impossibly futile. *It will pass,* I told myself, *you have to keep moving. That's what makes it pass.* By the time I got into my car I would be back to my purpose.

Was it all predetermined, I wondered? How could someone who believed he was responsible for his own actions watch himself throw off the comforting quilt and climb out of bed and know he was totally incapable of altering what he was about to do?

I quickly washed and shaved, took two greedy gulps from the large white mug Susan had set on the floor, and slipped into the shirt I had worn the day before. A few wrinkles, but clean enough. It would do for one more day, especially since I would see no one I knew in the plane or on the overnight train.

The sun's glare shone directly into my eyes as we drove toward Garden City. I turned to my niece. "Maybe you'd like to drive the car to Denver while I'm gone?"

"You read my mind, Uncle Charles," she said, her voice a little thin, as though she had been caught in a scheme.

"Not to mention." I said. "That'd be fun for you. Call your sister, get her to come down from Cheyenne."

"I'm glad you suggested that," said Susan. "You know, she thinks you favor me."

"That's too bad," I said. "I've always tried to do the same for her as I've done for you. I'm sure she knows that."

"I'm sure she does, Uncle Charles, I certainly am," said Susan, and she reached over to touch my hand on the steering wheel. "She just thinks you come see me more than you do her."

"I can fix that," I said brightly. "I'll go up to Cheyenne and visit her in a couple of weeks."

"That'd be swell," said Susan. "Is there anything I can do for you while I'm in Denver?"

"My gosh, I almost forgot," I said. Blessedly, she had solved the problem of how to bring up the subject, but I kept my voice light and joking. "There were some telegrams I couldn't get off at the Western Union."

"Sure, I can do that," she said. "I can make it up there tomorrow by one."

"No need. Between three and four will be fine," I said. "Just be there before the telegram office closes at four."

She leaned over and kissed me on the cheek.

"That's jake," she said.

"Jake," I repeated, slapping my hand on the steering wheel and beaming. "Have fun. It's a powerful car. Just pick me up on Monday at five-twenty."

Waiting to watch her Uncle Charles take off seemed like a dumb idea to me when she could get an early start to call Margaret for tomorrow's trip to Denver. I shooed her off and followed my niece's waving hand, growing ever smaller as she drove the Studebaker down the single lane dirt road away from the air strip, her long blonde hair and yellow scarf flying in the breeze.

Now I was alone, and I might as well tell you, I knew it. I looked at that big plane, looked big to me with its tailing dragging on the ground, and part of me wants to tell you I had second thoughts, but I didn't. I had my mind made up, that's what a plan is. I just didn't have any room for second thoughts; I had to do it and that meant I just had to be alone.

18

Even the simplest room at the Gotham Hotel was too fancy for me. Pretty tired Friday night by the time I got there, I didn't need but a room to sleep in. That room service is quite a deal and even if it wasn't a steak from Josh's herd it was pretty darn good. When I was just starting to eat, I looked at my watch. It was about the time the telegrams should come in.

The Equitable Trust raised the first question; that's why the prosecutor went looking for the clerk who handled the coded instructions. No two ways about it, he was stunned to find an Italian-American mother of three, who started as a receptionist seven years before, now in the position to handle telegrams in the code of the American Bankers Association. How'd you ever get there, he asked, without even trying to hide his surprise. After her husband lost his construction job, kids had to eat and bills had to be paid. She was plain clear in saying she knew how she got her job but that didn't mean she had to *stay* a receptionist. She started asking for more to do. Her bosses' hesitation gave way to little tasks and she kept asking. Finally, they gave her the job that required her to learn and keep secret the code.

Laurie McEnroe smiled and said, well, it was a big job. After a year they gave me the promotion that went along with it.

She was the only one left in the office after quitting time on Friday before a long weekend. Lori didn't need to go to the clattering teletype to know a telegram was coming in.

She could have left it till Tuesday. Aside from her, only two officers knew the secret language bankers used – and they were gone.

If you knew the code, you could tell a bank what to do, and you could trust what you were told. Knowing the code made her a vital link in that chain of trust, and she was proud of it. She valued that trust and she resigned herself to the knowledge that this is what comes with responsibility. She'd have to wait until it was finished. As far as she was concerned, if she had to stay a little late on a Friday, even Labor Day weekend, well, so be it.

It wasn't a long message — only a few words. She ripped the page off the roller and went back to her desk, unlocked the middle drawer, and took out the code book. Not that she needed it, mind you. She'd memorized the code the very first weekend of her assignment, but she had kept the book at her side for four years, just in case.

ALLUNGANDO: The test word. It proved knowledge of the code, on the part of the sender, but also hers, by telling her the number 326 was the total of all other numerals in this message, including the date.

EXEMPLAR: Deposit with a certain bank a sum of money for the credit of a certain other bank. Name of the CHASE NATIONAL BANK came as no surprise; after all, most of the coded telegrams she handled had to do with the Chase. The other bank, the one for which the credit was to be created, was new to her. An odd name, BANK OF TELLURIDE, but all the rest of the telegram was in order so she decided not to look it up. It wasn't important to her job to know who received the credit and this was already taking time out of her weekend.

BUNCADOR: The amount: $75,000.

EXAGITATE: Take care of this at once.

Well, of course. That word kind of offended her, in the way you can be offended by people you don't even know. The sender could thank his lucky stars that she had not left it till Tuesday, but still, it would have to be taken care of the next day, no matter who was telling her it was urgent.

She put the telegram in an envelope and wrote "Exagitate" across it. When asked why she did that with a word that offended her, she laughed that it was her little inside joke on the assistant vice-president. She took the envelope to the Transfer Desk and propped it up in the center of his desk. He had cleared the place more than an hour earlier proclaiming to all within earshot that he had drawn duty for the holiday weekend -- now, at least, he'd have something to do.

At six o'clock she left the bank. She remembered that she felt proud of her willingness to take time out of her holiday weekend to do the bank's work.

Remarkable woman though she was, she shared her devotion to duty with five other clerks in five other large New York banks.

Each clerk received and executed similar instructions from a different leading bank in Denver, passing on the same routine message: Deposit a sum of money with the Chase National Bank for the credit of the Bank of Telluride. For the two largest banks, I instructed the transfer of $100,000, but I trusted they would still be routine among the day's transfers.

The investigator discovered that on August 30, 1929, the clerks in those six banks would handle a total of three hundred twelve such requests for banks in St. Louis, Kansas City, Denver, Chicago, Baltimore, Atlanta, Salt Lake City, Miami, Boston, Philadelphia, Detroit, and Dallas. Seventeen of those requests came late in the day, between 5:31 and 6:00 p.m.

When the prosecutor said all of that was part of my plan, he was giving me way too much credit, but it just didn't make any sense to try to disagree with him.

All six New York banks followed the instructions and made the deposits. They did what I instructed them to do: create a $500,000 pool of credit for the Bank of Telluride.

The next day, all six of the Transfer Desks wrote out confirmations in longhand and put them in Saturday's mail to the Denver banks that had wired the requests.

As I finished my steak at the Gotham, I was counting on the system. Tomorrow, I would know if it worked.

19

Three p.m. on Saturday of the long Labor Day weekend, at the Central Hanover Bank, you might say the moment had arrived. The heat wave continued and it occurred to me that I might draw some unwanted attention as I made to enter the sweltering great hall in my black cashmere coat. I tried not to dawdle about before the vaulted front doors, knowing that everything I had put in motion converged with the touch of that long vertical bar in front of me. Before my hand grasped my destiny, the doors swung open and a guard, whose name turned out to be Murphy, stepped out and ushered me in.

I asked if he had been watching me.

"You might say I like to usher people into our bank," he answered.

Good business answer, I thought, even if evasive. Best I could tell nobody inside noticed Murphy's movement. My eye could see a row of empty officers' desks perfectly aligned opposite six tellers, barely standing after duty going on seven endless hours. You couldn't blame them for watching the last minutes tick off the massive clock that hung from the arched ceiling. I doubt they'd seen six customers all day. Truth to tell, I was counting on them not seeing me either.

At the far end of the room, on a platform raised six inches above the floor, the floor officer, sat behind his desk. I'd never met him, but in an instant I could see that I was lucky he was the man on the job today. He gave his full attention to the task of appearing to be hard at work. His job was to oversee the officers' desks, the tellers' stations, the front doors — everything. He did it so well, with such concentration, he didn't notice Murphy greet me, the only customer in the bank.

The burly Irish guard motioned with a big red hand and a ruddy smile for me to stay at the door. He went to stand by the floor officer's desk.

"Mr. Hayes, sir," said Murphy.

You could see Hayes was considerably annoyed when he looked up.

"What is it, Murphy?"

Edward Massey

"See that little man over there by the doors? He wants to see to you." Hayes followed Murphy's finger pointing across the enormous vault of the room.

There he saw me. I might as well tell you, I don't cut much of a figure. I don't like it but I have been called slight, and I wear spectacles. I'm sure I looked even smaller to him standing there under those towering doors. I do the best I can to turn out well with what I have, but I'm not saying I'm any Beau Brummell. I can't really judge how far away he was, so believe me when I say I swear he raised his eyebrows. For sure, he stared hard at me. I probably straightened my bow tie and maybe tugged a bit at the vest of my three-piece suit. I had to put down my hat. It was the light grey felt, almost white, that I liked so much with the high crown and wide brim. I had brought it for the simple reason that it went well with my coat. When I picked it up, I realized Mr. Hayes might never have seen one like it in New York. I suffered a chill moment of dread that its conspicuousness would bring a suspicion to his mind. Hayes testified later "that hat was a dead giveaway. He was not a New Yorker."

"Talk to me? Whatever for?"

Maybe Mr. Hayes didn't realize how well voices carried across that great hall. Maybe he wanted me to hear. He could easy see I was older than he was; he might have even guessed I was in my early fifties. Maybe that made him feel just a little bit self-important. His voice seemed to keep rising.

"Never seen the fellow before in my life. Did he ask for me by name?"

"Well, no, sir."

Murphy may have only been a guard but you could see he had the good sense to move closer to the desk to try to keep his conversation with the officer somewhat confidential. Hayes almost jerked in his effort to lean back keeping his distance from a mere floor guard. Murphy gave up his efforts to whisper.

"He sez he wants to see Mr. Pembroke. Sez he's the president of some bank himself. Seems like ..."

"He knows Pembroke?"

Now Hayes leaned forward and into Murphy almost touching his ear as he started whispering, his interest suddenly aroused at the mention of the senior vice president's name. He had been staring so I figured he could have seen the wrinkles in my pants by now, but he rose for a better view. You could see it took him a minute to sort through the questions in his mind. He found the one that satisfied his growing curiosity while being entirely consistent with his position. Resuming his full voice, he asked:

"What bank does he run?"

"Didn't catch the name. Don't sound familiar," and now when Murphy stepped in with his back to me for a whisper Hayes eagerly gave his ear for the information.

Because of the notes we had outstanding with them, Central Hanover had to be my starting point, well, sort of my ending point, too, so the whole transaction had to be done right here, right now. I figured it would help to come prepared, so I found out what little I could about the floor officers who might be on duty that day. Birch Hayes had been out of Fordham fifteen years, all of them devoted to this bank. You could see he was like most young bankers, he considered it his duty to be on the lookout for one more chance to make advancement come his way. He seemed to feel some urgency in this, probably because other people his age, some of them with Irish last names, were already assistant vice-presidents. Damned if he didn't deserve to be one of them.

Hayes might register the thought that he could not recall having ever heard of a bank president drop in on a Saturday, much less on a holiday weekend, but that wouldn't slow him down much. He knew how to handle the unexpected. That was why they'd made him a floor officer. Being the one officer, albeit a floor officer, willing to work on the Saturday of a holiday weekend wasn't the only reason he was on duty today. Of that he was sure.

It couldn't hurt that Pembroke, the senior vice-president, would hear how well Hayes had taken care of a client of the bank under unusual circumstances. He straightened up to a properly imperious demeanor, tugged down his gray wool waistcoat and ordered Murphy to bring me to see him.

Murphy came to escort me to Mr. Hayes, a wide grin showing he was sure in the knowledge that his big back blocked his face from view of the floor officer.

"Told him, I did, you act respectable enough, but humble, for a bank president."

I imagine Mr. Hayes chose to ignore that reference to his cultivated manner, since the only important question, now that he was aware I knew Mr. Pembroke, was how I could benefit his own career plans.

Murphy kept up his talkative way as we made our progress — almost like we were working buddies reconnecting after a long absence. When we got near the platform, I looked right at Mr. Hayes and connected with his gaze straight on. We smiled at each other. We bantered a bit. He was inspecting me. Fortunately I passed. He later told the prosecutor, I dressed fancy enough to be a bank president, but my hair might have wanted a clipping. Given that my hair was thinning and a bit gray, I took that as some compliment. I was mighty happy he didn't mention what was certainly true: that my three-piece suit looked just a mite rumpled.

"Mr. Hayes, this here's Mr. Wain," Murphy announced.

Hayes paused, long enough to make sure we knew who had authority over the introduction, then proffered his hand. I use that word because he just put it out in mid-air, kind of limp like. I grabbed it, squeezed hard, and shook it.

"Pleased to meet you, Mr. Hayes. My name is Charles C. Wain. My friends call me C.C." I just kept shaking his hand. "Sometimes they call me Buck."

He attempted to withdraw his hand and I continued to pump it. He didn't know what to make of that, seemed a little unnerved, and in his struggle to regain command, he asked primly, "By which name do you prefer to be called?"

"Don't really matter … maybe, maybe I'm just a little more comfortable with C.C."

"Fine," said Hayes, rolling into his professional courtesy smile. "Now, then, Mr. C.C., how may I help you?"

"Well…" I said and here was the moment. I twirled my hat in my right hand and got it started. "You see, I'm president of the Bank of Telluride. Telluride, Colorado."

From my valise I pulled out a file folder and I took my leather case out of my breast pocket.

Hayes watched my moves and I could feel him making his judgments: valise too big for a bank president, black overcoat too heavy for a warm day.

"We are a small bank, to be sure, a small bank in a small town," I said. There was no use trying to be something I wasn't. "Nevertheless, we have in the past had occasion to do business to our mutual satisfaction with your senior vice-president, Mr. Pembroke. That's why I was hoping to see him. Still, as you don't know me, Mr. Hayes…" I drew my credentials from the leather case and handed them to him. My grin was not meant to be ingratiating; at least no more than seemed obvious with the self-conscious truth of my acknowledgement, "I imagine you've never heard of my bank, Mr. Hayes."

"You must call me Birch." Hayes's eyes were wide open. He looked to me like he surprised himself. This suggestion seemed to have come from out of the blue. Maybe something I had done had allayed his doubts just a little bit. Anyway, he told the investigator that it really did seem as if he had met me before. It just seemed to be expected that the two of us would be on a first name basis.

"Mr. Pembroke is never here on Saturday," he said, "but I can assure you with confidence that he trusts me to handle any eventuality. I am certain he would say that it's unimportant whether or not I have heard of your bank. What matters is that you are a bank president."

"That I am," I chuckled. "President of a mighty small bank."

"Maybe so," said Hayes. "Position matters little, er, uh, I mean size matters little. What we have to do is make judgments about a man's sincerity and integrity. If they are beyond reproach, it matters little how big his operation. Now, please, have a seat while I take a look at these."

"Of course, take your time," I said, easing myself into one of the two chairs on his platform, a comfortable one I must say. Hayes offered a cigar from a fine, polished red box. The last thing I expected on this trip was to have a good cigar. "Oh, my heavens. Don't mind if I do."

He took one, too, and we both lit up and puffed in silence while Hayes pored over the credentials. He appeared satisfied with the paperwork and looked up through the smoke to seek one more confirmation.

"So, you know Mr. Pembroke from previous dealings?"

"Yes, I do. I've done business with the Hanover Bank. Both personal and on behalf of the Bank of Telluride," I told him. I looked him straight in the eye. "You might want to check that."

"Yes sir, I will. You'll see I am very thorough," said Hayes, warming to his role. "You won't mind a question or two. What was the nature of your previous dealings with Hanover?"

"I have borrowed money from you. I've repaid my loans, too. When they were due. You will have to check this, too, of course."

"Well, a customer who borrows and repays promptly is a customer worth keeping, I always say," the floor officer beamed with goodwill. He waited politely for me to respond, but it seemed like the time to admire the ash on my cigar. I figured I would just hold off speaking until Hayes broke the silence.

"I assume you've come to ask for a loan. I can tell you I have the personal authority to approve a loan up to ten thousand dollars. If it is for even more than that, I'll need to get the approval of a member of the credit committee. With Monday being a holiday, approval would have to wait until Tuesday."

I stood up and gently tapped my cigar on the rim of the crystal ashtray on Hayes's desk. His words spoke the truth. I was there looking for a loan. He probably misunderstood the meaning of my smile as I answered.

"Thank you, Birch, but, as a matter of fact, my bank presently has outstanding loans with Hanover."

My answer hung in the air while I returned to my comfortable chair. I took one long draw hard enough to make the ash glow red, then I resumed.

"The total amount is two hundred seventy thousand. I would like to give you a check to pay them off right now."

Mr. Pembroke had himself trained Hayes in banker's sangfroid, and I wonder if he ever knew how the young man betrayed just the slightest sign to his customer, his head snapped back ever so slightly, from the jolt he felt with those words. This was not Saturday banking as usual. This was real banking. Hayes could see himself looking pretty damn good in Pembroke's eyes come Tuesday morning.

There was nothing for me to do but let the silence grow. Hayes started to fidget; he wanted to get on with it.

"Right," he said.

"I am sorry to put you out, and I know it is very late for your people, but if you would just call Chase National, I believe you can confirm that my bank has five hundred thousand on deposit." There wasn't much more to say. He needed to know that I had the money – and I needed to know that it had arrived.

Hayes's eyes opened even wider. This was not at all what he expected. In truth, it was turning out to be a floor officer's dream. Every time a loan is paid off is cause for a private victory dance. It means the loan can no longer go bad.

Although Hayes had nothing to do with the loan, the way banks worked, he would earn the halo that went with handling the payoff.

I watched these thoughts work through him as he realized it was getting late. If he didn't act quickly, he feared he might be left behind. Perhaps to convince himself this was only a routine transaction, he said again.

"Right."

Hayes pulled out the banking directory and looked up the Chase's number.

"I'll call Chase straight away."

Volunteering to step away, I suggested the floor officer should be allowed to make his call in private. Hayes dismissed the very idea. Indeed, there wasn't really much to hear during the conversation — until Hayes, annoyed that the Interbank Supervisor at the Chase required him to do so, asked me to name the sum the Chase expected to receive. I obliged.

"Five hundred thousand dollars."

He conveyed the amount to the Chase man, listened intently, frowned slightly at the reply, and thanked his colleague in what appeared to be preparation to hang up. He pretended not to be acutely aware that I watched him through all this. I cleared my throat. Hayes glanced at me and I asked.

"Per chance, these pay off checks I will be giving you, could the Chase certify them? Today, if possible."

Hayes protested that the request was unnecessary, but repeated it over the phone, hastily adding that it was not the Hanover who was asking for the checks to be certified — after all, Chase's word was good enough for them.

"It's good procedure," I said. "Since they're just around the corner, I'll go over myself with the checks for certification."

Hayes waved that suggestion away with his hand and thanked the Chase supervisor for his cooperation in the most effusive and professional manner his training classes had provided. He replaced the telephone's handset.

"Now, how shall we do this?" he thought out loud. I knew he was not going to let me out of his sight. He glanced at his watch. "I'll have to send a teller. It is getting a little late. Our man will probably make it back before we close, but just in case, I'll dismiss the others. Murphy can stay behind to let him in."

"I surely do thank you," I said. I leaned forward to put the remainder of the cigar in the ashtray. "I'm sure sorry to put you to all this bother, but come Tuesday I want Mr. Pembroke to know these payments are money good because these drafts are certified."

"No apologies necessary, Mr…er, C.C.," Hayes replied.

"C.C.'ll be fine."

"Thanks, C.C. Mr. Pembroke will be happy. Mr. Cavelli over at Chase confirmed your funds. He told me he'd be happy to certify your drafts."

Hayes thought for a moment and, confident that smart management meant the small burden of a late errand on a Saturday before a holiday should fall on those with the least seniority, dispatched the most junior of the tellers.

I handed the checks to the junior teller, and habit took over. I took the young man, merely a messenger boy, by the elbow and escorted him to the front door of the bank.

When I closed the door, I took a seat on a bench directly to the right of the immense entrance way. I didn't forget that I had left my hat and valise in the chair; I just didn't need to return to Hayes's elevated platform until the teller returned from his mission. Besides, maybe Hayes wanted to be alone, and there wasn't any true need for him to pay any more attention to me right now. Well, maybe I misjudged that just a bit. Almost the instant I sat down he rose and crossed the room. At first, I thought he was going to sit down next to me on my bench.

"Excuse me, C.C.," he began, "I believe you mentioned that you wished to repay some loans to the bank. Perhaps we could use the time to attend to that small matter."

"That's very kind," I said, squinting as I looked up at the floor officer and into the late afternoon sun streaming through the cathedral windows. "But, as you said, it's getting late, and I'm sure you'll want to get home." I smiled to show that my only concern was for him. "I'll leave the checks with you, and you can take care of everything on Tuesday."

"Nonsense. No need to leave this business open over the weekend," Hayes hastened to object. Of course, I knew he would not be handling the transactions on Tuesday and someone else might get the credit. "I'll take care of everything right now"

Hayes led me back to the chair and seated himself once again behind his desk.

"Now," he asked, "could you tell me the particulars of the loan. I can locate the papers and mark it all complete, ready to attach that certified check. You did say it was for two hundred seventy thousand?"

"Yes, but I was using a bit of shorthand," I admitted. "I've just sent five drafts to be certified, so it's a little bit more complicated than just one loan." I drew out the single sheet of paper I had written and placed in my breast pocket. "I'll need to give you all the details."

"That's fine," said Hayes. He was not a man to be deterred by a minor complication. He uncapped his pen and inspected its nib, ready to take down the details of the transaction.

"First, my bank owes one hundred thousand dollars to Central Hanover and we want to retire that note. Then, there is a hundred thousand loan owed to you by a Telluride packing company. That note is guaranteed by my bank and collateralized by its stock. Of course, we want to clear all of that up as well. Third, I have a personal note of seventy thousand dollars. I borrowed those funds to give to my bank before the Central Hanover thought Bank of Telluride was creditworthy. That has to be repaid, too, of course."

"Well, if that's your wish," said Hayes, beaming, his words coming as close as possible to asking why I had said we want to clear all of that up. To be fair to the young man, it was hard for him to concentrate on what I was saying while his eyes were on the piece of paper, adding up the sums while he was talking. "Yes, sir, that's two hundred seventy thousand dollars, all right. But I thought you mentioned five hundred thousand. Did you want to put the balance on deposit?"

He had learned the importance of courting new business in his training, and I suspected this was one of the rare chances he had to put it to use.

"There are two more drafts," I added, "but there are no more notes to repay."

"Doesn't matter," Hayes said. "We'll handle them all the same." He reached in his top drawer for the proper slip. "And these two drafts will be for deposit?"

"Well, yes," I responded. My hesitation grew from knowing he expected the money to go in his bank. "But I'm afraid they'll have to be deposited at other banks. You see, I am transferring the funds to my bank back home. I hope that won't be a problem."

"No, no, of course not, we'll be happy to take care of that," said Hayes, trying to keep his voice positive to disguise his disappointment. He returned the deposit slip to his desk drawer and went back to his yellow legal pad.

"When the messenger returns," I continued, "I will give you a check for one hundred ninety five thousand to send over to Chase National for the credit of First National Bank of Pueblo and the further credit of the Bank of Telluride."

"Of course," Hayes said, writing down each step of the transaction, then looking at me. "That's very . . . efficient. It's a genuine pleasure doing business with you."

I acknowledged Hayes with a self-conscious grin. A compliment from Mr. Hayes was not my goal. I lost no time proceeding with business, "And one more draft for thirty thousand for deposit with the Continental Bank of Salt Lake City, also to the credit of the Bank of Telluride."

Hayes made further notes on his pad and announced, "That amounts to four hundred ninety-five."

"Correct. We'll leave the balance at the Chase," I said. "We already have a profitable relationship with your bank, but we've done comparably little with the Chase. I'm sure you understand."

"Why, yes, of course," said Hayes, looking toward Murphy who was standing at the door, watching for the teller's return. It was shortly after closing time. Hayes excused himself after offering me another cigar and descended the platform to dismiss the other staff, with the exception of the Saturday cashier, whom he now realized he would need to record the transactions. I suspect when he explained that something had come up, he was forced, to his annoyance, to promise an hour's overtime pay to satisfy the man.

Upon the young teller's return, Hayes returned to his desk and spread out the five drafts in front of him.

"Well, then," I said, rising from my chair, "I assume everything is in order?"

"Precisely," said Hayes. He stood up, too. That amused me. Perhaps it no longer seemed appropriate to him to be seated while I stood. He wanted to say something friendly. I stood waiting, hat in hand. At last Hayes brightened and said, "Excuse my ignorance, Mr. Wain, but I'm afraid I still do not know exactly where the Bank of Telluride is located."

"Oh, that's all right, Birch. C.C., remember?" I said with a chuckle. "You big city bankers wouldn't have any reason to know. Just a little Colorado mining town."

"Is that where Molly Brown was from? She was a client of ours." Hayes's expression brightened with relief as he seized on the opportunity to make small talk. "The Titanic happened before my time, but we here at the Hanover remember it all too well. After all, the Central Hanover lost more than one of its better depositors to that tragedy."

"She's actually from Leadville," I explained, "But you're close. Telluride's very much like Leadville."

I extended my hand. I noticed the cashier still stood at the base of the platform.

"Well, thank you again for seeing that my checks got certified. Now I'll leave you to your work, Birch. You've been very helpful and I deeply appreciate it."

"Any time," said Hayes, with a slight bow. "It is our pleasure to be of service to our highly respected clients. By the way, you're a long way from home. Do you have enough pocket money? Could I cash a small personal check for you?" He chuckled as he added, "I'm sure it would be good."

"That's kind of you, Birch," I said. "But no. I brought cash with me."

I started to move toward the door.

Hayes, satisfied with his little joke, barely heard my answer.

He did not notice as I left Central Hanover's endless Saturday before Labor Day. He was already busy with his instructions to the cashier. His thoughts were on Tuesday, the day he would claim praise from Pembroke ... and the day the system would perfect my transfers.

20

Tuesday opened to pandemonium, business as usual, at the New York Clearing House. That dark and dusty and venerable institution, established to wrest order from confusion, lived in chaos every minute right up to ten o'clock each morning. At that time, settlement was prepared. The hour the rest of the banking world put down its morning newspaper and its second cup of coffee, millions of pieces of perforated paper had begun to form a layer of dust on the Clearing House's suddenly calm floor. Yesterday's business was closed. The Monday holiday meant yesterday was Saturday.

You can know things that happened when you're not there and it's not the same as making them up. There are parts to my story that happened when I wasn't around. I need to tell those parts too.

Tuesday's checks waiting to be presented for payment made up a mountain far smaller than the average day's. On the day before holidays people usually do more business and more banking and write more checks needing to be cleared. Labor Day was different. People treated the Friday before Labor Day like the day before the holiday.

Saturday was the heavy day at the New York Clearing House. It came as no surprise to me when the senior executives told reporters that on that Friday people seemed to behave like it was the last holiday they would ever know. They said Saturday held an eerie resemblance to the frenetic activity of the days in 1913 before the Federal Reserve System had been established to maintain confidence in the monetary system.

The Porters Exchange made banking in the United States possible more than a century before. Porters scurried from bank to bank to exchange checks for bags of coin. That was a dangerous job and they had to figure out a way to replace it – which they did with The New York Clearing House. Banks sent their checks to a central clearinghouse in canvas bags with the general agreement that marks in a book are as good as coins in a bag. As with the coin of the Porters Exchange, the marks in the Clearing House books enabled banks that had accepted checks to receive their money. The clearing process might look highly structured but it maintained its original simplicity. It provided a place where payments could meet, mix, and move to their final destinations.

Paying and receiving and confidence building, all of it, occurred in two simple steps on the floor of the Clearing House beneath stately rows of overhead lights that hung from long thick cords. A credit was added to the Clearing House account of the bank that accepted the check. Upon receiving the credit, the bank surrendered the check. The transaction between the receiving bank and the Clearing House was complete.

For an instant, the Clearing House owned the check and the promise to pay.

The bank that had made the check would pay the money out as an amount subtracted from its account at the Clearing House. When this debit was recorded, the Clearing House would hand over the check, and all parties to the transaction were satisfied.

To do this the bulky and unwieldy checks needed to be moved only once. The bags from each bank were opened and sorted and subtotaled and totaled and delivered to each desk according to the check's bank of origin. All entries were made from those desks; most of the desks did the clearing for more than one bank of origin. The ledgers were presented to the settlement clerks and consolidated. Settlement was complete.

Certified checks received no particularly special handling. To be sure, they were sorted so that they were the first checks debited to the issuing bank's account, but that was more a bow to tradition than a practical need. The "certification" was to ensure that the customer had sufficient funds in his account, not the bank. Even a certified check for $100,000 drew no notice. A clearing clerk sorted through a hundred checks a day for more than that. Even two checks for $100,000 to be credited to the same bank would draw no attention. The clearing work was done at the desks of the banks on which the checks had been drawn.

On that slow Tuesday, the Central Hanover Bank sent one light canvas bag. As it turned out, they sent scarcely four thousand checks to be cleared. Forty of those checks, all jumbled in the assorted stacks of paper, exceeded $100,000. Two of those checks presented were in payment of the obligations of the Bank of Telluride.

On that slow Tuesday, the sorting yielded a modest stack of barely ten thousand checks to be debited at the Chase National Bank desk.

All the checks received by the Central Hanover Bank were presented and credited. All the checks made on the Chase National Bank were accepted and debited.

Cleared.

Settled.

Contracts created by Saturday's checks were legal and complete at ten a.m., Tuesday, by the time I was on my way to Grafton.

21

Not much I don't know about worries me. There were never monsters under my bed. The dark holds no terror. I arrived in Denver at nearly midnight after the long drive from Garden City and woke up at Brown's early Tuesday morning without an alarm clock. I looked at my watch. I will admit that I didn't think too much about the workings of the New York Clearing House, but by the time I got in the Studebaker for my nine and a half hour drive to Grafton, I knew my checks were legal contracts. What that meant to me was that my depositors would get their money no matter how it unfolded from now on. Of course, it would still take a couple of days to get the money, real money, in their hands. Someone would detect the loan I had created; I just needed a couple of days.

Not to say that young Lorenzo Swett was a monster. On the contrary, he was an admirable young man, doing his job, and I would have liked to have had him in my employ. His was a wonderful example of paying attention because he cared about what he did. It just never crossed my mind to think the discovery would come about in Denver that very day because one young man would be so alert.

Young Swett came from a banking family. There had never been a doubt about his career. Like his father and grandfather, he would be a banker.

His mother, however, had not imagined that her son's first job following graduation from Columbia University would be with the Denver International Trust. Denver lay far from Pawling, New York where I hear tell they have sprawling lawns that go all the way from the big houses down to the banks of the Hudson River. She saw life as one continuous act of preparing oneself for the next danger to befall one's offspring, fourteen years to prepare for the day she sent her boy off to boarding school, four years to prepare for the sheer terror of allowing him to live in Manhattan. And with all that preparation I don't imagine Emma Swilton Swett was ready for the shock when she learned that, immediately following graduation, her son would board a train and take it all the way to the Rocky Mountains.

The daughter of Edward Everett Swilton, President of the Equitable Trust Company International, had been reluctant to surrender her maiden name. For twenty-three years, Emma had harbored the hope that her son, however named Swett, would carry on the Swilton family tradition. Believe me when I tell you this, when she saw that train pull out, she was overwhelmed with fear that "little Larry" might even choose to remain in the Wild West.

Lorenzo fancied himself independent enough to refuse to let his banking career float in a direction defined merely by the fact his father and his mother's father were bankers. Still, he was not truly independent of his family. He found a bank job and secured it on his own – in Denver.

Transactions arrived at the Denver International Trust with the morning mail and someone in the mailroom examined each envelope to decide where it should go. If the address told too little, that same someone had authority to open the envelope and look at its contents. This Tuesday morning traffic compounded by the Monday holiday meant large volume; the sorting and routing was not completed until early afternoon. When Lorenzo Swett returned from lunch he found on his desk a daunting pile of envelopes and open advices.

The work was tedious. You can be sure it offered damn little excitement to a young man who had experienced the world of the Ivy League and Manhattan's inner circle. I imagine there were days duly recording advices and opening envelopes when he worried about becoming another Bartleby, but I don't doubt he discarded his worries. He had made his choice, and he was determined to make good on it. There is very little despair in a routine job when you know it will not be yours to do forever and that Tuesday afternoon Lorenzo steadily worked through his pile until he eventually picked up an envelope from New York's Equitable Trust Company International, addressed to *Credit Clerk*. It advised that the Denver International Trust's request for a transfer had been fulfilled with an overdraft of $70,000 from the Equitable Trust.

All he had to do was record the advice and move on to the next.

He lingered over that single piece of paper with the familiar crest at its top, a bit of home, something familiar in an unfamiliar land. He knew more about the Equitable than he did about any bank, including his father's. Perhaps, he later told Frank Simms, that was because his father was a banker and would not talk, or because his mother was a talker and not a banker.

Still shy of completing his third month on the job, Lorenzo had tried to peek in every corner of Denver International's business. As he made his quiet way through understanding Denver International's relationships, he would have noticed any connection with his grandfather's bank. He held that advice in his hand, and he could not be certain, but he doubted the Equitable Trust did any business with the Denver International.

To another, perhaps no more than an idle thought. For Lorenzo, the conclusion drew more thought. If the Denver International had a transfer to make, he could see no reason why it chose to do so through the Equitable or to request an overdraft to fulfill it.

Not to make too much of his suspicions, he knew when to ask advice and he drew on years of practice in achieving just the right tone of nonchalance as he leaned amiably in Carl Stewart's doorway.

"Carl, why would a $70,000 overdraft be coming our way?"

"The bank ordered a transaction that required more funds than it had on deposit," said Stewart. Recently promoted to assistant vice-president of the Interbank Department, he made no effort to look up from his desk; he was addressing a simple question of banking mechanics with a simple answer.

"I know that," said Lorenzo, frustrated that the person he counted as the closest to a friend he had among the bank officers would not be more open with him. This fell in Stewart's domain, so he tried a different question. "Tell me, how much does the bank have on deposit at the Equitable Trust in New York?"

"Not much," said Stewart.

"How much?"

"You are persistent," said Stewart, reluctantly drawing himself up from his chair. He pulled a large black volume from a shelf on the back wall. "It's so damn little, I don't remember it off the top of my head."

"Skip the lecture, just tell me."

"We have a $5,000 deposit with Equitable Trust," he said, his finger pointing to a line in the ledger. "That's a relationship deposit. Evidently we don't do any real business with them."

"Here." Lorenzo held out the advice. "Look at this. Doesn't that $70,000 overdraft mean someone here asked the Equitable Trust to send $75,000 in our name?"

Stewart quickly reviewed the advice, expression unchanged. His answer was like a pat on the head.

"Yes, Larry, that is how they would know to do it."

"Could one of our customers ask?"

"Goodness, no. Someone at the bank would have to make that request."

"But, Carl, who could it have been?"

"Who knows? Do you really need to know?" asked Stewart.

"We need to reconcile these entries," said Lorenzo by way of an answer. "There has to be an offsetting entry, so I need to know what it was for."

"Well, it tells you right there on the advice. We asked the Equitable to send $75,000 over to the Chase for our customer, the Bank of Telluride."

"Where is the Bank of Telluride?" asked Lorenzo.

"Oh, somewhere up in the hills. One of those mining towns," said Stewart, waving a hand to suggest a vague westerly direction. "I've never been there, myself. Harder than hell to get to."

"Why would we do that?"

"Beats me," said Stewart.

Lorenzo waggled the advice in his friend's face.

"Doesn't this bother you?" he asked.

"No. For god's sake," said Stewart. "It's done all the time. Ain't you never been around a bank before, son?"

The grandson of Swilton and the son of Swett chewed on his lip before answering. He had made a real effort, apparently successful, to conceal his connection with two great New York banking families. "Well, then, tell me this, who would do it?"

"Beats me," Stewart repeated.

"No, not that," said Lorenzo. "I mean who is the officer in this bank who does business with them. I want to see him."

"That'd be Ken Miller."

"Miller?"

I imagine Lorenzo's skepticism might have been audible. I am telling you his actions proved he was an alert young man. Now, he might have been around the bank for only three months, but, for sure, he already knew Miller never did anything for anybody.

When Lorenzo showed up at Miller's desk, I'm sure it was the way it always was, more than neat, empty. Nothing, not even a sheet of paper, and I'm sure Miller sat in his chair with hands folded in his lap, staring out at some point in space that held nothing either.

"Mr. Miller, do you know anything about the Bank of Telluride?" asked Lorenzo, direct, polite, but consciously short of obsequious.

"There's not much to know." Miller delivered his words with barely a movement of his facial muscles. "Their president's a bit dandified. Some call him Buck."

"Did you happen to loan the Bank of Telluride $75,000?" asked Lorenzo.

"Buck Wain asked me to make them a loan," said Miller. "Don't remember the amount, but it doesn't matter. He doesn't have any collateral up there. There's nothing left in Telluride but a mountain and hope. Maybe not even that."

"So you didn't make him a loan last Friday?"

"Oh, heavens, no. He came down here more than a month ago. Of course, I didn't actually say no. I sent him off to get us a repayment source before I would even consider it. He hasn't been back. Doesn't surprise me."

"Didn't do it," Lorenzo said to Stewart's raised eyebrows.

"Really?" said Stewart, curling the word as he said it. "No surprise. What did he say?"

"Didn't say anything. Didn't even ask why I wanted to know."

"Good old Miller," said Stewart, shaking his head.

"I think this is a mistake," Lorenzo continued. "We should notify them."

"Oh, great," said Stewart. "We are going to send a telegram to the Equitable Trust Company in New York informing them that the $70,000 overdraft was a mistake."

"Why not? You're an officer, you can sign it."

"Wonderful!" he laughed. "And how exactly do you say it? 'Thanks very much for the cash, but we didn't ask for it'?"

The young banker from New York said, "That'll do."

22

By the time I left Brown's on Tuesday morning, the New York Clearing House had settled Saturday's transactions, Lorenzo Swett had decided to question one of the advices he had received, and Laurie McEnroe was elbow deep in a pile of cables that confirmed her mixed view of holidays. A day off created a day of frenzy with two days' worth of work when she returned. She described her methods, picking up each cable as though nothing else mattered until its contents had been converted into action, even if it meant leaving cables unread. She had to be efficient. Touch each piece of paper only once. That was her motto. Laurie said that what bothered her most about the day after a holiday was that the traffic coming in during the day left a small stack of unread cables overnight, but what could she do? There were simply too many for her to complete in a day.

By the time she left for morning coffee at quarter of eleven Wednesday morning Laurie felt like she was back in her routine. She had cleared the day's new cables and organized her desk. All that remained were those few cables from Tuesday that had come in late in the day.

The second cable into clearing the previous day's leftovers called for more than her normal routine: examining its contents and calling on her Marist education to sort it, like souls into heaven, hell, or purgatory. The one from The Denver International called for consultation with the head teller. Being told you had sent someone $70,000 they never asked for was something you didn't see every day.

"Fuzz," she said, the nickname she had bestowed on Ray Pietsch, "I'm not sure where this goes, but this might be a problem for you to deal with. You might even want to show it to Ewell."

She handed the cable to Pietsch, a middle-aged man whose thick-rimmed glasses rested on a bulbous nose.

"This looks like a seventy thousand dollar question," said Pietsch, at first leaving unspoken his rebuke, then thinking the better of it. "You know we don't take these amounts to the vice-president."

Rules were rules and the rules at the Equitable Trust said you don't bother the vice-president unless there was at least a hundred thousand involved.

"Well, that's your decision," she said, in practiced deference to the head teller.

Laurie was a good worker and she recalled going home that afternoon happy. It had taken two days, but all her cables were cleared. She was ready for whatever the next day brought. The morning's seventy thousand dollar question was not even a memory.

Just before lunch on Thursday, Pietsch came to her desk, a cable in his hand.

"When did this come in?"

His tone made her stiffen and she felt her face redden. She made a slow and distinct effort to read the contents of the paper he held.

"A little before I gave it to you."

"When, exactly?"

She looked straight into his face, a map of little red lines leading everywhere and nowhere. She recalled her effort to be as precise as possible. What she didn't say, but what I'm thinking she knew, is that precision was the best way to create ambiguity.

"It might have come in yesterday; that's when I gave it to you, but it might have been late, maybe even after hours, traffic on Tuesday."

"Doesn't it have a time stamp on it?"

"You're holding it," she said. Before he could answer, she asked, "What did Ewell say?"

"He said," answering while he looked for the time stamp, "that you didn't give it to us soon enough."

Pietsch had asked to see Ewell Wednesday afternoon, more than three hours after Laurie had brought the matter to his attention. When he got his audience, after the coffee service had been retrieved on Thursday, the vice-president paid no attention to what he said. Ewell was a man who loved his information in writing. Spoken words seemed to disappear as quickly as they were uttered. He distrusted them. Besides, this message sounded almost like a joke, "Thank you very much for extending us the overdraft of $70,000, but we didn't ask for it."

Only when Pietsch forced the cable in Ewell's hands did he make progress. Like a talisman, the touch of that piece of paper was something he could trust and it calmed the excitable executive.

"My, this is serious," said Ewell. "We should verify this notification by writing Denver a letter."

At that, Pietsch ventured into the lion's den and suggested it might be quicker to pick up the telephone and call Denver. It came as no surprise to him when Ewell suggested he do just that.

Within ten minutes Pietsch was back in Ewell's office.

"A somewhat confident young man named Lorenzo Swett came to the phone. He insisted Denver International never asked for the money."

"Swett?" repeated Ewell.

"Perhaps, we would do well to call the Chase," suggested Pietsch, taking no notice of the tone of recognition in Ewell's voice, "and try to stop the transfer."

"Good idea. You make the call," said Ewell as expected. He surprised Pietsch when he said, "I will speak with them myself."

Smyth of Chase's inter-bank department told Ewell any transfers from Friday or Saturday were undoubtedly completed. Ewell's distrust of the spoken word must have made this conversation very difficult; he promised to rush over the documentation, after all, how could Smyth be sure if he did not have the paperwork.

Ewell hung up, unhappy. He had seen a chance to shine in Mr. Swilton's eyes and now his fear was that this business would reflect poorly on him. He instructed Pietsch to assemble all the paperwork – and to find out why that woman down there in charge of the incoming cables had not alerted them before Thursday.

23

Another young man who took very seriously what he did heard something amiss in a Senior Officer's bizarre request that he hold up a transfer authorized five days before. John Smyth couldn't be certain precisely what the Chase had been drawn into and what lay at the end of that strange telephone call. He drummed his fingers on his desk and stared blankly out his door to a beautiful half-acre of well-worn oak desks, each identical in appearance, each with responsibility for a different corresponding bank. Nearest him, at the inter-bank department supervisor's desk, sat the man to talk to, Leo Cavelli, a squat, bull-necked man wearing red suspenders.

"Too late," said Cavelli, shaking his big, earnest face in answer to the question. "If they asked for that transfer on Saturday, then we did it, sir. I was here and I know we got all our work done."

"Check anyway, will you," said Smyth. "It was to a Colorado bank on behalf of Denver International. Now Denver International has called Equitable and said they didn't request it. Maybe somebody in your department remembers something."

"Colorado?" asked Leo, his eyes growing larger. "I can't say about the Equitable. That's a thumper. What we had was a number of transactions right around closing time Saturday afternoon that all involved a Colorado bank. Funny name. Telluride. Easy enough to remember."

"That's the one the Equitable inquired about."

"Our transactions weren't with the Equitable, though. All of 'em were with Central Hanover. Some stuffed shirt over there called me. Said he had a customer wanting to verify his funds had arrived. Didn't see anything unusual in that. Still don't."

"Of course. And had the funds arrived?"

"Oh, yes," said Leo. "In fact, when I checked on it, money seemed to be pouring in for that bank. I just figured there was a syndicate had a closing on Friday. Six banks, I remember because I counted them, had sent money to the account on Friday or Saturday morning. And it was a nice round number, five hundred thousand, like a syndicate funding."

"Well, I told the Equitable I thought it might be hard to hold up the transfer."

"Hold up? Nothing to hold up. Transfer's done," said Leo. "I wonder what those people over at the Equitable do with instructions they receive on Saturday? Why should they be sitting around on a Thursday? Not in my department, and not when there are certified checks involved."

"What?" exclaimed Smyth. "We certified checks for five hundred thousand?"

"Near about! Four hundred ninety-five. Yes, sir."

"That certainly settles the request from the Equitable."

"Don't know about that, sir, but that money was gone by quittin' time Saturday night."

There's a whole lot I don't understand about what happens in big city banks, never have, never will. I was out in Grafton not knowing if anyone had come to suspicion yet and not knowing the few extra hours I got because Smyth had to go through the absurd ritual of proving that his problem qualified to get an appointment with his own boss. In Smyth's judgment no one could be told his deep suspicion of what had occurred until he had informed his boss. There's a man you'd want to have working for you. Good judgment, but it didn't matter none. He had to endure a detailed interrogation. Walter Winston Whitworth's secretary knew he trusted her judgment more than any subordinate. Something in Smyth's refusal to answer her questions or his look or tone convinced her to reverse her announced decision to ask the big man later in the afternoon if he wanted to meet with Smyth. He thanked her with one word: Immediately!

That meant three o'clock. Smyth presented himself promptly. The senior vice president's reputation for impatience suited Smyth just fine. He had a sense of urgency; he wasted no time on pleasantries.

"We have had a request to stop a transfer from the Equitable. I thought we may face similar requests from other banks."

Whitworth lowered his head and leaned far back in his chair.

"Did we do anything wrong?" he asked. "I'm the kind who likes to see the forest, Smyth, not the trees."

"No," said Smyth. He had thought it would be best to give the facts of the transaction to his boss, but he decided to stick to the forest. "We simply handled transfers and certified checks. Your secretary was not even sure I should bring this to your attention."

"Then why did you?" asked Whitworth.

"Because I had hoped we could head this matter off if we acted fast. Since then, since I first requested time to discuss this Equitable matter with you, Leo Cavelli has received three telegrams and two telephone calls about these transfers. Before I got into your office, officers of those banks showed up here to safeguard their transfers."

"My god, man, what did you do with those people?"

"Nothing, sir. Well, nothing other than I have three of them on the twenty-seventh floor, where I told them to wait for you in the Board Room. All three were steaming, almost literally given the heat."

"The least you could do is send the porter to bring them iced tea," said Whitworth.

I imagine Smyth suffered this Do-I-have-to-think-of-everything tone on a regular basis. You suffer that kind of treatment because you know which side your bread is buttered on, but on that day, I am pretty sure the press of business just made Smyth shake his head in wonder as he tried to stay on the point.

"As I was saying, we have now talked to all six of the banks who deposited money with us on behalf of this Colorado bank, five actually, and they ... well ... it appears they are having trouble verifying the orders."

"Preposterous!" said Whitworth. He started to laugh. "Even in my dreams our competitors aren't that sloppy. How is that possible?"

"It may not be sloppiness," cautioned Smyth. "The five banks who say they are having trouble verifying the orders are using, shall I say, polite language. One of the six Denver banks flatly denies it sent the telegram."

Whitworth breathed in deeply. He made a sweeping motion with his hands and spoke to Smyth with an exaggerated frown.

"I cannot afford any distraction from the margin committee meeting tomorrow morning. Now, listen closely. It does not do to jump to conclusions. In my many years of experience, and I have been at this banking game a long time, I have found it is best to get the facts before making a decision. I will give this my personal attention simply because I want it dispatched with now. Get that bank on the telephone. I'll get to the bottom of this."

When, minutes later, Whitworth found himself speaking with my head teller, Mr. Twicken, he learned that I was away in New York on business.

Satisfied with his demonstration of cutting to the core, Whitworth handled that information with simple efficiency. He told Smyth to find me in New York and report to him after the margin committee breakfast.

Friday's margin committee breakfast stretched on into the morning. Whitworth viewed the committee chairmanship as having far more importance than paying attention to Smyth's concerns.

In the end, the margin requirement remained at ten percent. Some bankers wanted a higher percentage. They argued that the entire financial system was facing a serious risk of crash if stock prices dipped even slightly. Just think, they warned: If you put up ten dollars and borrow ninety, then you have to put up another dollar when the price drops just one percent. But how are you going to do that? You only had ten dollars to start with, and when you lose one percent, you have to come up with ten percent more cash. That's a huge difference. To get the dollar, you have to sell a little bit. Maybe not this stock, maybe some other stock, but still you have to sell. And when you only need to put up ten dollars to buy a hundred dollars worth of stock, there are a lot of people who climb into the same boat, so probably a lot of people have to sell. And when a lot of people have to sell, two things can happen: With luck, the price simply drops, because there are people out there who have the money and want the bargain. But if too many people have to sell there might not be enough people who want to buy and then the price doesn't just go down. It crashes. To zero. And if you still owe ninety dollars it doesn't just go to zero. It goes to hell.

Other bankers, led by Chairman Whitworth, laughed at these Cassandras. They thought the margin requirement was too high. It could easily be cut in half. They confidently predicted the day when investment ratios of forty to one would be commonplace. They argued the talk of crash was a self-fulfilling prophecy and all such talk should just be stopped. Reduce the margin requirement even further.

More people would buy stock and when more people buy, stock prices go up. When stock prices go up companies are able to raise more money. So lowering the margin would pump money into the market and more money would create further expansion and everybody knew that expansion was the antidote to any potential crash.

No action followed the acrimonious debate.

"I'm amazed no one mentioned this at the margin committee meeting, sir. There are fourteen banks involved here," said Smyth, responding to Whitworth's expression of surprise to see him sitting at the side chair in his office when he arrived. Dispensing with time-wasting pleasantries may have offended the corporate manners, but it didn't retrieve the two hours he had been waiting for Whitworth to get back from the meeting.

"Nothing to discuss. We knew that. You told me that yesterday," said Whitworth as he threw his green leather folder on the desk. "Weren't you supposed to bring that Mr. Wain to me?"

"Not exactly, sir," said Smyth, ignoring the last question for the moment. "None of the Denver banks sent those telegrams. Yesterday they would not admit they sent them. Today all six have repudiated the telegrams. They are calling them fraudulent and unauthorized."

Whitworth had taken off his coat, half-listening to a fairly minor episode as he settled into the expectation of a good lunch in recovery from a disappointing morning. He sat down.

"Well, all the more reason to speak to Wain," he exclaimed, throwing up his hands. "C'mon, Smyth, produce this Mr. Wain to explain himself. Breakfast started before I could even my morning paper and I barely have time for my lunch. I have a busy afternoon."

"I'm sorry, sir," said Smyth. "As to producing Mr. Wain, we have called every hotel in Manhattan. He's nowhere to be found. I think we're going to have to take care of this."

Whitworth thumped a fist on the green leather folder. His eyes flashed with annoyance.

"Damn it, Smyth, this is not my problem. It's your department. Move fast and keep it quiet. We don't want this to get out."

"Too late," said Smyth. "It was in papers you missed. They're all upstairs."

24

Annie's father bought the farm outside Grafton in 1881. That was the year he and H.O. Chase organized the Bank of Grafton. They had this idea that prosperity would follow the arrival of the Burlington Northern. Father Martin took his young family and what money he had out west from Virginia. He came from good Huguenot stock and that meant he wasn't certain how much he could trust anyone, much less a New York banker. Sure, H.O. had founded the Chase National four years earlier, and that looked like a success, but father Martin didn't know much about how Chase treated his partners. Ever prudent, he divided his money in half. He gave one portion to Chase and he used the remainder for the farm. If one enterprise failed, he figured, he'd have the other to fall back on.

When father Martin died just after the Great War, I bought the farm from Annie's brother and two sisters. I knew how much the farm meant to her. I put the title in Annie's name alone, as quietly as I could. A secret act of love you might call it and best I knew it was still unknown to anyone, even to her. I've never been one to hide my assets or do anything too clever, but when it came out the farm was in Annie's name, that's just what they said, and it wasn't true. It was my secret from almost ten years before and I'm glad I could keep it as long as I did.

Annie had arrived in Grafton by train on the Saturday before Labor Day. She spent the day visiting friends before having dinner with her brother and sisters. They played a parlor game. The first one to name all seventy families in town won. They meant to test their move-away sister, and to keep from providing any help, they gave her first try. Annie laughed because what they had done was give her an advantage in that three of the families were right there at the dinner table. Even after twenty-six years in Telluride she could still name all but half a dozen families — "newcomers" who had moved in since we left town.

Her brother drove her out to the farm after church on Sunday. For the next two days she enjoyed her farm and her solitude, cleaning the rooms and ordering their contents, interrupted just enough by one meal with Leon Rawlins, the resident manager, and his family.

Edward Massey

Thursday morning I woke up with my hand resting on the space where Annie had been. Something about my hand touching Annie during the night soothes me and when the connection is broken I awake. Sound coming from the kitchen brought me by slow degrees to an awareness that I was listening to the country chorus of grease spitting and crackling in a cast iron pan. Eggs, and probably bacon, although Annie often made sausage patties from the loose pepper sausage that Mrs. Rawlins seemed to be able to produce fresh no matter when we came. The rough cotton sheets felt good as I stretched my arms up high in an effort to chase away the fatigue that lingered across my back and in my shoulders.

I had a thought; a little physical labor might be just the thing for this stiffness. It wasn't often that I actually worked on the farm. I pushed myself out of bed. Besides, I needed to make sure of a couple of things.

It was bacon, certain. I hoped she was making biscuits, too. That's what she had done yesterday. A good breakfast on our own farm. Wasn't that the life Annie and I had worked for? The bedroom was bright and straightforward, like just about everything in Annie's life, square with a door directly in the center and an upright dresser on either side. I stood there in the pale blue pajamas she had brought for me. They felt soft and rich, and as I got up and undid the top button I remembered how good it felt to put them on Tuesday evening. I had been living out of a valise for days. I don't consider that I dwell on much, but I will admit as I undid each button, the soft touch of that fabric reminded me I would probably not be wearing fine pajamas many more nights.

More than what the future held, the pajamas brought Annie to mind and the memory of my arrival two days before. I've never directed much attention to the intimacy between Annie and me. We enjoyed each other; we had our routine. That seemed enough. We made love from time to time, and neither of us felt obligated or burdened. It was part of our routine, not the center. But Tuesday night? That had been different.

Who knows where it came from; maybe there was something in my blood because I hardly noticed the nine-and-a-half hours of hard driving that got me from Brown's to the farm by dinnertime. Annie had just begun setting the table when she saw me drive up. She ran out through the screen porch, down the walk, and kissed me. This was not the waiting ritual we shared in Telluride. I exclaimed my appreciation for such a greeting, maybe I even teased her a bit, for I took notice of that, I surely did.

Minutes later a dinner of pot roast, boiled potatoes, and buttered carrots appeared on the table.

"I figured you've had enough of that fancy New York cooking," she said with an almost sly look about her, "now go sit down."

As usual, our dinner conversation started with her casual request that I tell her about my trip. She knew what she was in for. She had, after all, married a man who cared about details.

I'm afraid I didn't do justice to her potatoes, or her carrots for that matter. I launched into a detailed description of my first airplane rides — of how I watched out the window under the high wing of the Tri-motor Fokker F-10-A from the moment of take-off. After crossing the vast expanse of Lake Erie I was mighty glad to see solid earth under me again, even if the runway did look like we were going to land right in the middle of the city. Step by step I retraced each leg of the flight, including the landings in St. Louis and Kansas City. I was about to describe Susan waiting at the edge of the apron, sitting atop the driver's seat of the Studebaker and waving as the plane touched down, when Annie broke in.

"You must be tired," she said, and I swear I could see lights twinkling in her eyes, "after such a long trip."

Annie climbed into bed in her polished cotton nightgown. She snuggled up close to me with her back against my stomach. I wrapped my arms around her. I never admitted to tired, and once my hands touched her soft skin under one thin piece of fabric I felt a closeness to her that overwhelmed us both.

Our lovemaking over, Annie said, in a quiet and quizzical voice, "My?"

The next day I found myself looking forward to the evening. I discovered just how much I looked forward to it when I heard my voice praising my brother-in-law for his rigid punctuality. At the stroke of one, our coffee drunk and the bill paid, by me, Bradley left the Grafton Luncheonette and hurried back to the bank. I hurried back to Annie.

Edward Massey

The trip to town, to send a telegram to Twicken, and the little chat with my brother-in-law, had taken five or six hours away from Annie. It was all that I could bear.

I stretched my arms over my head and pulled off my pajama top, and then I slipped out of the bottoms. Carefully folding my pajamas on the bed, I smoothed out the wrinkles. They looked almost unworn. They would store well, I thought. I placed them in the second dresser drawer. The top drawer squeaked as I pulled it open. I reached for a pair of fresh underwear and a heavy cotton plaid shirt. From a hook behind the closet door I took down a pair of denim overalls.

Annie was still at the stove when I entered the kitchen. "Don't you look the Nebraska farmer!" she laughed, turning her head to greet me.

"What I thought you always wanted," I said coming up behind her.

"Either that or a banker," she said.

I put my arms around her and drew her toward me.

"What?" she asked after a quiet moment.

"Thank you," I said.

"For what?"

"Last night," I said.

"It wasn't exactly a complete surprise," she said. "Not like Tuesday."

"No," I said. "It wasn't. I didn't want to ask you, so I did everything I could to gauge your interest."

"Well, you're a good gauger," she teased. "Two nights in a row *is* a bit of a surprise."

I touched her cheek with my open palm, my fingers barely grazing her hair. She looked at me, eyes wide and expectant.

I was thinking how we had made love often during the early years of our marriage, before we purchased the farm. We were both forty-two then. When she came back from her trips to Grafton I would be missing her terribly, but she had things to do, things on her mind. Worst of all, she was as close to tired as I ever saw her. I soon stopped worrying about it. I remembered Thanksgiving, 1923, when I had made a big effort, and Christmas, 1925. And there was the time we had gone off to San Francisco together; I could not remember when that was.

"I think two nights in a row would be a nice habit."

"So you say," she said, turning back to the stove.

"What does that mean?" I asked.

"Well," she drew it out with a long pause, "you do seem more romantic these last two days and maybe even a little more relaxed, but you're going right back East, aren't you?"

I walked over and cut a piece of bread from the loaf on the counter. My back was to her. "Only for a couple of days," I said over my shoulder. I turned around with the slice of bread in my hand and said brightly, "Where's the jam? I've got to eat and get cracking. I've got chores to do."

"What are you doing with that bread? You knew I was making you biscuits. And when have you ever done chores on this farm?"

"My heavens, that is harsh," I said. I sat down at the table and opened the checkered cloth that covered the biscuits in their wicker basket. "By the way, it was nice to have a change of clothes to see your brother. How did the suits get up here?"

"Dear," she said with a sort of exasperation, pouring cream into her coffee. "You went away for a seven-day trip with the suit on your back and a valise in your hand. Do you think I didn't notice?"

"I didn't think about it," I said, spreading honey on a biscuit. "I barely noticed, myself."

"Oh," she said, serving the plates while drawing the simple exclamation out into its own statement. "I don't doubt that. You're always a little distracted, but you seem particularly preoccupied this past week."

"Have I really," I said softly. "I'm sorry, dear. I guess I'm a little worried about our friends."

"You've tried to help them," she said. She reached across the table and took my hand. "There's no limit to your trying. But there is a limit to what you can do."

Gently I squeezed the hand that had been offered. I looked out onto the mostly brown, slightly green field I could see from the kitchen. It had been mowed and no hay would be grown until spring.

"Maybe," I said.

"Is that what you've been working on so hard?" she asked.

She always amazed me a little bit. I never much felt the need to keep anything hidden from Annie, but whenever I worked on a surprise for her, some little mention showed that she knew what was going on. This was not something I could tell her about; I could not bring her into this, and somehow that created a signal that I had no idea was being sent and of which I became aware only when she made a mention.

We ate for a while in silence. That was my usual response. I stood up from the table, my second cup of coffee still half full, pushed my chair under the table and spent a moment looking at my cup. I reached down and finished it in a gulp.

"The storage shed needs sorting out," I declared, "and I have to talk to Rawlins before driving you to Lincoln."

Annie stood up, too.

"Leon Rawlins has been running this farm for ten years and you've never talked to him before. You'd do better to go back to town and jaw some more with Bradley."

"Now you exaggerate," I said. Somehow her words had a hurtful barb, and I felt it, but I also felt surprised to have that feeling instead of simple laughter. "My heavens, Annie, you are in a funny mood this morning. I had planned to find him and make sure he has everything he needs for the winter."

"A funny mood? Now, let me tell you, that's the pot and the kettle," she said. She walked to a heavy dark brown chest. From one of the drawers she pulled a carefully ironed white napkin. She brought the napkin back to the table and put three rolls in it, then added a fourth. "Take some of these biscuits with you. That's the least you can do if you're going to interrupt the man at his work."

"Hey, Leon." I expected Rawlins to be in the barn, pitching hay from the loft into a wagon hitched to the tractor, and I hoped my voice would find him up in the loft better than my eyes could.

"Mr. Wain?" he called down by way of recognition. "Ain't this a pleasure?"

"Do you have anything of importance in the storage shed?" I asked. "I thought I'd clean it out."

"No," said Rawlins edging over to the center eaves where he could stand upright, "don't think I do. What you doin'? You never done anything like that before, Mr. Wain."

"You and my wife," I acknowledged with half a laugh. In a louder voice, to make sure he heard me, "Nothing, really. Just making some room to store things."

Rawlins made his way to the crude ladder nailed on the side of the barn and climbed down.

"I can do that for you, Mr. Wain. You just tell me what you want done. You don't need to be doin' any chores around here."

"Heavens, man, you *are* starting to sound just like Mrs. Wain."

"Wouldn't want that," said Rawlins with a chuckle.

"Say, Leon," I said, "I was down at Sal's yesterday. You know, the barber? Saw some of your old friends."

Rawlins heard the different tone in my voice and figuring how to answer, he made a point of studying my neatly cut hair.

"He did a good job."

"Oh, that," his careful response made me laugh. "That was a man named Mueller. I had him come down to Denver from Telluride. Sal didn't give me this haircut, I just went in there to visit, sort of on the spur of the moment, on my way over to see Bradley Martin. Ran into ol' Blaine Hartley and his uncle, Jimmie Childs."

"Ain't that a miracle? Jimmie's two years younger than Blaine and still his uncle. Maybe Mrs. Childs was the miracle," said Rawlins. "Anywise, I imagine them two might not be too happy with your brother-in-law."

That was sort of what I was fishing for as I recalled Hartley's words. A mildly successful farmer, he had a fine crop but no one to buy it. If his potatoes didn't simply rot in the field, he figured he'd get pennies on the dollar and that wouldn't be enough to pay off his loan.

"Well," I said, starting to look around for something I could use for my chores, "when you go to a butcher you get meat, and when you go to a barbershop you get gossip. I gather what makes Bradley so popular with them is they've got a loan out with the bank?"

"Yep. Like most folks around here."

"Well, to tell you the truth, Leon, it wasn't exactly the pleasant chitchat I was looking for. And Jimmie is looking mighty thin, like he'd missed a few meals. Between us, I had to get out of there before somebody asked me to say something to Bradley for them."

"Fair enough," said Rawlins. "Ain't your place."

I gave up my looking around the barn. "Do you have a wheelbarrow out here? I need to get started. When I'm done, if you're finished and I won't be interrupting, we can go over what you need for the winter."

"That ain't necessary. There ain't nothing unusual coming up."

"It might be a harder winter than you think, Leon."

"Maybe," said Rawlins, looking intently at C.C., "but we can handle it. It ain't like you'll be out of touch or nothing."

I nodded good-bye. The man was right. Annie was right. We had never worked the farm; Leon Rawlins had. I'd been lucky. With a good income from the bank and a faithful tenant to run things, I'd paid off the mortgage in the first eight years. Mortgage-free these last two years I felt pretty certain Annie would be able to keep the place, come what may. The loss of the tenant was probably inevitable. Loyal as I was, Rawlins would have to produce some kind of income to feed his family. Still, I hoped he could. If Rawlins could survive, it meant Annie would also have an income.

Chores and lunch behind us, we drove out of Grafton. The weather turned gray and sharply colder in the dying afternoon.

"That Leon is a pretty solid fellow," I said. "He'll see things through."

"He has for ten years," Annie said.

I nodded. I didn't look at her. I had almost slipped. Maybe I should have talked to her of what was to come. I couldn't. It would be better for her if she never talked to me about it, no matter how it got between us today. The silence started to grow heavy between us.

"Bradley and I had lunch yesterday," I began. "You know him, twelve o'clock sharp at the luncheonette. I'd heard over to the barbershop that things might be a little slow around here, but Bradley wouldn't own up to it. Well, he did say there were some problems here and there, deposits down a little, but all in all I'd say he's been lucky."

"Any different from home?" asked Annie.

"Depends on if what Bradley says is true," I said. "I heard some farmers got problems. We got them at home. Like Tiedeman. Dixon's gonna want to foreclose on him. Won't do any good. There are a lot of people who think the way you deal with another person's adversity is to get tougher. Some otherwise good people go bad when it's time to help someone."

"Is he really otherwise a good person?" she asked.

"You mean Dixon?" I almost laughed. She had a bead on people. "You are tough. Your judgment about him is probably better than mine."

"Did you tell Bradley that Telluride's been in a slump?"

"He knew that but, yes, I did. Told him how people keep leaving town. How some folks just walk out their front door, even leave their dirty dishes right on the table. I let him know deposits are down eighty percent, but I'm not worried, and I told him so."

I pushed my spectacles back up over the bridge of my nose.

"Of course you're not," she said. She smiled at me. Her words seemed to carry two meanings, but in her smile I could always feel warmth, trust, love. "I know you. You always have a plan."

"Dearest," I said, feeling, as I always did, stronger in her smile, "I do have a plan, but for it to work . . . well . . . I don't know, like I said, some otherwise good people go bad when it's time to help someone."

"It must be painful," she said.

It was time for me to change the subject. As I searched my mind for a suitable transition, out of the blue, she asked,

"They still serve the meatloaf with mashed potatoes, gravy, and succotash?"

"They sure do," I chuckled. Annie had just the right touch, again. "I could'a had the same meal twenty-five years ago, including the apple pie."

I had returned home early yesterday to be with her. Now I was taking pains to extend my time a little more by driving her to Lincoln to make the train. I had told Bradley the trip to Lincoln was on the way to Olathe. I had to visit a bank, and I would go home from there. On the way, he said, maybe another couple hundred miles, obviously baffled by an act of such apparent inconvenience.

Silence had descended again. I cast about for something to say.

Edward Massey

The Telluride teas. Truth to tell, they were as incongruous as anything I could think of, but they were important to her. Fine ladies in long dresses, the cream of Telluride society, walked through the dusty town each week to the home of the hostess, sporting their wide-brimmed hats and white gloves. The clothes, the houses, the tea sets, the pretension all had been bought by the hardest kind of labor mixed with the hardest kind of living, and maybe just a little cheating and stealing. It truly was incongruous when I thought of Annie's flat out acceptance of fact; well, maybe she – and the other women -- had a point; maybe it wasn't such a bad idea to bring a touch of refinement to a town of ruffians.

"Will you do the teas again this fall?" I asked her.

"You mean my 'social'?" she asked.

"Oops. That's right. That's what I meant."

"First one's this Friday, after I get home," she said, brightening at the thought. "Why do you ask?"

"What?"

"Why do you ask about my socials?"

"Nothing," I said. "I was just interested."

"You've never been interested before," she said. "Do you object? They're community. I think it's important for us to be a part of our community."

"Of course."

"Well, something's going on?"

"Going on?" I repeated. Annie sat unresponsive, gazing at the fading countryside that rolled monotonously by her window. Again the silence seemed to unleash something cold and menacing, and I sought desperately to keep it at bay. "Do you think I have a woman or something?" I blurted it out, the unimaginable.

"Well, you will admit the last two nights were not exactly customary," she said.

"Is that a complaint?" I asked, vainly trying for a laugh.

"No, just a fact." She looked straight ahead, as though she held the wheel and needed to focus on the road.

"You're funny, you and your facts," I said, turning to her with a smile. "So, answer my question."

"What?" she said, still looking out the window at the fields. "Oh, you mean about another woman? No, of course not, not you. But there is something. I just can't put my finger on it."

At that moment I did not have the luxury of considering whether evasion was a lie. I never wanted to lie to Annie, but I accepted that I was in the midst of a decision that brought doubt on everything I did.

"Well, I'm going back East on business. I'll be back in a couple of days. Then, we'll see."

"See what?" she asked.

"Oh, for heaven's sake, Annie, nothing. Just a figure of speech."

I left it there. So much I wanted to say, but dared not. Because that would lead to questions and the questions could not lead to explanations. Knowledge, any knowledge, would only make it more difficult for her. The terrifying realization settled on me that the reason I never really thought she would abandon me was that I so much wanted to spend the rest of my life with her.

No matter how little my wants would govern what she did, I knew I could do nothing but trust her until after it was over. I had chosen not to speak to her because I did not want to put her at risk. I admit, I knew she would try to stop me. She would beg me to step back and see that I was not my bank. Beg may not be exactly the right word to describe how Annie would point out that the debts and the depositors were not my obligations. That was what she would say and she would say it because she wanted to persuade me to let it alone and I knew she was right and I wished I could believe it myself.

For a while we drove on in silence. The early autumn light shone bright on the flat ground and reflected off the hood of the Studebaker. A flock of geese passed low overhead in a perfect formation, suddenly changing direction and disappearing into the distance. The engine filled the compartment with a steady rumble. Only the presence of something silent and intangible kept us company as miles and minutes drifted by.

About two-thirds through our trip, just beyond where the highway joined the big road, Annie asked, "Will you drive straight through?"

"Almost," I said. "I'll probably stop over in Omaha." I was entering the outskirts of Lincoln. The chance to say more had passed.

Edward Massey

"Excuse me, dear," I continued, sensing her full gaze and briefly turning to face her, "but I always need to concentrate a little right here. I have to get onto 34 and then off onto North Ninth and then take Q Street up North Seventh. Once I get there, I'm okay. Let me take just a minute on these streets."

We pulled into the train station and I walked her, suitcase in hand, to her compartment. I reached out to hold her, her upper arms in each of my hands, and pecked her on the cheek. She slipped between my arms to hold me close and tight. When she released me, she looked me in the eyes, her eyes wide, saying nothing.

I waited on the platform and watched until the train started rolling. I could see her through the window. I waved at her. She waved at me.

Outside the station again, I stood at the car. With one hand on the door of the Studebaker, I drummed my fingers on the cloth top. I surveyed the sky, looked at my watch, and finally, opened the door and climbed in.

Those were my hardest moments. My life receded like that train that took Annie away. My life faced me on the roads I now had to take.

I remembered the one-way streets coming in. I started rolling slowly down the alphabet in the direction I had come. At the corner of North Ninth and R I turned onto 34 and I headed west.

25

Small Town Banker
Takes New York Banks
for $500,000

New York bankers, with crimson faces, vowed "to hang that seedy little banker from the hick town in Indian country."

That's the way the story broke. Years later Frank Simms told me he laughed out loud reading his morning newspaper that Friday. He bought his daily paper at the newsstand on his corner of York Avenue and he read it as he walked to work. He had to stop in the street. He was laughing so hard he couldn't walk, watch the traffic, and read all at once.

Well, I'm that seedy little banker. First thing I have to say is that I didn't take the New York Banks for anything. Second, I don't mind being called a seedy little banker. It's not as good as being called Buck, but I'll take it. Truth be told, I would have been just as happy if they had never put it in the paper.

When Simms got to the office he discovered the case had been assigned to him. The bankers who called the Burns Detective Agency told Simms their only concern was to catch the bastard and get their money back. I didn't do all of this to twist their tail; it was far too serious for that, but I laughed when Simms told me that.

"I'll allow as how I might have made them mad."

"Not just mad, Mr. Wain," he said. "Embarrassed. They wanted you found as quickly as possible so they could get this embarrassment behind them."

Simms had been told to report to the conference room on the twenty-seventh floor of the Chase National Building. He was a man who noticed and he noticed a good-looking young woman standing at the doorway. She pointed him to the empty chair next to the head of the table. Like a magnet, he drew questions from every man in the room. He could see each one had brought in a copy of the same newspaper he picked up on his way to work, and, for good measure, a few extras were strewn across the table.

He stood behind his chair and quickly counted sixteen men in the room. They all looked pretty much the same. He looked at the young woman who'd showed him in and smiled. She smiled back. He was ready.

Repeated instructions to keep the matter hush-hush assaulted him. He waited for the words that would give him this assignment, something like: "Find the culprit who persuaded the fourteen of us to co-operate with him in transferring a half million dollars from our banks to his." Not to breathe a word of it was all he heard.

Frank Simms had a habit of simple truth. The bankers told him they didn't like his attitude when he asked how he could keep hush-hush something he had learned about in the morning paper.

The agency got the case a few hours before Simms, a few hours before the first paper hit the streets. Now, barely half a day later, eleven City newspapers carried the story — and that didn't count the ones in German, Yiddish, Russian or Spanish. The whole town knew. Within hours the whole country would know.

Simms needed attention and patience from these men. The tall windows on the left side of this grand room directed bright light slanting across to the portraits of large, looming men on the right. He looked to the bankers crowded at one end of the enormous cherry table in the center of this majestic space, more chairs empty than filled. He tried to measure these men against the ones on the wall. That was why the portraits were there, so the ones under them would wonder if they measured up. Were the characteristics of attention and patience important to the men proclaimed great by portrait?

Scarcely after ten o'clock and already the temperature stood in the high eighties. Labor Day had been a misery. Now it was Friday. The heat wave had gone right on with no relief. Simms felt the room ready to explode. Voices crossed over each other in the heat — despairing over the prospect of finding some little man no one seemed to have met who could only be described in the most general terms.

"I don't give a damn about the description! I just want to catch the son-of-a-bitch. Can you do it?"

A fully stuffed, middle-aged man, flushed red all the way to the top of his balding head, stabbed his finger out across the table straight at Simms.

The chairman, Winston Whitworth, at the head of the table, paid no attention to the hubbub. He inspected the bright white tent cards neatly lined up on either side of the table, the name and bank of each person spelled out in perfect black script. By the smile on his face Simms could tell his bank's execution of this detail meant a lot to him.

When Whitworth finally looked up, Simms stuck out his hand: "Frank Simms, Burns Detective Agency."

The handshake was interrupted by the flush-faced banker thumping his fist on the table again. "We've been swindled by some seedy little banker from a hick town in Indian country, and I, for one, want to know how Mr. Simms proposes to catch the son of a bitch. I want to know!"

The man didn't really seem to expect an answer. Recognizing the choice of words, Simms also noted he didn't seem to care that the whole room knew who had leaked the story.

Whitworth turned a gentle hand to the gavel in front of him, the light tap not working, each tap heavier and harder. When he succeeded in his struggles to settle the room a bit, he introduced all the tent cards around the table. No surprise to Simms, every title included Vice President, some Senior, some Executive. There were two people at the table who got no tent cards and no introduction. Simms later learned they worked for the Chase, names of Smyth and Cavelli. A couple of regular guys, too, in his quick assessment.

Whitworth announced he would summarize for all concerned. Simms compared the summary to what he knew – and mentally marked up his opinion of Whitworth's attention span: someone had sent coded telegrams the previous Friday, exactly one week before, to six New York banks signed by six Denver banks telling them to transfer money on behalf of the Bank of Telluride to the Chase National Bank. Someone had showed up at the Central Hanover on Saturday afternoon and used this money to pay off all the Bank of Telluride's debts and to send the rest to other banks to hold on deposit for the Bank of Telluride. The Denver banks had now disavowed the telegrams. Whitworth made a point of noting that Hanover got its loans paid back but he failed to mention that the Chase certified the checks.

Simms also knew the D.A. had been called in by one of the banks. The D. A. was still trying to figure out if all these financial manipulations even added up to a crime. He said it looked a lot like six banks loaning money to another bank. Before Simms could decide if he should mention the D.A.'s doubt about these very confusing facts, the flushed bald guy gained a name, Simon Pugh, by virtue of his continued interruptions of Whitworth's introduction. Undeterred, he announced that his bank, the Harriman, cared nothing about the facts. What they wanted was fast action.

George Ethan, the only banker known to Simms and the one who had called in the Burns agency on behalf of the American Bankers Association, tapped his newspaper gently. His gestures as slow and steady as his voice, he said,

"I consider the whole scheme one of the most amazing financial manipulations on record. I think we can tell Mr. Simms what was done and how, even if we need to teach him a little about banking. The important task here is to find Mr. Wain. If anyone can do that, Mr. Simms can." He turned his head and looked down his side of the table. "Mr. Simms, please tell my colleagues how you expect to find this fellow."

"It won't be easy," said Simms.

Before he could continue, a tall, lean man rose from his chair. Three bankers fanned themselves with newspapers. Simms stopped talking and watched the room go still. With a slight bow, resting his right hand in the pocket of what Simms accounted a first-rate chalk-stripe suit, Mr. Pembroke greeted his colleagues nonchalantly,

"Gentlemen, the Hanover is not altogether certain that we should be a party to this gathering." He dropped his voice almost to a whisper, like he was sharing a secret. "As you know, we had nothing to do with these transfers."

"Nothing except get paid off, Pembroke," said Peter Grinnell, easily the youngest in the room, looking a little out of place with his bright red hair and a solid blue suit.

"That's not necessary, Mr. Grinnell," said Whitworth. "We have a long agenda today."

"Facts are facts," said Grinnell. "Speaking of which, I am not happy that Mr. Pugh leaked this goddamn story." Simms became more convinced this young cob was out of place as he held up the paper and started quoting at top speed:

> The search is on for Charles C. Wain, by all accounts a mysterious and nondescript little man who has left the major New York banks furious and embarrassed.
>
> All America is laughing while New York bankers are crimson with anger and vowing "to hang that seedy little banker from a hick town in Indian country."
>
> The furious New Yorkers are trying desperate means to find the little man and recover their funds. Detectives have been on the case for almost twelve hours and already they have many important and reliable leads.
>
> According to sources, the authorities have been tipped that Wain has booked passage on the Graf Zeppelin to Europe. The authorities have sent officers to New Jersey and are confident of apprehending the swindler.

"It just makes us look foolish." Grinnell shook the paper across the table at Pugh. "In as much as each of us just *gave* this gentleman between seventy-five and a hundred thousand dollars, we sure as hell don't need to draw any attention to ourselves."

"My God, man," shot back Pugh, "Those are normal amounts for banks to transfer. Nobody would notice them in an honest transaction. This was a swindle. We want our money back. If that takes getting everybody's attention, then we at Harriman are willing to pay the price. We want action. The Harriman National Bank has considerable experience out west. We know how to handle those people."

"Yes, I am sure you do," Whitworth said, somewhat absently. His main attention was on giving hand signals to a porter who had peeked his head in at a crack of the door.

A second later, three carefully dressed stewards in white gloves flowed silently into the room and dealt out trays of silver coffeepots and china cups. Simms concluded that Whitworth put great stock in being a good host, if nothing else. With a cup of coffee in front of him, Whitworth turned back to the table.

"Now, I know this little affair is an annoyance. We all know this meeting is not as important as other committees we share. It certainly is not as important as the margin committee that I sit on. Which, by the way, I will have to excuse myself to attend. All the same, it is our lot to deal with the responsibilities we are given. It will be a long and trying day, but if we attend to it, it can be the only one we need to devote.

"I am sure you have all heard about this new Federal Bureau of Investigation. I don't know exactly what they are meant to do, but apparently this matter is important enough that the federal people came to visit me in my office last evening. Based on what they told me, we best just take care of this ourselves. They actually told me they think this case is the kind of thing that can put them on the map. You know what that means."

"Not that I want to appear to support Simon," said Ethan, shifting slightly as the porter placed a cup in front of him, "but I, too, am concerned that we find him."

"We may never find him. Perhaps he was murdered by whoever masterminded this plot," said the elegant Pembroke. "After all, there surely must have been some brilliant mind behind the moves of . . . of, to use Simon's words, this seedy little banker."

"Could it have been an imposter?" asked another banker. "You know, someone else . . . maybe someone not even from out west. An imposter who claimed to be Charles C. Wain."

"Now, I could believe that," announced Pugh. "It would take a mighty smart man to do this. And he'd have to have an education! I just don't see such a person wasting himself out there."

Peter Grinnell reminded Pugh that someone from 'out there' was the first to spot the fraud.

"No, that was a New Yorker! He may be working for a Denver bank, but I believe he's the grandson of our chairman," interrupted Thomas Ewell of the Equitable Trust.

"It all comes down to the same concern," said Ethan, "That is precisely the reason we have the Burns Agency involved. We must find this man."

"My point exactly," declared Pugh. "Prescott Lamont will not tolerate any more of this dilly-dallying. He insists that we at the Harriman National Bank don't waste our time in inaction. We can thank him for meeting last night with the District Attorney, a personal friend of his, and now the DA will be posting grand larceny charges."

"Simon, not so fast," said a banker named Mark Peery. "I was at that meeting. Pains me no end to disagree with you, but I don't think the D.A. believes he has a case. I'm not sure any charges were posted last night."

Pugh leapt to his feet again.

"That's what we'll clear up. Today! Mr. Lamont has invited District Attorney Belder to talk to us over lunch."

"He what?" Whitworth looked stricken. "My God, man, we'll have to make arrangements."

"Winston," asked George Ethan, "how much time can we give Mr. Simms?"

Whitworth pressed the buzzer next to the gavel pad a second time before he broke off to look up at the clock on the wall directly in front of him. "We'll have to set up for lunch. Maybe an hour, not quite. For sure, not more."

"I don't need but fifteen minutes," Simms said. He wanted to learn what these people knew, not tell them what he knew.

"Proceed, Mr. Simms," said Whitworth.

"While it won't be easy," he said, deliberately repeating what he now considered to be a poor way of introducing himself, "it will be simple. Hard, but simple. We'll find this man we believe to be C.C. Wain by chasing leads. There's only going to be one good lead, so most of them will be dead ends. I don't doubt some of 'em will be deliberately misleading, but we'll chase 'em all down. That's why I say it won't be easy. It might take some time. But . . . we'll find him. We can start right now by reviewing everything you gentlemen know about him."

"Well, he's not in New York, that seems for certain," said Ethan. "Our people called every hotel yesterday and there wasn't a trace of him. Eighty-seven hotels, and no Charles C. Wain. We even had him paged. Of course, the Algonquin refused to page him in the bar."

"Didn't this all take place last Saturday? Why did you think he would be in the city yesterday?"

"I telephoned the Bank of Telluride yesterday morning," said Whitworth. "The head teller told me his Mr. Wain left for New York last week — "

"That would be consistent with what we know," Simms said, not noticing he was interrupting Walter Winston Whitworth.

" — *and*," said Whitworth, "he was believed still to be here."

"*And* who believed that?" Simms couldn't help using the same tone.

"Presumably, the head teller," said Whitworth.

"Uh-huh. This is a good example of what I was talking about. You don't know if that head teller was trying to help you or deceive you."

"All of that is irrelevant," said Grinnell. "What we really need to figure out is who this Wain is."

"Well," Simms said, "it appears we might already know. We know the Central Hanover Bank accepted him as president of his own bank, the Bank of Telluride."

"He is, after all, custodian of nearly eight hundred thousand in assets," chimed in Pembroke.

"What do the police think?" someone asked. "I assume you have spoken to the police."

"We have," Simms said. "They think proving the connection will be tough. Mr. Wain was in New York when the telegrams were sent and when they were received."

"He had accomplices," argued Pugh. "It was a conspiracy. He's got our money! This is getting us nowhere. He got that money under false pretenses and I do not see what you are doing to help us get it back. It's your job to get the proof."

"We have a man working on that right now, as we speak," said Simms.

Pembroke, of the fine suit and patrician air, said, "Why can't we simply track down the cash that's left and the collateral our bank returned when he paid off the loans? We could hold both. So far, your banks have been swindled out of $500,000 in banking paper, but it is not yet real money."

"That'd not be my area." Simms said. He was the best banking investigator in New York, but this was over his head. It just seemed to him that if one bank cashed another bank's check that was real money alright.

"The paper says Wain might be on the **Graf Zeppelin**," said Grinnell, bringing the room back to the hunt. "Have you checked on that possibility? You know the ship left New Jersey on Monday."

"He's not floating his way to Europe," Simms said. "He's a little guy from Conestoga, Pennsylvania. Charles Conestoga Wain. He went west and became a bank president, but he's still a little guy. He's trying to escape. He's just not going to Europe to do it."

Simms noticed one soft knock at the door and then Whitworth's secretary stepped in. He also noticed how the room fell silent. It wasn't so much her movement. She moved quietly. It wasn't her clothes, either. Her blouse was full, modestly cut, barely a trace of skin showed below her neck. She had a trim figure, but her long summer skirt with its wide pleats and some kind of flower pattern did nothing to accentuate it. These men had seen plenty of women as good looking as her or better. This was New York. No, it wasn't that. It was simply that she was a woman — the only woman — standing in the middle of a man's world.

She bent behind her boss to whisper in his ear.

"The District Attorney has arrived," announced Whitworth. "We'll take up the rest of our agenda after lunch."

Eyes watched the flowered print go back to the door; Whitworth nodded and the young woman pushed open the double doors. A middle-aged man, much younger than his halting steps, white hair carefully combed, white beard perfectly trimmed, progressed through the doors. Behind him followed a junior, more energetic man, carrying two large briefcases.

Pugh insisted that he perform the introductions. He started to walk the District Attorney around the room, but Belder didn't share his interest and quickly seated himself to the right of Whitworth.

The junior man sat quietly in one of the straight-backed chairs against the wall.

Without any visible cue, the secretary ushered in two stewards who rolled in trolleys and laid the sideboard. Two liveried waiters arrived and took up positions, ready to serve.

"Excuse me," said Belder to no one in particular, taking up a fork in his hand to wave at one of the stewards to bring his lunch. "I need to keep to my schedule. I have another appointment right at one."

"You go ahead, Mr. District Attorney," said Pugh. "I think I can set the stage for what we want done."

Belder cut into his tenderloin tips and withdrew his fork long enough to wave it for Pugh to continue.

"Gentlemen, as I told you, the Harriman has had considerable experience out west. When we financed the Union Pacific, we ran into plenty of difficulty, but we didn't let that stop us. We made our success by striking fast and hitting hard. And that's what we need to do right now. Catch this bastard and put him behind bars."

"How will that get our money back?" asked Ewell. "I am concerned that we will take the loss. Not that I want our Denver correspondent to take the loss, either."

"Find the culprit, find the money," answered Pugh.

George Ethan tapped his glass. He stood quietly waiting until attention was his. He announced his conclusion:

"Speaking for my bank, and for the ABA, the money has already disappeared."

"How can that be? There's no loss yet," insisted Pugh. "Chase just needs to stop payment. No one has to lose anything."

"The Chase can't do that," said Whitworth emphatically. "Central Hanover has already put those checks through the clearing house and made them legal."

"They were indeed legal," insisted Pembroke. "We just put them through in the ordinary course of business. Now it's up to the bank examiners to get our money back. That's what they're for."

Belder placed his utensils in the center of his plate and stood up behind his chair. "Gentlemen, if I may."

That was the year the drill team came into being and you'd have thought the bankers were in on it the way they put down their forks and turned their heads to face him.

"Oh, no, please continue with your meal," insisted Belder, pushing his coat back and slipping his hands into his pockets. "Although I am often accused to the contrary, on this matter my comments will be brief. First, let me say that the City of New York is delighted to be of assistance to all of you. Your institutions are what make our city so great."

Belder paused as the room broke into appreciative smiles, none broader than Whitworth's.

"Second, let me assure you that we have already spent long hours studying the facts in this case. We understand you have engaged private detectives to assist the regular law enforcement agencies. Thank you for the assistance. I am certain that together we will find our man."

He continued to stand behind his chair, glancing about the room in an almost offhanded way. Polite silence turned to stunned realization. He hadn't just paused. He had stopped talking altogether. The babble of confusion cleaved around one loud voice, Pugh's.

"Is that all?"

Simms could see Belder push back his shoulders forcing out his chet; he made a clearing sound deep in his throat. Every banker in the room leaned in.

"Gentlemen, it would be inappropriate for me to comment further. I cannot jeopardize an ongoing investigation. I will, however, say this: Grand larceny is a serious crime. It carries a high standard. If we can convict, the penalty will be harsh."

"What do you mean, 'If?'" exclaimed Pugh, rising to his feet. As though reminded of how to persuade a balking employee and displaying his certain knowledge that the District Attorney was just one such more, Pugh turned to the committee as a whole: "I am sure Mr. Belder is completely resolved to find this hick swindler."

Belder turned and stared into Pugh's words. He looked briefly into the now after noon sun and frowned in what looked to Simms like resignation.

"I admit that I have two questions concerning this case." He paused; his shoulders relaxed now, his chest no longer swelled. "No one ever saw this man?"

"No one except Central Hanover," said Peery. "They saw him, of course. He was there."

"But we are not one of the six banks involved," insisted Pembroke.

"Oh, you're involved," said Peery, "you just didn't —"

"What difference does it make," interrupted Pugh. "Whether we saw him or not, the man has our money and we want you to catch him."

"I am sure the police will do their job," said Belder, almost with a sigh. "Mine is not the role to catch him. I have just one other question. One other thing perhaps you can explain to me, Mr. Pugh, on behalf of all these gentlemen you seem to represent from these great institutions."

"And what is that?" Pugh pushed back against his chair, head poised in confident anticipation.

"Exactly where does the theft occur?"

Belder continued to speak, waving aside Pugh's repeated efforts to rejoin. "These funds were directed to a third party. Am I incorrect in understanding that the money went to pay off liabilities of the bank in whose name the credit was created? Is that normally how your bank thinks of theft? When a credit is created, isn't that normally called a loan?"

"It was a swindle," snapped Pugh.

"Alright," said Belder. "Do you have evidence of that?"

"The evidence," Pugh fairly shouted, "is obvious!"

"Well — as I said before," resumed Belder, this time to the whole room, his voice still confident, as though there had never been the least disagreement, "I really must take my leave. My one o'clock waits. Jeffrey?"

He held up a finger and the junior man leapt to his feet.

"I'll tell you one thing," said Grinnell as the door closed behind Belder. "Give him a week. He'll drop this case or let it die unnoticed. The way he sees it, six banks accepted the instructions as authentic, a seventh certified the checks, and an eighth cleared them. That's it. Who's going to get a jury to believe that was larceny? He's a politician. Mark my words."

"He doesn't see the opportunity," said Pugh. "But others will."

"Gentlemen," said Grinnell, "eighty years from now no one will believe we bankers accepted instructions to transfer money on the basis of Western Union telegrams merely because they were in code."

"So what can we do," someone asked, "if we can't trust one of our own?"

Simms tried to remember who had asked that question; he figured that question would be asked eighty years later, just like Grinnell's. All he could remember was that it led to a discussion that led to no real answer.

Pugh shouted louder than ever, causing Whitworth's secretary to cower when she came back into the room and handed him a note.

"Well," said Whitworth, this time wasting no light taps of his gavel. "It appears we are to be visited by the President of the Burns Detective Agency, Mr. J. Russell Cox."

Leo Cavelli groaned under his breath as he recorded the name in his notes. He was holding a ticket to the Dodgers doubleheader with the Pirates that afternoon. Before this business blew up he'd been figuring on leaving the bank by noon, since he had worked the Saturday before the holiday and it was a Friday anyway. The meeting dragged on. Bad news from the market the day before meant he had a heavy volume of inter-bank transfers to deal with. Now this, another guy coming in to talk. He'd never make it to either game. Simms learned all of this when Cavelli told him the only good news came when he checked the tape and learned the Dodgers had won him two bucks by taking the first game, six to five.

Simms's boss marched straight to the chair that Belder had vacated next to Whitworth. Cox placed his homburg on the table, resting it on the crown. Then he folded his overcoat over the back of the chair. Like everyone else in the room he wore a dark suit and tie. The lapels told the difference. On the bankers' suits they appeared flat and knife edged, on Cox's, rounded and thick.

Cox sat upright on the edge of his seat, hands folded on the table like a man at prayer. Whitworth viewed his comment as adequate introduction and Cox figured it was taking too long for someone to introduce him, so he started in on his own.

"Gentlemen, I have come here today because I have determined that this case warrants my personal attention. I assigned Simms because he has the right background, and because he has done an excellent job in the past — just as you would expect from a Burns operative. Now, he will perform a valuable function as my lieutenant because I will be assuming personal responsibility from this point on."

Cox looked at Simms just long enough to see if he had acknowledged the decision of his superior. He then cast a glance down the table at Simon Pugh. With a slow dramatic loop of his chin, he returned his head to center

"Upon further careful review, after making this assignment, I determined that the Burns Detective Agency needed to put a higher public face on this very visible case. Because I believe we can help the District Attorney, I will personally take charge of this massive manhunt. I will be in charge of coordinating the New York City Police Department, the American Bankers Association, and, of course, our own highly trained operatives. After all," he added with a tone he considered business intimate, "it is in the Burns tradition to give you your money's worth."

Cox stopped there and looked around for questions.

"No questions?"

Everyone seemed to be wondering where he was leading them. Simms certainly wondered. Simms thought Cox may have misunderstood the bankers' dumbstruck response. Cox concluded it was time to give them impressive results, now.

"Well I'm sure you'll be pleased to know that after less than twenty-four hours on the case, our operatives have already spotted C.C. Wain. In Kansas."

The room started to bubble with voices. It came as news to Simms.

"See? I didn't think he was on the **Graf Zeppelin**," Ethan was the first to speak. "Are you sure? Kansas? I heard he was sighted down in Mexico."

"Gentlemen, the Burns Agency is certain that Mr. Wain is in Kansas. In fact, gentlemen," he continued, his voice rising, "I am prepared to walk out of this room and announce to the press that after only one day on the job, Burns operatives will arrest C.C. Wain — today, Friday, in Kansas!"

26

That same Friday morning, My-Yut removed the gold-rimmed plates from the breakfast table and carried them into the kitchen. On my first day after we moved to Telluride, I walked home for lunch. Annie used the good china — and crystal and silver — to serve me lunch, and our first dinner together in the new house. Seemed fitting enough and I made no remark. The same good china – and crystal and silver – were spread out on the table for my lunch the second day. I asked her if someone special was coming that day.

"You," she said. "And me. There's nothing more special than my everyday."

She said the same to the ladies of Telluride when they exclaimed over her place settings the first time they gathered in her new home. I imagine she said the same on this Friday, truly a special day, first day of the season.

Each lady of Telluride had a day when she received guests. Annie had the first Friday of the month. When each new season opened in September it was her day.

Annie sat at the dining room table holding a smoothly curved coffee cup, enjoying the sense of calm that radiated up from the warmth in her hands. My-Yut had filled the wood-fired burner under the boiler almost an hour earlier, yet the room still hovered around shiver temperature against the crisp September day. She called My-Yut through the door of the kitchen. The short woman appeared silently on moccasin-clad feet.

Had enough wood been brought in the house for the stove and the fires in the kitchen and the living room? Annie distrusted the new steam heat I had installed.

My-Yut nodded. Her dark face shone against a bright turquoise blouse. "I bring wood in. Today. Every day."

"Of course," said Annie, fiddling with the lacy top button loop of her dressing gown. "It's the new season. I do like to get it all right."

She talked without expecting an answer. An answer would have been unwelcome, an interruption.

"It's not the ladies, you see. It's me. I like to get it all right."

She rose from her chair and walked past her Ute companion of twenty-five years, taking her coffee cup to the kitchen sink. My-Yut followed. She took the coffee cup out of the sink, washed it, dried it, and put it in the cupboard. Finished, she turned and faced her mistress.

"Some of the ladies think my day is the best," Annie said to the silent woman, "and I tell them they're all the same. They are, of course, and yet it really is, you know. I didn't get my day, 'At Home', just because Charles is President of the Bank of Telluride. I came into it after six or seven years, after Charles built the bank. Here it is almost twenty years later."

She flashed a quick embarrassed smile. This is one of those things I wasn't there to see, but I know sure as breath what happened. She did not allow herself to feel the first day in the season was an exalted position. Annie always tried to stay true to herself. She had been At Home on the First Friday through all these years and she did not want to treat it as anything other than a fact.

"What with the dead of winter and terrible summer heat, we ladies only get to open our homes eight times a year. That justifies a little excitement when September comes around, don't you think?" she asked rhetorically. My-Yut continued to stare back with wide unspeaking eyes.

Annie had the habit of ending her discussions with herself by sitting down. From a drawer in the center of a small white table with bright green painted vines encircling the legs, Annie pulled out a pad lined with tasks already set out for the day. She looked out the window past the spindles of the porch railing.

"I'll go check the yard. Then, I'll go down and talk to the Davis girl."

E.L. Davis's granddaughter had been coming to our yard to pick dandelion heads for four years. I had paid her a nickel each, knowing full well it was a terrific overpayment, but knowing, too, why I did so. When the accounting and payment had been completed, the little girl took her jingling pocket full of change and ran down the hill to my bank to make a deposit. Like grandfather, like granddaughter, a lineage traced from the entrepreneur who, helped by a few other stout men, built the town of Telluride.

"I hope she'll come up and take care of everything," said Annie. "She's fourteen now. You know, nickels aren't as interesting at that age as they once were."

"Yard no need," said My-Yut.

"Oh, you do a wonderful job, My-Yut," said Annie in a rush, "but I want to take advantage of our porch. You know, if the day stays bright, even if it is a little cool, it will be glorious to have the porch open. That's why the yard has to be perfect. Besides, you have enough to do."

She put her pencil on the notepad and tucked both into the drawer.

"If Charles were around, he could take care of the Davis girl and the yard."

I imagine she said that as she started to walk out the kitchen into the hallway because that was something she said quite a bit, just before adding *But I can't complain.*

The telephone rang and My-Yut answered with her deliberate movements, putting the receiver to her ear and making no effort to stretch up to the mouthpiece that pointed straight at her hairline.

"Hello," she said into the air. Without a further word, she offered the bone-handled earphone to Mrs. Wain. Annie's first thought was that one of her ladies had called to cancel.

"Hello," she said, pointedly bending forward to speak directly into the mouthpiece. "And who is this?"

"The name's Johnston DeLuz. Is Mr. Charles C. Wain at home?"

"Good morning, Mr. DeLuz," said Annie. "No, Charles is not here."

"Will he be at the bank this morning?" asked DeLuz.

"I rather doubt it," answered Annie. "He is out of town on business."

"So it would appear."

"Pardon me?"

"No use beating around the bush, Mrs. Wain. I'm calling you from Denver. I'm investigating the telegrams your husband sent to New York last Friday."

Annie stepped a little closer to the mouthpiece, taking in a deep breath.

"Investigating? Mr. DeLuz, I don't know what you're talking about. My husband was in New York last Friday."

Edward Massey

"Probably was," answered DeLuz. "That's why I'm supposed to find out how he arranged to send those telegrams from Denver on that selfsame day."

"I'm sorry, sir," said Annie. "I simply do not have any idea what you are talking about."

"Uh-huh," responded DeLuz.

The silence on each end lasted long enough for Annie to consider how she wanted to deal with this conversation.

"My dear, Sir," she let a tinge of impatience escape, "if by that you mean you disbelieve me, again, I am sorry. The fact is I can be of no help to you unless you tell me what you are talking about."

"Look, Mrs. Wain, I've traced those telegrams. I know where they were filed. I even know that three of the telegrams were sent by a woman, two by a man."

"That makes no sense and I don't see what it has to do with my husband. He wasn't even in Denver on Friday. He spent Wednesday night with my niece in Lamar and left for New York on Thursday."

"Is your niece a middlin' tall, attractive girl with long blonde hair?"

Involuntarily, Annie jerked the receiver from her ear. She stared at the box of the telephone, suddenly quite alive and a little threatening.

"We have their descriptions, Mrs. Wain, and we expect to make an arrest within twenty-four hours."

Their descriptions?

"Who, in heaven's name, are you talking about?"

She wondered if he was going to mention Connie.

"The ones who sent the telegrams from Denver."

Connie had been in Telluride last Friday.

"An arrest?" She asked, almost a whisper. "What in ever for?"

"For the five hundred thousand dollars they took with those telegrams," answered DeLuz.

"Five hundred thousand dollars?" repeated Annie, her voice rising just slightly then turning arch. "Are you kidding me?"

"Not at all. Your husband had five hundred thousand dollars wired to him in New York last Saturday."

"Now I know you're joking," she said, her voice almost mirthful. "How, pray tell, did he do that?"

"I don't know all the particulars, Mrs. Wain, but I believe you do," said DeLuz. "There's a nationwide manhunt going on. All I know is that my job is to find out how he got those Denver banks to wire him the funds."

"Manhunt?" she said, her disbelief out in the open, thinking she was hearing a joke. "For *my* husband?"

"If your husband is Charles C. Wain, yes, ma'am."

"This makes no sense," Annie said with growing impatience. "And exactly what was it he is supposed to have done?"

"It's not what he is supposed to have done, ma'am, it's what he did. Your husband arranged for some Denver banks to wire him five hundred thousand dollars, only he didn't do it alone. Apparently your niece helped him do it."

"Do what?" she said.

"Send the telegrams."

"But why do you think my niece was involved?"

"By your description," said DeLuz.

"My description?" sputtered Annie. "I didn't give you any description."

"Maybe not, Mrs. Wain, but you know I have it, so she must have been the one."

The sun was streaming through the oval window of our front door, filtered by the sheer white curtains. Annie moved forward as far as the cord would allow, until the rays came up to the waist of her cream and black dressing gown.

"Mr. DeLuz, I was at the beginning of a very busy day," she said. "Now, if you don't mind, I need to get back to what I was doing. Would you like me to tell Charles to call you when he comes in?"

"Yes, please do that, Mrs. Wain," he answered.

"Good-bye, Mr. DeLuz." She returned the earphone to its hook. The sun bathed the lower half of the stairway leading to the second floor. She sank down on the bottom step.

When she told me how she found out, she shook her head.

"I didn't think to ask him for his number."

27

Over at The Bank of Telluride, J. P. Dixon jiggled the key in the lock. He scowled over his shoulder, as much annoyed as surprised. David Twicken acknowledged the greeting with a smile and a broad wave of his arm.

"Friday morning. Today's the big day!"

Dixon frowned at the joy Twicken expressed in the problems they faced that day. He refocused on his task.

"It's eight-thirty, you're early," he said.

"Pity to leave this beautiful mountain morning," Twicken said, joining the vice-president on the top step. "Crisp, but beautiful. Still, I thought we could get in a few extra minutes. You know, preparing."

"Mr. Wain should be here," Dixon complained. "We should not have to face the bank examiners alone."

"He might surprise us," said Twicken brightly.

Dixon looked up and down Colorado Avenue. Empty.

"Besides, he's always here in spirit!" carried on Twicken, stepping back and bowing Dixon through the double doors.

Together they passed the three stations of the teller's cage to the vault and opened it. Dixon assembled what he thought might be needed by the bank examiners — journals, ledger books, statements of account — and carried them into the private office next to mine. Twicken created a neat little pile of the advices that the mail had brought on Wednesday and Thursday and gave them to Dixon. He had not yet had the time to enter them, but he knew what they meant. The bank's outstanding debits had been satisfied. All checks drawn on the bank would be honored.

He knew, too, that the ledgers showed all one hundred eighty-five depositors had withdrawn their funds since Tuesday. Each statement of account showed a zero balance. He had written up the withdrawals personally, starting Wednesday and finishing them all last night.

"Hey, Mr. Twicken!" Gus Spiros, owner of the one large grocery in Telluride, a kind of long-gabled warehouse down on San Juan near the tracks, opened the door at nine sharp.

"Gus, step right over here to my window," said the head teller. As he led the grocer to his station he asked Dixon if he'd be kind enough to send folks over to see him once they'd finished with any other banking business they had. At the same moment Amy Cole arrived breathless at her own window and Twicken repeated his request.

Twicken unlocked the drawer beneath his window and leafed through the thick stack of white envelopes. Each contained a certified check that he had made out in response to telegraphed instructions "to take care of the depositors" sent by me Wednesday morning when I went into Grafton from the farm. Twicken handed one of the envelopes to the grocer, who accepted it without a word and quickly departed. Gus had come the night before, right at closing, and Twicken had told him to come back. Obviously, word was getting around.

Dixon easily took on the air of a man much wronged, and that is how he looked as he scurried back over to address Twicken and Amy Cole in the low voice of conspiracy.

"We need to discuss how to handle the bank examiners in Mr. Wain's absence," he said.

Before he could say more, Silas Mercer, the carter, shuffled into the bank through the back door. He positioned himself in front of Amy Cole's window where he stood silently, his hands folded behind his back. His shirt undoubtedly had a dirty crease where he leaned over the side of his wagon to shake out the trash bins.

"Good morning, Silas." She had the warm voice of a young schoolteacher addressing her shy pupil.

"I need to take out four dollars," he replied, his head slightly bowed, his eyes looking for some place to settle.

"Before we do that, we have to take care of important business," she said, handing him two sugar cubes for his horses. "Now, would you mind seeing Mr. Twicken?" she continued. "He's handling the financial transactions today."

"Hello, Mr. Dixon," the carter called out to the vice-president, who continued to stand at Twicken's window. "I emptied the bins. Wasn't much."

"Thank you, Silas. Yes, it's been light," acknowledged Dixon. Turning to face the carter, Dixon flashed a quick smile and moved away. Silas Mercer slipped sideways to the head teller's window.

Amy had left her stool and whispered in Twicken's ear. The carter waited patiently as the head teller wrote a check for sixty-one dollars, pressed the certified seal into it, and put it in a blank envelope. From his drawer he withdrew four gleaming new silver dollars.

"There you are, Silas," said David Twicken, sliding the four coins and the envelope under the teller bars.

"What's this?" asked Silas holding up the envelope.

"A note from Mr. Wain," explained Twicken. "He's out of town, but he told me he wanted you to have it. You run along now, and don't open it till you get home, okay? And if you have any questions, just ask old Gus Spiros, he'll tell you what to do."

The carter looked puzzled, but he put the envelope in his pocket without a word. With his hands below his desk, Twicken went to the middle of the row of envelopes and found "Mercer" — a check for sixty-five dollars enclosed. He tore it in half, putting a piece in each of the hip pockets of his waistcoat.

Before Mercer was fully out the back door, the front door slammed open. Amy uttered an audible "oh" as three men spilled into the lobby. Each carried a brown expandable briefcase. Each wore a black homburg.

Dixon rushed to greet them.

"Gentlemen," he cried warmly, "I trust you had a safe trip?"

Twicken thought the bank examiners too well pressed and fresh to have arrived on the morning's train. That would have meant leaving Denver at seven last evening and getting into Telluride at four-thirty this morning.

"Impossible! It's impossible to get here," grumbled the first examiner.

"Lucky we made it in last night," said the second.

"Lucky we found a room," said the third. "Do you know there is only one hotel open for business in Telluride?"

"And what a grand hotel the New Sheridan is," said Twicken as he joined them halfway across the lobby.

"I'll grant you, we had a good breakfast. Steak and eggs. Not as good as Denver beef, though still good," acknowledged the first. "But it's damn difficult to get here, and a good breakfast don't make up for it."

"Ah," said Twicken, his arms outspread in welcome, "but now you are here. I dare say you'll find your task an easy one. If there were an early train, you could take it and be back in Denver for supper."

"There is no early train," said the first examiner. "I checked. I told you it's damn difficult to get here. And it's damn difficult to leave. Next train out is tomorrow morning."

Together, Dixon and Twicken guided the examiners to the empty office.

"Everything you will require is here," Dixon assured them.

"Too bad about the train," said the second examiner. "If everything *is* in order, I would've liked to catch an afternoon train out of here. This is such a godforsaken place, I couldn't even purchase a newspaper at the hotel for my breakfast."

"Unfortunately, our local paper recently stopped printing daily," apologized Dixon, and then he cheered up. "However, it is becoming a weekly. I believe there will be a Saturday edition. You'll have it for tomorrow's breakfast."

"We don't plan to be here for breakfast tomorrow — unless they feed us in time to catch the train out," continued the bank examiner who had missed his newspaper. "Where is your Mr. Wain? We need to get started."

Twicken stepped back from the semicircle around the doorway.

"Excuse me. Is there one of you I should be addressing as the head man? I am sorry to say, I can't tell."

"Don't be sorry," said the first.

"We're equals," said the third.

"In that case, *sirs*, I'll be at my station," said Twicken. "Not that you'll have any reason to need me."

Dixon watched Twicken disappear into the teller's cage. His look of confusion transformed into a plea for assistance. Twicken, seated at his station, acknowledged his vice-president with a smile and a nod.

The third bank examiner had taken a chair at the table in the meeting room and appeared to be settling to his work. Dixon smiled uncomfortably at the two men standing before him. The bank examiner repeated his question again and Dixon answered by calling in a loud voice,

"Mr. Twicken? Mr. Twicken, where is Mr. Wain?"

Twicken stirred only enough to raise his head.

"Not here yet."

The titter that escaped from Amy Cole's throat carried through the empty lobby to every cranny.

"Well," said the first examiner, "we'll get started without him."

With something of a bow, Dixon stepped backward out of the office, closing the door behind him.

At ten-thirty, the first bank examiner poked his head in my office to address Dixon taking up his perch as he thought appropriate at the president's desk.

"Sir, would you please ask your head teller to take us into the vault?"

Twicken joined them, as instructed, but not without first asking Amy to call him in the event someone entered the bank.

Customers had trickled in throughout the previous day, and to each he had quietly handed an envelope. In the locked drawer before him remained what was yet to be distributed — a little more than half — their contents already written up in the ledger as "withdrawn."

The first bank examiner put a pudgy finger on the open book he had placed between them. "Did you make these entries?"

"That is my function here," answered Twicken.

"Did you not find these entries to be a little un-*us*-u-al?" asked the bank examiner.

Twicken let the question hang between them.

"Sir," continued the first bank examiner, "every single depositor has withdrawn his funds from this bank."

"I was merely recording the day's business of the bank."

"And you didn't think this odd?" asked the examiner who had missed his newspaper. For the first time Twicken noticed that he wore glasses. Had he put them on while working on the books?

"You did not think *anything* unusual about all of these withdrawals?" echoed the third examiner.

"Unusual?" repeated Twicken. "Why? It was their money."

"That matters little," said the first examiner. "What you have here is a run on the bank."

"We do?"

"You have the makings of a crisis here," said the second examiner.

"Oh, I don't know," said Twicken. "We appeared to have some customers ask for their money the last couple of days, so we just gave it to them."

"That's just it," said the third examiner. "We think you should have closed the bank."

Twicken's voice was calm and his eyes barely graced those of the bank examiners as he continued to watch the front door.

"Mr. Wain would not have wanted that."

"Highly unusual," said the third.

"We've been monitoring this bank," said the second. "Loan losses and other deterioration. We knew of liquidity problems."

"We heard tell the reserves were impaired," said the first bank examiner.

"You've examined the books. I doubt you found liquidity problems," said Twicken.

"Beside the point," said the second, adjusting his glasses. "It's our job to determine whether to allow the bank to stay open."

"After all, you've allowed all of the depositors to get their funds out of the bank," said the third bank examiner.

"And is there something wrong with depositors withdrawing their own money?" asked Twicken, raising an eyebrow.

"All of these accounts should have been frozen," said the second bank examiner, "until we made a decision about closing the bank. After all, we have an obligation to protect the depositors."

"And, please, how does freezing the accounts protect the depositors?" asked Twicken. He could just make out Dixon standing at the door of the vault.

"We have an obligation to keep these funds on deposit for the good of the banking system," said the third examiner. "These few depositors should not have been able to withdraw their funds."

"Few depositors?" Twicken repeated. When the prosecutor grilled him, he just shook his head and said he had no idea how Mr. Wain had done it, but he knew his president had somehow made good every cent of every one of his depositors. Now he was being told it should not have been done, and the reason was for the good of the banking system.

Slowly, cautiously, he started again.

"Truly, gentlemen, I do not know what to say. I mean — didn't one of you say just a moment ago that every one of the depositors has withdrawn his funds?"

"I did," said the first bank examiner. "Furthermore, do you realize that you have a stack of advices in there that have not yet been written up?"

"Yes, sir, I do. I simply have not had the time."

"What they add up to, Mr...what is your name?"

"Twicken."

"Mr. Twicken, what they add up to is that all the bank's debits have been cleared by someone."

"That'd be Mr. Wain," said Twicken, "But, again, I am baffled. What is wrong with the bank's debts being paid off?"

"This is most unusual," said the second bank examiner. "The money is probably gone. I don't see how we'll ever get it back from the depositors."

"Well, one thing is for sure," said the first bank examiner, "we have to bring this to the attention of the Banking Commissioner. May I have the use of a telephone?"

"Oh, my," said Twicken, "I don't have the authority to make that decision."

The first bank examiner eyed him for what seemed like a long while.

"Does Mr. Dixon have such authority?" he asked.

"Well, he is my superior. Perhaps you should ask him directly?"

"Will you fetch Mr. Dixon for us?" asked the first bank examiner. He interrupted himself. "On second thought, I'll get him."

At the sound of his name Dixon made a dash from his listening post by the vault door back to the president's desk. Why, of course. They were more than welcome to use the telephone! Dixon pointed to the phone sitting on the desk and left the office to position himself discreetly by the teller's cage.

Minutes later the first bank examiner walked back to the vault and waved his arm to bring the other examiners, Twicken, and Dixon to its door.

"Mr. Ferguson Grant, Banking Commissioner of the State of Colorado," he announced, "does not attend to the routine assignments of his examiners. This examination was previously scheduled and Mr. Wain clearly knew it was coming. Unbeknownst to us, however, while we were traveling yesterday, the Commissioner's Office received certain telephone calls leading him to think this assignment might be of more than routine importance."

The bank examiner paused to allow himself to be interrupted. Twicken put his hand on Dixon's sleeve.

"The Banking Department of the State of Colorado," continued the examiner, "finds this highly unusual. A bank with all its deposits paid out in good funds. And now Mr. Grant informs me that there is a nationwide manhunt for this man Wain."

Dixon looked stricken, wanting to speak, his open mouth seeming to gasp for air, but Twicken's hand squeezed hard on his forearm.

"News to me," said Twicken evenly.

"For once, Mark's need for a morning newspaper would have served us well," said the bank examiner, for the first time volunteering a name. "It was in all the papers this morning. It's only you people out here in the hills who don't have the news.

"Anyway, whether you believe it or not, we are just going to have to close the doors to this bank. There are too many irregularities here."

"David," asked Amy who had overheard everything from her chair, "can they do that?"

"Well, I don't know," said Twicken. "I think we better get one of the Directors over here."

"Get the whole damn Board over here," said the examiner called Mark. "We want this bank closed by noon."

The bank door swung open and the late morning light splashed across the lobby.

"Paul!" called Twicken, cutting the examiners short. "It's still morning. You must have left Placerville pretty early."

"Not too early," said a short man dressed all in leather. "Maybe about six. It ain't but, what, fifteen miles?"

"Well, that's still quite a trek by this time on Friday," said Twicken.

"It ain't me, it's Jocine," said Paul Butler, a freighter, who would be slow to admit that jobs had come scarce these past few years.

"She's the one who made me open this account and put all my money in here. Now she's telling me to get up here and take it all out. I wouldn't a done neither."

"Oh, you can't take your money out," said the first bank examiner. "This bank is closed."

"Excuse me," said Twicken, turning on the examiner. Amy saw the head teller flush, then turn pale. "This bank is most certainly *not* closed, and you have no right to interfere with our customers."

"Who he?" asked Butler.

"Oh, some official from Denver," said Twicken, resuming his airy manner.

"Figures," said Butler.

Twicken returned to his window and dropped his hands into his teller drawer, looking straight ahead like a blind man playing the piano. Fortunately he had thought to sort the envelopes alphabetically. Butler was right up front.

"Well, can I get my money?" ask the freighter.

Twicken came out from behind the teller's cage and into the lobby, stationing himself between his depositor and the bank examiners. He looked hard at each of them. In another instant the hard look was replaced by a broad playful smile.

"Paul, let me ask you to come by a mite later," he said, grasping the man by the elbow in the familiar manner that everyone in Telluride associated with me and how I taught my people to take care of our customers. Without haste, in the bank's usual courtesy, he walked his depositor toward the door. "We're a bit busy here, see, with these gents from Denver," he said, loud enough for all to hear.

Twicken followed Paul Butler out onto the top step, pulling the door shut behind them.

"My God, it's a beautiful day," he said, looking toward the massive green wall of mountain above the buildings across the street and then east, into the sun, up to Imogene Falls. He raised his arms in a stretch and took a deep, dramatic breath. "Warmed up a bit, too."

"Well, David," said Butler, "you hustled me out of there right smart, but when will I get my money? Jocine is gonna wanta know."

"Oh, I have it for you right here," said Twicken, handing him the envelope he had just withdrawn from his coat pocket.

"Just a durn minute," said Butler, looking in Twicken's eyes while he slid a thick rough finger across the top of the envelope, popping it open in jagged edges. "What's this all about?"

"Just routine," answered Twicken. "I simply didn't want those folks in there to get mixed up with your affairs."

"Sounds fair enough. Thanks," said Butler. He peered into the envelope. "Say, I see this here's a check. I gave you good money. I expect good money in return."

"That is good money," said Twicken. "Certified. No matter what, any bank in the country would have to give you cash for that check." He patted the short man on the back to send him on his way.

"I'll have to talk to Jocine about this," said Paul. "She'll know what to do."

"You do that. She's a fine businesswoman," said Twicken, patting the leather-clad back once again.

Twicken turned and looked through the frosted glass of the door. The postures of Dixon and the three bank examiners told him they had been watching, but their actions and features were indistinct.

The first bank examiner met him as he entered.

"Lock that door," he said.

"I will not," said Twicken. "I have no authority to do that," he lied. "An officer will have to direct me."

"You!" the bank examiner pointed to Dixon. "You're an officer, are you not?"

"Vice-president," declared Dixon, almost jumping to attention.

"Then you lock that door."

Dixon looked at Twicken. The head teller stood still; nothing in his face or eyes showed approval or disapproval.

"Let me confer with my head teller," said Dixon. Dixon went into my office, Twicken followed. Minutes later they emerged.

"We believe only the directors can close the bank," said Dixon.

"My God, man," bellowed the first examiner, "Commissioner Grant has concluded that for the good of the depositors, this bank has to be closed."

"For the good of the depositors?" repeated Twicken.

This time it was Dixon who put his hand on Twicken's sleeve.

"Nonetheless," said Dixon, his voice displaying a confidence that caught Amy Cole by surprise, "until there is some legal authority, closing this bank is voluntary. In Mr. Wain's absence only the Board of Directors can make that decision."

"Then you get that damn Board over here immediately," said the examiner called Mark.

Josh Gibson arrived just as the afternoon rays started to slant across West Colorado Avenue above the roofs of the buildings, about an hour before the sun's daily dip behind the mountains.

"These gentlemen are from the Colorado Banking Department," said Dixon, starting a little hesitantly. "I would introduce you, but I never actually learned your names."

"John Casey" said the first bank examiner, stepping forward to shake hands.

"John Packard," with an identical tone and movement.

"Mark Norman."

"Well, pleased to meet you," said Josh, taking each hand in turn, his whole arm rising and falling in the continuous motion of a man working a pump handle. "Buck told me you were coming. You all need to go to dinner with me. We have good beef up here. We should, I grow it."

"We're stuck here for dinner, that's for sure," said Mark Norman.

"You are?" said Josh, the same smile only different. "Well, it ain't too bad here at night. Like I said, we got good beef. And maybe there's something on at the Sheridan Opera House. It ain't but afternoon. You'll have plenty of time to rest up. I'll meet you at the hotel later."

"Mr. Gibson," started John Casey, dismissing the pleasantries. "Are you a director of this bank?"

"Yes, sir, I am. I imagine that's why Miss Cole called me down here, to greet you officially."

The small lie was not much different from bluffing at poker, and Josh was known for keeping a straight face.

"No, sir, it is not. Mr. Ferguson Grant, the State Banking Commissioner, has ordered this bank closed, and your Mr. Dixon here refuses to do it. He says he does not have the authority."

"Closin' the bank?" Josh stared as though struggling to take in the meaning of the words. "Well, you know, I never thought of it before. I would guess Mr. Dixon's right, though. I suppose that would be a decision for the board."

"Precisely," said John Packard. "How many are on your board?"

"Five."

"Well, then three of you could vote to close the bank. That would make it official."

"Three would be a majority of five. Yes, sir, I imagine you're right there, Mr...?"

"Casey."

"I imagine you're right there, Mr. Casey. Only, you're moving a mite fast for me. Why would we close this bank?"

"For the good of the depositors," said John Packard.

"Say again?"

"There are some irregularities. Mr. Grant has been informed that your Mr. Wain tricked some New York banks into giving him $500,000. We need you to contact two of your directors and close this bank."

"Sorry, fellas, but you're not making sense to me," said Josh, making a show of lifting his high brimmed hat and scratching his head. "Now, I got to consider what you're saying about my friend. He's a right upstanding member of this community. Don't make no sense, but even if Buck did what you said, tricked them banks, why would we close this one?"

"As I've said before, it's for the protection of the depositors," repeated Packard, making no attempt to hide his irritation.

Josh looked around the room, buying a little time. "Mr. Twicken, will closing the bank protect the depositors?"

"I can't say, sir. All the depositors have taken their money back."

Josh's eyes opened wide in recognition.

"You don't say. All the depositors got their money?"

"Yes, sir. Certified checks. And the bank's debts are all paid, so there's no question that they're good."

"Did you receive one of those checks?" asked Mark Norman.

"Well, friend, as it happens, yes I did." *Call. And I raise you.* "Mr. Twicken, here, gave me one yesterday."

"What did you do with that check?" asked Packard.

Josh's answer came easy and straightforward, just conversation.

"Took it to the bank. Down in Delta." *And you don't even get to see the cards.* "I 'spect that check'll be honored."

"Depends on Mr. Grant," lectured John Casey.

"Who do you think we can reach?" Josh asked, turning to the group dubbed by one New York expert "the tiny staff of the Bank of Telluride."

"Mr. Davis is here," said Amy, "he was the one who told me where to call you." Alling Davis had his office just two blocks down from the bank. Twicken volunteered that he had seen Joe Wilson yesterday and thought he was still in town.

"So, Mr. Casey," said Josh, "seems like the horse is out, but you are promising me that if we close this bank down, Mr. Grant can be trusted to act in the best interests of the depositors?"

"Of course," said Casey. "That's why he's the Banking Commissioner."

28

Never seen an onion that big. Covered the whole patty and stuck out around the edge of the bun like the rings of Saturn. Out on that little square of a wooden frame they had for an entrance to the diner I stretched and looked into the sky clouding up all white. That stretch must have opened up some passages somewhere. I could still taste the grease of the home fries and a little belch brought up the taste of that big, fresh onion on the hamburger I had eaten. They grew onions in Wyoming, maybe that one came from right there in Lusk. How were the farmers around here doing? Seemed no matter what I saw or touched or read, it set me thinking about people working. Ordinary people doing ordinary work, the most important kind.

The blinding white coming on in the Wyoming sky forced me back to the task at hand. Worrying about farmers is one thing, like a habit, but what I had to think about was my driving. What you see up there in that Wyoming sky is a high arch of sparkling blue; only at that moment it wasn't. It had dropped flat and low and turned white. Someone had rolled a cover from horizon to horizon and roofed out the blue. The air was plenty warm, almost too warm for my overcoat and hat. Still, as soon as I got started, I knew I'd have to stop soon and put up the top. I didn't want to. I loved driving in the chilly air with the top down, bundled in my overcoat, hat pulled tight to my ears. What good was it to own a convertible if you didn't use it?

When I left the diner I looked forward to a crisp ride in the Indian summer afternoon. In less than half an hour what came up was way beyond crisp. This looked pretty big.

Damn, it was too early for snow, even up in Telluride, and certainly here. Too early or not, here it was. I just couldn't believe I hadn't seen it coming on. At home, in the mountains, I could sense the coming of snow. Out here, in the high plains, maybe the weather changed faster. Maybe there weren't any warning signs. Maybe I had something else on my mind.

By the time I latched down the driver's side of the top, big flakes drifted lazily out of the sky. The first snowflakes each year were a revelation, before they lost their individuality and became as interesting as sand. One alighted on my sleeve. It took its time melting, showing off its frilly eight-sided star. Strange how intensely I watched it. I thought I might remember that snowflake a long time, and as I write this, I guess I have.

What I needed to do was get up the road. Driving as fast as I could on the steep and tortuous roads out of Telluride was a test of skill – and a delight. Here, the roads were flat and straight. Driving fast here was not a matter of skill. Mattered little, I was curious. How fast could I go?

Half an hour ago I could see the horizon many miles away and at that moment it showed brown hills against a backdrop of white clouds. After the first inch of snow I would lose the horizon altogether, something that was going to happen all too soon, judging from how fast the snow had started to fall. Lucky the Studebaker was a powerful car, but I knew it took more than power and I would not be able to maintain my speed.

The snowflakes massed in a shimmering curtain over the long hood. The ribbon of road stretching ahead rapidly narrowed to a pencil line drawing my eye into no horizon, only a vast whiteness broken here and there by a tree.

I switched on the headlights. The wall of light yielded flakes that at the very last moment turned yellow as they smashed into the car.

Damn that lunch stop. If I had driven through I could have beaten the storm for sure. But then Lusk was around 80 miles before Newcastle and that made figuring lunch a little tricky. Just before noon I spied the diner. It wouldn't do to arrive at Newcastle in mid-afternoon on an empty stomach. The girl at the diner might have moved a little slow, but at the time I didn't mind taking almost an hour to get a good hamburger. After lunch, I sat at that wooden table feeling finished; not tired, just completed, with my loose ends tied up. Staring out the diner window, I could no more see the storm coming on beyond the miles of dry grass than I could see the future.

Now, I had to see the future, at least some of it, and I guessed I had maybe fifty miles to go. I had maybe an hour to get through this storm.

The thought that I had to make it through this storm started to seem a little prophetic. I distrusted those kinds of thoughts. They always came on when you had something on your mind and there was nothing predestined about this storm. Still, something seemed to fit. The snowfall, already steady and heavy, would get much worse. With time the driving would be impossible.

My sense of feeling finished had evaporated into thoughts of the bank examiners. They had arrived in Telluride sometime that morning. Seemed fitting, people needed to get ahead of the storm before the driving became impossible. Even as I tightened my grip on the wheel and struggled to maintain my speed, even as I distrusted thinking what it meant that the path was slippery, what I was really thinking about was Twicken and if he had fully understood the telegram I had sent him two days ago.

Going over it all again, I faulted myself for not being more explicit. Why had I written simply "Take care of the depositors"? Surely, I could have said something about certified checks. If anyone had asked me to enumerate my weaknesses, I would have put at the first that I gave my people directions that were vague or too broad. Of course, there had been a reason for that. I wouldn't deny it. That was what helped them to grow. Besides, I knew I could always step back in and fix it. Not this time.

I was out on that road alone. I traveled toward the disappearing horizon in isolation, and in confidence that the Studebaker and I could handle the storm.

No other car passed me in the close whiteness of the heavy snowfall. A strange sense of freedom rose out of the knowledge that I was so thoroughly cut off — a sense so strong it seemed like something physical. And in the next moment a dark wave was sweeping over me, eroding the firm ground of my confidence and leaving uncertainty and an unspoken fear. What if it had all been all for naught? What if the depositors could not get their money?

Twicken was a good man. He would think of certified checks.

But what if I had forgotten something?

An inch or two had already fallen, it was coming down hard. Involuntarily, I continued to reduce my speed as my senses stood on guard for the tires to start slipping or the tail to slide. I had chains. I always left prepared: chains, blanket, two flares, tow rope, tool kit, even a thermos of water. But putting on chains meant getting wet and dirty, and just that much more time. If I was careful I was pretty sure I could make it through.

I smiled at that last thought. I'd always figured that if I was just careful enough I could make it through. So far I had. Including all the way to New York and back to Denver. Care would get me to Newcastle, too. A nagging thought, like a single loose thread, told me that wasn't likely to be true about everything in my future. Whatever care I had or had not exercised, what I had done had taken the future out of my hands.

I dropped my eyes to the big round speedometer with its large numbers. Down to forty. Down to forty might have still been way too high. The nerves in my arms and sides and across my chest told me my machine was barely controllable. I looked up again across the long hood. The horizon had vanished.

"Damn," I said out loud. "Of course, it's true. If I'm careful I'll make it through."

I believed it. At that moment I thought nothing about what lay ahead for me, nothing except what I had to do to get through the snowstorm. When I come back to that moment, something I have done now hundreds or even thousands of times, what I realize is that in thinking nothing for myself I assumed a mute confidence that Connie and Annie would make it through.

The sign for the Flying V Ranch loomed out of the whiteness. Easing the brake, I turned off the highway, trusting the road I could no longer see to take me through the arch framed by two lodgepole pines painted black and holding up a big black V. My tires rolled quietly over the fresh snow.

To my view of things, being a banker in a small town meant maintaining a certain modesty in the world of men. I tell you that because at that moment I knew I was one of few people who could have driven those roads in that snow. Curiously, I allowed myself to have the thought and, without the need to say it to anyone, the thought cheered me.

The Studebaker rolled toward the main house, a huge thing in Tudor style. The white stucco disappeared in the wall of snow, but the black crisscrossed timbers flickered ahead, a dark beacon. By the time I reached the house I had slowed to a crawl and could see cars angled along the side of the driveway. The Flying V was full for a fall weekend. Nobody could have expected the storm. After lunch they probably just stayed put. How nice it would be to be snowbound with Annie.

With a hard right pull on the wheel I rolled into the first open spot. My oxfords sank into the snow, not yet high enough to cling to my socks, but high enough to soak the leather and possibly ruin them. I found my galoshes in the trunk and returned to the front seat to pull them on.

"Cabins is all that's left." Not menacing, just a statement. The woman was middle-aged and slightly overweight. The desk was enormous, decorated with elk horn.

"And might I ask my hostess's name?" I asked.

"Ada," she said. "Most everybody knows me."

"Well, that makes me a stranger," I said, hoping she heard the friendliness in my voice.

"Not for long," Ada replied. She turned the guest book around and handed me a pen. "Like I said, inn's full up. Everyone wants the inn. It gets cold out in them cabins."

"It's perfect for me," I said. "It can't snow forever. I'm just up here to do some sightseein'. Besides, I might be expectin' guests."

29

Finished stoking the fire, he dropped the last piece of the day's wood on the pile for his wife. Yesterday's coffee was beginning to warm. Larry Stein gulped down a cup, unwilling to lose any more time.

This was no ordinary day. This was the first day in the weekly life of his newly merged *Telluride Journal*. He made no bones about it during the investigation. The times had forced his daily to join up with that broadsheet and cut down to a weekly to survive, but he knew his old friend, Buck Wain, had given him one hell of a story to start out with.

Coffee could wait until he got a fresh cup over breakfast at the soda shop in the Nunn & Wrench Building.

Larry came out his front door before the sun cleared the peaks in the east, the little lawns on Fir Street still hoary with patches of frost. The inaugural edition – or the story – brought him out earlier than usual for his Saturday walk down to the office.

It was all he could do to keep from running down Colorado Avenue, eager as he was to pick up a handful of papers and get out in the street. He knew he had a front page and he wanted to hear what people had to say about it.

Papers stacked in bundles wrapped tightly in heavy twine lined the inside wall waiting for the early boys come to hawk them on the street. Stein cut open the top bundle. He began to read what he had hastily written not five hours earlier.

C.C. Wain Wanted for Half-Million Bank Swindle
Large New York Banks Fall Victim
Clever Scheme for Benefit of Local Bank

DENVER, SEPT. 6 — SPECIAL TO TELLURIDE JOURNAL — C.C. Wain, president of the Bank of Telluride, is the object of an international search following the revelation Wednesday of a $500,000 transaction, involving loans from six New York banks to the Bank of Telluride, which authorities alleged to be a swindle and characterized as one of the most amazing in banking history.

Bank of Telluride Closed by Action of Directors
Today

The Bank of Telluride failed to open its doors this morning, posting a notice on the front door that it had been placed in the hands of the state banking commission. This action was taken following a meeting of the directors Friday afternoon after a consideration of all angles of the case.

When he visited me, he told me liked that phrase about the transaction, involving loans. The friend in him felt shock and even a little grief, but he knew I thought I needed to borrow that money, so he wasn't going to give them the satisfaction of calling it a swindle before he called it a loan.

Then he laughed a bit self-consciously and with a sheepish sort of grin, he said the editor in him, and the proprietor of the newly merged *Telluride Journal* and *San-Miguel Examiner,* felt only gratitude. His quiet little banker friend had provided him a terrific lead for his last ditch effort to save the paper. Hell, like him, the paper had been around since Telluride had been called Columbia, and he didn't figure it was taking on too many airs to think there wouldn't be a town if there wasn't a *Telluride Journal.*

Damn those boys, where are they? Stein grabbed six papers and headed for the door. Before he hit the street, he turned back and charged into the adjoining room. A man in overalls and a faded flannel shirt stood bundling papers on a long table. Some years back Stein had hired Bill Essex and whimsically bestowed on the aging miner the high-sounding title of circulation manager. Essex took the title seriously. Stein never had reason to regret it. He liked the way Essex handled the four or five newsboys who worked for him. Best of all he liked the way Essex made sure that every drop where the *Journal* was sold had a full supply — and never ran out.

"Bill, when your boys going to get here?"

"On time," said Essex, pulling twine and snipping it, making no effort to turn around and address his boss.

"Uh? Oh, maybe I am early," said Stein. "Well, you got two boys who can holler?"

"Do I ever," said Essex, still bent over, talking and twining. "My boys could summon the angels right out'a Angel Falls."

"Good, that'd be loud enough," Stein grinned. "Put two of 'em up on either end of Colorado Avenue. We might be just a weekly now but, by God, we got us a good story to start it out with."

"Good's a word got lots of meanings," said Essex, straightening up from his twining and pressing both hands against the ache in his back. He was a small man, bent smaller from years in the mines. He turned to confront his boss.

"You think ol' Buck really did that? I ain't more'n a old dirt digger, but he just seems like an unlikely sort of bank robber."

"The paper doesn't say 'robbed,' it says 'swindled.' There's a difference, though I'm not sure our readers will know what it is," said Stein. He could see the creases in the old miner's face get deeper. "Don't rightly know about whether he did it."

"Mebbe," said Essex. "Mebbe you don't know. Seems like you educated people got too much on-the-one-hand and on-the-other for common sense. I know. He ain't no bank robber. As to swindler, I thought that was a fella who cheats another fella. Buck Wain never cheated no one."

"He's a good man, Bill, no question about that," said Stein.

"You couldn't tell it from the stories you wrote." He'd been coming round to this, once he could no longer turn his back on it, and now it was out.

Stein searched carefully for his next words.

"That means they're good stories," he said, speaking quieter now. "An editor has to be objective, even about his friends."

Essex picked up one of the papers he had not yet bundled. He looked at the headline and then back at the editor. "Well, like I said. Might be good for you. It ain't my place, but they's facts and they's facts."

"What are you driving at," asked Stein.

"Nothin. Not drivin' at nothin. I can plain out say it. They's some facts you didn't write about. Mebbe they's some facts you don't know about." Essex shrugged, signaling he had nothing more to say on the matter.

"Could be," said Stein, brushing the comment aside. "I don't claim to know everything."

He finished his sentence half backing away.

"Now, you get those boys out to holler."

Out on the street Stein walked past Fir up to the corner of Pine. The county car pulled next to the curb. Sheriff Pickett stepped out.

"Hey, Pickett, you seen my paper?" Stein held one up, headline face out.

"Been delivered yet?" asked Pickett, walking around the back of the Ford.

"No truck with dumb questions, huh?" laughed Stein. He handed him the paper. "I'm your delivery boy today."

Stein stood back to let him look at the headlines and deliberately avoided asking him about the story.

"Having breakfast at the soda shop?"

"Thought I might," answered the Sheriff.

"Besides, it's Saturday. It'll give you a chance to check on the soda tax."

"Could do," said Pickett, walking and reading the paper through the front door. "Last Saturday got missed on account of the holiday."

The Volstead Act did in the swinging doors. Ida Tarbull took the place over, put in a regular door, and started selling 'soda' to the townspeople. And paying the soda tax to the town. Ida brewed her own. The flatlanders who controlled the business down in Denver never bothered her, just as long as she kept calling it soda. And as long as there was no violence, the Sheriff thought it was in the best interest of the town to keep collecting the tax. A practical man, he declared he'd shut them all down, not just Ida's, as soon as Washington sent the town the lost revenue. Nobody was holding their breath.

Meanwhile, Ida's and the eight other soda establishments were considered important members of the community. None, though, served a breakfast like Ida's, not even the New Sheridan.

Pickett glanced up from the paper to notice that Harry Mueller, the barber, and Jim Duffy were already sitting at a table, well into a plate of eggs, sausage, and hash browns.

"You're a shit," Pickett said in a low voice to Stein. "I should'a known all this Thursday night. I could've been workin' on this yesterday."

"Spaulding," said Stein, uttering the Sheriff's first name with exaggerated patience, "you know I couldn't do that. Whatever you needed to know, you needed to know by official channels."

Edward Massey

"Hey, you two." Mueller was pointing to the two empty chairs at their table. "Sit yourself with us."

"What you got there?" asked Jim Duffy, his regular good cheer showing even in this simple question.

"Today's paper, first edition," said Stein, and he handed one to each of them.

Duffy reached in his pocket for a nickel.

"No, no, on me," said Stein.

Duffy placed the nickel on the paper doily in front of the editor of the *Telluride Journal.*

"Well, I'll be," he said as he scanned the headlines. "That ol' son-of-a-bitch."

Ida came over to their table, an unlit cigarette in one hand.

"Want a soda," she said directly to Pickett.

"Don't taunt me, Ida," he replied.

"C'mon, Sheriff, loosen up."

"I'll have coffee," said Stein. "I haven't had a decent cup yet today."

"Is that your new paper?" Ida picked up one of the copies lying on the table.

"Go ahead, take it," said Stein, "but for God's sake get me my coffee."

Larry Stein watched with satisfaction as Sheriff Spaulding Pickett, the barber Harry Mueller, Jim Duffy, the accountant for Alling Davis, the town's most successful entrepreneur, and Ida Tarbull, the owner of the best soda shop in Telluride, all read the first edition of his new paper.

Duffy finished first, put the paper down and sipped his coffee. Stein was still waiting for his cup.

"Guess I got my nickel's worth," Duffy said with an even bigger smile than usual.

"Ida! You gonna bring me that coffee?" Stein slapped the table, sending the nickel rolling to the floor.

"Hold your horses," she called back. "You should be glad to have a reader for this rag."

Ida counted herself one of the few new residents of Telluride, and she had arrived nine years ago. She knew as many stories about the people of the town as Larry Stein. She was a good listener. As to her own story, no one knew very much. It seemed they never asked and she never volunteered.

"That's some story, Larry," she said, bringing his coffee at last. She set down a pearly white mug and a small beaker of cream. "Do you think he did it?"

"Oh sure, he did it," said Pickett. Some of his conviction came from his lifetime as a sheriff; most of it came from his long friendship with Buck Wain. He might have been thinking back to the time in 1916 when we wrangled over the town's willingness to collect a fee from the girls down in the cribs at the same time they were telling those young ladies that what they were doing was illegal. I was the mayor then and, well, I just have to say, I would have none of it. It was either no fee or make them legal.

"But he's so ordinary. You know, kinda mild. You really think he could take them big New York banks like that?"

"Oh, he could take 'em," said Duffy. "Believe me. He'd know how."

"That sounds a little harsh," said Mueller. "C.C.'s my friend."

"Not harsh," Duffy protested. "Not harsh at all. Matter of fact, just the opposite. I admire the little fella."

From outside came the chorus of the newsboys.

"READ ALL ABOUT IT, TELLURIDE IN THE NEWS.
WHOLE COUNTRY LOOKING FOR OL' BUCK WAIN.
OL' BUCK MADE OFF WITH THE DOUGH.
READ ALL ABOUT IT."

"This'll boost circulation," said the accountant. "Couldn''a come at a better time. Be good revenue for you."

"Be better if we were a daily," said Stein.

"Like I said, he's so ordinary. Now that Annie o' his, she's all perfectly dressed and full 'a strong opinion. But if he did it . . . . well, she never scolded nobody that I know of." Ida shrugged and wiped her hands on her apron. "You got a good story there, Larry. Might even make for a good day here today."

She picked up Stein's already empty mug and walked behind her counter.

"He should come back here and try to get a new bank started." said Duffy.

"When?" asked Stein.

"When this is all over."

"He could by me," said Mueller. "I'm just a barber, but anything I got, he can have. Anyway, I don't know why we're talking about a new bank."

"Cause this one's done for," said Duffy.

"You'd know more about that than me, you, an accountant and all. And I guess that means I will lose some money. I'm a shareholder, but only a small one. Matters not, if this one don't re-open, I'd be a shareholder in any new bank with Buck," said Mueller.

"Hey, Ida, you gonna sell us anything but coffee?" called Pickett.

"I offered you soda," she called back from behind the counter.

"Damn, woman, you try me," said Pickett. "I just want breakfast."

"Okay, hold your horses," she said.

"He's made some mistakes with his banking decisions," said Duffy. "But this wasn't one of them."

"How do you know that?" asked Stein.

"My boss is on the board," he answered, a shrug and a smile.

"What about the city and county money?" asked Pickett, full of the questions a sheriff needed to ask. "Is that safe? I'd hate to go up against Buck if he made mistakes with city and county money."

"There's surety bonds," said Duffy. "I think that money's pretty safe, but those loans to the Denver Banks were damn risky. O' course, they all worked out. That's maybe what made him so bullheaded about bankrolling the Black Bear and some of them other loans to some other people. Buck was too hopeful about people."

"Reminds me of what Bill Essex said," said Stein.

"What's that?" asked Mueller. "I like ol' Bill."

"He was chiding me," said Stein. "Seems he thinks my story left out the good things about Buck, you know, like how he was the mayor for a while and how he owns the hospital. He'd probably want me to point out all those loans, too."

"Maybe it's just cover," said the Sheriff.

"Jeeesus, Pickett," said Stein. "I'm cynical, but not that cynical. Remember, this is our friend we're talking about."

"Are you allowed to say Jesus?" Pickett laughed at his own joke, but the traces of his smile quickly wore off. "Yes, he's been my friend, I admit. And for my friend, I hope he didn't do this thing. But your paper don't make it look too good on the facts. That's all I got to go on."

"My bet is that's only half the story," said Duffy. The cheerful little accountant looked at the Sheriff waiting for his usual barrage of questions.

"Looks like they got enough for me," said Pickett.

"No doubt," shrugged Duffy. "Given the side you're on. The bank examiners called all the Directors in to close the bank. The head teller, that David Twicken, said he didn't think it mattered much either way, seeing as how all the depositors got their money out. He said it right in front of the bank examiners. My boss said he used a curious phrase. The depositors had withdrawn their money."

"It was in the story, all right," said Stein. "Our dear Sheriff here just don't know what 'for the benefit of' means. That reminds me, Pickett, did you get your check? That's the one thing I did tell you Thursday night. To pick it up."

"What check?" asked Ida. She placed breakfast plates, steam rising even in the indoors heated by her wood stove, in front of Pickett and Stein.

"No, I guess I forgot all about it," said Pickett. "Think it's still there?"

"Is this none of my business?" asked Ida.

"No, not at all," answered Stein, taking a sip from the mug she'd brought back full. "I knew something was going on over at the bank on Thursday because David Twicken handed me a check for the exact balance of my account."

"And Jeremy Kearns got one," added Pickett, "only that didn't mean much at the time 'cause we knew he was leavin' town. Now that I think of it, Josh said he got one, too."

"You know, Josh probably knew a lot more than he was letting on," said Stein. "Buck warned us he was a lot deeper than we thought. He was the director who called the meeting to close down the bank."

"You're imagining things," said Duffy quietly. "I was over there on Thursday. Went there to make a deposit for my boss. Twicken pushed it back and gave me a check for him. Twicken even gave me one. He didn't seem to want that stuffed shirt, vice-president, Dixon, to know about it. Mr. Davis didn't know anything about it. That's for sure. He didn't know anything until the Director's meeting. Mr. Twicken said Mr. Wain told him to. It was unusual, but it was the right amount, so I never asked any questions."

"Do you think there's a check over there for me?" asked Ida, still standing.

"If you had an account, prob'ly," said Duffy. He sipped his coffee in thought. "What with those bank examiners forcing the directors to close the place down, I'm sure they're hoping nobody gets their money back. Your check might just be inside there, useless."

Ida's face sagged at the thought of her lost money. Duffy's pleasant oval face, sallow from too much of his life spent inside, suddenly brightened.

"You know, I'll bet you Twicken got them checks out a there. By God, I'll bet he just stuck 'em in his pocket. That Twicken's probably carrying your check around right now."

"What do you think C.C. was doing?" asked Ida. One thing about Ida, she may have thought me an ordinary little man, but she drew the line at calling me Buck.

"You're going to hear a lot of people talk about how he wanted to cover his tracks. Maybe he wanted to get back at them Denver banks," said Duffy. "Maybe some o' both, but he's been complainin' a lot lately about how nobody listens to him. He thinks a crash is coming. Maybe he just couldn't bear to see anyone in Telluride lose their money."

"You better be right about that public money over there," said Pickett. "I got my duty."

"It don't make for a long career to talk back to sheriffs," said Duffy, "but what we should do with that public money is build a statue to him."

"Fat chance," said Pickett.

"We don't know for sure if he did this. What's more, we haven't heard his side yet. I'll bet you ol' Buck saw trouble comin', what with so many folks leavin' town and pullin' out their savings. I'll bet you dollars to donuts his man Twicken's got a check for every poor miner, merchant, and wrangler in town. So, if you want to do your duty, Sheriff, you should build a statue to Buck Wain, right in front of your jail, or better still the county courthouse."

"That's a good idea," said Mueller.

"Quite a speech," said Pickett. "A statue to a man who robbed banks. That would put Telluride on the map for sure."

"Robbed banks to save his town," said Duffy. "He could've saved his bank by letting everybody lose their money. He didn't. Not many towns have a man like that."

30

That Sunday morning New York discovered fall was finally on the way. New Yorkers climbed out of bed to a cool, clear day of breezes that made memories of the sweltering end of summer just a week before. A stray newspaper drifted lazily down Fifth Avenue, past the lamppost at 64th Street. The doorman at 834 had already received a call down on the intercom that important visitors were expected for Mr. Whitworth and when he spied the offending sheet he raced out to the curb to grab it. He held it gingerly between thumb and forefinger to bring it inside to stuff in the bin, fearful it would smudge his glove. A quick look loosed an offended sound – two days old -- Friday, September 6, and certainly no reason to linger over the headlines:

STOCK PRICES BREAK ON DARK PROPHECY
Hoover Ends Summer Vacation Schedule
ROCKEFELLER BACKING NEW ART MUSEUM
STERN BROS • NEW FROCKS FROM PARIS

Financial news loses its capacity to threaten on a weekend and the breeze had banished the heat wave. Maybe it was the other headline he saw, 12 AMERICANS KILLED BY ARABS IN HEBRON, a story much discussed these days. Big stories he thought.

Maybe the breezes brought cool comfort through the open windows to the reading of today's paper, making most people pass over further study of the Middle East in favor of using Sunday's leisure on the weekly installment of *The Emperor of America*, illustrated by Gene Mack, and eagerly awaited on this day for being the last of twelve: "The Cardinal's Garden."

At the same time, the story that first broke on Friday, struck some readers as entertaining as any serial and still commanded front-page coverage:

U.S. ATTORNEY TAKES OVER HUNT
FOR FUGITIVE

The United States Government has taken the lead in the hunt for Charles C. Wain, the fugitive president of the Bank of Telluride who allegedly swindled New York banks out of $500,000.

U.S. Attorney Elliott S. Point said a Federal Grand jury would begin an investigation tomorrow. He was

confident it would bring one or more indictments for
using the mails to defraud.

Point has assigned the case to Deputy U.S.
Attorney Addison Mintz, head of the criminal
division. It is believed that a letter carrying a check
may have been sent through the mails in connection
with the fraudulent telegraphic orders.

Point also noted that certain of the banks were
members of the Federal Reserve System and this, too,
gave the government jurisdiction over the case.

Meanwhile, J. Russell Cox announced that Wain
had been sighted…

U.S. Attorney Elliott S. Point had many skills and one was
particularly honed. His every conscious effort served one purpose --
to stay alert to opportunity. His father worked hard enough and
steadily enough at the salvage business he started to put young Elliott
through college and law school. His father also bestowed upon him,
if not great wealth, at least a trim figure, one hundred fifty pounds
clung tightly to five feet ten inches. Opportunism and trim figure
endowed Point with a classic lean and hungry look, a look more than
matched by his attitude and zeal.

You have to be smart and work hard to make Law Review.
Making good on that opportunity got him the job at Davis Polk and
Wardwell. He liked the way they paid people, swim or drown. The
genteel yet powerful partners found his ambition too obvious. When
the Great War broke out they were all too happy to help him get his
wished for appointment in Washington, even extending some special
effort on their part owing to his slightly advanced age of thirty-one.

Lieutenant Point studied the way war worked in the nation's
capital. He concluded that a commission in the Army afforded no
tangible advantage save a certain social acceptability among a
Princeton crowd that wielded some influence at the time. That crowd
cared little for competence. Lieutenant Point just didn't know how
to use social grace as a way to achieve his personal goals. With the
same cheerful helpfulness he had received from the law firm, his
superiors were more than happy at war's end to approve his request
for a transfer.

They sent him right back to New York, to an appointment to the
U.S. Attorney's office in the Southern District of New York. Right

Edward Massey

away he grabbed a flashy start when his boss recognized that he was perfectly suited to the emotional rigors of a high-profile sedition case -- which nobody else wanted to touch. Victory led to being named Deputy U.S. Attorney, all within two years.

Now he had a perch. Peering down from it, Point continued to look for opportunity. Burning with ambition, what he saw on the career horizon was never more promising than to be a good second in command. A doomed role in his eyes and all he could do settled into a conviction that diligence – and his father's training – would be rewarded. Fate proved kind. In 1924 Al Smith mounted the marathon effort of losing the nomination of the Democratic Party in nine days and 103 ballots. To bring a Catholic that close to the Presidency, he took Point's superior to wage the battle.

You could never quite tell if he wanted you to know, for sure, that he was the youngest ever U.S. Attorney. He combed his thinning hair, unlike most other balding men, away from his crown. It exaggerated his pate. For sure, it did what he wanted: enhanced his career. That thinning hair and widow's peak provided newspaper writers and cartoonists the look that could be exaggerated to make him instantly recognizable.

Beneath the pointed hairline a long, thin nose dropped straight down to end with a slight hook over thin lips. On either side an eye swept back in a dark, sunken oval. The blue of his eyes was pale, almost colorless. Over the next five years his public image evolved under a top cartoonist's pen. The cartoonist's career and the U.S. Attorney's alike took flight with a hawk soaring above the landscape. Point wrote the cartoonist a note thanking him. He hung the best cartoon on the wall of his office with his diplomas and the photograph of himself with President Wilson.

On that Sunday the same cartoonist had the hawk flying once again, on page two of the *Sun*. The U.S. Attorney circled the canyons of Wall Street, ready to swoop down on -- me -- the hick swindler from the mountains.

Up on the seventh floor at 834 Fifth Avenue, the operator brought the clattering elevator to a jolting stop. He reached out his white gloved hands and pushed open a pair of handsomely carved mahogany doors.

The butler, his name was Charles, too, rushed out to meet U.S. Attorney Elliott S. Point and his retinue. He was horrified that they had been allowed to enter the foyer unattended. Blame it on this unexpected luncheon; he and cook had all they could do to get everything prepared on such short notice. They struck Charles as a group who had rolled from their bed directly to this apartment. He had no way to know they had already attended a hastily called Sunday morning conference.

With stately grace he ushered the five men into the living room, the library being too small for eight, and asked them please to sit while he informed Mr. Whitworth of their arrival.

Scarcely finished with his task, a loud buzzer sounded a second arrival of the elevator. Charles took two quick steps to the front of the double doors and then settled so that he might properly receive this newest guest. Pugh handed him his hat without a word and followed into the living room. Charles made it to his employer's study without interruption only to be told to come back after Mr. Grinnell had arrived.

Of course, the buzzer cawed again while Charles was crossing the black-and-white marble squares of the lobby, his hands fully laden with a massive silver tray holding coffee service and cups. The young banker saw he was occupied and politely proceeded about ten feet from the elevator doors to study the sculpted marble of a goddess whose shapely female body stood out from the wall separating library and living room. Charles tilted his head in the direction and Grinnell followed him to join the others, declining to sit while he awaited Whitworth's arrival.

"Told you Belder thought he had no case," Grinnell said under his breath, using Whitworth's extended hand to pull him just an inch closer. "Excuse us," he announced to the room, but looking directly at Point. "Mr. Whitworth and I need just a moment."

Without waiting for a response, Grinnell nudged the older man into the adjoining library. "We have a problem. They found the money, Winston, all five hundred thousand dollars!" He stopped, waited, and began again. "What's not with Hanover, is out in Colorado," he continued in a whisper, "in the hands of the depositors of the Bank of Telluride."

Edward Massey

Whitworth turned and walked into the living room. Grinnell had nothing to do but follow, muttering in agreement with Whitworth's comment, "We'll deal with this later."

Point extended a half-bent hand as Whitworth came through the door. Two busy, and important men meet with a well rehearsed ritual, a few quick words, a nod or two, down to business.

Whitworth settled in an Empire chair by the fireplace. Grinnell looked around, choosing a spot by the desk behind the sofa. Point continued to stand, gazing into the center of the room and across, out the windows, into Central Park. One hand hung limp by his side, the other disappeared into a coat pocket. His prow of a face was set hard, pointing into a storm that only he detected. His staff, perched at the edge of their Queen Anne chairs, watched him intently, awaiting any signal.

"There's a lot of work to do." Point's first words, delivered in his thin, reedy voice, cut across Whitworth's signal for his butler. Point was holding the newspaper that announced his involvement in the case, and now he scanned the faces in the room as he lifted it to chest height for emphasis. He held his head high as he spoke, one accustomed to addressing large audiences.

"Of course, the newspapers miss the point. They say, and I quote, 'The United States Government has taken the lead in the hunt for the fugitive bank president,' and so on. All of the attention is on the hunt. We are not a party to the hunt. Nor shall we be. He'll be found or he'll give himself up. That is not our concern. Our concern is what to do with him after he has been apprehended."

At that point, he paused. You know he did, well rehearsed. His gaze wandered out into the fragrant Sunday afternoon, to the far reaches of the park. Somewhere a blue balloon had escaped its owner and was drifting above the tree line, into a cloudless sky. The prosecutor dropped his eyes, confident of the jury's attention.

"Of course, this is a federal crime. That is why I have decided to take the lead.

"We have five people involved. Telegrams. Sent in code. Pre-arranged." He punched the air as he made each point. "What we have is an interstate conspiracy." Again, the seasoned prosecutor studied each face, even to the youngest lawyer, making sure they understood the gravity of his remarks. Pugh looked transfixed. At last he had found a rock.

"Everyone who participated is guilty."

"Who the hell participated," asked Grinnell, his voice belying his youth because he allowed it to show his frustration. He was not looking for an answer and continued. "And guilty of what? Belder says that if banks want to give someone half a million on nothing more than some telegraphed instructions, that's the business of the banks. We do look pretty stupid."

Point spun around to focus on the young banker. His acolytes were veterans of these opening statements. No one interrupted. It was not over.

"Belder has no vision. He couldn't convict even if he did. What is needed is leadership. We are taking the lead, and we have to focus on how to win this case. How to put this swindler behind bars!"

The faces of Point's team beamed. Charles sensed the moment and hurried into the living room proffering coffee. The buzzer cawed again and the elevator doors opened to Cox. Before Charles could free himself of the coffee service, Cox had wandered unattended into the living room. Pugh spotted him coming through the doorway.

"Cox! We have the government behind us — should we start with how Mr. Point can help us in hunting down this swindler?"

"Perhaps I did not make myself clear." Point scowled. "I have assigned my deputy one goal: maximum prosecution after he has been apprehended."

"You've given your deputy a tough job," said Grinnell.

"I've heard all the reservations," said Point. "It won't be difficult for a good prosecutor. Mintz is up to it."

Mintz smiled his appreciation. A year younger than his superior, he knew that he would remain stuck at Deputy U.S. Attorney for a very long while unless the U.S. Attorney had the sort of high-profile victory that catapults a man to the next level. He had an even better proposition than depending upon the whims of a presidential candidate he didn't know. Mintz's boss had lain the future of his career in his own hands.

"There are developments in the case," began Cox, anxious to assume the leadership he had convinced himself they were asking him to take.

Edward Massey

"You mean other than not arresting him in Olathe, Kansas?" asked Grinnell.

"Oh, you read the *Sun*, too," laughed Cox. "They certainly don't know much about investigating. The man who executed this swindle is no fool. He caught wind of our plans. From the newspapers, I suspect. It's to be expected that he would not walk into his own arrest."

"He's just a hick," said Pugh. "Of course, he's probably smart enough to get to Mexico."

"Mexico is easy to get to from Colorado," said Cox. "It might be hard to find him down there. Still, we are cooperating with the authorities. Burns operatives missed him in Kansas, but we got on his trail fast. We're only a few hours behind him."

"Does that mean you think you'll get this bastard today?" Pugh's tone was half hopeful, half cynical.

"Presently," replied Cox amiably. In a man so used to measuring his own importance, he recognized his intemperance of Friday had made him look foolish. He would not knowingly make the same error twice. "As I said, we are cooperating with all the authorities."

"I must say, I am confused," said Grinnell. "According to your report, Mrs. Wain was interviewed on Friday and she said her husband was headed for New York."

"Misdirection," replied Cox patiently. "Mr. C.C. Wain is in Mexico."

Point was impatient. He had made it clear, he did not care when the fugitive was found. He could indict, Convict, SECURE VICTORY, without the fugitive. This case was not about the man who did it, but about the man who prosecuted it.

"It matters little. The Grand Jury begins tomorrow. I'm perfectly confident we can use it to bring one or more indictments for using the mails to defraud. We'll subpoena everybody associated with this miscreant. His wife, his son, even his barber. I will make them all testify. The whole case is made by the fact that Wain could not have been in Telluride when the telegrams were sent."

"Nobody said he was," interrupted Grinnell. "The telegrams were sent from Denver."

"That's beside the point," replied the U.S. Attorney in his calmest, most reassuring way. He dropped into a seat, as though exhausted by their collective ignorance.

Charles recognized his opportunity and announced lunch.

The entire company moved to the dining room, a large windowless room brightly lit by two massive crystal chandeliers that cast playful rainbows against the gold-flecked wallpaper and a long fruitwood table. Whitworth apologized to Point for the interruption and asked him to proceed. Charles brought out chilled white asparagus.

"I was saying, you need to understand the power of the Grand Jury. I only need to explain to them the theory that binds the five people involved in the conspiracy. Three of those five people were women, all related to him somehow. A niece. A teller at the bank. When we find out about the third, she'll be related to him, too, you can be sure. They have a civic duty to tell all they know."

Charles circled the table, filling and refilling wine glasses, ignored as though invisible.

"All six banks are coming tomorrow to testify," confirmed Point. "Then we'll get the Grand Jury to issue subpoenas for the nieces and the teller. And don't forget the head teller. The barber. The son. The whole lot of them."

"You sound confident," said Grinnell, looking up from his plate.

"Why shouldn't I be, Mr. Grinnell?" He spoke softly, head tilted, his eyes narrowed as though bewildered by such a question. "He sent telegrams, but mail fraud is our vehicle. Recall that our man had the Hanover send a check for thirty thousand to the Continental Bank in Salt Lake. Presumably, they used the U.S. mails."

"I'm no lawyer," said Grinnell, "but the police doubt they can link Wain to the telegrams. Can just mailing a check from one bank to another hold up as mail fraud?"

Pugh almost spit out his wine in his haste to exercise his opportunity to step out once again as the logical one to take the lead.

"Oh, you don't need to worry about that," he said. "There's a letter somewhere, and we'll find it."

Charles had stepped between Mintz and Pugh with a platter of chicken breasts. Mintz leaned back to see around the butler.

"I'm glad to hear that, Mr. Pugh. We all know there is a risk with those telegrams. It is preferable if we can produce a letter suggesting the fellow's plans. I don't need to remind you that there are some who don't believe this was a crime at all."

"Which is precisely why I've appointed a prosecutor who knows how to prove a crime was committed," said Point, slapping a confident hand on Mintz's shoulder.

"Undoubtedly," exclaimed Pugh. By now, he had put down his glass and he stood to address the group. He leaned both hands on the table and bent his head for emphasis toward each and every one. "As it happens, Mr. Lamont has instructed me to assist the U.S. Attorney in precisely this area. To speak plainly, I believe the Chase has more information — in fact, the very information we need. I have an obligation, therefore, to insist you find it."

"Insist?" Whitworth had the look of a man who had been slapped. "That's intemperate, Simon, even for you."

"An obligation, then," offered Pugh, "that you make an earnest effort to provide the U.S. Attorney with the evidence he needs."

The room remained uncomfortably silent. Finding the money was one thing, but Pugh telling Whitworth what to do. That was quite another. Pugh decided to try again.

"Look, maybe the Chase could turn up something more tangible," he suggested, and he suddenly had the idea that sitting down would help him regain the proper posture, so he resumed his seat. "All I ask is that you put someone to the task of going through every piece of mail you have in every file concerning this Wain character."

"That could be done," said Whitworth, not ready to forgive Pugh, but unwilling to keep up the unpleasantness at his own table. "And what about the Hanover? They seemed to know him pretty well over there."

"Rest assured, I will make sure every bank involved goes through every file. We will turn up something."

Pugh had played his card. Whitworth knew he would appear petulant not to acknowledge it.

"Well, maybe I could assign someone to go through our correspondence," he said. "Tomorrow."

Seven months after MGM premiered its first 'all talking -- all singing -- all dancing film,' Frank Simms kept his promise to take his wife, Helen, to *The Broadway Melody*. When he emerged into the breezy and bright Sunday afternoon, it came as no surprise that his boss, Mr. Cox, had kept the press fully informed.

A newsboy stood under that big rolling sign on the New York Times building, the one with light bulbs that blink on and off progressively flashing the day's news. He held up the afternoon edition and hollered:

"Read all about it! Bank swindler sighted in Mexico. Read all about it!"

Simms figured the young man, maybe thirteen, had worked hard, maybe had a few fights, to win this rich corner. It was a pity it wasn't rich for him this afternoon. The more he yelled, the more the passers-by seemed to smile and even laugh at him.

As Simms stepped up to buy two copies out of sympathy, a great pudding of a man called out from under an ill-fitting bowler hat, "Hey, maybe he's in Hackensack!"

That was more than the hard-working boy could take. He rushed at the fat man and hit him weakly with the left fist that was not holding papers.

"Whoa, boy," gasped the fat man between bouts of laughter as he held the boy at arm's distance. With his free hand he pointed upward.

The boy relented and craned his neck to look directly above his head. Standing there the whole day, hawking his papers, his job was not to gaze aimlessly at the ever changing sign above him. Simms could see his shoulders sag as he saw the words crawling across those lights:

Wain . . . to be . . . arrested in . . . Canada . . .

31

Cavelli's search took him past five o'clock on Monday. He worked backward, all the way to the first correspondence the Chase had ever received from one Charles C. Wain, a clerk at the Bank of Telluride, twenty-seven years before. The inter-bank supervisor steadily made his way through the files. He said it occurred to him he was creating a sort of biography. Six years after I was clerk, I was president. Five years after I was president, the bank had two million dollars on deposit with the Chase. In fact, he became so in the thrall of biography, coalescing scraps into the traceable history of an actual person, rummaging through one file drawer after another, determined to cover or uncover everything, Cavelli nearly forgot that in the very first hour he had found two letters I had posted the previous May. The first was the letter of introduction I mentioned before, for my colleague in Olathe, Kansas. The second reflected my first plan to make a trip to New York, bringing a check to cash to pay off the bank's debts. I didn't specify a date for the expected trip, just "the next few months." Fact is I was still expecting to borrow the money from the Denver bank. I just couldn't be certain when they would approve the loan.

Cavelli concluded a day's labor had yielded poor fruit. He handed over what he had found. He reported the letters added nothing. All he had found was the president of a small bank, ambitious and hard-working, perhaps, but still like a thousand other correspondents, president of a small bank. The next day he repeated his disbelief that the letters were what he had been asked to find.

Whitworth took Cavelli at his word and described the letters as 'small pickings.' Pugh, as he was quick to tell anyone within earshot, had more insight into the process and he knew anything could be used against me. If Whitworth had letters, they were enough to send Pugh racing to the Chase offices Tuesday morning.

"We've got him. This is enough to get him for mail fraud." Triumphant, holding a letter in each hand, looking from one to the other, he pronounced. "Lucky I got you started on this, Winston. These letters are all that Point needs."

"That's a little optimistic, I must say," said Whitworth.

"Not at all, look at this. Here's a letter saying Wain will come to New York and he will need two hundred thousand dollars in large bills."

"How can that possibly constitute fraud?" asked Whitworth.

"There's no question Wain wrote these letters," said Pugh. "And it's clear as a bell that they have to do with the events of last week. He had this planned all along. We have to bring the Postmaster General in on this."

"The Postmaster General?" Whitworth looked bewildered. "In Washington?"

"Of course," answered Pugh, "but what does that matter? He can get up to New York right smart. There'll be another campaign. He needs the Harriman."

Postmaster General Ryan Benson arrived at Penn Station shortly after seven that evening. True to his word, Pugh arranged for him to be informed by the President's office that Mr. Lamont requested his presence in New York immediately. The U.S. Attorney had a car waiting for him.

Pugh arrived at Point's office before the Postmaster General's car, eager to greet Benson on behalf of the Chairman of the Harriman National Bank. It may not be a charitable thing to say, but I'll bet the little Pugh didn't even know what made him feel so downright uncomfortable when the large man with the honest face and forthright manner stuck out his hand. They were formally introduced and suddenly Pugh discovered he was being politely but unambiguously dismissed. *You understand . . . dull government work . . . so good of you . . . thank you . . . .*

In his captive audience of the man who was the president's campaign manager, Point recognized opportunity. He placed the letters in front of Benson with a flourish.

"Thank you," said the Postmaster General.

He damn near took no notice.

He already knew a young U.S. Attorney had investigated the letter that begged to introduce a professional colleague from Olathe, Kansas. Smyth at the Chase had assigned six clerks to search for any dealings with the named colleague or the Kansas bank. The bank in question had apparently opened an account at Chase in June with a five thousand dollar deposit. They could find no record of the predicted visit and since the deposit, no activity.

Tapping the second letter, the one with my plan to bring a bank check and cash it for two hundred thousand dollars in large bills, Benson looked at Point and said with simple disbelief.

"He wrote this last May and he didn't show up till last Saturday? I understand the foolish righteousness of these bankers. They want to believe this makes it fraud, but why do you?"

"Whether I believe it or not," replied Point, "is irrelevant. What I want to do is convince the Grand Jury . . . and, ideally, the public as well . . . that this letter is the foundation of Wain's mail fraud."

"And just how are you going to do that? Even I can see that he arrived in New York City three and a half months after this letter."

"To take the second step in his swindle," insisted the prosecutor.

"Where do you get that idea?" asked Benson. "He never even went to the Chase."

"Aye," said Point, swooping down. He saw prey. "But his checks did."

"I was told he took no money for himself in those transactions. That means, contrary to your reliance on this letter, he asked for no large bills." Benson leaned across the desk to speak directly into Point's face. "In fact, my friend, I understand that he did nothing but certify checks that were made out to other people."

"No wonder you didn't want the bankers in here," said Point. "Aren't you on the team?"

The man whose political instincts had guided the President into office pulled away from the U.S. Attorney, his distance a symbolic warning, one the ambitious prosecutor had no ability to understand.

"I aim to be on the winning team," he said. "That's how I got this job. And I do not see how this letter could possibly be part of the swindle."

"May I remind you," said Point, biting off each word, "it is my job to make that determination."

"If it blows up, it affects all of us, Mr. Point" said Benson. "You best remember, as I always do, you are an appointee. May I remind *you, you* are taking on something one prosecutor, an elected one, is backing off?"

"Belder's on the back nine," said Point. "That letter proves Wain was thinking about his scheme as far back as last May. It was premeditated."

"Of course it was premeditated," scoffed Benson. "How could making a withdrawal from a bank not be pre-meditated? But where was the mail fraud? That's what you're relying on. How are you going to get it?"

"No one disputes telegrams were sent," said Point. "That's wire fraud."

Benson's gaze had been drifting past Point to the wall beyond — the cartoonist's drawing, the photo with President Wilson, the President's letter of appointment, and on the side table an array of framed photographs of Point in the company of people of power.

"I would not want to bet my ambitions," he began quietly, a long pause after the last word, "on convincing a jury — much less the public — of a concept called wire fraud."

"Some of those checks he negotiated had to be mailed," insisted Point. "To someone."

"You're stretching," the skeptical voice warned. "He had all the money sent via banks; he couldn't know whether or not they were mailing them."

Point seemed about to respond but instead reached across his desk and picked up a small paperweight replica of the Flatiron Building. He had allowed himself to appear quarrelsome. That would not do.

"Of course, that remains to be seen," he resumed in a breezy sort of way, setting the paperweight gently back. "Fact is, it may not even matter. After all, we know for certain that the collateral the Central Hanover released was mailed. Back to the bank in Telluride."

"Right now all I see," Benson challenged, "is that every single one of those transfers was executed voluntarily by the bank and consummated completely. All legal."

"Ah, the devil's advocate," smiled Point. "I appreciate your warning. Just the same, I intend to show that this letter was meant to persuade the bank to have two hundred thousand in cash waiting for him. And I'll further show it was the first step in his fraud. With all due respect, it does not matter that he hit upon a scheme to make it look legal. My God, man, that's the very definition of a fraud. An illegal scheme that looks legal."

Benson shook his head.

"Counselor, no one needs to persuade the Chase National Bank to have two hundred thousand dollars in cash on hand. Again, what are you thinking? He didn't use the mails and he didn't take the money. That will certainly count for something."

"Not to my mind," said Point evenly.

Now it was Benson who was being dismissed, and it came to him as no disappointment. He had made the journey because the President's office had told him he should do so. But his instincts had been correct; it was a waste of time. What's more, the U.S. Attorney was a pompous ass. As the two men walked to the elevator Point asked Benson to remember him to the President. He suggested that Benson might also wish to make it clear to Mr. Hoover that, for this case, the Federal Reserve System and the U.S. Post Office would be in his good hands.

Next morning, Point had an announcement for his deputy.

"I've thought through our strategy."

Mintz was holding a cup of coffee. A few drops of morning rain still visible on his lapels, he started to say something but Point waved him off.

"Six banks were involved with the transfers. We'll file six charges of mail fraud. Everybody, the public and the press, will think we are filing a charge on behalf of each bank. The bankers will certainly think that."

"Do we have six charges?"

"We will," said Point. "There may be some misunderstanding, but a little misunderstanding never hurt."

"Each charge carries five years. Do you really aim to put him away for thirty years?" asked Mintz. "Or are you just trying to scare the sorry bastard into confessing?"

"Either way," said Point. "Those bankers really want him, and so do I. If we put the effort in, we'll find a letter mailed here, a package of collateral there, a cancelled note, whatever it takes. We'll find six examples of using the mail."

"Certainly is symmetrical," agreed Mintz amicably.

"Quite right," said Point. "There's one other thing." His brow was knit, his voice low.

"Yes?"

"I had to assure the Postmaster General that I would lead the prosecution."

Mintz looked stricken. "Was he dissatisfied with your staffing of this case?"

"Goodness no, not at all," exclaimed Point, offering a benevolent smile in way of comfort. "We didn't even discuss that. He simply wanted to be able to assure the President that I was personally protecting the Federal Reserve System and the U.S. Post Office from the damage this could do. Can't fault them for that, I suppose."

32

Up in the northeast corner of Wyoming, on the western edge of the Black Hills, seven or eight hundred people built houses spread out across miles of high plateau to live in and around the little town of Newcastle. If a person traveled north and west from Newcastle, he'd reach Devil's Tower, a monumental rock rising inexplicably from the plain. If he kept on going, sort of same direction, not too far, over pretty much nothing except high plain and rolling grass, he'd get to the Montana riverbank where, fifty-three years earlier, the blonde colonel led the members of his 7th Cavalry to meet their end. Or he could go in the other direction and travel almost due north on the old Canadian Highway and then a bit northeast and he wouldn't have to go too far to get to Deadwood, South Dakota, the town where James Butler Hickok held that final hand of two pairs — aces and eights. Not much more than three miles up he could see the hills rise that had already been staked out by some self-promoting artist in search of the perfect spot for his monumental sculpture.

These were the simple thoughts that filled my mind as I dressed and pulled on my shoes. The snow had stopped falling by the time I woke up on Saturday. The sky was clear blue; the early morning sun brighter than ever. It was a perfect day for sightseeing. The snow might pose a problem on some of the smaller roads, but I had chains. Of course, putting them on was a bother. Even so, it would be best to get a shovel from the Flying V before I set out.

I liked shoes that were almost boots; the kind that came up over a man's ankles. I shined them like shoes and they kept a good polish but I never had to worry because they protected me like boots. All I ever needed was the pair of galoshes I brought along.

A little hunger gnawed at my stomach. Comforting as it had been to sit in my cabin during the snowstorm, without chancing to go buy something to eat, the hamburger from yesterday afternoon had long since worn off.

I took a cautious peek in the ancient mirror on the closet door. I found no surprises. In a funny sort of way that surprised me. Everything was pretty much the same. Except for the galoshes, I looked like I was dressed for a day at the bank: brown tweed suit, white pinstriped shirt, bow tie. Pulling on my hat and coat I took one more look around the room, stepped out into the mountain air, and set off like a man with some place to go.

"Morning, Ada."

She looked up, a quick smile came and went, but continued in the eyes.

"Well, see you made it through the night. Want some breakfast?"

"Do I!" I replied. "You read my mind. Maybe you could tell me where to get some groceries?"

"You got plenty o' time. Dining room's back there." She pointed with a jerk of her thumb. "For groceries you'd be going down to Swenson's. Only thing's you might have a problem with the roads. We got plenty of food here. You won't need to go out."

"That's mighty nice of you, but I'm planning to go visit the Little Big Horn today. Is Swenson's on the way?"

"Don't matter none," said Ada. "If you can get out there, you won't have no trouble getting to Swenson's."

I ordered eggs, hash browns, toast, and elk sausage. The sausage had a mild taste of game underneath the sharp bite of black pepper. I finished and ordered a second helping. The coffee was cowboy coffee, a teaspoon of grounds and a gallon of water. Not as good as my own, but that didn't matter. It was a fine breakfast, and it left me feeling eager for my trip.

"Just in case," I said, taking my leave, "might I borrow a shovel?"

"That'd be fine," she said. I detected a note like friendship in her voice, and it pleased me greatly. "You know, you're taking a risk going up there in that car of yours."

"Not much," I said, "but thanks. It's a good car and it's got a good heater. Not that I need to worry about that. Even with all the snow, it's still early September. Won't be too cold today."

"Could be," she said. "Still'n'all, it'd be a lot easier travelin' if you just eased off a bit and went tomorrow."

"Can't do that," I said. "Got places to go tomorrow."

"Where's'zat?"

"Thought maybe I'd go up to Devil's Tower. It being a Sunday and all. Seemed like Monday'd be a better time for Deadwood."

"Sounds like you got it all planned out."

"A bit of a disease, but, yes, I have it planned out through Monday."

Edward Massey

Shortly after lunch on Tuesday, two men stepped out of a black car in front of the Sheriff's office in Newcastle, Wyoming.

"They're here." Deputy Black watched them coming up the walkway. Suits, overcoats, and hats, they must issue those outfits, he thought.

He had taken the call the day before. A yellow Studebaker cabriolet spotted at the Flying V. No, the caller would not give his name. Did they want to hear about it or not?

Black didn't know anything about any yellow Studebaker, or a missing banker, but he wasn't about to admit it — at least not to some nameless stranger. Sure, he wanted to know about it — of course he'd read about it.

The Sunday paper from Denver was still sitting on the marshal's desk, unread. They found the story on page nine.

"Helluva deal takin' your police bulletins from the newspaper," muttered Marshal Brattle.

"Think we can find the guy who made the call?"

"Nah," said Brattle, "not worth tryin'."

A call to the Flying V confirmed the information, and another, to the Denver sheriff's office, confirmed that the Studebaker and its owner were the object of considerable attention. Hold him, they'd said. Got nobody to hold, Brattle thought.

"He ain't goin' nowhere," he said.

The marshal and the deputy escorted two federal officers to the Flying V. They inspected the row of cars parked along the curb of the long driveway. All but two were black. Two had Colorado license plates. One was a yellow Studebaker cabriolet.

Brattle watched the federal agents check their guns, a round chambered, and return them to the holsters under their suit coats. His own revolver rested on his hip, where it had remained untouched for years.

Ada was behind the desk when they entered. Brattle introduced the agents. She eyed them, addressing herself only to the marshal. No, she hadn't seen the little man that day. She had told Brattle on the telephone that the fella wasn't staying in the main lodge. He had one of the cottages out near the campground. And, yup, she reminded him, it followed as how if his car was there he might be there, too.

The four lawmen walked up the hard-pack path edged by stones. The marshal sent his Deputy to the back of the cottage. The taller of the two agents took a position directly in front of the door, withdrawing his gun and holding it down to his side. He signaled the marshal to the right and the other agent, pistol now in hand, to take the left. Seeing the marshal standing empty-handed, he impatiently motioned for him to draw his gun.

With an eye check they were ready. The agent prepared to knock.

I opened the door.

I knew they were out there and I knew I wasn't going to make too imposing a figure up there with the endless sky and the monumental mountains, so it just didn't make any sense to let them make a fuss. I stood in the doorway, the same brown tweed pants, vest, and white shirt with bow tie that I had been wearing on my travels. My hair, such as it was, was combed straight back. I stroked my mustache to make sure it was straight and took off my spectacles and wiped them in a clean white handkerchief.

"Gentlemen," I said. These fine men had gone out of their way because of me and deserved a warm greeting. "It'll be dinner soon — would you care to step in and have a bite to eat with me?"

My fire burned pretty good in the hearth, you could tell it was there as much by the loud crackle it made as the pretty flickering flame you could see, and to be sure it filled the room with warmth and the scent of pine. I closed the door behind them and they stood awkwardly in a little semi-circle. The irony of it was not lost on me, and I'm afraid I smiled.

"Is this amusing to you?" snapped one of the federal agents.

"Oh, no, sir. I was just trying to be hospitable," I said, not willing to let him know that opening and closing doors for visitors was a practice I knew well. "So, let's have dinner."

"No time," said the same agent. "We've got to get you back."

"That's just it," I insisted. "It's a long trip back to Denver, after all, for everybody. You'll get hungry; hell, I'll get hungry, and that'll just take more time. It simply is not necessary."

I'm not really one who gets his way by insisting very much, but the five of us ate supper. Truth to tell, it was a small feast of sorts. I am a thrifty man. I couldn't stand to see any of the food I had purchased go to waste. You might say conversation remained sparse during the main meal. My guests were hungry enough, so eating took some attention, but the fact is they seemed a mite uncomfortable, perhaps it was just the question of chowing down with a man they had been sent out to arrest. A step, by the way, they had not yet taken.

When I served dessert — a couple of bear claws I'd intended for breakfast the next morning — the marshal took a long look at the lead federal man. He turned to me and broke what had been silence except for my efforts to draw them out.

"You seem downright relieved," he said.

It was a statement, of course, but everyone could hear the question.

"Really?"

The mild question was a technique I had developed over the years. It gave me cover, time to think.

"Maybe not relieved. More like not surprised. When you face up to the inevitable, there's no more struggle. You four showing up on my doorstep tonight was inevitable. Running and hiding is a kind of a struggle."

"Well, you haven't been struggling very long," said the second agent. "We haven't been looking for you a whole week."

"Not long," I said.

Now was not the time to smile. He deserved to be proud of his accomplishment. He assumed I was trying to escape. And he had, to be sure, caught me. Time was not part of his consideration.

"Just long enough."

I held the pot up high.

"More coffee?"

The marshal and his deputy accepted the offer and sipped coffee while the two agents searched the cottage. I cleared the table and piled the dishes in the sink along the wall.

"Don't you need to arrest him before you do that?" Called the marshal through the open door of the small bedroom.

"He knows he's caught," said the lead agent, emerging into the living room, and turning to me. "This it?"

He held the valise and four hundred dollars. The second agent trailed behind him carrying a change of clothes still on the hangar and a few toilet articles.

"Yup," I said.

Handcuffed, I rode back to town in the rear seat of the marshal's car. Black followed in the Studebaker. I wished I'd had a chance to say good-bye to Ada. All I could do was figure she'd understand. I rode in silence and soon I was caught up in watching the snow that still lingered on the pines fall away occasionally in little white puffs.

At the jail in Newcastle the marshal led me to a cell and the agents called their field office in Denver. Brattle checked the cell — water in the pitcher, blanket on the cot. When he returned to his office the agents were waiting.

"Congratulations," said the lead agent. He lit a cigarette.

"What for?"

He and inhaled deeply and gave a short, half laugh as he exhaled a column of smoke. "For the arrest, of course."

Brattle waited, and no further explanation came. "That's it? He's my prisoner?"

"You've just got to deliver him to the Sheriff in Cheyenne. For incarceration in the Laramie County jail."

The marshal edged around the agent, still standing at the corner of his desk, a hand on the telephone. He sat down and leaned back, his hands resting on his chest, fingertips touching.

"If this is half the case you say it is, that's some honor," Brattle said, looking up at the federal man. "Not fittin' for a small town marshal."

"Well, we've been told to pull back, leave the case to you," said the second agent, shorter, younger, colder. "Fittin' or not, it's your duty now."

"Makes no sense," said the marshal, not ready to be put off. "Why?"

"Not our business," said the first agent. "We just take orders."

"There's more to it than that," said Brattle. He reached for the phone, "If you don't know, maybe the Sheriff over in Cheyenne does."

"He doesn't, yet," said the agent, still holding his hand on the phone. "My boss said he only just found out. Something about the Denver banks not sending those messages in 'the code'."

"Code?" Repeated the marshal. "Is that like an Army thing?"

"That's how he got the money. Bankers have a secret code they keep locked up in a book. Seems only a thousand or so people in the whole country know about it."

"A thousand sounds like plenty to me. More than we got here in Newcastle." Brattle leaned back again. "What's that got to do with you taking him back to Denver?"

"Like I said, they use this code. 'Cept, turns out the Denver banks didn't use it. They don't use it to send any messages at all."

Brattle took another moment. "Well, I still don't see what that has to do with leavin' the man in my jail."

"Those New York banks want him shipped back East," shrugged the agent. "I guess they figure if the Denver banks aren't taking the loss, no crime was committed in Denver."

"Well, he didn't do it in Wyoming. That's for damn sure."

"Maybe not," agreed the agent, "but those New York folks aren't convinced the Colorado folks will, guess you might say, be *determined* in holding him until they get him back there."

"This don't sound like law. Sounds like politics."

"Maybe so," said the agent. "But we've been he's not going back to Denver. It's your case. He was arrested in Wyoming. He should be held in Wyoming."

"What am I supposed to do with him?"

The agent put on his hat and waved the second agent to join him. "Just take him over to Laramie."

33

Deputy Black called Wednesday at the jail bigger than the blizzard. Friday's snow, no matter how bad, should have succumbed to Wyoming's long Indian Summer. Mother Nature had more in mind and an unseasonable cold snap kept the snow on the ground. Snow, cold, even a little wind all did nothing to deter the steady stream of visitors determined to come see the marshal's new prisoner.

"Damn," said Black, "you're the most famous person ever occupied this jail, or the whole county for that matter."

"It's a bafflement to me, Deputy Black," I said, and it truly was. There wasn't any reason for those people in New York to be making such a ruckus and all I could figure was the more ruckus they made, the more people came out to try to get a gander at me.

Newspapermen, the County Attorney, and postal inspectors — two sets of them, one from Denver, the other from somewhere else they wouldn't say — all trekked to the town jail. Deputy Black found 'prisoner' an awkward word since by now he had told everybody in town about our supper Tuesday night at the Flying V cottage. He just started to use the word 'Visitor' and said it seemed more to fit the state of things. Who knows how the U.S. Attorney from New York found out about it, but he did, and he went out of his way to remind the marshal, by phone, twice, that the man in his jail was his prisoner, plain and simple, make no bones about it.

On the second morning, I was ready for breakfast when I spotted the marshal balancing a tray in one hand and struggling with a ring of keys in the other. The previous day it didn't matter much that he had brought breakfast in late. Dinner the night before had been pretty big and I was still satisfied. This morning was different. Besides, it was going to be a big day.

As long as I'm on the subject, the first night had not been bad. The bed was a standard issue iron frame bolted to the wall with wire springs and a two-inch mattress. It was not uncomfortable, but the mattress was thin and flat. At one point during the night it occurred to me that I might be able to get them better mattresses at a good price from a supplier I had come to know through the miners' hospital. The thought left as quickly as it came. It was simply one more thing I would never do.

Maybe things could get a whole lot worse than that first night flickered through my mind. I don't usually have thoughts like that and when I do they come as a surprise. Makes me wonder if I was ever grown up enough to take on what I took on.

Like I said, Marshal Brattle brought my breakfast late Wednesday morning. He scurried out of the cell with barely a word. I asked him if something was wrong since he had been so friendly and all before. He didn't even break stride going out the door of my cell calling a reassurance over his shoulder that nothing worse was wrong than him turning into a 'social secretary.'

After breakfast I asked to make a call to my niece in Cheyenne. About noon she called back. The marshal interrupted my interview with one of the postal inspectors to announce Margaret Smith was on the phone. The postal inspector wrote the name down and complained. His scheduled interview was cut short.

Marshal Brattle was curt with the barrage of interview requests. They were interrupting his only real job which was to persuade the sheriff in Cheyenne to agree to take me in his jail over there. He limited each to an hour and Deputy Black enforced the schedule.

The last interview of the day was with the County Attorney, a man blessedly uninterested in my escapades in New York City. That may explain why he stopped short of his allotted time. The marshal refused a second interview to the AP reporter because two in one day was just too much and because it would have meant scheduling my day past five o'clock. He told the reporter he was not allowed to inflict cruel and unusual punishment. He told him to come back tomorrow and he'd try to find some time after the postal inspector.

Now it was 'tomorrow' and Marshal Brattle, right on time today, tray in hand, pulled the outer door closed. With two short steps he stood in front of my cell.

"Figure it'd be o.k. to open this door and hand you your breakfast?"

"Normally, I'm not much of a desperado," I said, stepping back, "but you need to know, I'm a whole lot hungrier than I was yesterday."

"Starvation's not one of the usual punishments around here," chuckled the marshal. "Fact is, I would'a been on time yesterday but they called me about how to get you out a' here. It took more'n an hour on the telephone talking to that U.S. Attorney." Brattle looked down at the tray. "Besides, today there's treats. Ada came down from the Flying V. Brought you some rolls she made fresh this morning. You're get'n a whole lot better'n just my cooking."

Three large rolls lay alongside a pair of eggs, sunny side up, and a rasher of bacon.

"My sakes," I said. "I would have happily waited for breakfast again today. Bread dough rolls like these are a rare find."

"Ada'd like to hear that," said Brattle. "Nice words. A rare find."

"I am sorry to put you out with all that bother yesterday," I said, looking straight at the marshal as I accepted the tray. I sat down on the far edge of the cot. I held out a roll. "Can I invite you to share these with me? I'd be grateful if you'd sit a bit and tell me about the U.S. Attorney and all."

The marshal stood in the door of the cell, his body turned three-quarters so he could see into his office and the entry room of the jail.

"Best not to sit," said Brattle. "Besides, Ada brought me some of them rolls, too." He was silent for a moment, looking out toward the office. Then he looked at me, sitting on the cot, balancing the tray on my knees. "Seems like there's a question who's gonna take you back and when."

"Doesn't matter much, does it?" I said between bites.

"Mebbe," said Brattle, absently fingering the ring of keys, "but you're a whole lot more relaxed about it than the U.S. Attorney. He says you profited from this deal and he wants to make damn sure you're brought back there — 'back here,' he said, mebbe five times — to stand trial."

"I see," I said as I finished another piece of bacon.

"He said you not only profited, he also said you was aided in your schemes by several confederates."

"Schemes?" I repeated. I turned the word over in my mind. "Oh, my, I never thought of it that way."

"Well, what would you call it?" The question was blunt, but not threatening. Not unkind.

I shrugged and sopped up the last of my eggs.

"Don't know for sure when they're gonna take you back," Brattle continued, "but my guess'd be next week sometime. They're sending a U.S. Marshal. Figure he'll get here Sunday, then he'll take you over to Cheyenne, or maybe I will, on Monday."

We lapsed into silence. I drained my coffee cup, placed it on the tray, and placed the tray on the mattress.

"Maybe we best not be talkin' so much," said the marshal. He picked up the tray and stepped back into the hallway.

"Wait!" I called, springing up from the cot. I squared up my bow tie to make sure it was crisp at my neck. "I knew exactly what I was doing, and why. That ought to be clear to anybody who bothers to find out the truth." I waved my hand to acknowledge the cell that surrounded him. "I suppose I'll spend the balance of my life behind bars, but the way I see it, nobody but me has to suffer if this matter is handled properly."

The marshal had nothing to say.

"Truly," I said, my voice sounding a little lower and thinner to my ears. "I am sorry to have caused you all this bother."

"You're popular all right," said Brattle. He closed the cell door and turned the key. The metallic *click* made a slight echo in the closeness of the cell.

"I wouldn't say that," I said "More of a spectacle. I didn't mean to get all this attention."

"Well, it'll die down," said Brattle.

I stepped closer to the cell door. There was one thing I had not yet told him.

"I'm afraid I took the liberty of inviting someone over here. I hope you won't mind."

"Mind?" Brattle cocked his head and looked at me from the corner of his eyes. "Naw, it's the job. Only, I thought you didn't want to be no spectacle."

"Oh, it isn't that," I said. "I know that it's a bother to be my social secretary, but my wife came up to Cheyenne to be with her sister. So, I asked her to come over. I haven't seen her since…well, since this all came out."

"Family can visit."

"Thanks," I said "She might be here about suppertime."

Like all blizzards, the interviews subsided. The rest of the day was no more than a flurry. I got a little selfish and asked for some extra time to clean up for Annie. The marshal obliged and seemed happy telling everyone appointments would end at four o'clock. Turned out he had to disappoint that AP reporter a second time.

Word got out that Mrs. Wain was coming. The marshal came into my cell to tell me he had said nothing about it, but I confess to being friendly and chatty. It was just possible I might have mentioned something in passing to one of the reporters. Hell, there wasn't any good reason for my every word to go out on the wire service.

At five o'clock, Annie came through the doorway. I could see her from the moment the door opened. A comely woman, slim except she always complained about the last five or ten pounds, wearing a tailored light gray coat and a simple blue hat. The screen door slapped hard behind her. She stepped into the middle of the room. Deputy Black sat behind the marshal's desk on the right, a dozen men with notebooks and cameras milled around the small wood stove on the left. Brattle stood, alone, at the door to the cells.

Annie paused briefly to look around. In that moment, all could see her eyes, clear and determined and swollen. She took two forceful steps forward, stopping directly in front of the marshal.

"I am here to see my husband," she said. The words were steady and strong.

"Yes, ma'am" said Brattle. He made a motion to step around behind her. "May I take your coat?"

"Yes," she said, turning to let him reach for her shoulders. She stood quietly with her head held at a slight tilt, a single strand of pearls resting against a dark blue dress. She made no effort to make contact with the dozen pairs of eyes that followed her every move, but neither did she try to ignore them. Brattle had told them plainly, no photos, and no questions until after the lady's had a chance to talk to her husband. The reporters had grumbled, and Black had doubted he could keep them under control. Now, as they jockeyed for position, they still came across as a mob, but no one went against the marshal's words.

"Sorry," said the marshal as he returned from hanging her coat on a hook. "We got no hangers here."

"No bother," she said. "That coat'll be good for some rough wear."

"Yes'm," he said. "Right this way."

He unlocked the door, swung it open, and escorted her to the cell.

I stood at my door, left open by Brattle with the words, "This ought'a make it a little easier on her."

I had squared my tie and sharpened the creases of my pants between my thumb and forefinger. My hair was combed straight back. My eyes glistened under the circular lenses of my spectacles.

Annie came noiselessly forward, followed by the shuffle of reporters' feet crowding up to the outer wall of bars. She hesitated. She had hoped our meeting would be private. Well, so be it. She stopped just outside the cell, gently twisting her gray leather gloves in her hands.

I looked at her, hands at my side, body still.

"They said we could have supper together," I whispered.

Her chin quivered slightly. She crossed through the cell door. I met her with hands outstretched. She grasped them, and continued into my arms. Her body started to shake. I raised my arms to embrace her. Her eyes glistened and were moist and her chin nestled into my neck.

"Oh, Charles!" she murmured. "My poor dear husband."

She could feel my back shudder against her hands. I squeezed her hard. The composure that had carried me through what the reporting fraternity called the "perfect financial crime" melted. I could think of nothing more than she deserved better than my tears. I dared not speak.

Annie must have heard the voice from somewhere behind us say, "Look, he's crying." She rotated us slightly to put my back in the way of the view. She continued to hold me tight. Gradually, I separated myself and held her at arm's length.

"I know this is terrible for you," I said, pulling myself together, "but if I had done anything else, it would have been worse."

She pulled me back close to her and said in my ear, "I know. I know that's what you think, dear."

We stood like that for a long while until I pushed back once more. This time I took a crisp white handkerchief from my hip pocket and dabbed my eyes, then blew my nose. I folded it carefully and put it back in my pocket.

"Where's Connie?" I asked.

"He's in Denver," she said, holding both of my hands. "He thought he could do you more good there."

I thought about that comment. Complicated, something like that coming from a son in these circumstances, don't you think? I said, "Yes...very probably."

"Goodness, this is the first time I've seen you since you put me on the train," she said, attempting a brighter tone. "You're spiffed up and attractive as ever."

"You're sweet," I said. Now I kissed her. "I love you."

She squeezed my hands hard in reply. "You know," she began as though scolding a naughty boy, "you sent me off a week ago Tuesday without so much as a word. I had to find out from a private investigator. Over the telephone."

"Yes, I know," I said, my head bent. "I'm so terribly sorry I had to tell you a lie. I would rather have told you nothing, like all the rest."

The hour passed with our food barely touched. I didn't even know until later that Ada had made our entire dinner and sent it up to the marshal. The moment to part came.

I held her hands in mine. What do you do? What do you say? I smiled. I said it would be all right.

I felt sure of that, honestly. What I also felt sure of was that she should not take this on. I asked for no approval.

She left the cell to the crush of reporters pressed around her, shouting questions. The marshal tried to fend them off and lead her to the door.

Annie pulled up at the door of the jail and turned to face them. A slight quiver crossed her chin. But no tears.

"What would you have me say?" she challenged them, looking at everyone and at no one. "Say that I am proud of my husband."

"Bare Facts"
Detroit Free Press
September 21, 1929

New York pampers itself on its ability to knock off the weedbenders and appleknockers.

When a cloverkicker gets trimmed in Manhattan the birds sing an octave higher and industrials declare a dividend.

• • •

But once in a black and blue moon the tablecloth is turned and New York gets the soup stains.

This just happened recently when a champion hog caller from the sticks plastered a neat poultice on New York's smartest banks.

He knocked off the metropolitan cache for half a million of Andy Mellon's golden biscuits.

Thereupon, the New Yorkers ricocheted a yell off the rafters that is still splintering all the altitude and endurance records of financial weal and woe.

• • •

The sunburned tourist who accomplished this deed was just a little banker from the anonymous town of Telluride, Colo., out where the west begins.

Just to show how easy it is to manicure a leopard's tootsies, the Colorado boy figured out a scheme to knock New York loose from its wealthy complexion.

• • •

He did it with a couple of laughing telegrams and got the half million. Did New York take the rap by giving its clerks a vacation during laugh week?

It did not. It immediately chinned itself on the bar of justice and howled long, loud, and off key.

It demanded law, order and its concomitants. The Colorado boy was collared and cuffed by the laundry of the law.

• • •

This doesn't look like justice to us.

It looks like jealousy.

If New York had muscled Telluride, there would have been no burning of legal incense. It would have been just an item in the daily weather reports.

But when Telluride puts the obligatory stampede on Manhattan, then that's a horse from a different garage.

• • •

We have plenty of illegal admiration for the banker of Telluride, Colo. We hope he reforms. And gets a million the next time.

34

The clear early morning sky sent the chill of all eternity into the room with the soft cold light from the moon and stars. It would have been the chill creeping through the heavy quilt that woke Warren Hellman a few minutes before four. Warren lay in the old trundle bed his grandfather built, and I lay in my metal cot, six hundred miles away, but you will see why I know this.

Conscious of his stillness, motionless, slowly focusing on the familiar objects in the room, he wondered if he could go back to sleep. One bother was the pressure he felt in his bladder. As he tried to let himself float back into sleep, his plans for the day crept in as thoughts. He knew thinking and sleeping don't mix. He set the big thought aside, feeling neither urgency nor dread, and went back to what he considered non-thinking -- thinking about whether he could sleep some more. Today was just like any other day. Feeling some little pride in his decision to set thinking aside was still thinking and he was not asleep. He could feel that pressure in his bladder. At a quarter past four he crawled out of the quilts and padded across the cold wooden floor down the hall to the bathroom.

Warren had left his wife back at the house in town. Come out to the ranch alone, he needed make no effort to close both sets of doors that made the clever design, his own, of the indoor outdoor privy work so well.

He made his way to the cedar closet, crafted by his own hand from trees on his own property. No need for light, he dressed in the dark. His suit and tie gave him no problems, carefully hung the night before; and only a moment's fumbling burdened his efforts to find his black socks.

Out into the kitchen and into his normal morning routine. The fire in the wood stove came first. Only then did he find the lantern to light the wick. A mile from Delta, and from his bank, the ranch still lay beyond the reach of rural electrification.

Coffee pot on, lantern lit, Warren probably noticed his early rise put him ahead of schedule. He had a schedule, every detail planned out, for sure. He considered making bacon and eggs but thought better of it. Warren went to the big desk in the L side of the kitchen. The two bedrooms merited the privacy of walls, but the kitchen, living room, and office all shared the one large open room. This desk, a formality he affected in the rough and sparse ranch house, defined the country office of the president of the Bank of Delta.

Like so many people, since this ranch and country office was something he wanted for himself, something that put his special stamp on life, he was convinced the same would be good for me. I can't really say that I never wanted a ranch; it's more that I just never made the effort. Besides, we had Annie's farm and that was something she really wanted. What I can say for certain is that I never needed a country office for the president of the Bank of Telluride.

Warren had plenty of time, extra time, to take care of everything and be ready by nine o'clock, when the bank would open its doors in Delta.

He reached in the center drawer and found only second sheets, no letterhead. He paused a moment to consider whether he had letterhead anywhere else on the property. He drew out three sheets and three envelopes.

From the right-hand drawer he took the Waterman fountain pen his son had given him, engraved *Warren Hellman, 1926*, for his fiftieth birthday. He had always loved pens. He ran his fingers over the Sheraton pattern of the gold-filled overlay he had so proudly showed me on the day of his birthday party. He rolled out the cap and set it on the black and glossy barrel. He noticed some slight wear and two small nicks in the cap, but the Waterman imprint and the 0552 mark were crisp. He marveled at the signs of so much usage; he would have told anyone this pen got little use. To test the nib he wrote "Warren H. Hellman, President, First National Bank of Delta, Colorado," at the top of the first blank page. It gave him back a medium flex and wrote well. He continued on the same page,

To my dear wife, Barbara

Two weeks had passed since he had learned they were hunting me for something I had done in New York. He learned it the same day he learned they had shut down my bank, and the next day he read about it in the papers. We were friends the way competitors can be friends. He knew he could count on me to be his friend even if he had made that stupid loan to Josh; so, at first, he was wary because there was so much they said I had done, he could not really understand what I had done. He may have made some inquiries – and he may have just figured it out – but with time he knew I had laid my hand on the funds I needed to pay back my depositors.

Warren was a good banker and it would not have been too hard for him to figure it out. In the two weeks he had watched them make a furious pursuit of me in New York, trying to find me in Kansas, Mexico, Canada, everywhere but where I was. Out in Colorado what made the news was the desperate attempt to take back the money, or at least take back the collateral on the loans that were paid off, or take back something, anything.

As each headline told its fragment of the story, his amazement grew. By the time he left Friday night for his ranch office, he knew, perhaps only because it was clear to all, that the depositors had truly received their money from the Bank of Telluride. The funds I had sent out west stayed out west.

That was the day the Colorado State Bank Examiners arrived at his bank in Delta.

35

Capitalized at fifty thousand dollars, the Bank of Delta had attracted deposits from the local ranchers and farmers, and even a few miners, although mining was not all that important to Warren's little farming community. My friend had always wished for the rich deposits of miners and for a bank twice the size. It had amused him that the local depositors created by his lush, green town had been my envy, an opinion I expressed to him during frequent visits.

With hard work and time and success he grew the capital and the deposits until they allowed Warren to put out more than a million dollars in loans. Almost a third of that, with the help of banks in Denver, went out the end of the summer in that single loan to Josh Gibson. He knew I had not approved, and not just because Josh was a director of my bank, no matter what story Josh told him.

We had not spoken since then, but the truth is, I had been too busy with my own plans and I was just willing to trust that he knew me too well to believe I was carrying a grudge.

The bank examiners now called these loans "impaired." Delta's lush green camouflaged the hard times that were growing along the same riverbanks that brought the water. The depositors and the borrowers were the same people. The borrowers were not earning enough to pay back what they borrowed, much less make additional deposits.

Hellman was a good local banker and he knew that his borrowers — friends, practically every one of them — could pay off their loans in the long run. They were good loans. But that was not how it worked. That term, "impaired," allowed the bank examiners to treat them like bad loans without coming right out and saying it. Mr. Ferguson Grant, State Banking Commissioner, personally closed the Bank of Delta the night before. He was not about to have any more embarrassing incidents.

Hellman heard the percolating pot. He went back over his note before he signed it. What could you say to your wife? You couldn't very well explain about banking. Hell, that didn't much matter, anyway. He breathed in deeply. The coffee smelled good. He had stopped feeling the chill of the morning. You couldn't bear to watch what she was going to have to go through, but you couldn't say that, either. About all you could say is you loved her and because you loved her it was best this way. She would be better off.

He wasn't quite satisfied with the note, but he wasn't quite satisfied with the situation, either, and there wasn't much he could do about it. He signed the note and got up to get the coffeepot. Careful to protect the deep polish in the mahogany surface, he put the pot on an adobe tile. Sipping half a cup of coffee, he started the second note.

Only sips of coffee interrupted the steady production of the remaining two notes. By the time he was finished he could see the sun peeking over the hills in the east. The last cup of coffee in the pot poured out cold. He arranged the three notes in a line across the desk and took the pot back to the stove. It was still early.

He toyed with the idea of making another pot of coffee, decided against it, and the thought itself prompted him to go to the bathroom once more. He considered altering his plan, but it was as impossible to think about going ahead right now, rather than wait till nine o'clock, as it was to think about canceling the plan altogether. He had almost an hour extra. All he could think about was how he might explain things better in the second note.

It wasn't fair that they had shut down his bank; and part of what was unfair was that he wasn't even sure how it had happened. He had a bank that was the envy of bankers. One of the richest men in this part of the state, certainly one of the largest landowners, had even become a borrower. He must have wondered if maybe I had been right, that there was this drying up of business. But most folks said things were getting better, and the big loan should have helped make it better.

He was honest enough with himself to admit that before the loan it was getting serious. About half his borrowers were having problems with their payments. But Josh's loan let him get those problems down to about a third and that was a whole lot better. Of course, when a third of your income isn't actually coming in, you still can't meet the expenses and the interest the bank was obliged to pay out. Josh had made his first payment just fine, and if more folks did the same the bank would be all right.

How could they respond by shutting down his bank? It was like sending the bank to debtors' prison. Now those depositors were going to lose all their money and they would be doubly bad off because somebody would sell their loans and then they'd get pursued to pay them off anyway. So all his friends would be destroyed and he would be blamed because he was the one who made the loans to people who couldn't pay up now and there wasn't a damn thing he could do about it.

He looked out the window at his ranch and read and reread the second note but he couldn't figure how to improve his logic or his lot, and he left it unchanged.

My friend, Warren Hellman, reached for his deer rifle from the rack above the door. He took it back to the desk. He was always a punctual man. He looked at his watch. In two more minutes it would be nine.

36

The Colorado papers reported that the time was written down on each of the notes written by Warren H. Hellman, president of the Bank of Delta. The content of the first note was not divulged, it being private to his wife. The content of the second note was not divulged at the command of the Banking Commissioner. It was known there had been a third note, but the papers said it seemed to have disappeared.

That note, the third note, was addressed to me. Hellman's brother, the State Senator, was the one who found him, the same day. He also found a way to get that note to me without letting it fall into the hands of the U.S. Attorney.

Dear Buck,   September 21, 1929

Well it looks like we're both in a fix. Wish I had the brains to figure a way to take care of everybody the way you did. You did it first and I suppose they'd be on the lookout now, but give the devil his due, I just couldn't have thought it up.

If I upset you by making that loan to Josh Gibson, you need to know that was about the best I could come up with as my plan to save my bank. And you might say I thought you were being too fussy. It looked like good business. Turns out I was wrong.

I guess I been wrong about a lot of things. I'll never be able to make them right. It was a whole life I spent with this bank and this town and now it's gone.

I couldn't have done what you did and I can't face what you're facing.
Good luck, Buck.

Warren

37

Lights in Newcastle had started to flicker on throughout the town by the time the U.S. Marshal arrived. Three reporters had nothing better to do of a Saturday evening than slouch in straight-back chairs against the wall of Marshal Brattle's jail. Dinner dishes still in front of him, the Marshal rested his long legs on the desk. He made no effort to watch the cell behind, or the lone occupant of his jail, the object of all this bother.

I sat composing a letter on a board balanced across my knees.

The Federal man, Thompson, handed Brattle the transfer papers and asked if the warrant had arrived, shipped out by airplane on the eleventh.

"Don't got no airport," replied Brattle. "But the papers got here."

"Call the judge, then. I got to get going."

"Impatience comes with the badge, don't it," Brattle said as he dialed the call.

When he opened the cell door, he spoke to me in a low, private voice.

"Mr. Wain, we got to go to the judge now for the hearing. The U.S. Marshal's here to take you to Cheyenne."

I lifted the board, placed it on the cot, and stood up.

"You know, I don't really need a hearing."

Besides it didn't do to go before the judge looking the way I did. Tugging the bottom of my vest, I stepped to the front of the cell. I pulled at the top button of the shirt where there was no bow tie. Didn't help.

"Right enough, Mr. Wain. But you have to tell that to the judge. If he says so, you'll head out for Cheyenne straight away."

"It's not a hearing," interrupted the U.S. Marshal. "It's an arraignment."

"Okay, then," said Brattle, unfazed, "an arraignment. Like I said, if the judge sez it's ok, you'll go to Cheyenne. Prob'ly have a hearing there. After that, they'll take you to New York."

I lifted my suit coat off a hook and followed Brattle to the front office. The reporters scribbled what they saw and heard of our preparations to leave. One wished me 'good luck.'

"Mr. Wain," said Brattle, fidgeting with a pair of handcuffs, "I got this here order to put you in shackles when we move you to Cheyenne. I know I don't need to put you in no shackles, and I ain't gonna do it." He caught the U.S. Marshall glaring at him and fidgeted a little more. "Still, it's regulation to put these handcuffs on, and I don't see how I can take you outside without doing it. I'm sorry."

"Don't bother yourself, Marshal," I said, holding out my arms.

The judge met us in the foyer of his home, a rambling white Victorian on the edge of town. He wore a plaid shirt and faded blue jeans and leather moccasins with bright Indian bead work.

"Do you, uh…Mr. Wain…understand what an arraignment is?" he asked in a raspy voice.

With my first glance around the foyer, I noticed a small woman sitting in the next room by the fire. My god, this was unnecessary.

"I sure am sorry to interrupt your Saturday evening with your wife. Yes, sir, I know what I did and I guess I'm ready for the consequences."

"Well, now, that's not exactly an answer to my question." The judge scratched his head as if to emphasize that he was thinking out what to say next. "Let me explain. I have this here order to send you up to Cheyenne. They call that 'remanding.' So, I hereby remand you to the county jail in Cheyenne. I imagine you know they're going to hold a hearing to see if there's enough evidence to send you back to New York to stand trial."

The judge turned his back to us and held the warrant against the frosted pane of the parlor door as he signed it.

"He's my prisoner now," said the U.S. marshal, accepting the paper from the judge and leading the way out the door. He turned to address me for the first time. "Like I said, we'll leave straight away. Train's due in half an hour."

"Well, we better get your things together," said Brattle.

The U.S. marshal held up his hand. "I ain't no town marshal. I do my job. The order says in irons. He'll be in irons with me."

He put new handcuffs on me, let the chain fall with a clatter to the floor of the judge's porch, and attached the leg irons. Once finished, he motioned Brattle to remove the old pair of cuffs.

38

The U.S. Marshal walked behind me, touching my back, as we boarded the evening train from Newcastle to Cheyenne. He guided us into the middle of the car and sat me on the inside, next to the window. Always careful with his fugitive, he chose that arrangement because sitting on the aisle, especially at either end of the car, there was the chance I could jump up and run away from him in my shackles. I suppose he figured he had done his job and that was fine with me. There was nothing to do, but sit there and get to know him. Attempts at conversation brought only admonitions to be quiet and look at the scenery. The train pulled out and the darkness crept across the vast plains, slowly shutting out the light and the beckoning openness. My thoughts turned to the great mountains that had been my home. Neither mountains nor open spaces would be my home again.

I turned away from the window and at first the brightness of the compartment forced my eyes closed. After several minutes of silence I again attempted a little conversation. After all, friendly talk would help us both ease away the hours to Cheyenne.

"You had your eyes closed, go to sleep."

"Are you married?" I answered.

"Yes. Go to sleep, I said."

"She live in Cheyenne?"

"Bayonne."

"Really? Must be difficult for her, you traveling and all."

"Not always easy," he admitted.

And so it continued, slowly, almost imperceptibly, as small jagged pieces of the marshal's life fell into place, one after another, by my steady interest, questioning, and his willingness. After all, like I said, what else did we have to do? Besides, he was entrusted with a job; he deserved for me to believe here was a good man to get to know. Yes, Bayonne, New Jersey. A German wife. Two daughters, seven and four. Sure he had a mortgage, didn't everybody? By the time the train arrived in Cheyenne he had gone on to tell that he was the first in his family to end up on this side of the law.

"Brighter than Bayonne," said Thompson, outside the station, squinting at the sun now firmly planted in the sky. The U.S. Marshal

Edward Massey

maneuvered me into the back of the waiting Chevrolet and the sheriff's deputy drove the four blocks to the Sheriff's office next to the city and county building.

The sheriff walked through the door at eleven. Like his new prisoner, he was round, bespectacled, and mustached. There the comparison ended. He was round because with his rugged frame, the sheriff had played left tackle for the University of Wyoming, interrupted by service in the Great War. Where his career might have gone if it hadn't been for the war he had never stopped wondering.

The marshal presented his warrant and explained the case that had brought him so far from home.

The sheriff looked at the papers, and then pushed his big black Montana hat back on his head.

"Well, Marshal, I sure do want to thank you for coming all the way from back East to carry this here notorious fugitive from Newcastle to Cheyenne. You know, I hope all that bother was worth it."

"No bother," said Thompson, refusing to take the bait. He'd been through this before.

"Uh-huh," grunted the sheriff. He stared down at the papers that he still held in his hand. "This here's a warrant," he continued, sounding all business now, "not really enough for me to keep that man in my jail until much more than tomorrow. Tell you what; I'll put him up tonight. But somebody best show up with better papers than this pretty early in the mornin'."

39

U.S. Attorney Ashley B. Tate had his doubts. He knew no crime had been committed in Denver. Out west with a stalled career he may have been, but he still had friends in the big city. They told him the New York D.A. had quietly dropped the grand larceny investigation about the time U.S. Attorney Point stepped in. When the indictment arrived and he read it, he figured he would be able to understand all of this, maybe, but right now it didn't make sense to him. He allowed as how there was a chance it wouldn't make much sense even if the U.S. Attorney got a grand jury to issue an indictment — grand juries indicted almost everybody. Doubts or no, the good U.S. Attorney Tate had the problem of persuading the Laramie County Sheriff to hold the prisoner until the indictment arrived by plane. In the end dedication to shoulder the thankless tasks is what it took to advance a career stalled in Cheyenne, Wyoming. Dedication dissolved his doubts.

Best he could tell, Tate told the sheriff, what it came down to was those bankers in New York were mad as hornets. Not much more to it. But what the hell, he wasn't the judge. It didn't matter if he doubted those New Yorkers had enough to hold the little man, let alone drag him back to New York. What mattered was whether or not he did his job, shouldered his task. And his job was to persuade the Sheriff to hold the prisoner.

The Laramie County Sheriff didn't truckle much to U.S. Attorneys and he held out that he had a task to shoulder as well. Maybe this fellow thought he was free and clear. Maybe that was why he had refused the help of the lawyer his son down in Denver arranged for him. Maybe that was why he seemed almost cheery, sitting quietly down at the old wooden desk the Sheriff had set up for the interview, almost like a kid in a schoolhouse.

I pretended I hadn't heard all of this when the sheriff led Tate down the hallway to see me. There was no way I could pretend not to hear that he wanted the U.S. Attorney to know he was making no promises.

"You seem in good spirits this morning, Mr. Wain," Tate began cautiously. "Any particular reason?"

Like I said, I had heard what the two were talking about, only it wasn't hard to pretend otherwise because I hadn't been paying any attention. My thoughts had been on last night and without meaning to I let an unconscious smile spread into a big grin.

"Forgive me," attempting to assume the demeanor expected, "I am aware of the gravity of the situation. I wouldn't want you to think otherwise. It's just that…"

"Just what?" asked Tate. He leaned forward on his elbows, his hands clasped under his chin.

"Well, it's just that those other fellows back there gave me a fine reception last night, and their friendliness to a stranger just made me happy. You see, they held a sort of kangaroo court and charged me with coming in uninvited. Fined me a pack of cigarettes. I felt pretty cheap telling them I don't smoke. Sure would like to pay that fine, though."

Tate was a tall and lean man, given to a severe look. Even sitting he seemed to loom over me and the look that came over his face was more than severe, it was downright shock.

"Do you…" he faltered, and began again. "Mr Wain, is this all some sort of game to you?"

"No, sir," I said, and since what I was about to say was true, I made sure I stared right back at him, unblinking. "No game. It's serious business."

"Well, that's better," Tate said. "Now, pay attention, please. It's my job to make sure you know you have certain rights. I have to explain this hearing to you. You know there will be a hearing to order your removal to New York? You know you can oppose that?"

"Yes, sir," I nodded. "I'm not meaning to say that I know anything about what you need to tell me, but if it's all the same to you, I'd like to get back there as quickly as possible so that prosecutor can get the trial started."

Tate removed his glasses with a sweep of his hand. He set them on the desk. If I had to guess, I'd guess he was puzzled, but he wasn't too sure he wanted to know the answer to his next question.

"Now, I am not trying to give you any ideas here, and I am afraid that my mere question will give you the thought of a legal strategy, but Mr. Wain, well, do you mind telling me just why you are so eager to go back to New York?"

"Simple, really." I wanted to leave it at that, but he nodded his head in a sort of go on motion.

I set my palms down flat on the table. It wasn't that I was fixing to get up or anything, but I didn't want my hands distracting from any of the words I had to say.

"The U.S. Attorney has subpoenaed a lot of good people who had nothing to do with what I did. Now I know what he's doing. It's dishonest, but it don't surprise me. What's got me going is that, from what I hear, he's told them they all have to stay in New York until the trial's over. Well, those folks got their own lives to live, and that's hard enough. I never wanted to put anybody out by all of this."

"I see," said Tate, reaching for his glasses. "Well, be that as it may, my colleague in New York seems to be all fired sure you're going to resist us sending you back there. Now, I've got to cooperate with him, but I have a somewhat delicate job here. I also have to make sure you know those Denver banks didn't lose any money. You might have a case for fighting extradition. I don't want you to get one of those Eastern lawyers to come back and get you off scot-free because of me."

Tate stopped. He wanted me to make sure he had been understood.

"Say again," I said.

"What I mean is, I don't want to make a procedural mistake."

"No, about the Denver banks."

"Oh. Well, it's like I said. They're not out any money, so there's no case against you in Denver. It was just banker's paper for them. We know they never sent those telegrams."

"Really?" This was something I hadn't expected; but I didn't want to let on much more than polite interest.

"It's those New York banks that are on the spot," Tate continued. "That's why they want you back there. But you might have a right not to go back until the government can prove enough on the indictment charges to convince a judge to send you back. I'm not sure what the charge will be, but it might not be grand larceny."

Tate was searching for some way to tell me more. All the years listening to people ask for something that deep down embarrassed them – to borrow money they didn't have or to be granted release from a promise they'd made, usually in return for a new promise –

and I just knew how to sense when a person was doing something he didn't think it was right for him to do. I don't doubt the U.S. Attorney recognized his impulse for what it was — sympathy – and that made him all the more disgusted with himself.

"Like I said, I better go back." My voice was low, maybe a little tired sounding, but I didn't want a lot of discussion.

Tate frowned. He paused a long while, lost in his own thoughts. Finally, he spoke and from what he said, I guess he didn't want any discussion, either.

"Well, it doesn't make sense to me. I'll tell you what. You better get a lawyer over here. Like I said, I don't want procedural problems."

Our interview was over. I rose slowly out of the chair. I put my hand out to U.S. Attorney Tate.

"Thanks, Mr. Tate. You did your job. I better go back. There's no need to hurt those New York banks. Nobody has to lose in this deal."

40

That clerk of the court had to race down the long hallway of the U.S. Courthouse at Foley Square reminded how alone he was by the powerful echo of each strike of his heel against the marble floor. Self-conscious as all get out already, he stopped short at those imposing double doors and lifted himself onto his toes to peek through the small rectangular window. The young clerk saw the familiar rows of dark polished wood facing the tiered seats of the jurors, the prominent witness chair, the massive – and empty - bench for the judge. All spoke of a hallowed space, forbidden to entry, protecting the secrecy of the grand jury. Some hick two or three thousand miles away had brought down on his head the need to step through those doors with nothing more than a thin piece of paper as his shield.

"Telegram for the U.S. Attorney," he shouted, holding the flimsy paper high above his head.

This day marked the opening of the second week of grand jury deliberations and Deputy U.S. Attorney Mintz stood in front of his first witness from out west, my head teller, David Twicken.

U.S. Attorney Point rose from the government table and walked briskly down the aisle. Taking the telegram from the clerk, he had barely read it when he announced a five-minute recess "to confer with Mr. Mintz."

"We've got to ask for the indictment today," said Point the moment they closed the door in the lawyer's anteroom.

Mintz looked at his watch. "It's not quite one and we haven't had lunch recess yet. I just started with the head teller. I'll need two or three more hours."

"Doesn't matter. You can do that tomorrow."

"Tomorrow? But that won't work!" exclaimed Mintz. "I mean, the man only arrived yesterday, Elliott. I interviewed him this morning as early as I could get him in here. He's awfully vague. I tell you, we'll lose him if we give him time. I need the grand jury now."

Point shook his head. He held up the telegram.

"We can't afford the delay. Look, Wain's waived his right to examination before the United States Commissioner and has requested to go straight to his hearing before the federal judge in

Cheyenne. That can mean only one thing. The little bastard is looking to drag out the extradition hearing. No doubt some damn lawyer's told him the first rule of defense: dawdle, delay, disrupt. The longer it takes to get him back to New York the more this case will have cooled down. You know perfectly well the public can't stay focused on anything for long. The first big thing to come along — murder at the Cotton Club, a political scandal, anything — it'll push this right off the headlines and into the funny pages."

"As always, you are right that the better part of defense is outlasting the plaintiff, but this could just as likely speed things up," suggested Mintz. "After all, the guy can't be that sophisticated. Come to think of it, if he is, you have to consider that he could have gone through the Commissioner's examination and *then* asked for a hearing."

About that time he had to notice the color rising in Point's face. My bet is that he carefully shifted his tone. After all, he knew what had worked for him before with this boss, the earnest query of a junior man.

"Are you sure it's worth it?" asked Mintz. "Going for an indictment without the testimony of Twicken and his co-conspirators? His statements are vague, I admit, but at least he told us the bank operated at a loss since last February. That helps your case against Robin Hood."

"We can't afford the time to prove conspiracy," insisted Point.

He held up a hand to block further discussion.

"The indictment will work, you'll see. The Grand Jury will grant it because we ask for it. It will convince the judge that a trial is warranted because the grand jury says so. We don't need to wait for any more witnesses from out west. Of course we won't stop hauling them in to testify, that's just good and useful pressure, but we can get our indictment on what the bankers and the investigators told us last week. That'll stop any delaying tactics in their tracks. That little cockroach won't trifle with me!"

41

Twicken stood for a long while in the little green park across from City Hall. His hands shoved deep in his pockets, he stared at the statue of Justice atop the cupola of the magnificent granite and marble building. His early release from grand jury testimony had prompted an urge to meander, to explore the impressive government buildings of lower Manhattan. The Bank of Telluride could not compare with such grandeur.

Grandeur gave way to more practical thoughts. Satisfying his hunger brought out the tourist map to retrace his way back to his little hotel in Greenwich Village.

His greeting to the desk clerk upon arrival was an urgent request for a restaurant serving a thick New York sirloin with plenty of fried potatoes. He wanted a soda, too, but he had no idea how to ask for it.

"Maybe here," answered the clerk and handed him a message.

Twicken glanced first at the signature, *Josh Gibson.* He read with continued surprise Josh's invitation to join him for dinner at the Waldorf-Astoria. Twicken most likely he looked to the ceiling and called the young man behind the desk a 'providential messenger' — and startled him some, too, I'll bet.

My head teller was not an unworldly man, but he marveled that the subway whisked him uptown in less time than he figured it would have taken to walk from the Bank of Telluride to the New Sheridan Hotel.

When he emerged from the underground station and began to make his way to the hotel entrance on Fifth Avenue between 33rd and 34th Streets, the hawker screamed his news directly at its source: "Bank losing money! Indictment handed down!"

Twicken stared at the headlines. He told me he didn't know if he was feeling wonder or disgust. He was staring into the face of a reality he couldn't understand, one that didn't exist out west. His secret testimony had made it to the street before him.

There's no disloyalty in the truth, I told him when he described the numbness that came over him hearing, seeing his words. It left him standing at the door, staring vacantly at a plaque.

Edward Massey

> The Waldorf Hotel, built by
> William Waldorf Astor on the site
> of a farm acquired in 1827 by
> William Backhouse Astor, was named
> after the German Village from
> which John Jacob Astor, the
> founder of the Astor fortune,
> came. The Astoria Hotel was built
> by Caroline Schermerhorn, William
> Waldorf Astor's cousin, who joined
> the hotels.

The doorman waited patiently while the slender man in a seersucker suit and straw boater read the bronze plaque. At first the young man seemed lost and then, with a skill gained only by years of practice, the doorman sensed Twicken actually was reading it and he had finished. He pulled open the large brass door, and said,

"They're tearing it down, you know."

Twicken turned to the doorman, a beefy fellow stuffed into a green velvet suit trimmed in gold braid, beads of sweat standing on his brow.

"I wouldn't know," Twicken said. "I'm just a visitor."

"You don't say. Well, welcome to the Waldorf-Astoria. Yes, sir. Tearing it right down. Making room for a big, new skyscraper. Gonna try to build the tallest building in the world."

"That's too bad," said Twicken. "Looks big enough to me as it is."

"Oh, it's not too bad," reassured the doorman. "They're moving it uptown, over to Park Avenue. Even bigger. They'll do it right."

"No doubt," agreed Twicken.

He handed the doorman the newspaper and straightened a bit and followed the outstretched hand through the revolving door.

Standing at the entrance of the dining room Twicken could see the high sloping crown of a Montana hat showing above an open copy of the newspaper he had just given away. He figured the maitre d' had noticed it as well. The man only shook his head as Twicken mumbled never mind, he recognized his host.

"Ah, Mr. Twicken," said Josh, dropping the newspaper slightly, but not getting up. "Sit yourself down."

"Please, Mr. Gibson, call me David," said Twicken.

He could only nod weakly to Josh's suggestion that he should call a Bank of Telluride Director by his first name. He quickly covered over his discomfort by pointing to the maitre d' and saying,

"Excuse me, sir, but I don't think he likes you to wear that hat in here."

"I know," replied Josh. He punched the center of the newspaper with one hand. "My god, son, you're all over the paper here."

Josh started to read Twicken's testimony out loud:

'Did you assist in the transfer of money to the Bank of Telluride?'

'No.'

'Did you sign the checks that I have here, marked for entry as evidence?'

'Yes.'

'Why?'

'That is my function as head teller.'

'Did you have knowledge of the source of the funds?'

'The president of the bank told me it was a loan.'

'Did you then use those funds to pay out monies to the depositors?'

'Yes.'

'As instructed by Mr. Wain?'

'Yes.'

'Why?'

'Why? It is, after all, my function as head teller.'

"Please, no more," said Twicken, looking uncomfortable. "Why do you figure secret testimony is in the newspaper?"

"Dunno," replied Josh. "I just know they got the whole transcript right here. Got the indictment here, too."

"Apparently that's why they let me off early; they wanted to go for the indictment."

"Want to know what it says?" asked Josh.

Twicken eyed the waiter who hovered over them.

"Not really. Maybe we should order first."

"Sure," said Josh, lowering the newspaper just enough to look at the man in the tuxedo. "I'll have a steak. Rare."

"I was wanting a steak, but I've heard a lot about a Waldorf salad," said Twicken, addressing the waiter. "What is it?"

"Just apples," came the grunt from behind the newspaper.

"Oh, but it is very famous," gushed the waiter, "created by our own maître d'hôtel, Oscar Tschirky, that man standing right there."

Twicken's eyes followed the waiter's finger to the man who had frowned at Josh's hat.

"It was his own inspiration," continued the waiter. "Tart apples with celery and mayonnaise, and just a touch of lemon juice. If you like, we can add chopped walnuts. We prepare it right here at your table and serve it on a bed of lettuce."

Josh peeked over the corner of his newspaper and said,

"Go ahead and get some real food. I'm paying."

"No, really," insisted Twicken, "I'd like to try it. Something different from steaks at the New Sheridan."

"Listen to this bullshit," said Josh. For a moment, Twicken thought Josh was commenting on his order. "They indicted Buck on six counts of mail fraud. Each one good for five years. Look at this! One of them was for mailing back the collateral on a loan. Poor old Buck paid 'em off and didn't even touch that damn letter and it's gonna cost him five years."

"Jeez, that's thirty years," said Twicken.

"Damn straight," replied Josh through the newspaper. "Stinks. Here, let me read you this crap. 'The indictment set forth that on or about May 1, Wain and other persons to the grand jurors unknown devised a scheme to defraud.' Ain't that a mouthful! It goes on to name all the banks. Then it says, 'A part of the alleged scheme was to send or cause the sending to six of these banks telegrams to transfer sums aggregating $500,000.' And then here's where they got you in there. 'A further part of the scheme was to procure checks signed in blank by David Twicken, Head Teller of the Bank of Telluride.' Hmm...I'll skip some. 'The checks were deposited to apply to the indebtedness of the bank of Telluride and a further part of the scheme was to deposit the checks on behalf of the Bank of Telluride.'

"Why are they making something of that?" asked Twicken. "I told them it was my job to handle the bank checks."

"I don't know. There's a whole long section here I'll skip. It tells how they figure Buck worked his scheme. But then, I got to read you this: 'each of the six counts referred to a letter in furtherance of the scheme or a check sent.' Now, ain't that something. They say right out the whole damn scheme is based on telegrams and then they don't even mention them in the six counts they actually charge him with."

Two waiters arrived at the table. One carried a charger bearing a gold rimmed plate, itself bearing a large steak and a single, very large bloom of broccoli. The other carried a bowl containing the ingredients for the salad.

Josh cut into his steak before the waiter started tossing the chopped apples to coat them in mayonnaise. Twicken watched the production a moment and then asked,

"Why did they subpoena you?"

"Well," answered Josh between bites, "you know they're trying to make out that Buck had lots of other people involved. They want to figure I was one of them. He had $30,000 transferred to me."

"I knew that. I received that advice. All of that was reflected in the check I gave you."

"Go ahead, dig into them apples," said Josh, gesturing at the mound of salad that had been placed in front of Twicken. "He paid me every cent I had in the bank, the whole thirty thousand. Me being a director of the bank and the Norwood Cattle Co., they're trying to make it look all fishy. They want to keep this thing up about accomplices. Just listen to this, 'Authorities here are inclined to think that the scheme was too perfectly timed and carried out to have been accomplished by Wain without the cooperation of some person or persons who had some idea of what was to be attempted.' It just don't matter how much Buck insists he did it alone."

David Twicken had never before had a meal with Josh Gibson. It came as something of a surprise to him that the Director could talk and read and eat all at the same time. His steak was gone. His knife and fork were in the center of the dinner plate, next to the untouched broccoli flower.

Twicken took another forkful of salad.

"So, you're in on it, too, huh?" he asked.

"Me, you, hell, even his niece."

"Couldn't a been. I saw both nieces in Denver. They were just down there for a good time with Mr. Wain's car. They even got Amy to take the train and meet them."

Edward Massey

"Maybe so," said Josh, waving an arm at the waiter across the room. "Don't matter to them. They are trying to get their conspiracy going. They're calling that one from Lamar a 'mystery woman.'"

"That pretty little Susan? How's that?" asked Twicken.

"Just a minute, I'll read it to you," said Josh, holding up his hand.

He had the waiter in front of him and was asking if there was anything he could get for dessert that he couldn't get better in Telluride. The waiter harrumphed and went into a long explanation that included painting a picture with his hands. Josh accepted the waiter's suggestion and went back to his newspaper. It took him a few seconds to find the article. He took another minute to spread it across the table.

"Hell, I don't need to read it to you, it's just that they got these two postal inspectors who identified Miss Susan Martin as the 'mystery woman.'"

"Sounds like Charlie Chan and Sherlock Holmes," said Twicken. "Why are they calling Susan a mystery woman?"

"They're huntin' for a woman who sent the telegrams."

"Absurd," said Twicken. "There's no mystery. I spoke to Mrs. Wain. She told me the first she heard about this was when some private investigator called her the very day we had the bank examiners in. He had Susan's description before he even called her."

"Now, that's somethin'," exclaimed Josh.

Twicken wondered if Josh meant his information or the team of waiters who had arrived with a cart they wheeled. The one who sold Josh the dessert seemed to be conducting a quartet of complex movements that succeeded in commanding the attention of both of them. Soon flames leaped into the air above a saucepan of simmering bananas. The waiter ladled the brandy-glazed fruit over a large plate of vanilla ice cream and set it in front of the man with the hat. Josh's words and his spoon competed as he started a new thought and the dessert all at once.

"I can see what they're doing, but it ain't so clear to me they figure they're gonna be better off with a conspiracy."

After the second mechanical spoonful, he stopped and filled a teaspoon with the sauce and lifted it carefully to his mouth. Twicken marveled at the concentration he showed before the normal Josh exploded again to give the dish his undivided attention. No word was said until he abruptly stopped, this time after noticing the ice cream was more than half gone. He looked over at the sauce pan and saw more bananas and sauce.

"Will you hurry up with them damn apples, I want you to have some of this fancy stuff."

Twicken took a last forkful of salad before the waiter whisked away the plate and replaced it with another almost as large. Bananas and ice cream swam in the warm brandy that renewed the dying flames.

Josh bent back from his dessert and shook his head.

"Seems all out of kilter. They're tryin' to make it look like a conspiracy and a mystery. Tryin' to send him up forever. Don't make sense. Lucky that $30,000 he sent me ain't one of them six counts. Hell, that money ain't worth five years of his life."

Twicken finished his first bite and dipped his spoon again into the melting ice cream. Josh either took David's interest in the dessert to mean he had no response or he was just happy David liked his choice, because either way, he had more to say. As he talked out his thoughts, he waved his spoon in a circle and his voice got lower and deeper.

"He probably thinks I'm upset with him, what with him not making that loan on the ranch and all. I admit, it was a damn disappointment. But Buck operates according to some other kind of law. I know him. He's trying to do what he promised. All he's trying to do is take care of his depositors. Now he figures that's more binding than whatever law is on the books in favor of those big banks."

He looked into the deep and empty dessert dish. He put his spoon right in the middle of it and looked directly at Twicken.

"How d'ya figure they got the booze for that dessert?" asked Josh. "There's a law against it. Funny. There's no law against welching on your promise."

42

It was a day to be outside, walking, in the fine September sunshine, not confined in the grand jury anteroom. Two windows high up on the pale green wall were the only opening to the outside and they did precious little to bring that beautiful day inside. The little group, by now known as 'The Westerners' to the U.S. Attorney's people and the daily press, sat under the two long shafts of reflection in the dim that served only to remind them that they were there to await their turn.

My niece, Susan, was called first, shortly after nine. She looked a little flushed when she returned. During the hour lunch break Annie dipped her handkerchief in a water glass and held it firmly to the back of Susan's neck. They grilled Susan for two more hours. The clerk brought her back to the anteroom just after three. Then he took Heinrich Mueller. Mueller was my barber. To tell it in Heinrich's terms, a witness they had him made because to Denver he had trekked a haircut me to give. Some people have been saying I was a bit of a dandy, but that didn't persuade the U.S. Attorney's people. They insisted there must have been some reason for that trip other than a haircut. In truth, there had been, and they never found out -- a 1901 penny I kept in my desk at home and had meant to carry on this journey — a penny from the year I married my Penelope.

Connie offered his cousin a cigarette. That didn't go down too well with Annie and she wasn't one to leave her disapproval unspoken. Her reproach mattered little – or maybe not. Susan declined.

After he lit up, Connie broke the silence with a simple, how was it?

Susan started out by saying everyone was cordial, showing good manners all around. She walked over to the door and looked through the window, turned back to face the Westerners and dropped her voice to a whisper. Strange. The court recorder was typing everything down. Susan said that when she went in there what she had in mind was to set the record straight. She wanted it to be accurate and honest. But when she tried to answer some questions, she was told yes or no was all she was allowed. But there was no yes or no, she tried to protest. Then Mr. Point would go off and tell the grand jury what he thought and Susan wanted to interrupt but was told to answer only the questions she was asked. To top it off, what really confused her, he didn't even talk to her about the things he had quizzed her on in his office the day before.

Mueller abruptly returned, surprising The Westerners who were all prepared for a long vigil. Less than an hour had passed.

"Did Connie's lawyer get you out?" asked Amy, jumping to her feet when the barber came into the anteroom. She had not yet testified and her fear exaggerated her youth. She wore the green dress that Josh had admired what seemed so very long ago. The fearful little girl folded and unfolded her arms across the dark green stripe of the aggressive young woman.

"He's not my lawyer," corrected Connie. "That lawyer I tried to arrange for Dad out in Cheyenne suggested him. All I know about this fellow is he was a candidate for District Attorney." Connie stubbed out another cigarette in the grimy metal ashtray on the table in the center of the room.

"A colorful fellow, that Ivy Dan Hanson is," said Mueller with a hearty laugh, producing a cigar in camaraderie with Connie. "Yet, he helps none. He's not even allowed to go in there. Did he help you, Miss Susan?"

"Well, they said I was permitted to go out in the hall and talk to him. So, I did, once," she said. "Mostly his advice was, 'Tell the truth.'"

She continued to sit next to her aunt. Annie's hand stretched into Susan's lap to hold both of hers.

"That's about all he can do," said Connie. "He can't speak to you. He's not even allowed to speak to the jury. And there's no judge in there."

"So why are you out?" asked Amy. Her voice almost formed an accusation, wavering with the fear that she would be the next one called. "Didn't they have questions?"

Billowing smoke picked up the green tint from the walls. "That Mintz asked two or three questions," answered Mueller. "Then, hoop!, all of a sudden, the big man looks at his watch and jumps up and says it's getting late. If any more they have to hear from me, he tells the jury they will hear it tomorrow."

"Did he interview you before you went in there?" asked Susan. Mueller shook his head. "Funny," she continued, "like I said, I was surprised none of what he asked me about yesterday came up today."

Connie's face carried a look of alarm. "Be careful, Susan."

"Why?"

"You're sworn to secrecy. The court can find you in contempt for discussing this with us."

"But...." The others watched her lapse into thought and soon saw the comprehension. "Oh, I see. My testimony is secret. Yes, Mr. Hanson told us that. But Mr. Point is using it like in reverse. What we tell the jurors, he's not supposed to repeat to the press. But what we tell him beforehand . . . . That's why he interviews everybody first, so he can decide which things not to ask in there, if it won't help get Uncle Charles. And he can smear Uncle Charles with anything we say. That's it, isn't it? Well, then, what I told him is that Uncle Charles gave me six sealed envelopes, all right. And, Amy, I told him we made an adventure of it. He didn't like that. He kept saying Uncle Charles told us to send them from Western Unions all over town. He knew that wasn't true because I told him in the interview Uncle Charles wasn't even in Denver and all he told me was to make sure they got sent between three and four. "

"Did you read today's paper?" asked Connie. "Point told the press that Dad gave you six sealed telegrams and that you sent them from all different locations. Makes it look sinister, doesn't it."

"Did I do something wrong for Uncle Charles?"

"Not at all, kid," Connie reassured his cousin, two years his junior. "You got to wonder, why's he still calling people before the grand jury now that he's got his indictment. He doesn't need to convince them anymore."

"Mrs. Wain?" the door flew open and the words of the clerk filled the anteroom.

"Yes," said Annie, standing up to address the voice that came from out in the hall.

"Would you step outside, please? Mr. Point wishes to speak to you."

"Oh, it's all right," she said, cool and firm. "Tell him he can come in."

She brushed out the wrinkles in her long blue skirt and stood quietly facing the door. One by one her four companions stood up. All five faced the empty doorway. They heard a slight commotion outside.

Point stepped just through the door and planted his feet, shoulder width, knees slightly bent, as if prepared for the Westerners to rush him.

"I trust you have not been discussing your testimony."

It might have been a casual greeting, delivered just so.

"Naturlich nicht," Mueller responded in the mother language he had not spoken for more than twenty years.

"Good," said Point, his eyes and his attention only on Annie. "Would you please come with me, Mrs. Wain?"

"Oh, that won't be necessary," she said. She smiled at him, not warmly, a smile that dismissed the question.

"I just have a few questions I need to ask you," he said, making an effort to sound friendly.

"Yes, I should expect so," she said, not smiling.

"It is my responsibility to screen what goes before the grand jury," he said, breaking his stare at Annie to glance from face to face. Annie watched him spread his arms. She recognized his summation in the grand gesture. She did not reply. He waited a little longer. The first contest was lost. If anyone was to break the silence, he had to speak. "In that regard, I will need to know what you knew."

"I knew nothing," she said.

"Oh, come now, Mrs. Wain. We have information."

"What information?" she asked. Annie had a manner about her; she could always be very courteous even when curt.

"You and your husband were very close…"

"Are!"

"…are very close. Exactly. He must have told you everything."

She opened her mouth. Closed it. A moment of animation dissolved into slow languid movements. She took a handkerchief out of her small pink handbag and touched it once to her right eye. The slight breath she drew through her nose could be heard in the room.

"He told me he was going to New York."

"Please, Mrs. Wain. That is why I want this interview in private. You know the grand jury is sealed. Your testimony will be secret. Nobody needs to know."

"Mr. Point!" Connie exclaimed.

Annie quietly put her hand on his sleeve.

"I have no testimony to give," she said. "My husband told me nothing. Nothing of his plans."

"If you persist in this, this attitude, Mrs. Wain," said Point, looking at all of them at once, "I will be unable to offer you immunity."

"That's neither here nor there," she said.

"Then you will waive immunity?"

"I will waive nothing," she answered. This time when Point moved to speak, she raised her hand, "But I refuse to be interviewed."

"Then you are refusing to cooperate," he insisted. "There are a number of important questions. Do you refuse to answer them?"

"Not at all. You'll simply have to call me before the jury," she said. "I will not answer them here."

"I will not call you if you do not answer my questions here and now. You will not have your chance to testify before the grand jury."

"I know you're not required to inform the grand jury of evidence that favors my husband. You're allowed to present anything you want to. Tips. Rumors. You can even say things that you say you alone have been told. And we all know Charles has already said what he did. He's better off if I don't say anything about him before the grand jury. At least then I can say good things about him in public."

Point tried a different approach. "Oh, Mrs. Wain, you exaggerate. I have only an indictment. I still need the evidence for a jury to convict."

"In the public's mind, he is already convicted." She glared at Point "You know that as well as I do. That's what an indictment does."

"If you think he has been unjustly indicted," said Point through a wolfish smile, "then you should welcome the chance to address the grand jury. But if you don't cooperate, I'll not give you that chance."

"Mmm," she said, appearing to give his offer — or threat — serious thought. She took the time to sit down. She looked up at him.

"Tell me, what prompts a prosecutor to bring excessive charges against a good man?"

"The purpose of the grand jury is to protect those accused of crimes." He dropped his smile, adopting again his posture of addressing the room as a whole. "You should take comfort from its presence. If you truly love your husband, you will not refuse to cooperate."

"I repeat, I will be happy to testify before the grand jury," she said.

Connie could take it no longer. He edged around the table, beyond his mother's reach. Point took a step back.

"Mr. Hanson told us the grand jury has two functions," he said. "It screens evidence to protect defendants from unjust indictments and it acts as the government's investigative arm, the sword of justice. Looks like the protection works mighty poorly and the sword works only too well."

"Hanson probably told you that, too." Point was back into his balanced, defensive stance. "Reason enough to be glad he wasn't elected D.A."

He turned one last time to Annie. "When I go out this door and outside this building, there will be a horde of reporters. I am prepared to tell them that you will not be called before the grand jury and that you refused to answer important questions. Are you prepared for that?"

Annie stood again.

"You may go, if you please, Mr. Point. We both know the truth."

43

They'd brought me my own clothes before taking me to court. They even let my sister-in-law wash and iron my shirt and bring fresh underwear. Standing in my cell, tying my bow tie and pulling it straight, without benefit of a mirror I might add, I reminded myself clothes don't matter all that much. You don't have to be a peacock to have pride. Still, I needed to correct what was going on. It would be just that much harder trying to persuade the judge while standing before him in prison issue stripes.

The handcuffs did not bother me.

Two guards, both with pistols in big black holsters and both so tall I had to crane my neck, brought me before the judge. One bent down and whispered in my ear.

"You're the best groomed little man we ever had here in Cheyenne."

I had barely time to thank him before the judge started with his questions. To the judge's question was it my voluntary act to waive my hearing, I asked,

"May I say something?"

The judge nodded.

"I hear the District Attorney in New York is saying there are at least five people involved in this."

"The U.S. Attorney," corrected the judge. "This is a federal court."

"Yes, sir," I said. "The U.S. Attorney, then. I think he mentioned that nice little girl who is the teller in my bank and my head teller. He even mentioned my son. That is not true." I said each of the last four words as carefully and firmly as I could.

"Not true at all," I repeated.

"This is your hearing, Mr. Wain," admonished the judge. "We're not talking about anybody else here."

"Well, that's my point, your honor," I said. I stood as straight as I could. Good posture always seemed to punctuate determination. "No one else was involved. I thought this up all by myself, and I did it all by myself. It's true, I asked some of those good people to do certain things I needed done, but they were just following my instructions. They knew nothing of what I was doing."

"That, Mr. Wain," said the judge, taking off his glasses, "does not come under my jurisdiction. My role is to find out if you want me to hear testimony why you should not be sent back to New York."

"If we do that, can we keep the others out of this? Can't I just tell you I did it and then have you tell that U.S. Attorney to let those people alone and send them home?"

"No," said the judge. "If you want a hearing, we can do it Monday."

"If you schedule a hearing on Monday, your Honor, and if I convince you I did it alone, will that mean those folks in New York can go home?"

"On the contrary. The U.S. Attorney may be waiting to see if you are trying to delay your extradition, and a hearing will be more of a delay," said the judge. "In fact, the longer it takes to get the trial over, the longer your friends will have to stay in New York."

"But I said I did it!" I was pleading.

"Well, you'll have to say that at your trial. Even with a guilty plea, they might have to stay until the trial is over. A plea would just make the trial blessedly short."

"So there's nothing I can do?" I asked. I could feel my good posture start to go.

"You can go back to New York, Mr. Wain."

"Yes," I said, my eyes staring at nothing, "yes, I aim to."

The judge slowly moved his head back and forth in disapproval or in wonder. It was impossible to say which. All he said, very deliberately, was

"So, do you waive your right to a hearing?"

I roused myself. When you face up to something, you should face up to it forcefully.

"Yes."

The judge read a prepared order. Marshal Thompson and a guard were assigned to escort me from Cheyenne to New York City. He read the order. I noticed the small figure of a blindfolded lady over his head.

44

Postmaster General Ryan Benson held his position because he gave the President good advice -- in blunt terms. This time he spoke his words of advice to a different president through the telephone from his vast office in Washington.

"You can forget about such extreme measures."

"The senior Senator from the State of New York supports us, Mr. Benson," said Prescott H. Lamont, standing in his grand office on Wall Street, one befitting the president of the Harriman National Bank. "He is deeply concerned that the banking industry in my state not be damaged by this swindle."

Lamont loudly did not mention that the Senior Senator from The State of New York was chairman of the committee that watched over the U.S. Post Office. Lamont know how Benson earned his position. Benson knew the New York banker was a big contributor. He considered several ways he might respond to the veiled threat. If a banker wanted to play power politics, Benson could play. In the end he chose soft words to regain control,

"Let me look into it."

Benson put down the receiver and stared at the phone, deep in thought. He called for an assistant and instructed him to find the exact location of the train carrying the collateral, the released securities the New York bankers were trying to capture. He called a second assistant and asked him to find out when he could talk to the Colorado Senators, Bessemer and Edson. The call to the Telluride postal inspector he placed himself. He checked his directory. The name was Grange.

He listened to the crackling connection in the receiver and it was like he could see the telephone line itself stretching into the frontier. When a voice came at the other end, Benson identified himself by name.

"Don't know no Benson," the voice on the telephone replied.

The Postmaster General nearly laughed aloud. Well, he might call the President by his first name in private conversation, but he wasn't dealing with Washington now. He had the power and prestige of wealth, the right schools, and political office, but the American West would require a different sort of approach.

"Maybe not," he said in the easy voice of an old campaigner, "but do you know who the Postmaster General is?"

"Can't say as I do," answered Grange. "He don't get out here much."

Benson gave in to a chuckle. Clearly, this wasn't going to be easy, but he couldn't begrudge respectful recognition of a careful man.

"Well, I am the Postmaster General, Ryan Benson — I don't expect you believe that."

"Got that right," replied Grange.

"I'll tell you what, Inspector Grange. Somewhere in your office is a U.S. Post Office Policy book. In it you will find the code for calling the Office of the Postmaster General. You call me back. I'll answer the telephone."

"How do I know this is legit?" The voice rose and fell and the line crackled loudly. Benson approved of the question.

"You don't. Here's the thing. If you find the code and call and you talk to the Postmaster General but he turns out not to be me, you apologize and say some imposter called up trying to impersonate the Postmaster General. He'll think so highly of you, it will advance your career. If you hang up the telephone and do not call me back, since I am the Postmaster General, I'll think so poorly of you I will end your career."

"That's clear enough," said Grange, hanging up so abruptly he left Benson holding a dead phone.

Within minutes the call came back.

Grange was one of my depositors and by the time that call came in he had one of those checks from Mr. Twicken. Grange was as careful as Benson figured him to be and he was as honest as the mountain air is clear. Grange spent no time trying to figure why the Postmaster General needed to have information about mail trains arriving from Denver that could have connected with New York over the past four days or so. He answered almost before the question ended: Not a single train had arrived for two days due to heavy rains.

Benson thrilled at the thought that he had this unknown Telluride Inspector in his command. He could be trusted.

Benson knew what such a delay would mean to the New York bankers. If he agreed to commandeer the collateral, a wise political move that may benefit the President, by the time they got their hands on the securities, the funds would all be dispersed. He had an easy decision to make.

"Here's the thing, Inspector Grange." Benson confided, relying on his long tested ability to size up a good man. "You use that code to stay in touch with me personally. No matter who calls you, whether it's a U.S. Attorney in New York or the head of some big bank, don't interfere with any of the mail on any of those trains. Not unless I tell you."

On the same Saturday, young Peter Grinnell of First National Bank chaired a meeting of the concerned banks. Regrettably, Grinnell explained, the Chase's Winston Whitworth was tied up with yet another meeting of the margin committee. Blessings, he astounded the assembled bankers by saying, seemed to come in pairs, as the Harriman's Simon Pugh also had business elsewhere.

"We have just one item on our agenda today," began Grinnell. "To deal with the loss. Mr. Wain is in custody, perhaps in no small measure as a result of our efforts. Recovering our funds, however, might be more complicated.

"Mark," he continued, addressing the vice-president from National City Bank, Mark·Peery, "when we talked yesterday, you had an idea that I thought warranted further discussion. Would you repeat it for the sake of the others?"

Mark Peery never suggested any idea that he had not already made sure was approved by the group. The possibility that he might suggest something that proved unacceptable to his peers froze him. The look on his face was blank as stone. When he spoke it was with obvious reluctance.

"Very well." He hesitated for a long moment. "Simple, gentlemen. Almost too simple, you might say. I merely suggested, and in private I might add, never with any thought he might bring it out today. Anyway, I suggested to our Mr. Grinnell that we might do well to ask the man to return the money."

"Indeed," said Alistair Pembroke of Central Hanover, after a thick silence. "And then what? Drop the charges?"

"That would be the understanding," said Peery.

"But what if he doesn't have it?" asked the American Bankers Association's George Ethan. "It's already distributed. And our lawyers have just informed us Colorado is prepared to make us go to court rather than give the money back."

"I was afraid of just this misunderstanding," said Peery. "I don't like to work this way."

"Duly chastened," acknowledged Grinnell, "but we just don't have time to work any other way. Do you have a solution?"

"I dare say," acknowledged Peery. "If he doesn't have it, then we'll have him promise to return it when he does. No worse than a loan. And if we could get our hands on the collateral that was released, we'd have security for half the money. Shares in a cattle company and his old bank might not be much, but that would be better than nothing."

"Who could ever miss Pugh?" muttered Grinnell. "Much as I hate to admit it, he probably knows most about any progress with the Postmaster General. Seems the senior Senator from Colorado has turned Pontius Pilate on us and washed his hands of getting that collateral."

"Do you really think it would work?" asked George Ethan.

"We have to ask Mr. Wain to return the money. He's still president of the bank, under supervision of the Colorado State Banking Commissioner. He can certainly sign a promissory note. Our Mr. Wain is responsible for the loss. Let him make it right."

"This is impossible!" Pembroke was on his feet. "Makes us look like a pack of fools."

"I'm afraid I have to agree with Alistair," added George Ethan. "It just doesn't look good, does it, letting him take out a loan to pay off his depositors and then if he pays it back, saying all is forgiven."

45

The taxi stopped on Third Avenue before it reached the corner of East Seventh. Half a dozen steps up Third Avenue and another half dozen down East Seventh stood the sign hanging over the sidewalk, "McSorley's." Yesterday the wind had been so strong it blew the sign off its S-shaped hinges and so chill they cancelled ball games. Today was the first day of fall and people took advantage of the fickle weather gods to spill out into the streets in shirtsleeves.

Elliott Point climbed out of the back seat. He blinked in the warm midday sun and glanced at his watch, noon on the dot. He looked up and down the unfamiliar street at the crowd of people, turned away, and bent over the front window to pay the fare. He kept his head down and made the six steps to McSorley's.

He walked through swinging doors into a room so dark he felt spasms in his eyes. The barman stood behind the zinc-topped surface. Mirrors, glasses, glass shelves, the empty bar reflected the glow from the door behind Point. This was not his world and since Point was a man who only felt things in relation to himself he must certainly have felt something come over him, something like discomfit. Sawdust and pigs feet and hard boiled eggs didn't bother him, but the rules were different here. He was not in charge. He could not bend the rules to his benefit and he could not be in charge.

Point held out a hand, introduced himself, title and all to be sure, and added "Denny sent me."

"Pleased to meet you." The barman had a firm, moist grip. Point took in the large rough face and the faded stains on the apron that covered a white shirt, no longer clean, and a frayed black tie. "What's your pleasure?"

"Lemonade," said Point. Too hasty, he thought. Exposes my lack of control. He quickly added, "I'm here for lunch, actually."

"Of course you are," nodded the bartender, "That's all we serve."

He took a glass and poured from a pitcher on the counter. He pushed the glass in front of the standing Point.

"Denny did say you might be by."

Point's forced smile gave way to raised eyebrows, the muscles in his face going on alert. The U.S. Attorney lifted the glass of lemonade in front of the mirror, saying nothing, smelled it and set it down.

In slow circling motions the barman began to wipe a nonexistent smudge off the zinc countertop.

"Not much of a crowd today," the barman commented in a casual manner, "it being Saturday and so fine a day. All the better for you. Tis. We have a good table."

He walked the length of the bar, threw up a hinged section, and joined Point on his side of the counter.

"It's Farley, Kevin Farley," he said. He raised his hands in a shrug and pointedly looked around the near empty room in a way that could only mean 'proprietor.'

"And, so they say, a good barman," responded Point, reaching for his glass, and lifting it high in salutation. "Not that I know much about that."

"Well, sir, I haven't pulled a pint these eight dry years," said Farley. "And that's the God's truth." He took long enough to wink at Point before he rolled out a confidence, "But Connor, my night barman, I can't speak for him."

"I assure you, I'm just here for lunch," said Point. "And maybe a little conversation. Nothing official."

"If it's conversation you're wanting," said Farley, guiding Point past the empty front tables, "you came to the right place. That is, if you can stand the conversation you'll be getting!"

The barman guided Point to a table against the far wall. He found himself standing before five men, each seated in front of a large plate of corned beef and cabbage. Three continued to eat without looking up. One, somehow out of place in this company, sat before his food, knife and fork untouched. The fifth, clearly in a position of some authority, paused from his meal to study the new arrival.

"This here's Elliott Point," said Farley, "the U.S. Attorney, don't ya know. Denny sent him over to say hello."

"I'll be blessed," declared the man who had looked up. "Seems to be the day for it." He rose from his chair, putting out a hand.

Point eagerly seized the offered hand and responded with his best hail-fellow voice. "A pleasure to meet you, Mr...?"

"Cunniffe. Mo Cunniffe."

Point beamed at the smallish man, thin sandy hair atop an impish face deeply creased by the lines of countless smiles. Not much extra flesh on his frame, but the hint of toughness. Over Cunniffe's shoulder, Point noticed the man who was not eating. It was obvious he was uncomfortable. Even in the dimness he could see the complexion was darker, not ruddy Irish.

Cunniffe saw Point's eyes and stepped back from the table. "Sorry, but I figured you two fellas already knew each other. After all, you have a big case in common. This here's Ferdinand Pecora, Chief Assistant to the District Attorney."

"No case in common, Mr. Cunniffe. All Mr. Point's," said Pecora. "It's customary to defer to the U.S. Attorney."

"We have met," said Point flatly.

"Figure it's as good as a starting gate?" The tone was a skilful blend of question and statement.

"Excuse me?" said Point.

"High stakes. Important people involved," said Cunniffe, in a matter of fact summary. He swung his arms broadly. "No need to be coy here, Mr. Point. What we do here is talk politics. Pecora, here, I'm sure you know, is looking to get the nomination for District Attorney. And no doubt you are here to listen to the fine Irish music?"

Point tightened up and his back straightened. That prow of a face started pushing further out to sea. Then, he thought he knew the situation and as though washed over with a wave of understanding, the sharp angles on the prow relaxed.

"Oh, you politicians," laughed Point. "You're all the same. Seeing opportunity everywhere."

"I'm no politician, Mr. Point," said Cunniffe, demonstrating how the ever-present smile had carved the lines on his face. "Sure, I've got a few friends here and there, but I'm just a simple businessman."

"Well, then you'll agree with me," said Point. "I've got to put this Wain fellow away. For the good of the free enterprise system."

Cunniffe laughed. "I think you're out to win — "

"Of course!" interrupted Point.

" — and I've no argument with that. Indeed, if you're going to do it at all, you had better win!"

Cunniffe stopped. Point looked at the Irishman, waiting for more.

Apparently the conversation had just become tastier than the corned beef. Point noticed that the three men sitting at the table stopped eating. Cunniffe knew very well how to draw out a silence, but chose to move the attention to the other man who had come seeking his approval.

"Mr. Pecora has such strong support from his boss, our good District Attorney Belder, that he has to come here lining up Irish Democrats to help with his nomination!" Again, the Irishman's face wrinkled in mirth.

"I cannot listen to such talk," insisted Pecora. "He's been good to me."

"Well, yes," said Cunniffe. "He may have done you a favor. He could have given you the case Mr. Point has."

"Really, Mr. Cunniffe." Point playfully put his hands to his chest as though he'd been wounded. "You sound as though you have doubts about this case."

The Irishman smiled on. "Well, Mr. Point, we don't see the D.A. jumping in, do we?"

"The District Attorney's standing back until he sees how the Federal case goes."

"Just what Mr. Pecora said," smiled Cunniffe. He pointed to an empty table next to his. "Sit down. It's a good table. Denny's. He probably won't come today, but if he does, Kevin'll bring him over."

Point gave his order to a waitress, her red hair piled high and held tight with a large clip. He'd have the same as his companions.

"Aye, you're Mr. Point," said the waitress, nodding her head in acknowledgment. "Kevin told me you were here. Pleased to meet ya."

"You'll find people friendly here," said Cunniffe, "but bein' friendly and wantin' you as governor might not add up to the same thing."

"You flatter me," declared Point, gaining confidence that he could parry when tested. "As I see it, Roosevelt will certainly be re-elected governor next year. As to what he does in '32, well, Hoover appears to be blessed with prosperity. Mr. Roosevelt may or may not wish to go against such an opponent. So let's just say that a prudent person would be ready for whatever opportunity presents itself." The food appeared almost immediately. He leaned back while the waitress placed the steaming plate in front of him. He thought something more needed to be said. "I think it is best to be very careful on such subjects."

"You're right, there's time," said Cunniffe. "But I hear a little money is being raised for your campaign — not that you're actually running, mind you! Still, it might go better if you get this conviction. But I'm not so sure."

"Oh, I'll get it," said Point, turning his attention to his food.

Pecora still ate nothing.

Cunniffe watched them both.

The meal continued in silence for several moments.

"So, everybody has testified now?"

Pecora's question surprised Cunniffe, breaking the silence. It hung in the air like a challenge.

"Everyone except his wife," answered Point.

"Going well?" queried Pecora. "Belder tells me you're pursuing a conspiracy theory."

"Conspiracies are hard to prove," mumbled Point, pushing his plate aside. "Of course, we have what we need. Complaint and warrant were sent out to Cheyenne by airplane."

"I don't understand. Why are you going for a conspiracy if they're hard to prove," asked Cunniffe, his face a study of Irish innocence.

"No need. Belder has it wrong again, of course," Point said. "I am confident we will be able to show that Wain benefited personally. That's why he didn't include others in his scheme."

"So, you cannot really prove a conspiracy — "

"Oh, it's not that," insisted Point, cutting off Cunniffe. Then, directly at Pecora, "It's just that it would take longer, and I think we all want to get this case behind us. He is, after all, the guilty one. The others are really just dupes, in a sense."

"Well," said Pecora, still as if speaking privately to Point, "it's a matter of philosophy. I'd rather go after bankers who actually cheat their clients. And let the evidence speak for itself."

"I've no doubt you would," flashed Point. "But first you would need to have a track record to get in that position."

"You've picked a good one," Pecora parried with a hint of laughter, appearing to ignore the last remark. "Of course, the little man had a novel idea; something that I think bears consideration, but those bankers looked so foolish. Just going forward with this case gets them off the hook. You have unerring judgment."

"Thank you," said Point. "Everybody wants in."

He continued, addressing no one in particular, proving to all he had not understood Pecora.

"Get a case with a little publicity and they all want a piece of it." His thin lips looked severe as he raised his hand to hail the waitress. "Take the Chief Postal Inspector."

"Goodness me," Cunniffe declared, his face glowing with mirth, "now there's a title! And what does the good fellow do for all of that, I wonder?"

"The Chief Postal Inspector, Mr. Cunniffe," said Point, suddenly shifting to the sharp, clipped voice he used before a jury, "is the person who oversees the investigative arm of the Post Office. Oversees more than a thousand inspectors nationwide. Reports to the Postmaster General. It's his office that investigates mail fraud. But it's the fellow's first big case since his appointment and, frankly, he bungled it."

"Isn't that a little harsh?" protested Pecora. "For good public servants who are merely trying to step into your limelight?"

"Oh, that doesn't bother me," said Point, spreading his arms broadly. "I'm not in this for the attention. I merely refer to the fact that he allowed the Colorado State Banking Commission to get their hands on two hundred seventy thousand in securities that Central Hanover returned out West through the mails."

"I read about that," chimed in Cunniffe. "The banking commissioner told the Post Office to have the securities delivered to his office. So what's the problem with that?"

"The Chief Inspector was apoplectic," said Point, his grin showing the pleasure he took in others' misfortunes. "It means he lost custody. It means he lost his personal opportunity to be the savior of the New York bankers.

"You see, so long as the Post Office has the mail, the sender technically owns it. The sender is Mr. Charles C. Wain and it could be confiscated as part of the investigation. But once it's delivered, even if delivered to the Banking Commission, it's the property of the recipient. In this case that would mean the Bank of Telluride."

Edward Massey

"Sweet Mother of Mary," whistled Cunniffe, shaking his head, "Do you think that little man knew that beforehand?"

"He's probably too simple to have figured all that out," said Point. "Takes a deeper understanding than you would expect him to have. All it proves is that the Chief Inspector is a damn fool. He should have consulted with me. I would have told him to work it out quietly and turn it over to me."

Point looked around for comment and interpreted the dumb-struck silence as a signal to continue.

"You see, we could claim their value as restitution to the banks."

One of the three who had not yet spoken a word scratched his head.

"Are the banks out anything if they get repaid?"

The barman passed the table. He nodded in the direction of the unfinished platter.

"Not to your taste?"

"On the contrary, best I ever had," insisted Point. "You people have great food. It was just more than I could manage." He placed two bills on the table and got up.

"Aye," said Kevin, clapping him on the back. "You'll go far. You've got the blarney."

They shook hands while Mo Cunniffe stood up. As Point started toward the door, Cunniffe followed with him.

"You know," he said almost whispering in Point's ear, "Denny said to help you, so I will. But between you and me, Mr. Point, I think you've arrested Robin Hood."

46

Business gets done everyplace and they were going to a ball game. The official black car carried the boss. It pulled to a stop even with the curb at the Murray Hill apartment building. Addison Mintz swung open the door and settled into the back seat.

"Thanks for the invitation," he said.

"Don't thank me," said Point. "Thank Prescott H. Lamont, our dear president of the Harriman National Bank. It's his invitation. He said to bring you along."

"Any idea why?" Mintz's question was automatic, idle, like his attention on the Park Avenue buildings passing by as the Buick picked up speed.

"Checking on our progress, no doubt," said Point. "A burden we bear."

I know you have a right to doubt me when I tell you what he thought, but I know the man and many like him. Point rode along in silence as the car traveled under the el. A tight smile crept over his face, betraying the mental rundown of his list of accomplishments for one day, such a list: laying down the law to the Postmaster General before breakfast, building political support at lunch, now off in the afternoon to deal with important men in banking, all in the name of justice, and all in the same day.

They crossed the bridge into the part of New York called the Bronx and drove along the river where they caught sight of the stadium. The growing backup of cars pulled them to a dead stop. Mintz craned to look out the window. The stadium was awe-inspiring. The building was already two years old, but he had not yet been there. He barely heard Point talking.

"That crafty little banker likes the headlines. He's a schemer. He'll play for the jury's sympathy."

The car lurched forward — they were almost there. They had made the trip in just over twenty minutes, in plenty of time to witness the organized chaos of pre-game — infield practice, scrubs running in the outfield, pitchers throwing on the sideline. Too bad they hadn't come early enough to watch batting practice. Mintz wanted to melt into the commotion all around, but his boss had something on his mind and that meant he was obliged to stay focused and say something in response.

"Are you thinking we should have left it with Belder?"

"Ha, we saved his skin," said Point. "And his man Pecora knows it. I talked to him at lunch. They're amazed."

Mintz watched people walked across the plaza to the gates.

"They didn't want it, boss. I've only seen the one photograph of the guy, the one in the paper, but I'd say he comes across as pretty sympathetic."

"Part of the act. Deception." Point's words hung in the air. "He's a sleazy little swindler, and I'll make everybody see it."

"Yes, sir," said Mintz. He knew his boss.

The car finally stopped at the curb and the driver opened one door and escorted them to an unmarked entrance to the stadium. A blue uniformed guard nodded to Point and motioned him through.

"You've been here before," said Mintz.

"A couple of times," allowed Point as he continued up the small incline and then back into the sunshine. "I told you. It's a burden we bear."

Below them lay the green field and the men in white with fine black pinstripes.

Point started down the aisle toward two men sitting in a box of eight seats to the left of the dugout. Mintz let out an appreciative laugh.

"First base dugout!"

Simon Pugh spotted the U.S. Attorney and tapped the shoulder of the man sitting next to him, deep in conversation with a uniformed player. Mintz saw the round contours and friendly face of someone he recognized. The other man waved his hand in annoyance, refusing to be interrupted. Pugh stepped out of the box and extended a hand as Point approached.

Point stepped aside and said, "I trust you have met Addison Mintz."

"Haven't had the pleasure," said Mintz, as Pugh muttered, "Of course."

Now all three men entered the box. Lamont leaned over the rail and laid a hand on the man's shoulder to hold him in place.

"Babe," he said, "may I introduce you to our U.S. Attorney, Elliott S. Point."

"Pleased to meet ya," said Ruth, presenting a countenance the size of home plate.

"Thank you," said Point. Mintz stared wide-eyed. Lamont apologized sociably that he had not known Mr. Mintz's name and he pointed out that the third man worked for him. Pugh fidgeted.

"The Babe was just telling me that our good friend Miller Huggins is in St. Vincent's today for a slight operation."

"Really," asked Point. "How slight?"

"Don't look good," said Ruth. "Couldn't be. They had me managing a game." The Babe chuckled along with them. "Seriously, I hope they're telling the truth. Hope it's not serious." He started toward the dugout with a wave, "I better be going."

Lamont turned to his guests as the Babe picked his way down the dugout steps.

"Truth is a scarce commodity. The Yankees were eliminated last Saturday, and they had Babe stand in for Huggins at Sunday's doubleheader. Since then his coaches have stood in. I think he is quite ill, actually."

"Sorry to hear that," said Point.

Lamont smoothed out the overcoat he had spread on his seat and turned to the three standing men.

"Please, sit down."

He placed Point to his left. Pugh and Mintz sat directly behind. Almost immediately Lamont began to relate the highlights of the Sunday games Ruth had managed. The first game went quickly as all Tom Zachary needed was the one run Ruth manufactured with a single, advancing to third on a bungled pick-off play, then ambling home on Bill Dickey's first hit in twenty-two times at bat. The Yankee pitcher shut down the Indians one to nothing. The U.S. Attorney listened without comment. The singing of the national anthem fell exactly between Lamont's narratives of the first and second games. After the cheering, before they could even sit down, Pugh could stand it no longer.

"You know," he said to Point, loud enough for Lamont to hear, "he did not commit the perfect crime."

"Do tell," sputtered Point. "In my business, Mr. Pugh, there is a general disbelief in the perfect crime."

"I'm afraid our Mr. Pugh is a little direct at times," said Lamont, placing a hand on Point's sleeve. "It seems the Westerners are growing a bit obsessed by this. They're the ones who insist he has committed the perfect financial crime."

"I know what you mean. I had a long talk with that town marshal. They're soft on him. A Westerner, you know, one of their own. You can bet I'll be using one of my U.S. marshals to handle his transport to New York. I'm not about to take chances."

"I read," said Lamont equably, "that he told the officers who caught him that he was thinking of giving himself up. And now he has said he would waive his hearing."

"That little man has something up his sleeve," said Mintz. "There are days when we're not sure we can understand it."

"It delayed nothing," interrupted Point, asserting something no one had disputed, but hoping to distract attention from Mintz's comment. "We have used the time to round up witnesses. Everything's in place."

"The jury will be people who read," said Lamont. "They'll know he said, 'I did it to protect my depositors —'"

"He took the money to pay off his creditors."

Point's interruption surprised Lamont. It was a minor infraction, but people didn't interrupt the President of the Harriman Bank. He paused as if politely attentive, and when he resumed speaking Point did not have the ears to detect the coolness that had crept into his tone.

" — to protect my depositors, who are the only important creditors any banker has.'"

Point brushed the words aside with a wave.

"Our little Robin Hood can say all he wants about looking out for his little depositors. It's mail fraud, and it will stick."

"I told you, Prescott," beamed Pugh, "this man wants him as much as we do."

"Admirable, Mr. Pugh, that we share a mutual goal," said Lamont, interrupting himself to cheer the leadoff single by Combs. After Metzler's triple in the top of the first, Wells had held the White Sox.

"We're starting well," said Lamont. "You know, Ruth is looking to break out of a home run slump. Maybe he'll do it now."

Point made no attempt to interrupt Lamont's interest in the game as they watched three straight outs, including Ruth's strikeout. With a smile, Lamont turned to Point.

"Apt. I was about to say it appears conviction will prove a difficult task for you and your staff."

"Difficult," agreed Point, "but you'll find we're up to it."

"Are you a real fan," Mintz asked Lamont in an effort to help Point carry the load.

"Not really," laughed Lamont. "It's easy to follow the Yankees."

"Even easier with numbers on their backs," volunteered Mintz.

"To be sure," said Lamont. "Of course, everyone knew Ruth batted third in the order." Lamont continued watching the game. The pitcher singled to score the first run. "Good, Wells helped himself."

He watched the White Sox come up to bat again. His guests and employee waited. Without turning his head, he said,

"I'm not sure I would conclude that they're going to cooperate with your conspiracy theory."

It took Point a moment to register he had been addressed.

"Dropped it last week. We have the indictments."

"It looks bad," muttered Lamont.

"What?" asked Point. "Why do you say that?"

"Oh! I'm sorry," responded Lamont in a reassuring tone, "I meant for the Yankees. The White Sox have the bases loaded."

Point looked out at the field and saw three men in plain gray flannels standing on base. The scoreboard showed the Yankees ahead.

"It's a good day when you're winning," said Lamont, "but the lead can be snatched away, at any moment, even right now."

Mintz heard two meanings in Lamont's words and tried once again to lend support to his superior.

"Do you see any validity in Mr. Wain's claim that he did all of this to protect his depositors?"

"Not much," answered Lamont. He watched as the opposing pitcher grounded into a double play.

Mintz was not prepared for the sudden attention when Lamont turned directly to him and said,

"I imagine you followed Professor Fischer's speech last week."
Mintz shifted uncomfortably.

"No. I'm not even sure I know who Professor Fischer is."

"Yale," said Lamont. "Economics. Last January, Fischer said we've entered an era of permanent prosperity. Last week, at Whitworth's committee on margins, he said he thinks the market is still a bargain. It will go higher."

"That's good news," said Mintz.

"It certainly is," chimed in Pugh.

"I'm inclined to agree," said Lamont. "Certainly the people over at National City and the Corn Exchange Bank must think so, with the merger they announced today. But still people never cease to amaze me. The outlook is good enough for two banks to merge to become the biggest in the world, and yet it isn't enough to get the whole committee to go along with lowering the margin rate."

Lamont turned back to the game. "It's always best to end the inning."

He watched the field without a word as the teams changed. The box watched him.

"Have you ever actually thought about why he did it?" asked Lamont as the new inning started.

"He wanted the money," said Point automatically.

"That's not good enough," shot back Lamont in a tone as tough as any judge. "He took no money. If he said he did it for his depositors, Mintz is right to ask. What did he think his depositors were facing? Why do it for his them?"

"They were facing the product of his defalcation," said Point, wondering where this was going. "I told you, he's a common swindler."

"Whether you can convince a jury of that — " Lamont paused and watched the longest drive of the day, Gehrig's, sail over the bleachers and come down in the last vacant rows. Foul. " — may have a profound effect on your future, Mr. Point."

Point waited until the commotion from Gehrig's drive settled down. He touched Lamont's elbow to draw his full attention.

"I will convince them. You and I both know the banking system is not failing. He has bad loans on the books. He's incompetent. So, he tries to cover up his own mess. It doesn't much matter whether it comes from incompetence or theft, it's still by his own defalcation. For damn sure, he isn't trying to save the whole town from any failure of the banking system."

"Uh-ha," said Lamont and turned his attention to the field. They watched without conversation as Chicago scored two in the top of the seventh. As they stood for the seventh inning stretch, the Yankees appeared safely ahead, 8-3.

"You know," Lamont said to Point, "sympathy's a powerful tool, but good executives never let it get out of hand. If Huggins dies, and the fans voted, they would make Ruth the manager. But Ruppert won't make Ruth the manager."

"I assure you," said Point, "this situation won't get out of control."

"Good," said Lamont "Anything else is bad business. Very bad business, indeed. One hopes that little banker will not be allowed to go unpunished. No, that would be most unfortunate. For so many people. But then, I needn't tell you, Mr. Point, that eight very important institutions have been embarrassed. They would remember if you deliver for them."

"I'm not thinking about that," protested Point.

"You have me convinced," smiled Lamont. Most of the fans headed up the aisles. "You know, I never leave early."

47

The train from Cheyenne had one car for passengers, two freight cars, and a caboose. And above all a regular schedule.

The U.S. Marshal arrived at the Sheriff's office before full daylight. He gestured for me to hold out my hands. He snapped a cuff on each wrist, bent down and closed ankle cuffs around my pants. He clipped a chain to the handcuffs and bent down once more to fix the other end to the ankle cuffs.

48

One thousand miles of grasses and grains weave a hypnotic spell. Limitless horizons escort the train from Wyoming to Chicago. I live with a soaring optimism. The knowledge that everything will work out and all is possible traveled within me even as I rode in my shackles on the hard upright bench. I don't fidget much, as a rule. It was easy to sit very still. That way the iron bindings caused not too much discomfort. It was even easy to nod off, though I fought the impulse best I could. I didn't want to sleep during the day. I wanted to look out at the open spaces and sky and waving grass.

Efforts to engage the U.S. Marshal and his new companion took too much energy. I just stopped. Besides, Connie was on my mind. I hadn't talked to him about any of this. All I could do was assume that my son would understand. What a great burden. It would fall less on Annie's shoulders. She had the farm and her family. Connie, on the other hand, had a career ahead of him, which now would certainly not include banking, and he had a wife and his wife had a family. I figured that both his wife and her family would take to a period of doubting Connie. There was not much I could figure to say to Connie. About all I could say was that it was the right thing to do. Of course, saying that kind of thing was pretty much useless.

Once again I found myself gazing at the plain and the sky, stretching out together to touch each other in some distant place, on some distant horizon. Maybe Connie and I could come together on some distant place, for until then, I knew that what I had created for Connie was dashed hopes and what I was feeling was my own unnamed sorrows. The sorrow sprung not from a foreboding that it would work out poorly for the boy. He was in his twenties and he would get on. I can't say I really knew what his hopes were but whatever they were, they would have to change and I would no longer play a role in shaping those hopes and I, for sure, could no longer help turn them into reality.

I could see Chicago rising from the Plains like a muscled giant clad in concrete. The sight had the power to arrest thought. My watch told me we were hours away. All those very big buildings silhouetted against the vast blue-white sky energized me to try again to have a conversation with my guards. You couldn't say their response was any more welcoming. They did go so far as to promise we would have breakfast in Chicago before the train continued to New York. That was sociable enough, I guess. Don't get me wrong. They just wouldn't talk, but they didn't treat me poorly. They had offered me coffee and water, all of which I had refused to drink after the very first time I asked permission to use the lavatory. The swaying of the train coupled with the awkwardness of the chains made me wet myself. As I shuffled back to the bench I struggled against the handcuffs and the chains to cover the dark spot on my suit pants. There I sat and you can imagine I was resolved not to budge until we reached the next station.

The mound of sliced ham that came with my order of eggs at the station café was a sight to behold. I was hungry, and the coffee tasted good, and I had just begun to eat when a reporter discovered me and asked for an interview.

He startled me, appearing out of nowhere and unexpected. No, I admitted, it wasn't so much that I minded. It was just plain curious. I didn't know what to make of folks interested enough in me to bother to track me down. I tried, and anyway it was good manners, to defer the request to the authority of the U.S. Marshal. That was a trick that didn't work. Marshall Thompson probably thought it would shut up my questions for a while and he could eat in peace. All he did was wave his fork to signal the reporter he could proceed.

The reporter was a youngish man not unlike my Connie, and I told him that if anything I could say might help him in his career, we could talk while I ate. To my surprise, the words came easily enough to me and I discovered I had a lot to say. Over the ham and eggs and a second cup of coffee I told him I'd been working steadily for years to pay off my depositors. I reckoned I had returned the money of thousands of people since troubled times started coming to Telluride years ago. Truth to tell, I first told the young boy I had saved the money of thousands of people, but I caught myself and got it corrected. It might have started out with troubled times, and it might have been because Telluride was failing. But I wasn't taking on any airs. It was their money and it was on deposit, all I did was return it.

Everything I had to say, pretty much in my simple way of saying it, found its way into the New York newspapers the next morning. They arrived on kitchen tables even before I got to Penn Station.

49

The train slowed down when we came in underground and then as slow as it was going, it stopped with a jolt. The conductor, a negro man about my age with beautiful gray hair, not thinning like mine, a man who had ignored the agents and noticed my shackles and offered me coffee, tea, or water several times, all of which I continued to turn down, proudly announced we had arrived at Pennsylvania Station, New York, six minutes early — 8:54. Passengers eagerly filed out the narrow corridor, awkwardly gripping belongings that had a way of bumping into knees and seat cushions. I followed single file behind Thompson and in front of the second agent who I knew only as Sullivan. The line was slow and something seemed to be holding us up. When finally we reached the doorway a woman and her young girl were approaching the exit from the other direction. Thompson stepped down onto the platform and damn near pulled my arm out because there I was, framed in the doorway, pulling back, bowing slightly, and waving as best I could the mother and daughter to pass in front of me. At that very moment a volley of flashbulbs flared, their loud pop followed by a low hiss, like so many snakes, and an acrid scent of burning glass and metal. The photograph they took ended up covering the front pages of the next New York editions, captioned in one of them as "Robin Hood and Lady Marion. This gallant little man in chains bows to the lady and her child."

I could barely see the last step onto the platform for the flashbulbs. A wall of noise, mostly calling Mr. Wain, some venturing Buck, seemed to come from just beyond where my eyes could see. I suppose they were yelling questions at me, too, but I can't remember any as it was all one big blur of shouts and flashes. One reporter shoved a newspaper into my hands and pulled the U.S. Marshal aside, pulling with him my manacled right wrist. Amid the noise and jostling, I took no notice of their exchange in whispers but I can tell you I noticed the small yellow envelope the reporter shoved into the marshal's pocket as Sullivan kept a tight hold on my left upper arm.

Working their way through the crowd the two lawmen pulled me to a large black car waiting on 34th Street. It takes a little lining up when you are attached to somebody, but all three of us got into the back seat. I wondered at the sight of the reporter climbing in next to the driver, but only faintly because these were New York City things that I didn't know anything about.

I have no idea why that newspaperman handed me the paper, but I still held it in my hands and my eye caught an article. It said President Hoover's son had graduated Stanford with an outstanding record and now would matriculate at the Harvard Graduate School of Business Administration. Well, that came as no surprise. Hoover was a good business man. And this showed he was probably a good father, too. At least one who could be a good influence on his boy. I hadn't made up my mind about Hoover, except that he obviously didn't see what was coming.

Connie might have pursued graduate studies, but that didn't seem possible now.

A short tug at my chains brought me out of those thoughts about who was right. I looked up to find myself in front of a building inscribed with the Gothic masthead of the *Evening Journal.* There was always the chance we were stopping here to drop off that reporter, but I really thought it had more to do with that little yellow envelope. It mattered none. They had me and each one of them had their little opportunity to profit, so it was just one more bob in the roiling sea that I had jumped into the moment I walked into the Central Hanover Bank. That was beginning to seem like years ago. Could it really have been scarcely a month?

Soon I was sitting in a warm and overheated office, cluttered with papers and people. I slumped deep into a comfortable overstuffed chair. I lost track of the lawmen, sitting quietly somewhere behind me. Truth to tell, I think I dozed off a minute before a pleasant man in a vest offered a cup of coffee. This time I accepted gratefully.

The reporter from the train station produced a sugared donut. I accepted that, too, with a wink and said,

"Ah, my yellow envelope."

They asked me the sort of questions I had come to expect. I was ready and willing to answer. It wasn't unpleasant, really, to sit there and talk for a while. Nearly two hours had passed when there came a loud bang at the door and three men burst noisily into the room.

They announced I was a fugitive.

The judge and the U.S. Attorney had been awaiting my appearance in court since ten and it was past noon. Those men had been sent to find me and drag me back, if that's what it came to!

If someone hadn't spotted the Journal's car at the train station, they might be looking for me still. That shows you how much I registered when we arrived; I didn't even notice the big gothic logo on the side of the car when we got in.

Thompson rose to his feet when they entered. He wasn't completely unprepared. Sure they were to deliver their prisoner, he acknowledged, and deliver him they would. But no one had given him a deadline. Hell, trains can be late. Almost anything can happen. And that's all there was to it.

The two newspapermen insisted they were only doing their jobs, just like everybody else.

Only one voice was missing from the chorus. They didn't need me for their debate, and that chair was awfully comfortable. I think I might have dozed off a bit.

50

The second Thursday in October was the day. Just past 8:30 a.m. the guard came to take me to the car for the trip to the Federal Building. He was tall and slightly stooped, or at least that is how he looked to me when he bent down to apologize for putting on the handcuffs. I had heard similar words before, but I knew he had no choice. I smiled at him and at that moment he maneuvered slightly, creating a small corner of privacy.

"Mr. Wain," he said quietly, "I just hope the judge goes easy on you. You know, for what you did for those people back there out west."

"That's very kind," I answered, looking up at him. I should have told him that's the kind of sentiment that makes it possible to see a thing like this through. I just motioned with my bound wrists pulled in front of me. "May I ask your name?"

"Ben Simpson. Call me Ben. I hope you'll remember me."

"Oh, I will, Ben. I expect I'll have a long time to remember you."

Two guards took me in a black Model A on the short drive from the jail to the courthouse in Foley Square. They were good enough to point out all the landmarks. I must say we passed an imposing assortment of government buildings. They told me they were all locked together in a tiny triangle from the days when the whole of New York City occupied only the tip of Manhattan Island.

That trip took the better part of half an hour and was a pleasant trip. The one from the steps to the courtroom took about twice as long and wasn't.

My lawyer, Ridenour, a nice enough man I had met once in my cell, stood at the top of the steps, right between the columns. The sun shone down on him and still he shivered in his topcoat and scarf. It was cold for this early in October and gusty winds whipped through the downtown streets. He looked miserable.

"I'm sorry to put you out like this," I said.

I've seen those looks before. You know, deliberate, determined, eyes looking straight ahead and not quite at you; face without any expression, everything designed to appear neutral. I know when you work so hard to hide what you feel. Hard as he tried, he looked miserable. I was about to tell him not to worry when he abruptly took my arm. My shackles made me stumble as he started to lead the way into the building.

"Let's go," he said. "We're going to see the U.S. Attorney."

I detected a note in Ridenour's voice, not so neutral, mind you, definitely more triumphant than his posture. He had some maneuver going on. Like I once said, I don't think much about what I don't think about, but it was staged.

Point and Mintz were waiting for us in the marshal's room, standing like set pieces on either side of a grand portrait of someone obviously important and long dead. The guards left the room and Ridenour immediately protested.

"I want to know your plea," interrupted Point disregarding every word of Ridenour's protest.

"My client does not need to be manacled for this discussion," responded Ridenour testily. "You promised."

"What does it matter?" answered Point. "This won't take long, and then he has to be transported to the court."

"Nonetheless," insisted Ridenour. "We had a deal."

I shot a look at him. Ridenour made a deal with a man you can't trust. You never do that. Point wondered aloud what a promise mattered. No surprise.

I said nothing. No, I wasn't respecting Ridenour's unspoken command. Hell, I had just discovered I had a lawyer who made a deal with a man you can't trust.

The two of them were locked in an absurd dance of wills back and forth and I just watched and tried to make out what possible use was being put to this.

Right judgment may have been sullied, but Ridenour prevailed. Point yielded up a slight motion of his prow and that sent Mintz to the door to retrieve one of the officers.

"Okay," said Ridenour, "now we can proceed."

"I want to know your plea," repeated Point, speaking directly to me.

"I have told the venerable U.S. Attorney," Ridenour said, "we will plead not guilty. He wants to hear it from you."

I just stood there between the two of them, not even looking up. My sakes, those handcuffs left reddish rings. I rubbed each wrist with the other hand to see if they would go away.

"Oh, my goodness," I said, looking at one wrist and then the other. "I already told Mr. Point, I took the money from those banks."

"Then you admit that you used the United States mails to defraud!"

"Oh, no sir," I said. What he said was offensive and I figured it was time to set him straight. "I took the money, alright. But I don't know how many times I have to tell you, I would never consider mail fraud. I spent half my life protecting the folks in Telluride from that sort of thing."

"Well?" smiled Ridenour.

"This is irresponsible!" shouted Point. "Are you prepared to let me put your client away for life? I assure you, if you plead him not guilty, he'll die in prison."

"Only if you convict him," said Ridenour. "But, tell me something, Mr. U.S. Attorney, if you're so sure of your conviction, why are we talking?"

"Gentlemen, I think we're getting nowhere." It was Mintz, speaking up for the first time. "We haven't heard a word from the accused."

The young man turned to me and made a gesture that I figure was meant to encourage me to say something, but Point flashed him a dark glance.

Mintz knew not to press for my answer and a good thing, too, since I couldn't figure if he had not just heard me or if I was missing something. I figured the best thing to do was just watch the two of them. His boss's face quickly returned to its hard, passive veneer. His lips etched a smile.

"Right. It's a waste of time. We'll let the judge settle the matter."

51

When you come back East from out West, everything is a first. The Judge's chambers were like that. I never had seen a room that big inside a building. And large isn't the only thing. That room was duded up to be solemn with a dark green rug and deep mahogany walls holding leather bound volumes in row after row from floor to ceiling interrupted only by darkly painted portraits. The judge's welcome amounted to a general nod he granted the four of us. He pointed wordlessly to the heavy fabric covered chairs. Everyone sat except me. The guard guided me to a spot in the center of the room and left me standing alone. The judge sat behind his desk and planted his hands on it, palms down.

"I understand you are confused regarding the nature of the charges against you, and that this confusion is affecting your consequent plea." He stopped, sat back in his chair, addressing the entire room. "I have agreed to this meeting in order to address this point. If we can resolve this confusion prior to trial, that, I believe, is in the interest of us all. If you cannot agree, however, I assume your attorney will enter a plea of not guilty."

Point and Ridenour erupted together each asserting his understanding and each convinced his lawyering had been upheld.

I stood waiting. They were just words and they simply did not mean anything real to me.

"Mr. Wain, you are being charged with mail fraud. If you want to admit that you committed this crime, the way you do so is to plead guilty."

"I'm sorry, your Honor, but let me be clear here." I said.

I knew they gave him this impressive and solemn room to make sure you knew he was the judge and it did intimidate a little man like me, it really did, but for so many years I had advised successful men as often as I had addressed the concerns of simpler folk. I treated them all equal, leastwise, I tried to. They were all equally my responsibility. It was no different here.

"I admit I instructed the New York banks to transfer money to the Bank of Telluride. I've said that before. Nobody much wants to hear it, but I needed to borrow that money to pay off the debts of the bank, and the most important debt of any bank is its depositors. I swapped one debt to people who couldn't afford to lose it for another debt to the people who were going to make them lose it. Oh, I know it wasn't the regular way to go about borrowing money, but I tried the regular way. Time and again, and it just didn't work. So I had no alternative but to do it the way I did."

"Yes, Mr. Wain, I know all of that," said the judge. I listen to people and I can hear. His voice had a softness to it. He was willing to be patient. "But what we have here is a matter of the legal charges. Mr. Point and Mr. Ridenour are trying to reconcile your willingness to admit what you did with what the law requires. Counselor, perhaps you should instruct your client further on this matter."

Ridenour rose, but he didn't need to tell me anything, I just waved him away. I took a step forward to speak a little more directly with the judge.

"Your honor, where I come from it isn't considered seemly to toot your own horn but, honestly, don't you think I could have come up with a better scheme if I had wanted to commit mail fraud?" The judge's smile added some energy to my appeal. "Why can't the government just charge me with what I did? Why can't you simply tell the prosecutor to do that?"

The judge raised his eyebrows in Point's direction.

"We are charging the defendant with mail fraud," said Point, speaking from his chair to demonstrate that whatever conversation I might have with the judge was irrelevant. "We need not explain and it needn't be discussed."

He stood and made a show of preparing to leave. The judge's eyes followed Point's antics without a word. His silent expression made it clear that the U.S. Attorney was not the most powerful man in the room.

Abandoning his tack, Point stepped right up close to me.

"Mr. Wain," he began, clasping his hands and assuming the exasperated tone of a schoolmaster, "Mr. Wain acknowledges that he deceived six New York banks into transferring money to his control. I have heard all about how he says he used it to good purpose. Even allowing that he might have used the money for his own benign — but nevertheless alienistic — purposes, that does not mitigate the fact it was still illegal. Indeed, the fact he *says* he believes he did not use the mails to defraud anybody is irrelevant. What we will prove is that he has a history of defrauding everyone. If you take someone else's money and give it to the Salvation Army, you go to jail. In this instance, Mr. Wain took that money by using the U.S. mails. Furthermore, he used it to his own benefit. And that is something that we shall prove beyond any doubt."

"Mr. Point," said the judge, leaning back in his big chair, "this isn't the courtroom and you do not need to convince me. Nevertheless, in the off chance that your opening statement has convinced the defendant, I ask you, Mr. Wain, do you care to change your plea?"

"Well, I am disappointed," I said. "I told the judge in Wyoming I wanted to bring this trial to an end, and he told me I had to come here and plead guilty to what I did. That, sir, is what I want to do. Now you're telling me the government doesn't want me to plead guilty to what I did. The government wants me to plead guilty to somethin' I didn't do. Ain't that just like the government?"

They weren't telling me why they needed to go about this nonsense and it seemed downright silly to me. I can say that now, but much as I wanted the judge to know I was his equal, you wouldn't catch me saying something like that in his room.

"Mr. Wain," said the judge, "you have a capable lawyer. Surely he discussed the charges with you. You were charged with mail fraud. You must have known that's what we're about to deal with in the courtroom today."

"Of course," I said. "Mr. Ridenour's done a fine job explaining everything to me. He even explained we could delay this trial further if he asked for a bill of particulars. I don't want to delay it. I don't want to delay it, and you can ask him, I told him in no uncertain terms, I did not commit any mail fraud."

"Well, that would be consistent. I was told Mr. Ridenour intends to enter a not guilty plea," responded the judge. "Perhaps you should let your lawyer speak for you."

"This is just foolishness," I said. "I don't want a long trial. Mr. Ridenour's told me he wasn't so sure these fellers could get a conviction. And I believe him. Of course, that means four or five weeks of keepin' a lot of good people here on five dollars a day when they got nothing to do with this in the first place. All that fiddlin' and inconvenience, and what for? Just to try to beat the system? It's just plain foolish. I said I took that money. I had to. If the government wants to put me in jail for it, then just tell them to charge me with what I did."

"Mr. Wain," said the Judge, "I am unable to know whether the government would like you to plead guilty to larceny. What I am capable of knowing is that for you to do so, the government would first have to charge you with larceny. As the case stands now, they have not done that. Maybe they have not done that because they are afraid you would change your mind and plead not guilty. Then they would have to prove it. The government can make the case it wants to make. This trial is to determine if they can prove the charge they make against you, and they have chosen to charge you with mail fraud. That, sir, is all there is to it."

Authority makes itself known and the judge had just told me the audience was drawing to a close. To the judge and probably to my own lawyer it was just a simple matter of making a decision.

It won't come as any surprise to you that I didn't hold out that I had any too much authority of my own. The best I could manage in reply was,

"Well, I don't like it."

52

The Yankees didn't win the pennant in 1929. The Athletics had won the first two games of the World Series at Wrigley Field and Thursday was a travel day to get them all over to Shibe Park. I figure that was about as good a reason as any for the gallery to be packed at ten o'clock. Frank Simms didn't agree with me. He said people showing up at my trial didn't have anything to do with the World Series and now I feel a little self-conscious about mentioning this, but he said all those people came out just to see the little man who had robbed big men to give the money to even littler men. He went so far as to say there were quite a few people who felt like they were connected with me. He even seemed to think it was important that damn few of the big men in their suits and stickpins showed up to watch me get prosecuted. Hell, I didn't think nothing of it. They had more important things to do and they just delegated that job. Seems most publishers didn't agree with Simms's assessment, either. One of them flat out told me nobody cares about a banker who did the right thing. So, I always figured it was just the lack of competition and nothing to do on a Thursday in October that filled up those galleries.

I straightened up my suit and tie and pulled down my waistcoat. A smudge filtered the light through my spectacles and I cleaned them with a fresh handkerchief Annie had brought me. One of the guards held open the door in the corner to the right of the judge's bench. I stepped through and a guard on either side escorted me all of twenty feet to the center of the space between the judge's bench and the lawyer's desks. They left me there, standing alone, with my handcuffs pulling my arms in front of me.

By ten-thirty the judge still hadn't appeared. I'll allow as how our little meeting in his dark room had set back the starting time of my trial, but standing there almost fifteen minutes trussed-up and abandoned while the judge delayed seemed like a deliberate act of, well, of spectacle. I am not immune to seeing these things; I just don't automatically assume they are for my benefit. The judge had someone in mind to reprove with this delay. I was just beginning to think out who when I heard Mr. Ridenour's voice yell some words I couldn't make out across the room. Some scuffling went on behind me.

The bailiff came up to my left side and opened the manacles locked at my hip. I thanked him. He asked me to turn and hold up my arms for him to unlock the cuffs.

That turn gave me my first chance to search the court room. Instantly my eyes found Annie.

Sitting a couple of rows behind my lawyer's desk, she looked as trim and crisp as she ever did. Lucky for me she was a smallish woman, but it really struck me how downright little she looked amidst all those big New Yorkers. Her hair was perfectly arranged in a soft, loose curl, but for the first time I could see it was slightly graying. Damn. Maybe I caused it.

I simply looked at her, no gesture, no expression. She looked back, a composed look, and glowing. I think I mentioned how her touch could make my life seem special. Her look carried her touch.

Judge Arthur K. Lantern arrived. Of course, he apologized not one word for the delay, and started the proceedings like we were the ones who got there late.

He asked me to identify myself, my residence and my occupation.

The courtroom was silent and I thought I was speaking to the judge but the court reporter asked me twice to speak up, she couldn't hear my answer.

". . . as to occupation, of late I was president of a bank . . . ."

The papers the next day said something seemed to have defeated me. The papers like to report an opinion and parade it as a fact. The fact is, he knew all of this and I was not feeling very smiley or chatty. I'm normally a pretty easygoing little fellow and I had certainly got along well with everybody over in the Federal building, but this was court and the judge wasn't there to be my friend.

I felt no dread standing there, I looked small and rounded and slumped and soft because I am. I never cut a big figure and standing there with that judge looking down at me, I was supposed to look inferior.

The judge asked for my plea. Ridenour stepped forward.

"Your Honor," he began, but he didn't get any farther. I turned and looked at him. I stopped him with a look and he went mute.

Then I turned a little more. I knew the courtroom was watching as I looked behind him into Annie's face. She saw what was on my face; throughout our marriage she had told me I never needed to ask her permission, but I just kept looking at her, and at the nod of her chin I knew I had what I had been seeking.

"As you know, your Honor," I began, remembering to keep my voice loud enough to carry to the court reporter, "I have admitted that I tricked those banks into sending the money to Telluride. I'd be prepared to let them say that's what I did."

People rustled in their seats behind me; maybe, despite my best efforts, they couldn't exactly hear what I said. There wasn't any more to say and it died down pretty much when the room concluded I had come to a stop. Judge Lantern's face was impassive; I stared hard but he gave me no signal. He didn't appear ready to speak, neither. So, I just started talking again and this time I tried to speak up enough to help those people behind me hear better.

"Look, I know the fact those bankers were fools doesn't make me innocent. It makes for the reason why I had to do it and it makes for the reason why I could do it, for damn sure. But it doesn't make me innocent." I was surprised by the laughter. I stopped talking for a minute. It was just better to let that laughter die down. "I know that. And I know I have to pay a price for what I did."

"Mr. Wain," the judge said, as calm and patient as could be, "we have had this discussion. In fact, for the benefit of the courtroom, that is the very reason we are late getting these proceedings started. I need you to plead guilty or not guilty."

The only honest and true answer was neither, but he would not accept that and it was his court room. It looked to me like I had to choose between an honest answer that would cause a whole lot of people more difficulty than they deserved or a dishonest answer that would take care of this problem once and for all.

Wasn't that the damndest thing? That was what this whole situation was all about.

"Guilty."

Judge Lantern gaveled hard to restore order. Even after he stopped hammering on the little wooden plate, he waited to make sure he wasn't dealing with anything more than a low background rumble.

Edward Massey

"Are you pleading guilty to each and every count?" he asked.

"Lettin' this trial run on isn't going to do anybody any good," I said.

Those newspapers reported my words as timorous and my manner overwhelmed. You know, they might have been right -- and it might mean I don't know what those big words mean because there wasn't anything more to say. I turned to acknowledge U.S. Attorney Elliott Point and his deputy Mintz standing in front of their desk.

"I told them I wouldn't give them any trouble."

"You do understand you are pleading guilty to six counts of mail fraud?" asked Judge Lantern.

"I told you, I do not want to plead guilty to mail fraud," I said. "I told you guilty to something I wasn't guilty of once. That's enough."

Now it was my turn to get a bit exasperated and my tone may have been a bit more forceful than I wanted. What I wanted was to whisper, to speak privately with the judge.

"Yes, you did," responded Lantern, noticeably not whispering, "but I believe we have been over that, too. Those are the charges the government has filed."

In a voice deliberately loud he repeated,

"I have no choice but to ask you the question in this way. Do you, Mr. Charles C. Wain, plead guilty to the six counts of mail fraud?"

"Yes ... sir."

A long moment passed. The entire court room respected a silence that seemed to make everybody disappear except Judge Lantern and me, facing each other. This result, my pleas, might have come as a surprise to him. He certainly had every reason to believe it had not been worked out earlier in judge's chambers.

I talk to a lot of people without using words and the man on the bench was offering me one more chance to change my mind. I remained, watching him, trying best to show him I understood. He had no choice but to ask the question in his way and that left me no choice but to answer it in my way.

The courtroom could not take the silence and moved to a low rumble of discomfort.

The judge shook his head and again tapped his gavel. He began to speak in that loud, artificial voice, the one meant to signify that what he was saying now was 'official'.

"You have pleaded guilty to six counts of mail fraud and this court will accept your pleas. Do you have anything to say before this court sentences you?"

"Yes, sir," I said matter-of-factly, "I do. I would like to tell you about the people of Telluride."

The judge nodded and lay down his gavel. He sat back in his big chair. You might even say, leaned.

"Proceed."

I looked around the courtroom, my body turned partway to the jury — eleven men and one woman who would have no opportunity to pass judgment on me. I paused a moment, took a half-step back, and looked up, directly at the judge.

"Well, sir, the people of Telluride work hard. There aren't many left, must be down to five hundred by now, but they're a hard-working bunch. The ones who've stayed on are good people. Those who pulled up stakes and left were good people, too, only they had to leave because there aren't any jobs in Telluride. Not any more.

"Anyway, of the ones who are still there, about half of them or more, maybe three hundred, are women and children. That makes it about two hundred working men. Did I say two hundred? It may not even be that many, because I recollect we had one hundred eighty-four depositors in our bank, besides me, that is.

"That's about the number of families depending on about that number of men. Those folks have nothing more than what they earned and what they saved. They work in the mines and with the cattle and the sheep and even a couple of them out lumbering. We don't have many farmers up there. There're a lot of farmers over in Delta, 'cause Delta's got water and good dirt. But we don't have farmers up in the hills. Anyway, miners are a hardworking lot. Some of them have degrees like Jeremy Kearns, the engineer who lives right next door to Mrs. Wain and me. Well, he used to, 'til he moved out, too. But about ninety-nine out of a hundred of them don't have degrees and they've got nowhere to move. They just work with their hands down in the dirt and the rocks. Some of them don't even speak much English. That doesn't stop them from having families, and they feel just as responsible for their families as anybody else. Oh, I didn't mention, there's a newspaper and ten shops and they're all run by fine people. They put in long hours and work just as hard as anybody.

"Now, you see, all these folks help each other out, the way neighbors are supposed to do, and they all support the Bank of Telluride. I'm fifty-three years old and I've been president of the bank for a good long while. At first, Telluride was a dream town; everything worked almost like magic. Then hopes just closed down, along with the mines. When things were going well, people made regular deposits, and they were willing to let me loan that money out to other people, and to other towns, all the way down to Denver. Fact is, most of the loans went to Denver 'cause that's where the big banks are.

"Anyway, recently, well, these last few years, actually, it's been a lot harder. It's the mines mostly, although we don't see the prices for cattle we once saw. That's when people started leaving town, and when the ones who tried to stay on had to start takin' their money out of the bank. Then some of those ten shopkeepers had a hard time making their loan payments because people weren't coming in to buy so much any more. I saw all of this happening, but I knew it wouldn't be that way forever. Hell, even if we do have only five hundred, we'll have two thousand again someday. Those mountains are too valuable. They'll get used for something.

"Now, here's the thing. There's a lot of people who have asked me what it felt like to see my bank fail. Well, I'll tell you. What I feel is that these people need a chance to be able to make it through.

"I wake up in the middle of the night sweating and freezing at the same time. Damn right, I do, but it's not because of what's happening to me. I didn't want to see anybody leave town, but if they thought they had to, I had to make sure their money was there for them. If someone needed his money to live on, I needed to make sure it was there. And I'm tellin' you, Judge, it wasn't going to be there the way things are going.

"O'course, that doesn't do much good, my saying that, 'cause I've been telling everybody for months now. There's a mess comin' up and I don't know if we can keep it from happening. O'Course, nobody believes me. What's worst, nobody believes they had anything to do with it or they can do anything about it. Well, I'm here to tell you, I sure do know we can do something about it to protect our depositors.

"We need to guarantee people they'll get their money back, so I tried to get a loan. I needed to give my people their money back.

"I went to Denver. I told you, that's where I'd loaned the bank's money out in the good times. It was only right and proper that they'd return the favor. But the Denver banks told me the loans we were holding didn't have good enough collateral because some of our people had missed payments. Hell, I knew that. It wasn't any secret. Those Banks knew about those missed payments because I told them about those missed payments. But those loans are going to be good, I said, because those are good people. They just need a little more time. To top it off, most of those folks had put their land up as collateral for those loans. I offered that collateral, too, but the Denver banks told me the land didn't have any value because it wasn't producing income. Land that had brought millions of dollars, and most of that to Denver.

"I was looking for the help, sure. I couldn't do it alone. The people of Telluride were going to get hurt and they didn't deserve it. When I set up to be a banker and I took their money, I promised to give it back when they asked for it. And I aimed to keep that promise. And if that meant these big New York banks had to lose a piddlin' little bit of money to make that happen, well, then that's how it had to be.

"But you know, it didn't have to be that way. It just had to be a loan. That was what I asked for in the first place. If they had just asked me, I'd of promised to give it back, too."

I stopped. That was all I had to say. My voice had started out quiet but when you talk about something you love, your voice gets stronger.

53

Judge Lantern waited patiently. When no more words came, he broke out of whatever he was thinking with a shake. He cast his eyes around the bodies jamming his courtroom. They came to rest on me, standing alone in the center of the well beneath him. The judge spoke again in his loud, official voice. Again, he summarized the charge. He restated his understanding that my plea was guilty to each and every count. Once more he looked down silently at me and once more he seemed to shake himself.

"Do you understand the severity of the penalty you face?"

I nodded. He shook his head.

"I am going to say this very distinctly. Each count . . . carries with it . . . the sentence . . . of five years." He paused.

I could see his look. I could see what the judge was trying to do. He was trying to understand what I felt. I had just been told I could go to jail for thirty years. If I got out, I would get out in time to die.

It took some while for him to gavel down the reaction of the room.

"Mr. Ridenour, before I pronounce the final sentence on your client, do you have anything to add to his statement?"

"I certainly do, your Honor," said Campbell Ridenour, practically leaping from his chair. "You have heard his statement, your Honor. Surely you must take into account that this was a banker who had been led into his crime entirely by altruistic motives. He did what he did for the good of others. He benefited not personally. Indeed, his behavior should be considered exemplary, an example..."

"Your Honor!" The wail of U.S. Attorney Point interrupted Ridenour. "This tiresome Robin Hood story is not only improbable, it's simply untrue. It is the old story of attempting to cover up one's misdeeds when the day of reckoning is at hand. There is no banking crisis in this country. The Bank of Telluride failed because it was scuttled from within."

Lantern hammered Point to silence and motioned him to sit down. Ridenour objected, too, but the judge silenced him with another rap of the gavel.

"Mr. Point," said Lantern, but before he could continue, Point took that as license to erupt again.

"There is no altruism in this miscreant's efforts to cover it up. I have evidence of forged notes, of efforts to set up false trusts in order to defraud widows, of — "

"Enough!" shouted Lantern. "I had intended to allow you a statement, but now that won't be necessary. It seems that you have already made it."

He assured Mr. Ridenour that he understood his plea for clemency and then he looked directly at me.

"Mr. Wain, just why did you commit this very serious crime?"

Maybe my speech had taken something out of me. How was it that the judge still did not understand? All I really wanted was to have this over with and be left alone. Now I felt a little tired. I had the passing thought that I could have fallen right down to the floor and gone to sleep. Of course, I couldn't; I had to answer the judge.

"Your Honor. My depositors depended on the bank, and the bank depended on me."

"Do you mean that the people of Telluride whom you have described as good people would have wanted you to commit a crime?"

"Not at all, sir. I never put the question to them. It was my duty."

"Are you saying that it was your duty to defraud?"

"It was my duty to obtain a loan to protect my depositors. When it came down to it, I was their deposit insurance. There are no government programs to turn to. I tried by every means available to me until I finally succeeded.

"Yes, your Honor, yes. It is my duty to protect my depositors. More than duty, it is a moral obligation."

54

When judge Lantern spoke again it was with a changed voice, formal and objective. Whether he was shocked or just putting on a performance, the words had a life of their own and seemed to have little to do with the man saying them.

"Mr. Wain, you have been examined concerning your sanity. I do not believe you are insane. There are no emotional conditions extenuating. The theory of the defense is highly improbable. Your crime was deliberately planned. The law leaves little room for such actions to be excused as altruism. Are you, perhaps, a Robin Hood? The U.S. Attorney would have you the author of acts of forgery and dishonesty, even milking the estate of a widow held in trust. This court realizes the U.S. Attorney is raising the specter of crimes for which you are not accused in order to sully any merry image the public may hold. Fortunately, I need not comment. And without comment and without allowing that the reasons you may have had for your criminal act had any mitigating effect, I do note that your behavior was cooperative after taking brief flight. You saved the government time and money by not contesting your extradition here. You have, today, again saved valuable time and money in your guilty pleas. You have accepted responsibility and shown contrition.

"For these reasons, and again not for any reason of endorsing your belief that what you did was for the good of anyone other than yourself, I determine that the latter three terms of five years should run concurrently with the first three terms of five years. You will be eligible for parole after serving one-third of your sentence based on your good behavior while incarcerated."

Frank Simms was there, watching. Even if the judge did bend over backwards, what it came to was still fifteen years. Maybe, Simms later told me, he thought the judge got as close to the result he wanted as he could. Judge Lantern knew he was sentencing a good behavior prisoner. That meant I would be eligible for parole in five years, the term of one count of mail fraud. Sometimes Judges have to do the best with the worst and Judge Lantern might have been trying to achieve the sentence he thought was best -- even if it was the heaviest sentence for mail fraud ever to have been imposed in any U.S. court.

I watched the judge. For the moment I know we were thinking the same thing. We were staring off into my future.

We were interrupted by a slight commotion. Annie left her seat and made a motion to go to me. The female warder stopped her at the gate and took her arm and looked up at the judge for guidance. He nodded and Annie was released into my arms.

My trial and my testimony and the judge's decision made for a day or two of news.

Point may not have got the mileage he expected. Life goes on.

Two weeks later, on Black Thursday, everyone was talking of other things.

55

Pierre Robichaud
Telluride, Colorado
1931

Atlanta, Georgia
December 18,

Dear Pete,

There are rules in this institution as regards to letter writing and so I hope you will understand that I was not allowed until today to write and acknowledge the Christmas greetings you sent me. But I suppose Mrs. Wain made you aware they were received and related to you how much I appreciated them. Queer how many of my former friends, or should I say few, have ever written me or even let me know in any way that they knew I was alive. The way of the world, I guess.

Since I have been here, I have held down a job, now 22 months. I must say I have been happier here than I was the two years before, when I could see what was going to happen. I think I did all that was humanly possible but you know the story as well as I do. When I came in here, I thought I had provided for my family and money for when I got out, but I had not counted on the Post Office. They have kept all my mail and one of those letters, still unopened, has a check that represents all I have left in the world. My lawyer tells me the New York banks are fighting over who owns it and that might take ten years. Thank God, Annie still has the farm and I trust you won't breathe a word of this.

Which I guess brings me to the ulterior motive for writing this letter. If you could conveniently do so, and without material harm to yourself, or risk to your business and your family, as I do not know the circumstances right now, perhaps you could make me the loan of $200. I need a little money all the time in here and the six cents an hour I get paid at my job is just not enough to take care of the little things.

I can repay you when I get out of here, but that is the rub for we do not know when that will be, although I recall from the Judge I will be eligible in October, 1934. So, if you would propose an interest rate, and I insist, I would gladly repay it at interest when I can.

Well, Pete, life is a fine thing to live. I remember one old man saying, "Every dog has his day, and I guess I had mine as a pup." If you can't make the loan, don't worry. If you can, rest assured, I will repay you.

Sincerely yours,
Charles C. Wain

56

"I have this day taken an Emergency Banking Act . . . . Tomorrow, the bank holiday of these past six days will end . . . . Each depositor's savings will be insured."

— Franklin Delano Roosevelt
First Fireside Chat, March 12,
1933

57

Good behavior prisoners automatically come up for parole. According to the judge's word when he sentenced me, I was slated to come up for parole in October 1934. Automatic might mean something different than I thought it meant because that schedule, and, I guess, the judge's words, seemed to have no effect on the parole board at the Atlanta Penitentiary. October 1934 came and passed. Even for a good behavior prisoner, it usually took two or three appearances before the board would grant a parole. Coming up on the summer of the sixth year of my sentence, I hadn't even been called for my first time. It looked like there was going to be a long wait before I got out.

The assistant warden came into the cotton duck mill to find me in May. It was about the time it started to really heat up, but I couldn't figure why they were calling me off the line. They had never taken concern for how the heat affected an old man before.

He told me a letter from the Judge had been delivered to the prison. You can imagine my surprise when he told me the Judge seems to have told the Parole Board of his desire to see his intended sentencing guidelines be carried out.

He was quick to add that no judge up in New York was going to cut a path with any Parole Board down in Georgia. I figured that for true. I wasn't that important at all. If it was anything got their attention said the assistant warden it was the fact somehow they might have overlooked me. Hell, the Depression brought on a budget crisis that meant no one could afford the expense of keeping one extra prisoner after he was eligible for parole.

The assistant warden had read my file six years before and understood not one word. It was all too complicated. If the feller was a banker, the only two bank crimes were robbery and embezzlement. The assistant warden found no mention of a gun, so this feller was an embezzler.

Still, I hadn't caused a problem in six years. I'd survived the predators in the yard probably because they saw an old man. Old men, like old women, do not stir the juices of young men. I'm not sure the assistant warden heard anything of me from that first day when he read my file to that day when the judge's letter arrived.

Edward Massey

About all there was to hear was that I helped the prisoners out from time to time with little problems. Age and usefulness accorded me a measure of protection.

The assistant warden wasn't the kind of man to wonder about all this. What he knew was enough and mostly he just knew I was an operator on the line at the cotton duck mill. The prison made cotton duck and sold it under the label Albany Mills. No one knew it was prison labor.

Rumor had it that Albany Mills was in fact a personal business of the warden. Of course, I had heard the rumors. If it was true, I probably could have helped the warden some, but since he never asked, I never needed to know if he owned Albany Mills. My job was to operate that machine. I did it. I served my time.

Six years was too long for the public to remember much of anything. Violent crimes filled with sex and blood are forgotten in less time. I never counted myself as the "Robin Hood of the West" and no matter what they said mine was a pretty tame crime that could not have been remembered vividly, not after the cruelest hardship the country had ever known.

The crisis I had seen coming was now being called The Depression. It might have vindicated me, all right, except, the pain was so great to so many people and so hard to take. My little piddlin' effort was wiped from memory. So was I.

The Parole Board had no idea who I was. They had honestly lost me and they hardly cared. The judge's letter left unexplained why it claimed urgent need to free me now. Even those words might have fallen on deaf ears had the warden thought the mill was short handed. The person who delivered the judge's letter sat in while the warden and the Parole Board discussed the demand for cotton duck. It was slack, like the demand for everything else. Like I said, with the budget crisis and all, the warden found it to his benefit to recommend parole.

Now, in the space of two hours, my status changed from prisoner to parolee. It would take three days to prepare my papers and I would be released. I wanted to let Annie know. She had told me when she moved into the boardinghouse and since then she had visited me on every visitors' day. I had a telephone number.

I was told parolees were free men and were allowed unlimited telephone calls, or telegrams, provided they could pay for them.

When they swung open the doors to my freedom, no crowd, no reporters surged on me. No one surged at all. The headlines of 1929 and the crime I committed had vanished, swallowed up in the crisis a simple little man with nothing but his dirt common sense could see was coming.

There was a guy in our prison, came there after the Pecora hearings, and he taught me a new word. He told me what I had done was a Quixotic gesture. Maybe he was right, but I wasn't tilting at windmills, I was doing the one thing a man is supposed to do, live up to his promises. And when they swung that door opened, I still believed in what I had done and I still believed that it could be done by all the banks to save their depositors.

Annie stood alone out on the road, next to a simple black car, tears in her eyes. That was enough for me. After the first moment it took to think of myself outside the gate, I kissed my wife. Annie handed me the keys. Getting in the driver's seat, I drove us off to the rest of our life.

Atlanta was as good a place as any. We stayed in a hotel that first night. Perhaps Annie anticipated my shy desire because she proposed room service as soon as we arrived. She said without even so much as a wink that she had moved right out of the boardinghouse and we had so much to plan and to do.

"We used to talk about opening a bakery if things got rough. We have a little money from the farm," she said.

She knew what I was thinking. How would I ever support her? I remembered the conversations, all long ago, about what we would do if we had nothing else. I also remembered the most painful letter I had received in prison.

"I always thought baking a noble profession," I said, respecting her choice, now as then, to treat the sale of the farm as simply one more fact in living a life. "There's something biblical about turning flour into the staples and pleasures of life. Of course, it might be a little hard to make a go. There's infinite demand, every meal of every day, but then there's also nearly infinite supply. All you're doing is replacing labor, and the one thing people have today is the need of a job."

Edward Massey

Annie smiled at me. She kissed me and I knew what she was thinking. Too much analysis.

"Well, we could go back home," she said.

"Not just yet."

Before selling the farm, Annie had sold the house and moved to Nebraska to be nearer her sister. She discovered that communities have a strange chemistry. She said a lot of people in Telluride thought me a hero, and, in the end, that mattered little. One or two or maybe even five people of the five hundred judged Buck Wain harshly. One or two may have even tried to profit from my pain and they told the world they held me to be no better than a common thief. Just that little dose of malice — like vinegar in the wine barrel — could sour a man's reputation.

She agreed. Let's not go back home just yet.

58

Lorenzo Swett and Frank Simms met at the Hay-Adams hotel to have a much deserved drink before both left town. With a flourish they saluted the repeal of Prohibition and raised a toast to The Banking Act of 1935, finally, the law of the land. Their task was finished. After more than two years of intense work, on the day of the signing, their assignments complete in the eyes of the Congress, neither had a per diem for one more night's hotel room in D.C. Simms planned to drive straight back to New York; Swett would catch his train to Denver. They had met in dozens of conferences and hearings and along the way they had picked up the habit of promising to have a drink when it's over. Most men don't follow through with promises made like that, during the intense pressure of common work, but Lorenzo Swett and Frank Simms were remarkable men. This was that drink.

Young Swett had been in the capital since before the inauguration. His mother was very happy when the Chairman of the Senate Committee on Banking and Currency, the ailing Senator Norbeck from South Dakota, found him out in Denver. Mother Swett's father might have had something to do with that. Before even the President took office, Senator Glass was started on the path of legislation that he hoped would reform commercial lending and he needed a smart aide who knew the banking business. Virginia Democrat that he was, he knew the ways of diplomacy and power. He turned to his Chairman, the outgoing Republican, Norbeck, for help. His Chairman asked the people he knew, particularly the ones who were pledging to give money for Mount Rushmore. It's the way of the world.

Soon after Swett arrived in Washington, the committee's investigator discovered him and asked him to interpret documents and facts he'd turned up but didn't understand.

Investigator Simms's job had been to get all the research in place and do everything necessary to push Steagall's amendment. Steagall's amendment, turning bank deposit insurance into permanent law, had been the price the Representative had exacted from the reluctant Senator Glass for his joint sponsorship.

Frank recognized immediately what Chairman Steagall wanted, but he never knew exactly how he ended up working for a patrician congressman from Alabama. True, he happened to be in New York City, at the heart of the banking scandals, and he later learned Steagall personally called the Burns Detective Agency asking who they could recommend for banking investigations. Simms figured his boss probably wanted him out of New York and out of the agency. The committee wanted independence for its investigators and that gave his boss the opening to suggest that no mere leave of absence would suffice. He would just have to be terminated.

Simms and Representative Steagall had gone over to the North Wing of the Capitol for the bill signing and then to the Senate Chamber for a little drop with Glass and Swett.

Now, on a 97-degree summer afternoon, the two aides sat at the bar in the air-conditioned lounge of the Hay-Adams hotel hoisting their long promised drink.

Lorenzo asked the waiter for the humidor. Simms could smell the sweet scent of the box's cedar lining as Lorenzo chose a Montecristo robusto.

"I might get out of banking," said Lorenzo, tilting his head back and letting out a column of very expensive cigar smoke. "This kind of stuff, it's not what I had in mind when I went out to Denver International."

The words caught fire in Frank's brain. Denver International? Simms kicked himself. What did it take for an investigator to make a connection?

"Jesus! You're the one who caught on to those telegrams?" Simms stood straight up off his bar stool.

"Huh?" stammered Lorenzo, caught off guard.

"You know, that thing with the banking code and the President of the Bank of Telluride. It was Denver International that caught on and called one of the New York banks. The Equitable I think. Yeah, that was it. The one discovered it was some guy out there from a banking family." Frank paused a moment and climbed back up on his bar stool. He turned to the smart young man he had known two years as the legislative aide to Senator Glass. "You, it turns out! I knew his name, Charles C. Wain, but I never knew your name. I knew about the banking family because the guy at The Equitable was worried he might lose his job. Don't know why but the person out in Denver was the son of his boss."

"Grandson. That was Ewell. Works at my grandfather's bank," said Lorenzo, adding with a chuckle, "Still does."

Top investigators make connections that are there for all to see but seen by few. He said, slowly, drawn out,

"So, we're both here because of that little man."

He looked around the lounge of that famous hotel. Every person looked comfortable, in his place, like he belonged. Frank turned his attention back to Lorenzo.

"You must have been a hero out there. As I recall, none of those Denver banks lost anything."

Swett studied the roll of his Habana.

"I never gave it much thought," he said.

Simms wondered briefly if the young man's modesty was also truth, but he let it go in pursuit of another connection he was making.

"Well, think of it, now. The Pecora Commission never looked into Wain or what he did, but it showed us, for sure, those New York banks were talking out of both sides of their mouth. Even if they lost the whole caboodle, remember it was only seventy-five or a hundred thousand per bank, it was pennies compared to what their own executives were making off with."

"Now that you mention it, Pecora exposed Mitchell and National City as the worst of the lot. Glass wanted his head. He pretty much preached buying stock on margin right to the crash. Pecora exposed he made forty times his salary selling stock to the public."

Simms remembered Mitchell, they couldn't get him for cheating the public, but they did get him dead to rights on tax evasion, and he still got acquitted on the criminal charges.

"Yeah, but he wasn't the National City guy on the committee. Meek guy, good guy, the one who suggested they ask Wain to give the money back. He might not have known exactly what his bank was up to."

Simms asked the waiter about something to eat; hors d'oeuvres would be set out on the bar at five.

"Almost all of them got off, but there was one didn't," said Simms, nursing his beer. "Pretty damn near the closest thing we got to justice. One bank was really out for Wain's blood. That was the Harriman National. Their guy, Pugh, made all kinds of noise. Then Pecora goes and nails Harriman, himself."

"Isn't that the guy who was falsifying bank records?"

Simms nodded and looked at his watch as three Negro waiters, their white coats perfectly pressed and starched, appeared before him. Five o'clock sharp. In what seemed no time they laid the whole surface of the bar with a feast so perfect and symmetrical it seemed to him almost too beautiful to touch. He reached for the bite-size crab cakes and put one in his mouth whole. He'd just stuck another one in when Swett asked,

"Whatever happened to Wain? I never even followed the case once we knew we weren't going to take the loss."

"I had already been re-assigned," Simms said, "but I did go to the trial. He pleaded guilty. I never understood why. I mean, he did it, and he admitted he did it, but they charged him with mail fraud, and I don't know why he pleaded guilty to that."

Swett grunted, exhaling smoke, food still not as interesting as a good cigar. He slowly studied his cigar and then pointed it straight at Simms.

"Simms, do you realize what we just did? We passed a law providing for 'payment to depositors in an amount equal to the deposit and subject to withdrawal on demand.' My God, I wonder if we should get hold of the Senator. It'd be downright embarrassing if we still had the guy in jail for doing just that."

"Well, that's what Steagall thought," said Simms. His answer came out matter-of-factly, something like old news, apparently not as interested in my fate as the little plate of delicacies he'd put together.

"They sent him up for a long time," said Swett. "Maybe he should get a pardon."

Frank Simms looked at this sensible young man over the little plate he held in his hands. What were the limits of professionalism? He popped a third crab cake in his mouth and chewed slowly. With half a mouth full remaining he realized the Parole Board's action would be public record.

"Judge Lantern thought so." Simms finished his last swallow. "Did you know the judge grew up in Hyde Park?"

59

Annie never complained about the early hours the bakery imposed on her. She even reminded me she was a farm girl. Early hours held no burden for her. I regretted them. I regretted more that I was such an accurate economic forecaster.

As I feared, the Depression left people with a lot more time on their hands than money. Baking touches the soul of every meal but few families could afford to go outside the house for the luxury of store bought bread or cake. It would take a war to change that. Nobody likes to face it, but only the war got us out of the Depression and by then the bakery was two years gone, along with the last of our savings and my hope of repaying the $200 loan I had borrowed from an old friend while in prison.

60

That last day in Atlanta Annie stayed home to finish the packing so we could make an early start. I said I could close the bakery by myself. All it took was settling with the landlord and turning the key. No employees. No mortgage.

We owned few things but Annie treated everything with great care; she took the clothes from the closets and the drawers and carefully arranged them. I had preserved the one suit and she packed it with concern for each crease, placing tissue paper between the folds, as if I was going to the bank tomorrow. When she folded the coat, my leather case fell out and hit the floor, spilling its contents.

Annie picked up each piece of paper, carefully resetting the seams. She noticed a yellowed piece of paper that looked like newsprint. She thought it not too personal to look. She opened the fold. What she read she remembered seeing once before, an editorial from the *New York Times*.

It was dated Friday, October 11, 1929.

> Everyone will continue to repeat Judge Lantern's question to the defendant before sentence was pronounced: "Just why did you commit this very serious crime?" In fifteen years Wain may be able to figure it out himself.

When I returned, all three suitcases were outside the screen door on the stoop of our cottage apartment. As I packed them in the trunk of the car, she asked where I thought we might go. I answered without hesitation.

"Grand Junction. Maybe Everett will give me a job."

61

Violence dominated the front page of the Grand Junction *Journal*, a pleasant paper serving a peaceful town on the western Colorado border.

Banner headlines announced that Germany had invaded Poland. A wire photograph showed Polish horse cavalry charging an advancing line of Tiger Panzers.

The *Journal*'s second story crossed only two columns but its headlines showed above the fold. Local entrepreneur J. Walter Everett had been shot and killed at his Biltmore Club. There was no photograph.

Grand Junction might strike big city folk as a quiet place, but it was an open town in a high piece of country flat on the border with Utah. Things went on there, with pretty much no questions asked, that proved a powerful magnet to the men from Utah when they could get to it. Except for the winter storms, they could make the two hundred eighty miles all the way from Salt Lake City with just a little bit of trouble and about seven hours of hard driving.

The Biltmore was a men's club. There a man could find a friendly game or, if he was of a mind, a friendly touch. J. Walter Everett had started the original Biltmore Club in 1924 another one hundred twenty-five miles up the canyon, in Telluride, with a loan. He didn't know me and I didn't know him at the time. I was president of the Bank of Telluride and I told Everett I recognized a good business idea when I heard one. I had hoped the venture would help revive the town and bring back the good times, like when the mines were all operating and the girls in the cribs were making deposits once a week or even more. Everett ran a good and prosperous club and repaid the loan in half the two years that I had given him. I recognized a good business idea, but more than that, I recognized a good man.

He'd been shut down for more than two weeks the summer of '29 when he finally had to come see me, by now an old friend, and tell me he needed his money from the bank because he was moving the club down to Grand Junction.

When I walked into the Biltmore Club that day in 1937 to ask for a job I will admit I was counting that Everett might be one of those few men who was eager to return a favor.

-279-

There could have been a lot more embarrassment. Last time I'd seen Walt I was a bank president, now I needed a job, and there was a reason needed telling.

"I don't know nothing about it, and I'm less interested," he said, "except to say it hurt like hell to know it was happening to you at the time."

"That's not quite logical, Walt," I was touched by his prevarication, but I could not leave it without the truth told. "I need to tell you clear where I've been for eight years. I went to prison and…"

"I don't want to hear it," Everett repeated.

"I have to tell you," I insisted, "for your own good."

"Well, I've been pretty good at keeping track of my own good for quite a while, but I have been looking for somebody to keep track of things. Can you do that?"

"Yeah, Walt, I think I could do that."

Everett took me into a caged room and introduced his bookkeeper to her new boss.

I kept track, all right. I kept track of everything from the books right down to the polish on the brass that held the velvet ropes. Everett had only one thing to do, pay attention to his customers, and business boomed until that evening when one of the guests in a friendly game turned unfriendly and went out to his car for the gun he had left behind.

Those were the rules of the club; leave the guns outside, but when he returned our guest wasn't interested in the rules.

I don't cut too big a figure as a bouncer. You might say I'm small and you can't miss the spectacles, but at the front door, I had one thought, to obstruct the re-entry of this angry man.

"Out of my way, bookkeeper," he sneered, using the official title that by now many in town knew belied my true role as Everett's business manager. "I'm not kidding, you little four-eyed twerp."

I can't really say that I stood my ground between Everett and the bellicose customer, and I can say I was quite aware of the large handgun that was clearly meant to solve the problem. There was only one avenue available, turn on my boss. Summoning the sternest voice I thought I possessed, I said,

"Everett, you go back to your office, right this minute."

Truth to tell, I may have forgotten my station for a moment there. I never even questioned, I simply assumed, that my command would be obeyed. Surely, Everett would understand it was the customer I needed to pay attention to.

I turned to calm the customer, offering quiet talk and a night upstairs as honored guest of the house.

The angry guest preferred to remain angry. He swung the pistol down hard across the left side of my would-be peacekeeper's head and into my neck. I wasn't much of a defender. I have never even once in my life put my dukes up and he was so fast, I didn't even raise a hand. In one movement, the gunman had knocked me to the floor and leveled his pistol at J. Walter Everett.

He fired once, hitting Everett in the chest. He turned and ran out the door.

The police had no trouble finding the man. I was well aware of all the club's customers. The newspaper article called me quite a precise fellow and noted that I supplied an accurate description as well as a name.

The last paragraph of that same story, where it jumped to an inside page, mentioned my name. The reporter did this, no doubt, for the sake of thoroughness, never once imagining that he was informing the Rocky Mountain West and anyone else who cared to know what had become of Telluride's Charles C. Wain.

62

Annie woke up when I came through the door at four on the morning of the Everett shooting. She reheated the hot chocolate she had made for my return three hours before and set it before me with the simple question of what was wrong when she noticed the blood and bruises on the side of my face.

"It's time to find another place to live," I answered.

She started cleaning my wounded face and neck. Before she put the bandage on, I told her what had happened. She cried a moment, for Walt and his wife, not for us.

I told Annie I pictured the headline would read FELON DISCOVERED IN GAMBLING ESTABLISHMENT. That, I figured, would put Everett's widow in an impossible position.

"We might as well start getting packed, it's already morning. Reno's a good place to go."

She finished the bandage and told me where to fetch our suitcases, the three she had been given as a wedding present. Since we were leaving town we had no need to discuss what would be taken and what left behind. Everything would be taken. Annie finished packing and inspected the cupboards.

Before I took the suitcases to the car, she asked,

"Do you know what you'll do now?"

"Something they can't take away," I said. "Where I'll be of use to people. And where I won't fail you."

63

Frank Sherman Simms was out in Sparks for his grandson's graduation. Florence was using their daughter's kitchen to make bread dough rolls — a special treat for her grandson. Only when she made rolls for one of the grandkids did Frank get any these days. He was first in the kitchen. He was enjoying the last of his allotment when he came across the article in the Reno paper.

An article about an 83-year-old Fuller Brush man brought Frank to a halt in the middle of that roll. Better part of a page devoted to a door-to-door salesman who had enrolled in the local community college to study journalism. Seems like the old gentleman had decided to write his memoirs.

A Fuller Brush man writing his memoirs? Simms studied the photograph. Not such a remarkable face — curved and soft, pleasant and friendly, behind a white mustache. There'd been no reason to pay attention to an elderly salesman turned writer in a strange town. He remembered wondering if maybe he should take up writing his memoirs. That's when, finally, he noticed the name, under the photograph.

Charles C. Wain.

Frank Simms started noticing things he had skipped over, like the fact I said I'd lived in Telluride "during the good times." And that the good times "passed the town by."

He remembered delivering that letter. Congressman Steagall had been frantic to get that man out of jail before the President signed the Banking Act.

Simms started reading again.

64

The editor had asked why I was spending my last years selling Fuller brushes, years most men were retired. Annie had died by then, but I told him what we talked about. I told him I had to have something useful to do that would be a help to people. He wondered if I found my writing was getting in the way of that. I allowed as how I didn't know yet. I figured I had a story to tell. After he sent out that first reporter, I finished paying off my last obligation and I had finished a first draft. Maybe the story would be a help to people.

Simms took the last big bite of breakfast roll and chewed slowly, shaking his head. Frank Simms went through the article one more time and he said now he was sure. It was that little fellow who had the odd habit of saying he'd done what he did because of his promise. Frank knew and the Congressman and the President knew what he did for that little town of his was no different from what FDR did for the whole country just a few years later. Simms helped, in fact. FDR that is. How long ago? The paper said I had settled in Reno before the Second World War. That'd be some four or five years after he had taken the letter to the prison.

Thirty years now and that had been a big story back then. For one moment in 1929, the whole country heard about that little banker. Simms had even been part of it and he recalled the big effort by bankers and prosecutors to make people think poorly of me. Some went so far as to say I was deranged. Maybe I was, thought Simms, but I sure as hell knew where the country's banks were headed. Two weeks later the crash made everybody forget.

And the newspaper article didn't say a thing about it. He wondered if that's what I meant when I said I was taking that class so I could write my memoirs. And he told me later he wondered if he was going to be in it.

65

The next afternoon Simms made his way to the newspaper office in downtown Reno and found the city editor, a Mr. Presley. Turned out somebody else had visited him to ask about that guy in the article. Somebody's widow, Presley said, had stopped in the day before. She'd run what she called a gentleman's club, out in Grand Junction. Her husband had left it to her, but she couldn't make a go of it when the war came. She'd moved to Reno, figuring she could always get a job helping run a club. That's what she was doing when she saw the paper's story about an 83-year-old Fuller Brush man taking a college journalism class. He looked older now, of course, in the photograph, but then there was that phrase about his being twenty-five years in Telluride. She told the editor the story of her husband's murder and the little bookkeeper who had tried to save his life.

If it's the same man, Presley told her, he seemed damn near blind now and could use her help. He's probably broke.

Well, if it was the same man, she knew he wouldn't take her help. That wasn't what she'd come for, Presley recalled. She wanted the editor to know that there was a lot more to that man and he might want to look into it.

"She refused to tell me more," Presley said. "It was strange. She said was there was a lot of misinformation about him and she left."

Presley planned to look into it, but there was a lot of work in running a newspaper. He had not yet got around to calling me. Plus, he'd written one story about me. He wasn't all that sure his readers would be much interested in another. That came as no surprise to me. He was one of them told me he wasn't all that sure anybody would like to read my book, either.

"Well, he would be the same fellow she remembered, all right. I don't know anything about what went on in Grand Junction, but she was talking about that little banker from Colorado who ran up against some big boys in New York."

The editor nodded. He didn't ask how I made out. Simms thought even curious people aren't interested. Good times create distant memories. They won't be interested until it happens again. He shrugged. He had only gone to ask the editor if he might have an address or some way to reach me.

Hillside Court, Reno
January 28, 1959

Mrs. Pierre Robichaud

Dear Amelie,

Well, thanks a lot for that fine letter. And you wrote back so quick. It was good of you to take care of it about as soon as you got back from California. Like I said in my letter, Pierre was real good to me sending me that money. I knew it was sometime in 1931 or 1932 and I'm glad you still had that letter so's you know the amount, $200, is right and we got the date for the interest straight, January 1, 1932. You didn't mention what you figured would be a proper interest rate, but I know I promised to pay your husband at interest, so that's what I aim to do.

Funny, that's what sort of started all of this. People don't know much about it anymore. Of course, I don't remind them, either. Still, they just had an interview of me over at the newspaper here in Reno. Seems they'd heard I was taking a journalism class learning to write my life story and thought that was so peculiar they had to interview an old man like me. The young reporter was like to died when I told him I still went to work every day as a Fuller Brush man. Sorry to meander but what I was meaning to say is that he asked about my life and I just told him I was in Telluride for around twenty-five years and there was some good times and some bad times. I've been here in Reno coming on to twenty years and that seemed to interest him the most.

Of course, it's not like it used to be here. I came out here in '39 and not because of that Charlie Chan film, either. It was a booming place and Bill Harrah had just opened up his Tango Club here, but I told Annie I wouldn't be able to get a job there and I was right. That was when we started with the Fuller Brush business. This is a nice little apartment here. We had another room for me, you know to keep the records and the samples, but now it's too big for me with Annie gone. She died a little while back. I was glad to still be here when she died. I mean she'd been through a lot with me and she always stood by me, so this has been about my best chance to repay her. But you know about all that what with Pete's passing. I know why you talk about him like he's still here. He was a very special man. You know, I always thought he was the best entrepreneur we had. I guess it comes as no surprise to you why I borrowed money from him. (I mean aside from the fact I needed the money, ha, ha, a little joke.) You know there comes a time when you are so alone, you wonder if there is any one person who will help and maybe you don't pick just one person because if Pete had said no, I would have had to ask someone else.

But anyway, Pete was the one person to pick and the $200 check came right back almost the very next mail. Now, Christmastime, 1931, that must not a been very easy. I hope you didn't have to go without none. I never told Annie. I never expected to need the money, but I was trying to save her from selling the farm. Course that didn't work out either. You might be asking yourself why I never asked Josh Gibson, him being more my age and such a close friend. Truth is, there were two reasons. First thing is I figured he might not be able to spare it and my asking could put him in a real uncomfortable spot, if he had to admit that to me and all. Second reason is why I didn't go back to Telluride. You didn't ask. You're like Pete that way, but everybody else does.

Well, here's the thing. Josh lost everything. And you know, I think he might have blamed me a little because I wouldn't make that loan to him that old Warren Hellman, bless his soul, did. When that Delta bank failed, the Denver banks came right in and took Josh's farm. Course that don't make any sense, but the world's like that. Lucky for him his son out at Princeton made a good living writing stories about the West. Anyway, some of my good friends weren't too anxious to be good friends with a criminal. Well, of course, they had their Depression to deal with too. They weren't thinking too much about me and I couldn't expect them to. You know, most of them were also investors in the bank, and I knew what I was doing was going to lose the investors their money, but I knew they had more money on deposit in the bank than they had invested in it. And they'd been receiving dividends right along in the good times. So, I lost their investment for them, but I saved them more than that. Anyway, this is going on too long. All I was saying is that the real reason I didn't go back to Telluride is all those people wanted to get on with their lives. You know, that young man Kearns, who left town? He went on to become president of that big copper mine. You know, that kind of thing. They didn't want to be reminded. It's too hard on folks to keep explaining you don't mind.

Gosh, this letter's going to be over three pages. That's long winded when all I was trying to say is that being you didn't say anything about the interest I promised, I'll have to try to be fair and I hope you'll agree. We had a depression and then a little bit of inflation and now these last few years a recession. Maybe you don't care about all of that but I wanted to tell it to you for my reason for believing 2% is a fair interest rate. Now if my calculations are correct (I'm a bit rusty being out of banking these many years, ha, ha, another little joke.), that's 26 years and 27 days and it makes the interest $135.19. That's compounded, simple interest wouldn't be fair. I have been able to save that much (of course, I knew that before I wrote you the first time) so the check is for $335.19.

I am sure glad to have that taken care of. But being as old as I'm getting, I can't help but tell you it scares me a bit. Funny, how it took thirty years, but everything's taken care of now.

All the debts have been paid.